New York Times and
Jane Porter has wr
women's fiction nov
Mills & Boon in 20(
finalist, Jane is know
and sensual novels,
alpha heroes, exotic locations and happy-ever-afters. Today Jane lives in sunny San Clemente, California, with her surfer husband and three sons. Visit janeporter.com.

Kelly Hunter has always had a weakness for fairy tales, fantasy worlds and losing herself in a good book. She has two children, avoids cooking and cleaning and, despite the best efforts of her family, is no sports fan. Kelly is, however, a keen gardener and has a fondness for roses. Kelly was born in Australia and has travelled extensively. Although she enjoys living and working in different parts of the world, she still calls Australia home.

Also by Jane Porter

Bought to Carry His Heir
His Merciless Marriage Bargain

The Disgraced Copelands miniseries

The Fallen Greek Bride
His Defiant Desert Queen
Her Sinful Secret

Stolen Brides collection

Kidnapped for His Royal Duty

Also by Kelly Hunter

Claimed by a King miniseries

Shock Heir for the Crown Prince
Convenient Bride for the King

Discover more at millsandboon.co.uk.

THE PRINCE'S SCANDALOUS WEDDING VOW

JANE PORTER

UNTOUCHED QUEEN BY ROYAL COMMAND

KELLY HUNTER

MILLS & BOON

First Published in Great Britain 2019
by Mills & Boon, an imprint of HarperCollins*Publishers*
1 London Bridge Street, London, SE1 9GF

ISBN: 978-0-263-27330-4

MIX
Paper from
responsible sources
FSC® C007454

This book is produced from independently certified FSC™ paper
to ensure responsible forest management.
For more information visit www.harpercollins.co.uk/green.

Printed and bound in Spain
by CPI, Barcelona

THE PRINCE'S SCANDALOUS WEDDING VOW

JANE PORTER

For Lee Hyat.
Thank you for being my first reader, my friend,
and my cheerleader.
This one is for you!

PROLOGUE

PRINCE ALEXANDER JULIUS ALBERICI had known change was coming. His June 27 wedding to Princess Danielle would require a return to his Mediterranean island kingdom, Aargau, for prewedding festivities. After the ceremony and reception, a two-week honeymoon had been planned, and then he'd finally be free to return to Paris with his bride, where he oversaw an international environmentalist group focused on improving sustainability in fragile ecosystems.

His work was his passion, and Danielle had expressed support for his work—a positive in an arranged marriage. She'd also agreed at the time of their betrothal to live wherever he chose, understanding that ultimately they'd end up in Aargau as soon as Alexander needed to step into his father's shoes and ascend the throne.

But that day—replacing his father—was supposed to have been years away, decades away, as his father was a strong, athletic man and a vigorous, powerful king. Or he had been, until his winter cold lingered into early spring, a nagging cough that wouldn't clear even with antibiotics. And then in mid-April came the diagnosis of lung cancer and now King Bruno Titus Alberici had been given months to live. *Months.*

It was unthinkable, unfathomable. Alexander had never been close to his father—King Bruno might be beloved by the people, but he was cold and unforgiving behind closed doors—yet Alexander couldn't imagine the world without his fierce, unapologetic father. Now his father was determined to manage his death, just as he'd managed his life—without emotion or weakness. To that end, there would be no changes in palace life or protocol. Alexander's late-

June wedding would not be moved forward. Bruno's illness would not be made public. There would be no changes in wedding date or venue. There would be no acknowledgment of ill health. There would be nothing to alarm the people until an announcement had to be made, which in King Alberici's mind was notice of his death.

His mother, the queen, agreed with the plan because that was what she did—supported her husband. It had been her role from day one of their marriage, and she'd fulfilled her responsibilities. Now it was time for Alexander to fulfill his, which was to marry and have an heir so the monarchy would live on.

Alexander stirred restlessly, feeling trapped in his cabin, even though it was by far the largest on the ship. He pushed open the sliding door and stepped out onto the balcony, leaning on the railing to stare blindly out at the sea.

This trip, organized by his closest friends, had been a mistake. He couldn't relax. He felt guilty being on a pleasure cruise when his father was growing weaker at home, and yet both his parents had insisted he go, determined that he keep up appearances.

The trip was to have been a last hurrah before the wedding preparations began in earnest. Princes didn't do bachelor or stag parties, so instead, Prince Alexander Alberici's best friend, Gerard, had organized a week cruising the Aegean and Ionian Seas. Troubled by his father's swift decline, Alexander had left the details to his friends, knowing they were far more excited about this last adventure—concerned that it might indeed be their last adventure—but now wished he'd been part of the planning, at least when it came to approving the guest list.

The yacht itself was impressive. Large, new, and the very definition of luxurious, with two different pools, a hot tub, a sports court, a disco, and a movie theater. But the luxurious appointments couldn't make up for the fact that it was a boat, and they were all trapped together—not a problem if everyone was on good terms, but inexplicably Gerard had permitted Alexander's cousin, Damian Anton Alberici, to bring his girlfriend, Claudia, along.

It wouldn't have been an issue if Claudia didn't also happen to be Alexander's ex-girlfriend, and their breakup six months earlier had been acrimonious at best. He'd been stunned and uncomfortable when he discovered Damian was now dating Claudia, but to bring her on this trip? Why make it awkward for everyone?

Alexander's jaw tightened, his gaze narrowed on the pale rocky island ahead, each island so like the last.

The tension on the yacht just made him eager to return home, which was saying something as home wasn't exactly pleasant, either. His mother was struggling to come to terms with his father's terminal diagnosis. Virtually overnight his father had wasted away, his strong frame increasingly frail. The palace staff, sworn to secrecy, were incredibly anxious, tiptoeing around, walking on eggshells. And yet no one discussed what was happening. But that was because they didn't talk in his family, not about personal things. There was no sharing of feelings and certainly no acknowledgment of emotions. There was only duty, and he understood that all too well.

The sooner the wedding took place, the better, and Princess Danielle Roulet would be a good match. She was lovely and well-bred, and fluent in numerous languages, which was essential in Aargau's next queen. She was also sophisticated and would be a stylish princess, something he knew his people would appreciate. It was not a love match, but it would be a successful marriage because they both understood their duties and responsibilities, and best of all, the wedding would give the people of Aargau something to celebrate, which was sorely needed when the crown would soon change hands.

Now, if he could only get off this yacht and get back to his family—who did need him, despite what his parents might say, or not say—because Alexander was finding nothing pleasurable in this last bachelor getaway.

CHAPTER ONE

JOSEPHINE JUST WANTED the yacht to leave.

Why was it still here? The Mediterranean was huge. Greece alone had hundreds of islands. Couldn't the yacht go somewhere else? The luxury pleasure boat had been anchored outside the cove of her tiny island, Khronos, for two days, and after forty-eight hours of endless partying, blaring music, and shrill laughter, she'd had enough.

The revelers had even come onto the island earlier in the day, their testosterone-fueled speedboat racing them to shore. Jo had hidden behind the cliffs and trees above, watching as the dozen hedonists descended on her beach.

The young women were stunning—tan, lithe, and beautiful in tiny, barely-there bikinis—and the men were lean, chiseled, and handsome. While the women splashed in the surf and then lounged on the beach, the men sprawled on chairs and towels in the sun, looking like indolent princes. They were there to party, too, and there was plenty of alcohol and other things that made Josephine wrinkle her nose in disgust. Only one of them didn't drink, or smoke, or make love on the beach. Sometimes he sat on his own, but other times, people surrounded him. He was clearly the center of the group, the one with the wealth, the sun around which all the others orbited.

She watched the revelers out of curiosity and with a sprinkling of disdain, telling herself not to judge, but the interlopers on her beach clearly enjoyed a pampered, decadent lifestyle, a lifestyle for those born of privilege, or those lucky enough to be invited into the elite circle. Her dad used to say she was critical of such people because she'd never be one of them, and maybe there was some truth in that.

But she liked to use her brain, and she enjoyed her work assisting her father, who was one of the world's leading volcanologists, which was why they lived in the middle of the Aegean Sea, taking advantage of Greece's volcanic arc.

Her work included documenting her father's findings, and she'd proved indispensable to his research. He was the first to admit that he wouldn't have his enormous body of work without her assistance. But late in the day, she'd turn to her passion—drawing, sketching, painting. She had run low on paper and canvas again, but her father would be returning in ten days, and he always brought back fresh supplies for her.

This afternoon she carried her sketch pad with her to the rocks overlooking the sheltered beach cove, thinking she'd draw the scene below—well, not everyone, but the one who'd caught her attention. The one man she thought was by far the most fascinating. He appeared otherworldly with his thick dark hair and straight black brows over light-colored eyes—blue or gray she didn't know. But even from a distance the lines of his face appealed to the artist in her: his jaw was square, cheekbones high, his mouth full, firm, unsmiling.

Her charcoal pencil hovered over the page as she studied the face she'd drawn. His features were almost too perfect, his lower lip slightly fuller than his upper lip, and she just wished she was closer so she could see the color of his eyes.

Even more intriguing was the way he sat in his chair, broad shoulders level, chin up, body still, exuding power and control. Josephine glanced up from the sketch to compare her work to the real man, and yes, she'd captured the sinewy, muscular frame as well as the hard set of his jaw and chin, but his expression wasn't quite right. It was his expression that intrigued her and made her want to keep looking at him and trying to understand him. Was he bored, or unhappy? Why did he look as if he wanted to be anywhere but on that beach, with these people?

He was a mystery, and she enjoyed a good puzzle. It gave her mind something to focus on, but now he was rising, and everyone else was rising, gathering their things and heading to the boat.

Good, she told herself, closing her sketchbook, and yet she couldn't help feeling a stab of disappointment as the speedboat whisked her mystery man back to the massive yacht anchored outside her cove, because he was, without a doubt, the most interesting man she'd ever seen, and now he was gone.

Later that evening, Josephine was returning from doing her last check of the equipment in the cottage when she heard loud voices, as if in argument, from just outside the cove. She crossed to the beach, listening intently, but this time she heard nothing, just the sound of the yacht engine humming. Was the yacht finally leaving?

As usual, it was brightly lit and pulsing with music. On the top deck she could see couples lounging and drinking. There were others on a deck below and then others at the far end of the yacht, in the shadows.

The yacht was moving. She could see the moonlight reflecting off the white wake. She was sorry to see her mystery man leave, but glad the noise would be gone. The music was terrible. She was still standing there when she heard a muffled shout and then saw someone go overboard. It was at the back of the yacht, where people had been on a lower deck in the shadows.

She rushed closer to the water's edge, attention fixed on the point where the person had gone into the water, but no one resurfaced. Sick, panicked, Josephine worried that someone could be drowning. She couldn't just stand idle while someone died.

She yanked off her sundress and dived between the

waves to swim out to where the yacht had been anchored for the past two and a half days. Diving beneath the surface of the water, she struggled to see in the gloom, but all was dark, so dark, and the reef dropped off dramatically not far from her, the coral giving way to deep water. Josephine swam with her hands in front of her, searching, reaching, lungs burning, bursting, and just when she was going to push back to the surface, she felt fabric, and then heat. A chest. Shoulders. Big, thick shoulders. A man.

She prayed for help as she circled his neck with her arm, hoping for divine strength because she needed superpowers in that moment, her own lungs seizing, desperate for air.

With a groan, she pulled up and he rose with her. Not quickly, but he was floating as she swam, his huge body heavy, but she'd never swum with such resolve. She'd grown up in the ocean. She'd spent her life swimming, deep, exploring caves and the reef, and even though spots danced before her eyes she told herself she could do this because she wasn't alone. She had faith that she was meant to be there when the body fell overboard, and she was meant to find him, and she was meant to save him.

And she did.

She surfaced and, gasping for air, towed him to shore. Once she'd dragged him out of the waves, she kept pulling, hoping she wasn't hurting him as she wrestled him onto the firm damp sand. Once she knew they were out of the surf, she rolled him onto his side, allowing water to drain from his mouth and nose, before settling him onto his back. It was only then she realized it was him.

The beautiful brooding man.

The one who'd barely seemed to tolerate the others.

The one who suffered no fools.

She'd never had to resuscitate anyone before, but her father had taught her years ago, and she remembered the basics, although guidelines kept changing every year or two. She pinched his nose closed and then breathed into his mouth with five strong breaths, followed by thirty chest compressions. She put her ear near his mouth and listened. Nothing. She heard nothing. She repeated the cycle with two strong breaths into his mouth and another thirty compressions. After each cycle, she listened and watched his chest, checking for signs of life.

She wouldn't give up. *Breathe, breathe, breathe*, she chanted in her head, repeating the cycle, praying as she did, asking for divine help, not at all prepared to lose him.

Breathe, breathe, breathe.

Live, live, live.

Just when she was sure her efforts were pointless, his chest lifted—not much, but it moved, and it was enough to give her hope. Determined, Jo breathed into his mouth, those two strong breaths, and this time she felt air exhale from his lips and saw a definite rise and fall of his chest. His breath was rough and raspy, but it was a breath. It wasn't her imagination. He was alive.

Her eyes stung with tears. Her hands began to shake as she shoved her long, wet hair behind her ears, overwhelmed and exhausted. The sheer enormity of it all hit her, and she sat back on her heels, shoulders sagging. She'd saved him. But now what? What was she to do with him?

Her adrenaline faded, and she began trembling in earnest, wiped out. She didn't know how she'd managed any of it. She was a good swimmer, a strong swimmer, but it was a miracle she'd been able to find him and pull him to the shore. He needed medical help, and she had no way to call for assistance. Her radio was broken. Her dad would be bringing a new one when he returned, but that wasn't for days. Ordinarily, she wouldn't mind being cut off—she'd gone weeks before without communication—but this was different.

Her brow creased as she glanced out toward the sea, the mouth of the cove empty, the moonlight reflecting brightly on the water, the only sign of the yacht a distant glow of yellow light on the horizon.

How did no one notice that he'd gone overboard? How could they go without him?

Gently, she stroked his hair back from his brow, only then noting the blood matting the thick hair at his temple. He was injured, and from the nasty gash on his forehead, he'd been injured before he'd fallen—or been pushed—overboard.

She'd heard raised voices. She'd heard a fight. It was what had drawn her attention—that and the hum of the yacht engine. From the mark on his brow it looked as if someone had struck him. Why?

He blinked, trying to focus. His head hurt. Pain radiated through him. He struggled to sit but the world tilted and swam around him. He blinked again, not understanding why everything was so blurry. It was almost as if he was underwater and yet, through the haze, he saw a woman leaning over him, her face above his, her expression worried.

He struggled to place her. How did he know her? Did he know her?

The effort to think was too much. He gave up trying to focus and closed his eyes, sinking back into oblivion.

Pain woke him again.

A heavy, brutal pounding in his head made him stir, his eyes slowly, carefully opening, trying to minimize the ache in his head.

It was day, either early or late he didn't know because the light was soft, diffused.

A woman was moving around the room. She wore a loose white dress, the gauzy fabric fluttering around her bare legs. She paused at the small square window, her brow creasing as she gazed out. Her hair was long and straight, falling almost to her waist.

For a moment he wondered if she was an angel. For a moment he wondered if he had died and gone to heaven. Not that he deserved to go to heaven. Strange thought, but true. He struggled to rise but immediately felt nauseous.

Biting back a curse, he slowly sank back against the pillow, realizing he wasn't dead—or at least, he wasn't in heaven. He couldn't be, not if he hurt this much.

His muffled groan must have reached the angel girl, as she turned in her white dress, the delicate fabric floating behind her as she moved toward him, so young, so beautiful he was certain she wasn't real.

Perhaps he was feverish. Perhaps he was hallucinating, because as she knelt next to him, the sun's rays seemed to narrow and cast a glow around her, highlighting her long golden-brown hair, her smooth brow, and the high, elegant cheekbones above her full lips.

Maybe hell was filled with angelic beauties.

He was finally coming to. Josephine moved forward, crouching at his side. "Hello," she said in English, before it struck her that it was unlikely English was his native language. Most of the conversation she'd heard on the beach had been French, while others had spoken Italian. "How are you?" she asked in French.

He blinked and struggled to focus, his eyes a brilliant blue, contrasting with his long, dense black lashes.

She tried Italian next. "How do you feel?"

His brow tightened. He grimaced, responding in Italian. *"Tu chei sei?" Who are you?*

"Josephine," she answered, as he slowly reached up to touch his head, where a crust had formed on his cut. "Careful," she added in Italian. "You've been injured. It's finally stopped bleeding."

"What happened?"

"You went over the side of your yacht."

"A yacht?" he repeated in Italian.

"Yes. You were with friends."

"Dove sono?" he murmured, his voice a deep rasp. *Where am I?*

"Khronos. A small island off Anafi," she answered.

"I don't know it."

"Anafi is very small. No one knows Anafi, and Khronos is even smaller. It's privately held, a research site for the International Volcanic Research Foundation—" She broke off as she realized he wasn't listening, or at least, he wasn't processing what she was saying, his features tight with pain. "Do you hurt right now?"

He nodded once. "My head," he gritted.

She reached out to place a palm against his brow. He was cooler now, thank goodness. "You were running a fever last night, but I think it's gone now." She drew her hand back, studying him. "I'd like to see if you can manage some water, and if you can, then we'll try some soup—"

"I'm not hungry. I just want something for the pain."

"I have tablets that should help with the headache, but I think you should eat first. Otherwise I'm worried it'll upset your stomach."

He looked at her as if he didn't understand, or perhaps he didn't believe her, because his blue eyes were narrowing and his mouth firmed, emphasizing his strong jaw, now shadowed with a dark stubble.

He'd been striking from afar, but up close he was absolutely devastating, his black hair and brows such a contrast to his startlingly blue eyes. His features were mature and chiseled. Faint creases fanned from his eyes.

As his gaze met hers and held, her pulse jumped. "It's been almost a full day since I pulled you out of the sea—"

"How?" he interrupted.

"How?" she repeated.

"How did I get here?"

"Your boat. Your yacht—"

"I don't understand this yacht." The wrinkles in his forehead deepened. He struggled into a sitting position, wincing and cursing under his breath. His hand lifted to his temple, where the wound was beginning to bleed again. "When was I on one?"

"The past few days. Probably the past week or more." She sat back on her haunches, studying him. "Do you not remember?"

He shook his head.

"What do you remember?"

He thought for a moment, and then his broad, sun-bronzed shoulders shifted irritably, impatiently. "Nothing." His voice was hard, his diction crisp. Authority and tension crackled around him.

Her jaw dropped ever so slightly. "You don't remember who you are? Your name? Your age?"

"No. But I do know I need to find a bathroom. Can you show me the way?"

He had questions for her later, many questions, and Josephine fought to hide her anxiety over his complete loss of memory. She prepared them a simple dinner, talking to him as she plated the grilled vegetables and lemon-garlic chicken. "I think you must be Italian," she said, carrying the plates to the small rustic table in the center of the room. The table divided the room, creating the illusion of two spaces, the sitting area and then the kitchen. "It was the first language you responded to."

"I don't feel Italian." He grimaced. "Although I'm not

sure what that even means. Can a person feel their nationality?"

"I don't know," she answered, sitting down across from him. "But I suppose if I woke up somewhere else I'd be puzzled by the different cultural norms."

"Tell me about the people I was with."

"They were all about your age. Although some of the girls seemed younger. They all looked…polished. Affluent." She hesitated. "Privileged."

He said nothing.

"Everyone seemed to be having a good time," she added. "Except for you."

He glanced at her swiftly, gaze narrowing.

"I don't know if you were bored, or troubled by something," she added, "but you tended to be off on your own more than the others. And they gave you your space, which made me think you were perhaps the leader."

"The leader?" he repeated mockingly. "The leader of what? A band of thieves? Pirates? Schoolboys on holiday?"

"You don't need to be rude," she said slowly, starting to rise, wanting to move away, but he reached out and caught her, his fingers circling her narrow wrist, holding her in place.

"Don't go."

She looked down to where his hand wrapped her wrist, his skin so very warm against hers. She suppressed a shudder, feeling undone. She was exhausted from watching over him, exhausted from worrying. It had been a long night and day, and now it was night again and she felt stretched to the breaking point. "I'm just trying to help you," she said quietly, tugging free.

He released her. "I'm sorry." His deep voice dropped. "Please sit. Stay."

His words were kind, but his tone was commanding. Clearly he was accustomed to being obeyed.

Her brow furrowed. She didn't want to create friction, and so she slowly sat back down and picked up her fork, but she felt too fatigued to actually eat.

Silence stretched. She could feel him watching her. His scrutiny wasn't making things easier, and she knew his eye color now. Blue, light, bright aquamarine blue. Blue like her sea. Reluctantly, she looked up, her stomach in knots. "I thought you were hungry," she said, aware that he hadn't yet taken a bite, either.

"I'm waiting for you."

"I've lost my appetite."

"The company you're keeping?"

She cracked a small smile. "The company's fine. I think I'm unusually tired tonight."

"I suspect you were up all night worrying about me."

It was true. She hadn't been sure he'd survive. There were complications for those who'd nearly drowned. "But you made it through, and here you are."

"Without a memory, or a name."

"I suppose we should call you something."

"Perhaps," he said, but it was clear from his tone that he didn't agree and wasn't enthusiastic about being called by a name that was probably not his.

"We could try names out, see if anything resonates."

He gave her a long, hard look that made her stomach do a funny little flip. "I'll say names and you tell me if anything feels right," she pressed on.

"Fine."

"Matthew. Mark. Luke. John."

"I'm fairly certain I'm not an apostle."

Her lips twitched. "You know your Bible stories, then."

"Yes, but I don't like this approach. I want my own name, or no name." He stabbed his fork into his dinner but made no attempt to eat. "Tell me about you," he said, turning the tables. "Why are you here on what appears to be a deserted island?"

"Well, it's not deserted—it's an island that serves a scientific purpose, housing one of the five research stations for the International Volcano Foundation. My father is a professor, a volcanologist. We were supposed to be here for a year but it's been almost eight."

"Where is he now?"

"Hawaii." She saw his expression and added, "He is a professor at the University of Hawaii. He juggles the teaching and the fieldwork. Right now he's back in Honolulu, lecturing, but he'll return end of the month, which is now just nine days away."

"And he has left you alone here?"

She hesitated. "Does it seem strange to you?"

"Yes."

Her shoulders shifted. "It's actually normal for me, and I don't mind. I like the solitude. I'm not much of a people person. And the quiet allows me a chance to do my own work, because when Papa is here, it's always about him."

"What about your mother?"

"She died just before I turned five."

"I'm sorry."

She shrugged again, uncomfortable with the sympathy. "I don't remember her."

"Would she approve of your lifestyle here?"

"She was a volcanologist like my father. They worked together for ten years, doing exactly what he's doing now, but in Hawaii, so yes, I think she'd approve. Perhaps her only disappointment would be that I haven't gone off to college or earned all the degrees that she did. I've been homeschooled my entire life, even with the university courses. My father says I'm more advanced than even his graduate students, but it's not the same. I've never had to be in the real world or compete with others for work. I just work."

"What is your field of study?"

"I'm a volcanologist, too, although personally I prefer the point where archaeology intersects with volcanology."

"Vesuvius?"

She nodded. "Exactly. I've been lucky to work with my father on the volcanology of the southwestern sector of Vesuvius, where archaeological and historical data have allowed scientists to map the lava emitted in the last several thousand years. I'm fascinated by not just the lost civilizations, but the power of these volcanoes to reshape the landscape and rewrite the history of man."

"It doesn't sound as if you've missed anything by being homeschooled."

She smiled faintly. "I haven't been properly socialized—my father said as much. I'm not comfortable in cities and crowds. But fortunately, we don't have that problem here."

"Your mother was American, too?"

"French-Canadian, from Quebec. That's how I ended up Josephine." Her smile faded as she saw how his expression changed, his jaw tightening and lips compressing. "You *will* remember your name," she said quietly. "It's just going to be a matter of time."

"You spoke to me in French, didn't you?"

"I tried a number of languages. You responded in Italian, so I've stuck with Italian. *Est-ce que tu parles français?*"

"Oui."

"And English?" she asked, switching languages again. "Do you understand me?"

He nodded. "I do."

"How fluent are you?" she asked, continuing in English, testing him. "Is it difficult to follow me?"

"No. It doesn't seem any different from Italian."

He had almost no accent, his English was easy, his diction relaxed, making him sound American, not British. She suspected he'd been educated at one point in the United States. "Would you mind speaking English then?"

"No."

"But should it give you a headache, or if it creates any stress—"

"No need to fuss over me. I'm fine."

She opened her mouth to protest but thought better of it. He was a man used to having the final word. So who was he? And why did he, even now, ooze power?

"Tell me again about the people I was with on the yacht," he said. "Tell me everything you know."

"I will after you eat something."

"I'm not hungry anymore."

"That's strange, because my memory seems to be fading, as well."

He gave her a hard look. "I'm not amused."

"Neither am I. You've been through a great deal, and we need to get you strong. And as I am your primary caregiver here—"

"I don't like being coddled."

"And I'm not known to coddle, so eat, and I'll tell you everything. Don't eat, and you can fret by yourself because I have things to do besides argue with you."

His eyes narrowed and his jaw hardened, making a small muscle in his jaw pop. For a long moment he just looked at her, clearly not happy with the situation, but then he reached for the plate of chicken and took a bite, and then another, and did a pretty impressive job of devouring the rest. He lifted his head at one point and met her gaze. "This is good, by the way. Very good."

"Thank you."

"You made this?"

"Yes."

"Here?"

"Yes."

"How?"

"I have a freezer, and I use the kiln outside for roasting the potatoes and baking. The rest I prepare on the stove."

"A kiln?"

"It makes excellent flatbreads, and pizzas, too. I learned how to cook in a kiln when we lived in Peru. That was before here. I loved Peru. My father loved the stratovolcano." She smiled faintly, remembering his excitement and obsession as Sabancaya roared to life, spewing ash and rumbling the mountain. If it weren't for the village women, Josephine would have been forgotten. Instead they took her and her father in and helped teach Josephine to cook, and as a thank-you, Josephine would look after the children, giving the hardworking mothers a break.

"Where else have you lived?"

"Washington State, Hawaii, Peru, and Italy, but that was brief, before here. We've been here the longest."

"Was every place this isolated?"

"No, this is definitely the most remote, but I'm truly happy here."

"Is that why you just watched us on the beach and didn't come introduce yourself?"

She laughed as she reached for his plate. "I think we come from different worlds. I am quite sure I'd be an oddity in your world."

His brow creased. "You think so?"

"Absolutely. I wouldn't know how to drape myself over and around handsome men." Her lips twitched. "I can't for the life of me just lie on a beach. I need to be active, and instead of sunbathing I'd be catching fish, and examining the water table, and trying to figure out the volcanic history of the exposed rocks—" she broke off. "Not your kind of girl at all."

"What is my kind?"

"The kind that looks like a swimsuit model. The kind

that doesn't lift anything, not even her own swim bag. The kind that pouts when you don't feel like talking."

"Interesting," he drawled, blue eyes glinting.

"How so?"

"You didn't like my friends. You never said that earlier. This is new information."

"I shouldn't have said anything. It's not factual and not important—"

"But revealing about you."

"Exactly. There is no reason to share my feelings on anything. I should be focused on assisting you. Who I am and what I feel isn't relevant in any way."

"You're allowed to have opinions."

"I'll voice them if they'll be helpful. Me judging your female friends isn't helpful. It's just me being petty and unkind and unnecessary."

"Why do I feel like you are a rare breed?"

"Because I am strange. I don't fit in. I never have."

"Sounds a bit defeatist, don't you think?"

"I would agree with you if I were here licking my wounds. But I'm here by choice, because I'm happy here. I sleep well here. I can breathe here. I don't feel odd or different, and on Khronos I don't second-guess myself, and that's a good thing."

"You're saying society makes you uncomfortable."

"Absolutely." She carried his plate and fork to the small sink in her very small kitchen and felt his gaze bore into her back as she filled the small plastic dish tub with water to let them soak. "But I've been raised outside society so it's to be expected."

"Have you ever lived in a city?"

"Honolulu."

"Is that a proper city?"

She turned and shot him a disapproving look. "Yes. Honolulu has some beautiful architecture and it has a fascinating history. Hawaii isn't just beaches and surfing." She didn't tell him, though, that she didn't enjoy going back to Oahu anymore because it was too urban for her now. There were far too many cars and people and it had been overwhelming, which was why she'd elected to remain behind on Khronos while her father went to teach.

She turned away from the sink, wiped her hands dry on a dish towel and carried the water carafe to the table. "There were maybe twelve of you that came onto the beach," she said, taking her seat again. "Seven men, including you, and five women. The yacht was huge. One of the biggest, most luxurious yachts I've ever seen. Your group would come onto the beach during the day and everyone would swim and sunbathe, eat and drink." She shot him a long look. "There was lots of drinking. Everyone seemed to be having a good time."

"And the night I went overboard?"

"There was music playing—as always—and a party. As always. Your friends were on the top two decks—the top deck you all used as a disco, so the music and dancing were there, but there were others on the second deck, and I wasn't sure if they were in a hot tub or a pool, but people there were just hanging out, talking and laughing. But what got my attention on that last night was the arguing at the back of the yacht. I heard voices, or thought I heard voices, and things sounded like they were getting a little heated. It was what caught my attention and what drew me to the edge of the water."

"*I* was arguing?" he asked quietly.

She hesitated, frowning. "Yes. No. I don't actually know that it was you. I just heard arguing, and then there was a shout and a splash. I couldn't see that well and for a second wondered if someone had maybe jumped overboard, but when the person went under and didn't resurface, I panicked and raced out."

"Saving me."

She tapped her fingers on the table, suddenly uncomfortable. "I didn't know it was you. I just knew someone was in trouble."

"That couldn't have been an easy swim."

"No, but I was terrified you were going to drown. I couldn't let it happen."

"You risked your life for a stranger."

"What is the point of being a strong swimmer if I can't save someone now and then?"

She'd deliberately kept her tone light, wanting to ease the tension.

He didn't smile. "I would have died without you."

"But you didn't. Now we just need to get your memory back, and all will be well." She gave him a bright smile and then rose, moving around the room, adjusting the shutters to give them more of the evening's breeze, and then taking her broom and sweeping out some sand that had found its way inside.

She could feel his gaze on her the entire time and it made her skin prickle and heat. She felt herself flush and her pulse quicken. He watched her the way surfers watched the waves—with focus and quiet intensity. It was unnerving and she suddenly wanted to adjust her skirt and gather her hair. She wanted to be pretty and worth the attention—

Josephine gave her head a shake.

She couldn't try to be someone she wasn't. She'd done that in the past, in Honolulu, for example, and it had been disastrous. "Judging from your accent," she said crisply, giving the threshold one last hard sweep of the broom, "you could be from Belgium, Luxembourg, France, Italy, Switzerland, Monaco, Sicily, Malta, Aargau—maybe even America. You've certainly managed to nail the American drawl."

He grimaced. "I don't feel American."

She returned the broom to the corner. "Then we can cross the States off the list." She did a quick count in her head. "Leaving nine possible cultures or nationalities."

"We're whittling down the list."

She laughed, and then her laughter faded as she studied the huge bruise still darkening his brow. "I just wish I knew how that happened," she said, nodding at his temple. "Were you injured in the fall? Did it happen before you went over the side?"

"I've wondered the same."

She studied his expression, debating if she should reveal her worries, but then he said what she'd been thinking, his voice deep, his delivery slow and thoughtful, "Because if it wasn't accidental—that would change everything, wouldn't it?"

CHAPTER TWO

HE DIDN'T KNOW his name. He didn't know where he was from. He didn't know what he did, or where he lived, or why he'd even be on a yacht "with friends." He didn't know if someone had meant him harm or if he'd simply had an accident and fallen overboard.

But there was one thing he did know, and it was this: he wanted her.

He woke thinking about Josephine and fell asleep thinking about her and it was all he could do to hide the physical evidence of his desire. He wasn't a boy. It shouldn't be difficult to control his hunger, but the fierceness of his desire made him wonder if he'd ever felt like this about anyone before or if this was typical of him. Desire. Hunger. Impatience.

Perhaps the intensity of the need was due to all the other unknowns.

He tried to distract himself with reading the books on the shelves in the house. When he was tired of reading, he swam or lay on the warm sand, soaking in the heat of the sun. But inevitably, as time passed, his thoughts turned to Josephine. He wanted to see her. He just wanted to be near her, so he'd pull a shirt on, one of the shirts from her father's closet that she'd lent him, and assist her with her work. He'd help with her notes, or he'd water the garden—anything if it meant he could be at her side, as he'd come to crave her shape, her scent, her smile.

She was beautiful and brilliant as well as innocent and earnest. He was certain she was a rare gem, a jewel among even the world's most beautiful women, and he said that to her one day, after they'd emerged from the sea following a swim.

She smiled at him, amused but also shy. "Thank you for the compliment, but seeing as you don't remember anything of your world, I'm not sure it's valid."

"I don't have to compare you to know that you're smart and kind. You're also cheerful and optimistic, and you make me happy. I have a feeling I'm not always easy to please."

"You certainly weren't cheerful on the beach with your friends. In fact, you were often quite aloof, sitting off on your own, staring out at the ocean. I would watch you and sketch you—"

"Sketch me?"

She nodded, blushing. "It's what I like to do when I have free time."

"I haven't seen you draw since I've been here."

"I do when you're not around, or late at night when you're sleeping."

"What do you draw?"

"This and that." Her blush deepened. "Mostly you."

He loved how her pink cheeks made her eyes look even more green. She was so fresh and pretty. She reminded him of a mermaid…a siren from the sea. "Why draw me?"

"You fascinate me."

"Why?"

"You have to know." Her lips pressed, her expression suddenly reminding him of a prim schoolteacher. "Don't make me spell it out."

He was enchanted by the line her full lips made and the firmness of her chin. His fingers itched to reach out and trace her pink cheek and the shape of her mouth. And just like that, his body hardened, the desire hot and insistent. "Apparently, my head injury has made me a little slow. Be kind and explain to me why someone like me would fascinate you?"

Her chin lifted higher. "I'll only tell you this one time."

"I'm listening."

"You're unbearably attractive—"

"Unbearably?"

"You're very intelligent."

"Can we get back to the unbearably attractive part? Is it possible to be *unbearably* attractive?"

"Yes. You've proven it. Let me continue." She tapped her fingers as if counting her points. "You have a sense of humor—when you want to."

"I suppose that is a drawback, being unpredictable."

Her lips twitched. "You have rich friends. That yacht was enormous. But that's really more of a negative then a plus."

"Why a negative?"

"From an environmental standpoint, it's terrible."

"I agree."

Her brows arched. "You do?"

"I do. I'm always worried about the environment."

"You are?"

He nodded.

She frowned, a faint link forming between her eyebrows. "That's interesting," she murmured.

"Is it?"

Josephine nodded. "You're starting to have a clearer sense of self. I think some of your memories are returning. This is a good thing."

He felt a sudden wash of unease, and he didn't understand it. The return of his memory should be a great thing, and yet all he felt was a pervasive dread. "Let's talk about you instead."

"Why? I'm a boring academic—"

"Not boring, and academics are exciting."

She laughed. "Are they?"

"I went to school with brilliant women. There is nothing sexier than a smart woman—" he broke off as he realized what he'd said. He'd gone to school with brilliant women. And he knew he hadn't meant high school or grammar school. He'd meant university, and the words had been so comfortable, so natural. He also knew that calling university *school* was very American. Had he gone to school—college—in America?

He could see from Josephine's expression that she'd heard the reference, too, and understood it, as well.

"Your memory *is* returning," she said softly, breathlessly.

"You're healing me," he said. "All this sun and swimming."

She smiled back at him. "It's not as if there's a lot to do here. No TV or video games."

"But even if you had those, I don't think it's something you'd do. You love being outside. You're at home in the sea."

Her cheeks were pink, and her eyes were bright as she tucked a long strand of sun-streaked hair behind her ear. "I've always grown up next to the sea. First in Hawaii and then here. I can't imagine not swimming. If I go too many days without getting wet, I feel off. The sea always restores me."

"You are a fish."

She laughed. "My father says the same thing. He says that I have scales and they dry out if I'm out of the water too long. Thus my close proximity to the beach."

"So maybe not a fish but a mermaid."

"Maybe," she answered, smiling, feeling strangely shy and sensitive because everything inside her seemed to be shifting and lurching. Changing.

She'd noticed it before, and she'd tried to suppress the feelings, but she couldn't pretend it wasn't happening, or real, any longer. She couldn't pretend that he wasn't aware of her. She couldn't pretend that there wasn't something taut and electric between them, because there was something about the way he looked at her, something in the intensity of his expression that made the air catch in her throat, making her heart gallop. The way he looked at her terrified her and yet, at the same time, thrilled her. Being near him was wonderful, confusing, exhilarating. No one had ever looked at her as if she were so important. No one had ever made her feel so beautiful. Every conversation made her feel alive, and she didn't know why because there was nothing terribly revealing said. And yet he fascinated her. He'd fascinated her on the beach when he'd been just a mysterious stranger, and her fascination only grew with every day because how could he—this gorgeous, handsome stranger—want her?

And yet, being wanted was doing something to her, seducing her, making her question everything she believed. She'd always thought that she'd never have sex with someone, not unless he was her forever love, the man who would marry her, the man who would share a life with her. Looking into his eyes, she figured she was losing out on something beautiful. This felt special. It felt like a once-in-a-lifetime opportunity, something she wasn't prepared to miss.

It helped that she knew the attraction wasn't one-sided.

It was clear from the heat in his gaze that he desired her, and the knowledge was a heady power. An aphrodisiac that made her restless and curious. He could make her feel so much with just a look. How would she feel if he touched her? *Kissed her?*

She didn't let herself think further than that. She'd never experienced more than a couple kisses, kisses that hadn't inspired her in any way, making her think there was no need to repeat the experience. Until now. Somehow she sensed that kissing her mysterious stranger would be entirely different. Maybe even life-changing.

But did she want that?

She looked hard at her stranger, who truthfully was no

longer a stranger, but someone who was quickly becoming very important to her.

She'd spent so much of her life alone, or alone with her father—which was virtually alone since he rarely spoke, his head always down, buried in his work. She understood her father's fascination with his work and his commitment to research, but every now and then she wanted…more.

She wanted to be seen.

She wanted to be known.

She wanted to be…loved.

Growing up as she had had taught her tremendous self-reliance, but there were times she felt that her life had also left her empty and aching for more. More connection. More expression. More emotion.

Usually these thoughts and feelings happened late at night, and she'd blame fatigue and the need to sleep.

But she was feeling these things almost constantly lately. The arrival of her mystery man had changed something within her.

His arrival had made her aware of the world out there and that there was more to the world than she knew. But even with that knowledge, she also knew she was happy on Khronos. Most of the time she wanted nothing but her work and the sun and the sea. Most of the time she was utterly content.

She needed to be content again.

Abruptly, Josephine rose, moving away, trying to escape the heat suffusing her skin and ache filling her chest. Her father had left her here to manage the foundation's station. She needed to stay focused on her responsibilities. "I'd better get back to work," she said huskily.

"Can I help?" he asked.

She shook her head. "I'm just going to check the solar panels. You relax—"

"That's all I've done the past few days. Show me what

you're doing, or what needs to be done, so I can help while I'm here."

She smiled tightly. "Okay, follow me."

The old Greek cottage had been constructed of stones, without the charm of whitewash, and while it looked ancient and almost abandoned from the front, there were clean, well-maintained stairs behind—stairs that rose up to a clearing filled with a mass of solar panels and equipment, and another smaller stone house.

"That's where the foundation keeps all the seismic monitoring equipment. The equipment is connected to portable seismometers along the edge of the island, as well as some in the water. You see, we're sitting practically on top of a volcano. Khronos is just the tip, which is why we have the seismometers to detect rock movement in the earth's crust. Some movements may be the result of rising magma beneath the surface, which could mean an awakening volcano. We also have equipment here that monitors gases like sulfur dioxide, as an increase in sulfur dioxide could be an indication of magma near the earth's surface."

"And if that should happen? What do you do?"

"It hasn't happened in the past ten years, so I think I'm safe. Odds are, I'm safe."

"You're pretty nonchalant about something potentially catastrophic."

"Some people are terrified of volcanoes, particularly supervolcanoes, but there has never been such an eruption in human memory, and did you know there are actually quite a few people who choose to live near a volcano because they're drawn to the geothermal energy, the minerals and the fertile soil? I'm a fan of geothermal energy because it's very clean, and the resource is nearly inexhaustible.

"Speaking of energy, come see," she said, walking farther back along a compact dirt path that cut deeply through the rough, rocky terrain dotted with a few gnarled olive trees. "Twenty years ago the foundation was powered by those wind turbines before us. Unfortunately, they were prone to breaking down and the repairs were costly, and then new, improved solar technology became a better answer, so eventually no one bothered to repair or replace the turbines."

"They do look forlorn," he said, taking in the line of tall wind turbines that covered the top of the island.

"Luckily for us, solar works incredibly well, allowing the foundation to live completely off the grid. We use solar energy for almost everything. Light, heating, cooking, powering the radio—when the radio actually works—and now for desalination."

He'd been studying the solar panels, but she noted how his interest was piqued by the mention of their desalination system.

She walked him back to another frame, this one with its own set of panels, plus tubes, dials and black rectangular features, and motioned for him to crouch down beside her. "This is our baby and my personal favorite because this one gives us all our fresh water. In the beginning, we had to bring everything in, including gallons and gallons of water. We'd collect rainwater when we could, but if we had no rain, we'd begin to panic. Now, thanks to a partnership with my father's university, we're able to turn salt water into drinking water using only solar energy. Although there are over eighteen thousand desalination plants across the world, this one is unique in that it combines solar energy with brand-new technology allowing a family to generate enough clean water for individual use."

"How is it different from traditional desalination?"

"You're familiar with the desalination process?"

"Salt water is brought to a boil, creating steam. The steam is run through a condensing coil."

"Right. The traditional method is very energy inefficient and requires expensive, complex infrastructure. Over half of the cost of a distillation plant is spent on energy."

"So this is membrane distillation?"

She was impressed he knew that much. Perhaps he'd studied science in school, or something environment related. "Yes and no. The university took conventional membrane distillation, where hot salt water flows across one side of the porous membrane and cold freshwater flows across the other, and added in a layer of carbon-black nanoparticles. The carbon-black nanoparticles attract light, heating the entire surface of the membrane, converting as much as eighty percent of sunlight energy into heat, giving us more water with less energy. It's ideal for us with a compact footprint, but it will also revolutionize the way the world desalinates water because the nanoparticles are low-cost and commercially available."

"Fascinating," he murmured, studying the section with the nanoparticles and then the tubing where water dripped into a clear canister. "By integrating photothermal heating with membrane distillation you've created more productive and efficient technology."

"I haven't. The university program did. We're lucky the scientists and engineers agreed to let us work with it here. We've had it eighteen months now and it's transformed our lives." She nodded toward the small garden off to the side. "Tomatoes, cucumbers, lettuce, carrots, and more. All possible now due to a never-ending supply of clean, drinkable water."

"I'd heard about an American university developing something like this, but it's amazing to see it in use here on Khronos and to know it's not just theoretical."

"It's a game changer for the world."

"Indeed," he murmured, and yet he wasn't looking at the system but rather at her; his gaze locked on her lips and she felt his scrutiny all the way through her.

Heat bloomed in her cheeks. She felt overly warm, her skin exquisitely sensitive, and she looked away, trying to hide how flustered she felt. She wanted his kiss and yet she feared it, too.

She wasn't experienced, and she knew most women her age would have had a number of significant relationships by now. She suddenly wished she'd had a more conventional life, a life where she'd had dates and boyfriends so she'd know what to do and how to respond.

She wanted to respond. Could he tell?

"You're bored," she said huskily, rising and brushing the coarse dirt from her hands.

"I'm not," he answered, rising, as well. "I'm fascinated by everything here. Not just by how you're managing to survive in the middle of nowhere but by you and this father of yours. I can't imagine any other father leaving his only daughter defenseless in such a remote spot."

"I'm not defenseless. I have the radio—" she broke off, lips tightening. Her heart was racing and her stomach churned and she felt close to tears and didn't know why. Nothing had happened, and yet somehow everything was happening and she seemed to be losing control. "Normally it works. I've never dropped it before. I've never broken it before. That accident was a fluke, just like you being here is a fluke. I've spent four years on Khronos and we've seen plenty of yachts, but none have ever stopped here before. And we've certainly never had any castaways, either—"

"Why are you afraid?" he asked, interrupting her torrent of words.

"I'm not." And yet her voice was high and thin, breathless.

For a long moment he was silent, studying her, and then he reached out and lightly traced her eyebrows, the right and then the left. Her breath caught in her throat as the touch sent sparks of hot sensation shooting through her veins. She stared at him, deep into his eyes, as he continued to explore her face, his fingertips light as they caressed the length of her nose, and then her cheekbone, and finally down along the line of her jaw.

"You are so beautiful," he murmured, his voice deep and rough.

She felt his voice and his touch all the way through her, an erotic rasp that teased her senses, making her skin flush and her body ache.

"No makeup, no designer clothes, no expensive blow-outs. Just beautiful you," he added. "I didn't know women like you even existed."

"You say that now, but if you put me next to your lovely ladies from the yacht, you'd see how I'd pale in comparison."

"I don't think there is any comparison. You're extraordinary. Your mind. Your passion for your work. Your beauty. You're perfect."

"You're going to give me quite an ego."

"Good. You should know you're special. One in a million."

She drew back to look him in the face. He didn't turn away, letting her look, allowing her to see the flare of heat in his eyes.

"If you really feel that way, would you kiss me?" she whispered. "Unless that's not how you feel—"

"I've wanted to kiss you from the moment I opened my eyes and saw you in the room looking like an angel."

She swallowed hard. "I'm no angel," she murmured, even as her pulse beat double time, and her gaze drank him in, lingering on the hard, clean line of cheekbone and the shadow of a beard darkening his strong jaw. He shaved every morning, using her father's kit, but by late afternoon he had that shadow again. And then there was that mouth, his wide, firm mouth, his lips lovely. She'd loved drawing his face and loved his mouth most of all, wondering what it would feel like against her own. Wondering what he'd taste like. Wondering if kissing him would be different from kissing alcohol-fueled Ethan in Honolulu two years ago. That kiss had been so awful and sloppy that it had killed all desire to date.

He closed the distance between them, his hands circling her upper arms, bringing her in against him. His blue eyes glowed bright, the heat in the depths holding her, trapping her. Life seemed to slow, and the world shrank to just them.

Josephine could feel the thudding of her heart, and his hands wrapping around her arms, his skin so warm. She shivered at his heat and the way his hard chest pressed against her breasts, making her conscious that she was braless, and her nipples were tight and yet tender, and so sensitive to every breath he took.

This was what she wanted. This was all she wanted. Just to feel his mouth on hers…

His dark head dropped and very slowly his lovely, sensual mouth captured hers, sending sharp hot sparks of sensation through her. She heard a whimper and prayed it wasn't her. His hand rose to cup the back of her head, holding her still while his lips traveled over hers, teasing, tasting, discovering. She shuddered as more sparks of feeling shot through her, the heat making her melt on the inside, her brain flooded with wildly contradictory signals. She wanted more, so much more, even as another part whispered that she was out of his league.

"Second thoughts?" he murmured, lifting his head, his blue gaze meeting and holding hers.

"Um, yes. No. No." Because truly, she'd never felt so alive and so full of yearning about anything, but this was crazy. Her feelings were crazy. Excitement filled her veins, making her feel daring and wild…two things Josephine was not, nor ever had been.

And yet, it felt so good to feel excited and alive.

It felt so good to be touched and kissed.

"Tell me what you're thinking," he said, stroking her cheek, sending rivulets of fire through her, fire that she could feel in the tips of her breasts and deep between her thighs.

"Because it's obvious you're thinking."

"I know, and I'm sorry for it—"

"Don't be. Talk to me."

She drew a quick, shallow breath before blurting, "Do you think you could be married?"

"No."

"So you don't think you have a…a wife…somewhere?"

"No."

"How can you be so sure?"

His broad shoulders shifted. "Just the way I know I'm not American. It doesn't feel right. It doesn't sound right. It doesn't sound like…me."

He released her and she took a step back, and then another, not because she wanted to be apart from him but because she couldn't think when she was close to him and this conversation was important. "Your memory is returning."

"It must be."

"What sounds like you? Could you describe yourself? Who do you think you might be?"

"European. Wealthy." He grimaced. "Mediterranean, most likely. I think I run a company, or own my own company, and I'm good at it. I feel like I have quite a few employees, so my company can't be small. And I have a nagging suspicion that I'm a perfectionist, and, quite possibly, not easily pleased." He looked chagrined. "And if that is all true, I've just described a man that sounds like a pompous ass, which makes me despise myself, even though I don't yet know myself."

She laughed. "Considering that you don't know yourself, I think you're being a little hard on yourself. After spending the past few days with you, I think you're a better person than you described. My gut says you're a very good person, as well as something of a loner, because even when you were with your friends, you were still a bit distant, and rather alone."

"Probably because I'm an unlikable prat—"

"No!" She interrupted with a throaty gurgle of laughter, and the sheer joy in the sound stopped her. Was that really her giggling? Sounding so impossibly girlish and happy? Josephine went through life very seriously. She was committed to facts, not feelings, and her life revolved around work and being useful and practical.

"What are you thinking now?" he asked.

"Is it that obvious I have a tendency to overthink everything?"

"I like it. I like you. Don't ever apologize for being you, Josephine."

The commanding gruffness in his voice made her throat swell closed. She felt a ridiculous need to cry. It had been such a strange and wonderful few days with him here, and everything inside her felt full and tender and new.

"We should head back to the house so I can focus on dinner," she said.

He caught her by the wrist to stop her from escaping. "You never answered my question. What were you thinking just a moment ago?"

She suppressed a shiver as he stroked the inside of her wrist with the pad of his thumb, setting her alight. "That I'm happy," she said unsteadily, trying not to look at his mouth, trying not to remember their kiss earlier, because it had been perfect, and he made her feel beautiful and perfect, and standing close to him made her shockingly aware of how much she wanted to feel more. "And…" She gulped a breath and then lifted her chin, determined to finish her thought. "I'm happy you're here."

CHAPTER THREE

THE SKY WAS putting on a show tonight, the sunset a stunning orange on top of red, while waves crashed onto the beach—but the beauty was lost on him. Tension rolled through him. He didn't yet know himself, but he sensed parts of himself. It was strange and disorienting as well as infuriating. He didn't like not knowing himself, and he didn't want to be called by a name that wasn't his.

He wanted his name, and his identity.

He wanted to be himself, whoever that was, good or bad. He'd take the good and bad, fully embracing both because it was beyond frustrating to feel and think without a foundation of self, never mind self-knowledge.

Every time he heard himself say *I think*...a little voice inside him stopped him, questioning him. *Are you sure? How do you know?*

So, hurrah, his memory was returning, but it wasn't fast enough. He was impatient with the process. He didn't want pieces of himself; he wanted *all* his memory back. He wanted his life back. It wasn't enough to sense things about himself. He needed to *know*. He needed the truth.

The darkness inside him threatened to engulf him tonight and it crossed his mind that this life of hers was not him, which just made him want to know what his life was. He was by no means bored on Khronos, and he was enjoying being with Josephine, but this quiet island of hers wasn't his life.

He knew with certainty that his life wasn't quiet.

His work wasn't calm.

His world had stress and chaos and deadlines and people.

"Here," Josephine said, emerging at his side on the

beach, a glass of wine in her hand. "I think you could use it."

He arched a brow.

"It's good wine," she said, smiling, her full lips curving, the sweet lift of her lips reminding him of their kiss earlier, and how soft her mouth had been beneath his, and how good she'd felt in his arms. Hunger stirred and he imagined doing all sorts of things to her that weren't innocent and would probably shock her.

But she'd enjoy it, and he'd enjoy her pleasure.

"And I need it because…?" he asked, smashing his hunger, not needing one more torment tonight.

"You're pacing this poor beach like a caged tiger. I'm hoping a couple glasses of Father Epi's merlot might help you relax."

He took the glass from her. "We've never had wine before."

"I don't normally drink, but this is a special occasion."

"Is it?"

She nodded, color suffusing her lovely cheekbones. "I thought we should do something different tonight. Make tonight special. Hopefully it will provide some diversion and distract you from whatever is bothering you."

"You don't need to worry about me."

"But I do."

"Why?"

"I care about you." Her shoulders lifted and fell. "Which is why we're having dinner alfresco tonight. I've set a table for us and we will enjoy dinner outside and watch the sun set, and you'll be my first real date. Unless that is too awkward?" She bit into her lush lower lip for a moment, struggling with her confidence. "Am I horribly awkward? I'm afraid I am."

"There is nothing awkward about you," he answered huskily, reaching for her and drawing her close. "I would enjoy a dinner date with you very much, *bella*," he murmured, his head dropping to kiss her soft, warm mouth. For a moment she stiffened, and then in the next, she leaned into him, giving herself up to him. He traced the seam of her lips with his tongue and when her lips parted, he claimed her mouth, too, his tongue teasing hers, tasting her, wanting her. She shivered against him, and he kissed her jaw and then the side of her neck, feeling her shiver again as he kissed his way down to her collarbone, the air catching in her throat. She was so sensitive. He battled his desire, keeping his need in check.

She wanted a date. She wanted romance. He could do that.

"You don't have to do anything," she said quickly, breathlessly. "I'm taking care of the dinner and I've already set the table. Want to come see?"

He nodded because he did want to see, very much so. He offered her his arm, and she shyly tucked her hand through the crook of his elbow. They left the beach, returning to the little house, which looked altogether different with the glowing fire outside in a fire pit and a small round table covered with a vivid tablecloth with bright birds and butterflies against a black wool background. There were two place settings on the table, and tall tapered candles glimmered in the center. It was charming and rustic and he was touched that she had gone to such pains for him.

"That's not a Greek tablecloth," he said.

"No, it's from Peru. My dear Azucena made it for me before we left. I was supposed to save it for my hope chest—" She broke off when she saw his confusion. "Do girls not have hope chests where you're from?"

"I'm not sure. What is that?"

"It's where you save things for your wedding. Linens and quilts and other things to help you begin your new home once you're married."

He noticed she wouldn't look at him as she talked, and color darkened her cheeks.

"I'm not planning on getting married," she added, moving around the table, adjusting the plates and glasses, "and it seems like such a waste to leave this lovely tablecloth in a chest forever, so I brought it out tonight. It's pretty, though, isn't it?"

"It is." But he wasn't looking at the cloth. He was looking at Josephine as the candlelight illuminated her profile. She'd changed at some point from her casual sundress into a long blue skirt that she'd paired with a white peasant-style blouse. Her long hair had been pulled into a loose knot that she'd attempted to secure with what looked like wooden sticks, but long tendrils of hair were slipping out and curling loosely at her neck and around her face.

Her cheeks were flushed and her eyes bright as she glanced at him, and her expression was nervous and shy, sweet and hopeful, and it was the hopefulness in her green gaze that made his chest tighten and ache.

He had a feeling his life was full of beautiful women, but none were like her. How could they be? Who could possibly be as smart and beautiful and yet also so capable? He marveled at her ability to make do with so little. She complained about nothing.

"Why won't you marry?" he asked, wanting to touch one of those long, loose tendrils that had slipped free from her chignon to rest on her smooth, tanned shoulder.

"It's just unlikely," she answered, giving him a smile. "It's not as if men wash up on my beach often."

"I did."

"Yes, but it took me eight years to rescue my first prince."

His brow creased. "Prince?"

She smiled, and a small dimple appeared near the corner of her mouth. "Like the story 'The Little Mermaid,' except I don't intend to give up my soul in order to marry or in order to make him—or anyone—happy."

"I confess, I don't know the story."

"How can you not know it?"

"I was an—" he stopped and looked away, perplexed. He'd come so close to saying *I was an only child.*

But was he?

And was that why he didn't know the story?

"It's not an American story," she added, "although Disney did a version of it. It's Hans Christian Andersen, and his stories are invariably really sad and depressing. I think they were meant to scare children into good behavior, but they gave me nightmares so my dad told my mom not to read them to me anymore, but of course I remember the ones that upset me most."

She glanced at him. "But no depressing conversation. Dinner is ready. Shall we eat?"

Josephine plated their dinner—roasted lamb fragrant with garlic, oregano, thyme, rosemary, and lemon juice. She loved cooking Greek food and tonight's lamb paired perfectly with the merlot and the sky, the stunning sunset fading to just a wisp of red and purple on the horizon.

He held her chair for her as she sat down, a chivalrous gesture that made her feel safe and protected. "Thank you," she murmured, watching as he took the seat opposite her, the candlelight reflecting off the bronze of his cheekbones and his inky-black hair. She felt a sizzle race through her as his blue gaze met hers and held. It was hard to think clearly when he made her feel so much, her pulse racing, her body humming with nerves and excitement.

She wanted him to kiss her again.

She wanted him to hold her and make her feel all the things she'd felt earlier, because this magic wouldn't last. He'd be gone before she knew it and this time here, together, would be just a memory. A memory she'd cherish forever.

"I can't imagine a more inviting table setting, or a more beautiful dinner companion," he said, lifting his wineglass. "To you, Josephine. Thank you for everything."

"It's my pleasure," she said, lightly clinking the rim of her goblet to his.

He sipped the wine and nodded. "This is really good wine."

"It's Greek, made by Father Epi in the monastic community Mount Athos. It's my father's favorite and what he always brings back with him."

"I'll have to remember it."

She felt her lips curve. "I'd rather you remember your name and those important things like where you live and what you do." Her smile faded. "Your family must be frantic. If you were mine, I'd be beside myself."

"It'd be nice to know who they are."

"I'm sure they are heartsick, as are your friends."

"Hmm."

She shot him a speculative look. "You don't think so?"

His jaw hardened, his gaze narrowing. "They didn't come back."

She'd thought the same thing many times. Carefully, she added, "Maybe they didn't know where you disappeared. It is a huge sea."

"Whoever I fought with knew I went overboard. Why didn't he sound the alarm?"

"If that person did know…you're still in trouble. That person is dangerous. He or she meant to do you harm. Otherwise the yacht would have circled back. Your friends, the rest of them, would never have left you."

"That's the first time, you said *he or she*." His gaze met hers and held. "Until now, you've always said *he*. Do you think it was a woman?"

"I don't know. I shouldn't have said anything. And I shouldn't speculate. I was never close enough to your group to hear conversations. I only watched from afar, and to be honest, I only really watched you." She felt her face go hot once again. Her shoulders twisted. She didn't know where to look. "You were the most interesting."

His gaze locked with hers and held, and what she saw in his eyes made the air bottle in her lungs and her skin heat. He wanted her, desired her, and it struck her for the first time that it wasn't because he was grateful she'd saved him—which was what she'd always told herself until now—but because he liked *her*, Josephine Robb, social misfit. It shouldn't matter that she could speak a half-dozen different languages but didn't know anything about popular American culture, but it did whenever she returned to the States. While women her age discussed fashion and the current social-media sensation, she felt foolish and exposed, a fish out of water.

It was all she could do to eat her dinner, and it was one of her favorite meals. Chewing, swallowing, talking, smiling became a challenge because she could feel him from across the table; she could feel his energy and it was dizzying. Her breasts peaked, her body felt hot, like liquid, and she pressed her knees together, trying to deny the sensitivity between her thighs.

"You've become very quiet," he said, as they finished their meal.

The candlelight flickered, casting a dancing shadow across his face. Her gaze followed the shadow and light as it moved over the slash of cheekbones, the strong forehead, the line of his nose, and the utterly masculine jaw. He was handsome and virile but also hard, with a toughness, a fierceness, at his center that made her think she wouldn't ever want to be his adversary. Far better to have him in her corner, on her side.

"I should clear the table," she said huskily.

"No, you shouldn't," he answered, his gaze focused intently on her.

She felt her mouth tingle beneath his scrutiny, and her face warmed, the skin feeling taut and sensitive. The heat in his blue eyes took her breath away, making her heart pound. Awareness rippled through her, desire coiling low in her belly with a need and a desperation she'd never felt until now. He'd awakened something within her that made her restless, even frantic.

She didn't just want him; she needed him.

There might never be another who made her feel this way. Beautiful and valuable. Excited and alive.

"Come here," he said, leaning back in his chair.

He didn't extend a hand, nor were the words sharp or frightening, but the command was undeniable. He expected her to go to him. He knew she'd obey.

And she knew it, too.

She rose on shaky legs and walked around the small table to his side.

His dark head tipped, and his gaze slowly traveled over her, from her hot flushed cheeks to her full mouth and down over her shoulders. His attention riveted on the tips of her breasts pressing against the thin gauze of her blouse, and then finally moved down over her waist and hips.

The hunger in his eyes made her tremble. She wasn't frightened, and yet the heat in her body now seemed to center low, pooling in secret places that made her damp. She felt as if he was slowly turning her to wine and honey.

"I want you," he said, and his deep voice had a rasp in it that made her nipples tighten. "But I'm trying to be respectful," he added. "I'm aware of how much I owe you—"

"No."

"I do. I owe you my life."

"Then don't want me. Not if it's because you're grateful. I don't want to be wanted out of some misguided gratitude—"

She broke off as he reached out and pulled her down onto his lap, his hands locking around her waist.

"I don't want you out of gratitude. I want you because I can't sleep at night anymore because my body aches for you. I want to touch you and taste you and be in you. The only reason I've held back is because you're innocent. I'm hoping to God you're not, because then I wouldn't feel like such a bastard for wanting to take you and make you mine."

Her thighs clenched as heat ricocheted through her, the desire as sharp as a razor's edge.

"Tell me you're not a virgin. Tell me this wouldn't be your first time." His gaze, so hot, blistered her, while his deep voice scratched her senses, gravel-rough.

"It would be my first time," she answered unsteadily, "but everyone has to have a first time. Why can't it be with you?"

"Because I don't think I'm good for you. I don't think I'm what you need."

"How do you know that?"

"I don't."

"*Exactly.* We don't know very much of anything except that I'm as attracted to you as you are to me, and I like how you make me feel. I like this, whatever this is, between us and I want more of it, not less."

His jaw flexed, hardened, just as she could feel him harden beneath her bottom in undeniable proof of his desire. His erection made her feel even more sensitive and she exhaled in a rush, overwhelmed by the sensation coursing through her. "I want you," she said thickly, sliding her hands up his chest, exploring the hard, warm plane of muscle. "I want you to be my first."

Her words were like gasoline on an open flame.

He wanted to strip her bare right there and feast on her. He wanted his mouth on every inch of her. He wanted her, oh, so very wet and writhing beneath him.

He could make her squirm and shudder and cry out his name.

If he were a gentleman, he'd release her, push her off his lap and tell her to go to bed.

He'd go for a swim to cool off and he'd swim until he burned off this terrible need.

If he were a gentleman, he'd wait for her to fall asleep before he returned to her father's room where he slept every night.

But he wasn't a gentleman. He didn't know very much about himself, but he knew that much.

Head dropping, his lips brushed hers, not because he was being careful with her but because he was feeling cruel.

He wanted her to ache for him.

He wanted her to crave him the way he craved her, and so he teased her lips and teased her with touches that were light and unsatisfying, his caress brushing her shoulders, the sides of her breasts, the outside of her hip, every touch designed to make her arch and flex, her slim back a bow drawn taut.

She was breathing harder now, short gasps, and her mouth lifted, trying to find his. She wanted his kiss. She wanted him.

He grazed the pebbled nipple of one breast with the back of his knuckles, a fleeting touch that made her whimper and her body gyrate on his lap. Her eyes were cloudy, the pupils so dilated her eyes looked almost black now.

He brushed the other just to make her dance again, and she did.

He nearly growled with pleasure. She was his.

Finally he took her mouth, his lips claiming her, his hunger barely leashed. As he took her mouth, he drank in her groan of pleasure. Her mouth was both hot and cool. She tasted fresh and impossibly sweet, and as his tongue traced the seam of her lips, her mouth opened to him. His tongue plunged in, sweeping, stabbing, punishing.

He didn't know why he wanted to punish her. She was nothing short of heaven, an angel here on earth.

Maybe that was why he was angry—and not with her, but with himself.

He didn't deserve her.

He shouldn't take her.

He shouldn't be the one to steal her innocence.

For God's sake, she'd kept a hope chest, filled with desires and dreams and hopes, and tonight she'd brought out a special tablecloth, and now he was going to take her virginity?

He shouldn't do this, he shouldn't. He didn't even know if there were other claims on him. He didn't think he was married—he wore no ring; there was no tan line—but could he have a significant other waiting for him somewhere? Worrying about him?

Missing him?

He broke off the kiss and lifted her, putting her on her feet before walking away, putting distance between them so he couldn't reach her easily.

For a moment the only sound was the crackle of the fire and the hum of the ocean as waves broke on the shore.

The rising moon cast a pale glow and he knew if he turned, he'd see her where he'd put her. She hadn't moved. She stood frozen, staring at him, waiting.

Wondering.

"I can't do this," he ground out. "I can't just take your innocence because I want to. It's wrong, at every level."

"Not even if I give you permission?" she said.

He heard the wobble of hurt in her voice and he glanced over his shoulder to see that yes, she was exactly where he'd left her. She looked rooted to the spot, except she no longer glowed. Her lips were pressed together and she looked pinched. Wounded.

And he'd done that to her, as well.

Pain twisted within him and he hated himself for putting her through this. He ought to know better. He was a man, not a boy.

"You should be protected," he said roughly. "It's what your father would want for you, and what you need. I can't just wash up on your beach and claim you—"

"Why not? Why not if it's what I want?" The bruised tone was gone, replaced by something stronger, fiercer. "I'm twenty-three, almost twenty-four. This isn't the Middle Ages. I am not a ward, and I do not belong to a man. I can decide for myself what is best for me."

He laughed, the sound mocking and unkind. "And you think I'm best for you?"

Her chin notched up. "I think you can teach me what I want to know."

He lifted a brow. "Teach you?"

"As you can tell, I haven't had a lot of experience. I've actually had almost no experience. There have been kisses," she added flatly, "and some uncomfortable groping, but that is all. As you can see there are not a lot of men here, and I'm happy here, so I'm relatively…untutored…when it comes to sex. Which is why I want you to be my first so I won't feel so…foolish…the next time."

The next time.

Her words flamed his temper. Primal emotion flooded him, making his blood boil and his shaft throb and ache.

He hated the idea of her with anyone else. He hated to think of any man touching her.

"You say you owe me your life," she added, her winged brows arching higher, as imperious as a queen. "Well, I don't want your life. I just want you to bed me. I want you to show me how it is between a man and a woman so that

I can be confident in the future. It would help me feel less awkward when I have sex in the future."

"You keep calling it sex. Why not lovemaking?"

"Because I'm a scientist and haven't been raised with euphemisms."

"But when you're with someone you truly desire, it's not just sex—it's bigger and more powerful. Transformative, if you will."

"Would it be that way with us?"

"If it's right."

"And if it's not?"

"It would feel like two bodies touching, rubbing, with hopefully a release in there somewhere."

"Sex can be bad, then?"

"With the wrong person, yes. With the wrong person it can be disconcerting."

"Even for a man?"

"It's a profoundly intimate act. I always enjoy it best in the context of a relationship."

"Ah." Her head nodded once, a thoughtful movement. "That's why you don't want to do it with me. We have no relationship. It wouldn't satisfy you."

"On the contrary, we have a very unique relationship, and making love to you is all I've thought about these past few days. But if I were to take you to my bed, I'm not sure I could, or would, let you go."

"Then don't," she answered simply.

For a moment they stood where they were, just looking at each other, the crackle of the fire mimicking the crackle of heat in his veins, making his shaft longer and harder, making him ache for her.

She patted the chair he'd left. "Come back here," she said coolly.

It wasn't a plea but a command, just as he'd commanded her earlier.

"Come sit down again and let me sit with you, like we were," she added. "Let us see how this goes without your conscience telling you things. I have a conscience of my own. I don't need yours deciding what I want or need. I can and will do that for myself."

He'd found her innocence seductive, but this version of Josephine was far sexier and even more compelling.

He sauntered toward her, aware of how her gaze boldly moved over him, giving him the same thorough examination he'd given her earlier, before her attention focused on his hips and the rigid length of him thrusting against the fabric of his trousers.

The tip of her tongue touched her lips and he wanted to roar with need and lust. She might be innocent and yet she had a sensual nature which called to him, stirring him. He took his seat and leaned back in the wooden chair, his brow lifting, challenging her. "Your Highness?" he taunted lowly.

She sat down on his lap, legs together, facing him. "Now what?" she whispered.

He didn't answer her with words. Instead he drew her arms behind her back and wrapped one hand around both of her wrists, holding her captive and still. He liked her like this—helpless and his. He liked how her breasts jutted and her lips parted, her breath coming fast.

He kissed the corner of her mouth, and then her mouth, feeling how her lips quivered against his.

He licked at her lower lip, his tongue finding all the nerve endings inside. She wriggled on his lap, hips rocking, and he longed to reach down and rub her between her thighs. Part of him wanted to shock her, while another part wanted to soothe her. She was passionate and responsive and utterly gorgeous…and right now she was his, all his.

"Can you feel me?" he growled, kissing the side of her neck, his teeth scraping across her skin. "Can you feel me between your thighs?"

She nodded her head, a jerky nod, even as his tongue flicked her tender earlobe and then swirled inside the shell of her ear, making her groan.

"I can feel you," he murmured, tugging on her hands, drawing them lower so that he held her hands against her butt, making her back arch even more. Her white cotton blouse clung to her small, high breasts, the thin fabric outlining her nipples. His head dropped and he sucked on one nipple, drawing on it hard.

She gasped, and whimpered, grinding down against him. He could feel her through his trousers, her body hot, wet.

With his free hand he worked the blouse off one shoulder, revealing the simple white cotton bralette, the thin fabric cup damp from his mouth. He stroked the pebbled nipple, making her squirm again.

"I can feel your heat and your need," he said, his lips just below her ear. "You are so wet, and it's so sexy."

She shuddered at his words.

"What I want to do with you is very hot and rather indecent. I'm afraid it would shock you."

She was finding it increasingly hard to breathe. "How so?"

"I would like to touch you, everywhere, and discover with my hands and my mouth what you enjoy. I'd like to kiss you between your thighs and use my tongue to make you come—"

"Would you enjoy that?" she asked, interrupting him.

He laughed softly at her wrinkled nose, her expression indicating disbelief.

"I would like it very much."

"You're telling me the truth?"

"I will always tell you the truth. No lies between us. It would ruin everything."

She stared deep into his eyes. "I do trust you," she said quietly, firmly, as if giving him reassurance. "Which is why I want you to be my first. You're supposed to be my first. I've been waiting for you."

"As much as I like the sound of that, I'm afraid it doesn't make sense."

"But it does. It's science," she said, "the laws of something or other. Nature or physics. If I could think clearly, I could tell you why it's meant to be, but I can't think clearly, not with you kissing my neck and everywhere else. You're clouding my rational brain."

"I should stop."

"No. You should most definitely not stop." She drew her head back down to his, kissing him sweetly, persuasively. "Promise me?"

"Promise," he answered, rising with her in his arms. As he walked, he kissed the side of her neck, making her breath catch in her throat. He was already hard and hungry, but that faint hitch in her breath made his body burn and throb.

She was gorgeous and sensitive and she made him feel so many good things. He wondered if he'd ever felt like this before. He couldn't imagine desiring anyone as much as he desired her.

He headed to the stone house, hesitating in the center room, not sure which way to go. Josephine pointed to her room. Her bed was small, considerably smaller than her father's, but it would still be plenty big enough for the two of them.

In her room, he sat down on the edge of the low bed and drew her between his thighs. His hands ran up and down her sides, stroking the length of her, savoring the feel of her. She was slim and toned and yet she had lovely curves, perfect breasts and generous hips, and a firm backside that was meant to be touched.

"What do I do?" she whispered as he reached for the hem of her blouse.

"Nothing. Let me," he answered, lifting her blouse up and then untying her sarong so that the fabric fell to the ground. Next to go was the plain white bralette and matching white panties, and once they were off, she was his, and beautifully bare. He smothered his groan of appreciation. "You are so beautiful," he said, drawing her even closer to kiss one pink-tipped breast. Her nipple puckered, tightening as his lips brushed the sensitive tip.

His body throbbed all over again, his erection straining against the zipper of his trousers. His tongue swept the peak lightly before his mouth closed over the damp tip. She shuddered as he drew on the nipple, her slim back arching. His hands settled on her hips, holding them firmly, thumbs stroking her hip bones.

She practically danced in place, making soft little whimpering sounds. She was so sweet, so innocent, and he battled to keep his desire in check, not wanting to rush.

The first time was special. The first time should make her feel good and beautiful.

He kissed his way to her other breast, giving the dark pink nipple the same attention and then some, pulling harder on the tip, working it and feeling how her body responded, hips rocking harder, her legs now trembling.

He stroked down her hips and then to her outer thighs and back again. He stroked lightly, awakening every nerve he could as her breath became increasingly shallow. She was practically panting as he caressed up the inside of her knee, up her smooth taut thigh to tease the curls between her legs. But instead of touching her then, he caressed back down her thigh and then up so that his knuckles grazed her. She bucked a little against his hand as he trailed a finger where she was most sensitive.

She was trembling against him now, her hands on his shoulders, holding her up. He slipped a hand between her thighs, finding her slick folds. She was so tender, so warm, so wet. He desperately wanted to put her on the bed and part her thighs and lick her, and taste her, but he didn't want to overwhelm her. This was clearly all so new to her, and so he contented himself with stirring her and heightening her senses and her pleasure. He wanted her fully aroused to make sure her first time was as comfortable as possible.

She shuddered again when his fingertips traced her delicate lips and then her nub. Her breath even shuddered as he stroked her, oh, so lightly there.

"I can't stand anymore," she said lowly, hoarsely.

"Sit. Switch places with me," he said.

Her expression was uncertain and yet she did as he asked, and he used the moment to strip off his clothes before kneeling in front of her, his hands circling her ankles. He stroked the fine bones in her ankles and then up over her shins and calves to her knees, and then down again, working the backs of her calves. He could feel her relax, her breath grow deeper and slower. Gradually, he shifted his attention higher on her legs, stroking up her thighs and down again, and with each stroke he pressed her legs back, opening them gradually to him. She stared at him, fascinated, her husky breath the only sound in the dark room.

The moon wasn't yet high enough to see her well, but he could see enough to be painfully aroused—pale skin, her thick honey-brown hair tumbling over one shoulder and breast, and the triangle of curls at her thighs. She gleamed in the dim light, her long limbs exquisite, her small, full breasts perfect. He felt beyond hungry; he was ravenous and he wanted to feast on her. Instead he was careful, and he leaned between her thighs to press a tender kiss in the hollow where her thigh connected to her pelvis. She groaned softly as he blew lightly on her inner thighs, focusing the air on her curls. She jerked against his hold, her breath hitching again.

"This is a kind of torture," she murmured.

"The best foreplay always is," he answered, parting her there to slip his fingers across her. She was hot and so tender, her soft flesh like liquid velvet. He kissed her on her nub, then used the tip of his tongue across her.

She shivered and cried out.

His body went rock hard, so hard he felt as if he'd pop out of his skin. He wanted her, wanted to be buried in her sweet wet heat, buried so deeply that they were one, forever one, making her his, and only his. He kissed his way back to the junction of her thighs, kissing her lightly, soothing her before rising up and shifting her back on the bed and slowly extending his body over hers, covering her.

Her arms wound around his neck, her fingers at his nape.

"Kiss me," she whispered.

And he did.

Josephine closed her eyes at the hunger in his kiss. His lips were firm and the pressure of his mouth parted her lips. She shuddered at the feel of his hand under her breast and then on her breast, fingers stroking the tight, peaked nipple, sending rivulets of feeling throughout her body. Her hips pressed up against his, his thick shaft extended across her belly. She'd always wondered what this would be like, and he was right; she'd imagined it as a clinical sort of thing, but there was nothing clinical in the heat and texture and sensation.

He made her feel so wonderfully alive. She couldn't imagine this moment with anyone else, just him.

He lifted his head to gaze down at her. There was something in his expression that made her chest tighten and her heart thump with pain.

"You promised," she whispered. "You promised you wouldn't stop. And I won't regret this, I swear to you." She caressed his neck and then her hands went to his shoulders. "Don't be afraid."

He laughed low, as though amused. "I'm not afraid, and

I'm glad you're not afraid, either. The first time isn't always comfortable, but it'll get better."

"I've heard that, too."

He kissed her, smiling against her mouth, and then his smile faded as the kiss turned hot and electric. She opened her legs for him, allowing his hips to settle between her thighs. He entered her slowly, taking his time, and Josephine had to draw a deep breath and tell herself to relax when it began to pinch and then burn, and then there was all that fullness and that pressure inside her, so different from anything she'd ever felt before. He was right. It wasn't comfortable and she wondered how anybody enjoyed this.

He must have sensed her panic, because he held still and kissed her, biting and then sucking on her lower lip, distracting her from everything but his teeth and tongue. Gradually the sting eased and the pressure was less overwhelming. He rocked his hips a little, shifting inside her, and as he eased out and then in, she found herself holding her breath again, but this time because it was a strange fluttery sensation that felt new but good.

"Do that again," she urged.

He laughed softly. "Many, many times," he answered, withdrawing again to thrust in more deeply. The fluttery good feeling happened again and continued with every thrust, and the pleasure built, the sensation erotic, making her arch and dig her heels into the mattress of the bed.

He met the lifting of her hips with a deeper, harder thrust, and the pleasure continued to rise, pressure and pleasure swirling, tightening so that she felt almost dizzy from it. She didn't know what she was waiting for, or reaching for. She just knew he couldn't stop, and she wanted whatever it was that he was doing and making her feel. Emotion and sensation joined together, hot and intense, as she tried to grip him with her body, wanting to keep him inside her where he felt so good, but he wouldn't be stopped and her skin grew hot and damp, and she felt the heat sweep through her, her skin prickly and tingling all over.

She panted with the need and tension, her body wound up, too wound up, and she didn't know what to do or where to go with the tension, and then he reached down, between them, and touched her where she was so very sensitive, circling her nub even as he drove into her, and his touch there, as he thrust deep inside her, made her shatter. She stifled her cry by pressing her mouth to his chest, but the waves of pleasure didn't stop. The climax continued, hard and intense, breaking her into a million shimmering pieces. She felt like stardust strewn across the sky and it was earth-shattering, heart-stopping.

Even as she was still floating like stardust, her mind so scattered, she felt him groan and stiffen, his hoarse guttural cry not so different from her own.

Josephine's arms tightened around him and she held him fiercely, desperately thinking her life would never be the same.

It could never be the same.

He would forever be a part of her now because she had just given him a piece of her heart.

He woke up in the night and glanced around, wondering what had woken him, and then he realized it was the moonlight streaming through the window, falling across the bed in white streaks of light.

The moonlight illuminated Josephine's elegant profile. Her features were delicate and refined, reminding him of a fairy-tale princess. Every day he discovered something new about her, and tonight he'd discovered her passion. Part of him felt guilty for taking her virginity, and yet another part of him agreed with her—they were meant to be. Destined to be together. She was beautiful and brilliant, innocent and earnest, and temptingly sweet.

His head dipped and he pressed a light kiss to her temple and then another to her cheek.

She stirred and moved closer to him, her slim warm body pressed to his. "What's wrong?" she murmured sleepily.

He stroked her long silky hair back from her cheek. "Nothing."

"You're awake."

"The moon woke me."

"I'll close the curtain."

"No, don't. Then I couldn't see you, and I want to see you."

Her lips curved, her cheeks rising with her soft smile.

He dropped another light kiss on her lips. "You're a jewel, Josephine. A rare jewel."

Still smiling, she nestled even closer so that her cheek rested on his chest. "Thank you for the compliment, but seeing as you don't remember anything of your world, I'm not sure it's valid."

"Let me be the judge of that."

"Yes, my lord," she said with a faint laugh, her breath a light caress against his bare chest, and then she fell back asleep, and he lay awake for another hour, just holding her and watching the big full moon high in the sky.

This wasn't his life, or his world, but in some ways he was quite certain it was the best life he'd lived, as well as the best world.

Josephine woke the next morning and stretched and smiled as she felt his arm tighten around her. He was here. It wasn't a dream. She was so glad because it had been the best night of her life.

She slipped from bed and pulled on her bikini and then headed outside for an early-morning swim. As she swam she heard the buzz of a helicopter. It was far from the beach, but the hum grew louder. She stood up in the water, hands over her head, waving frantically as the helicopter moved toward her and then headed in a different direction, flying away.

She ran back toward the house. He was just leaving her bed, pulling on the pair of her father's shorts she'd given him along with the other clothes. The shorts were huge and so he anchored them with a belt as he raced back outside with her.

"It came so close," she said, running toward the beach. "And I waved, and I thought it must have seen me but then it went away."

"Maybe it did see you. Maybe it's gone for help."

"Maybe."

They spent the rest of the day on tenterhooks waiting for the helicopter to return or a glimpse of a boat, but the morning turned into afternoon, and then dusk fell. "I'm sorry," she said to him where they sat side by side on the sand.

"I'm not," he answered, turning his head to look at her. "I'm glad. This gives me more time with you. It gives me more time to discover you and all the different ways I want to know you."

"But we made love."

"There are so many ways to make love."

She chewed her lip, hiding her smile. He made her feel so excited and nervous and shy and hopeful and all those emotions kept rising in her, bubbling up, making it impossible not to smile.

"You like that," he said, his voice dropping, growing husky.

She blushed, even as her smile stretched wider. She shouldn't smile. She shouldn't encourage him, and yet she loved how he made her feel and how amazing it had been to be his last night. His weight, his scent, his heat…the friction and the pleasure.

"I did," she said unsteadily. "I loved it. I loved being with you. It was…perfect."

"And that was just the beginning," he answered, drawing her toward him, pulling her on top of him as he lay back. She felt him beneath her, hard and warm, his chest crushing her breasts, and his erection pressed to the apex of her thighs, the heavy rigid length making her impossibly aware of his desire. His hands shifted from her waist to her hips and then lower, to cup her butt, his hands so warm on her that she felt as if she was melting.

He cupped the back of her head, kissing her deeply, making her whimper with need. She wiggled against him, her hips dancing over him, encouraging him, practically begging him to take her.

She wanted him to fill her and stretch her. She wanted the maddening pressure and then the explosive release. She wanted everything he'd shown her last night, and even more wild and fierce tonight.

Passion—she wanted the passion he'd awoken within her.

And then he was lifting her and he was sliding lower, holding her thighs apart until he settled beneath her, his face under her most private place.

She pressed against his shoulders, trying to escape, but he held her knees firmly, keeping them wide-open so that he could her kiss there, between her thighs. She shuddered and swallowed a cry.

"Take your bikini bottoms off," he told her. "Now."

It was a definite command but also unbelievably sexy, and she peeled them off, trying not to panic. This was what she wanted—him. Them. Earlier today she'd wanted him to want her like this; she'd wanted him to show her all the things she didn't know, and he could, she thought. He could teach her and share with her, helping her discover the world that lay beyond Khronos's beach.

"Come here," he growled. "Kneel over me."

She'd wanted to be daring; she'd wanted to take risks but this was terrifying. "I'm not sure—"

"I am. I want you. I want to taste you again. Last night was not enough."

Heat rushed through her, heat and need and fear that perhaps this was all a dream and once she opened her eyes, he'd be gone.

And then his mouth touched her there, and his tongue found her between the slick folds, and she cried out as he stroked her and sucked on her, drawing the sensitive nub between his lips and then his teeth, tugging and licking until she felt as if she'd explode out of her skin.

He slipped a finger inside her, finding more sensitive spots as he sucked on her, and she couldn't fight the intense waves of pressure and pleasure building. She screamed as she climaxed, and the orgasm shuddered through her, making her body writhe and bend.

He lifted her up and turned her around so that she lay in the sand, and he stretched out over her. She stared up at him, so dazed she could barely focus.

"You liked that," he murmured, pushing her hair back from her face.

"You could say that," she whispered, reaching up to tug on his shirt. "But I'm feeling greedy. I want you. I want what we did last night. That was heaven. Please take this off. Your shorts, too."

"We have to be careful," he said. "I wasn't careful enough last night. I didn't pull out fast enough."

She struggled to follow what he was saying and then she understood. Careful as in careful not to get her pregnant. Careful as in birth control. "Oh. Right. Smart." Why hadn't she thought of any of that?

But then, there was no time for thinking about anything, not when he was settling over her, handsome and naked and beautiful. She'd never met anyone half so beautiful. And then he was kissing her again and lowering himself to cover her before he entered her, his thick shaft stretching her and filling her so that her breath caught and she had to relax to accommodate him.

But then when he began to move, slowly, the uncomfortable sensation eased, and the pressure became a good pressure as he found the spot inside her that liked being touched. "Again," she said, lifting her hips. "Do that again and again."

He laughed softly against her neck. "My pleasure."

And then she didn't want to talk anymore, not when she was feeling so much heat and sensation and emotion.

With him, like this, she felt beautiful. Together with him, like this, everything was perfect.

The days passed, one after another. The sun shone brightly every day, long hot days that only cooled in the late afternoon as the wind blew. They spent most of their time together. He felt guilty that she wasn't working very much, but he knew that it was just a matter of time, too, before her father would return and everything would change. Maybe that was why he couldn't get enough of Josephine, craving her body and warmth. Or maybe he couldn't get enough because she felt like sunshine and life—so open and warm and affectionate. Her smile did something to him, creating strange pain and pressure in his chest. He feared what he didn't know, and yet it only served to make the present even more important. It made *her* more important. He wasn't going to lose her, either. She was his. She belonged with him. He knew that much.

"My father should be back very soon now," she said, curling up against him late one afternoon, her hand on his chest, her fingers lightly caressing his skin. He loved the way she touched him. It felt right. She felt right in his arms, in his bed. "Just three days, and when he returns, he will know who to contact," she added, "and what to do."

The news should please him. Obviously, he knew they could not remain like this forever. But he dreaded reality, unable to fathom the future or the truth of it all when he was so removed from it here with her.

She misinterpreted his silence, because she looked up at him, giving him one of her radiant, reassuring smiles, which never failed to put an ache in his chest. "My father will like you. Very much."

He couldn't answer her smile, not when there was so much heaviness within him. "There is a whole world out there that we don't know."

"But we will discover it together, yes?"

He kissed her brow and then the tip of her small, straight nose and then, finally, the lushness of her lips. Almost immediately desire flared, the warmth of the kiss sparking hot cravings. He pulled her closer, wanting to lose himself in her rather than at the edge of the unknown. The unknown wasn't his friend. But she was. Here on Khronos, she was his world. She was his everything.

"I love you," she whispered, as he entered her, thrusting deep.

He didn't say it back, but then, he didn't think she expected him to.

Later that night, he woke up and glanced toward the windows, looking to see if it was light. But there wasn't a wall of windows where he expected glass to be. The window was on a different side of the room, and it was a simple square window with a simple grid in the middle.

He frowned. This wasn't his room. This wasn't his home.

He swung his legs out of bed. The ground was very close. It jarred his knees. His bare feet arched against the roughly cobbled floor. Why was he here? He didn't belong here. He lived somewhere grand. He lived somewhere…

His throat worked. He swallowed as the past returned, colliding with the present, because he *knew.*

He knew his name. Alexander.

He knew who he was. He knew what he was.

Alexander glanced around the room, understanding where he was. Not in Aargau but in Greece, on this island with Josephine who'd rescued him.

He looked over and there she was, still sleeping in the bed. Her bed. Her cottage. Her island, not his.

Her long honey hair spilled across her bare shoulder. Her thick lashes rested on her cheek. She was stunning even in her sleep. His very own mermaid.

She'd saved him. He would have died—drowned—if not for her, and then when he was still weak, she'd taken care of him. And then last night she'd told him she loved him, and he hadn't answered her with words, but he'd shown her how much her faith in him mattered to him by making love to her for hours, worshipping her body since something inside him kept him from giving her his heart.

He'd thought that maybe he couldn't give himself to her fully because he didn't know who he was. It was what she'd said, and he'd hoped maybe it was true, but now he knew why he couldn't love her. Because she wasn't his, and he wasn't free.

He was Prince Alexander Julius Alberici of Aargau, and he was betrothed to another.

CHAPTER FOUR

HE NEEDED TO tell her.

Alexander needed to tell her that his memory had returned, that he knew who he was.

But he also knew that once he did, everything would change. Forever.

He wasn't ready to lose her. He wasn't ready to lose the warmth of what they had. He'd never felt like this with anyone, and he'd never been wanted like this by anyone. She didn't even know who he was, or what he was, and yet she wanted him.

And so that day, all day, he watched her, paying attention to everything, committing to memory the sunlight on her hair and how it illuminated her stunning profile. He watched her walk and that way she'd almost skip because of the joyous bounce in her step. She was so buoyant, so happy, she radiated light and goodness.

Hope and strength.

He hadn't been raised with women like her. He hadn't ever known that women like her existed. His mother had been born a princess and had been raised strictly, taught to be conscious and vigilant about the image she presented, conscious of her elevated place in society. Lovely Josephine was nothing like his mother. She was free and lacked conceit and arrogance. She was humble and practical and so quick to smile and laugh.

He'd dated many women over the years but there had never been anyone like Josephine.

And his fiancée, Princess Danielle, was nothing like Josephine, either.

The heavy rock returned to his stomach, the weight reminding him that his past and future were about to collide and it would be painful and ugly.

No, he couldn't think of the future now—it wasn't here. And he couldn't dwell on Princess Danielle, either.

He didn't want to think of anything but Josephine, acutely aware that they were on borrowed time and that the real world would intrude soon, and once it did nothing would ever be the same.

"What's wrong?" Josephine asked, coming up behind him to wrap her arms around his neck. She leaned against him, kissing his cheek, her body so warm against his back. She smelled of sunshine and lavender and the honey-vanilla-scented shampoo she used on her hair. "Is your head hurting again?"

Not his head, he thought, but his conscience.

He'd spent the past week making love to her, promising her the future, even as another woman counted down the weeks, anticipating their wedding in the Roche Cathedral across from the Alberici palace. He was going to end up hurting one if not both of them. He reached up to cover one of Josephine's hands. "My head is fine," he answered quietly. "I just keep thinking about the future."

"It won't be so bad," she said, her voice gentle.

She was always so gentle with him, so patient. As if he deserved tenderness and patience when he was anything but tender and kind himself.

She wouldn't like who he was, he thought.

She wouldn't like Prince Alexander Julius at all.

The emotion was intense and uncomfortable, so uncomfortable that he couldn't allow himself to go there. Instead, he pulled her down onto his lap and kissed her, his hand fisting in her thick hair, warm from the sun.

But kissing her only made the emotion hotter and fiercer. He didn't want to let her go. There was no way in hell he wanted to lose her—she was the first woman he'd ever needed, ever craved—but at the same time, Alexander didn't know how he'd reconcile his duty and responsibility to his kingdom and Princess Danielle with his feelings, and Alexander knew too well that in his world feelings didn't matter. Feelings, in fact, were inconsequential. What mattered was fulfilling one's duty.

He'd tell her tomorrow, he vowed, breaking off the kiss. Her green gaze met his and held. She looked at him with such trust, such love. His chest tightened, guilt pummeling him. He'd never been dishonest with anyone before. How could he hurt her? How could he do this to her?

She wouldn't stand in the way of his wedding to Danielle, either. She'd tell him to do the honorable thing. She wouldn't ask for anything for herself.

Her hand rose to lightly skim his cheekbone and then his mouth and finally his jaw. "What's wrong? Tell me."

He wanted to. God, how he wanted to, because there were still things he didn't remember and things that weren't clear. Like the trip on the yacht with his friends. He wasn't even sure which friends had been there. Shouldn't he remember that? And he didn't remember the beach, and he didn't remember a fight, and he didn't remember going overboard.

If his memory had returned, why were those details still blank?

"I just want to remember the yacht," he said after a moment, hating the turmoil within him. He'd always known himself. He'd always been confident. No, he didn't like this new version of himself. "I want to remember my friends and the circumstances that brought me to you."

She rubbed the line of his jaw and then lightly dragged her fingernails across the stubble of his beard. "I do, too. And then when I know what happened, I will find your friends and give them a piece of my mind because how dare they treat you so shabbily! How dare—"

He stopped her words with a kiss, and as he kissed her he felt a shaft of pain through his chest. She was, without a doubt, the very best thing he'd ever known, and soon he'd break her heart. And just maybe break his, too.

Josephine woke with a start, a familiar sound puncturing her dreams. It was a boat.

Her father's motorboat. She flung back the covers and practically jumped out of bed, trying to absorb the fact that her father was home two days earlier than expected.

A strong muscular arm reached for her. "Where are you going?" he murmured sleepily.

"My father's home," she answered, heart hammering, trying to imagine her father's reaction if he walked into the cottage and found her in bed with a strange man. Her father was tolerant but it would have been too much for him. She dragged her hair into a ponytail. "You stay here. I'll go speak with him."

"I'll go with you."

He stood unashamed before her, tall, muscular, tanned, *naked.* Heat rushed through her, and her hands shook as she pulled on a sundress, covering her nudity, suddenly aware that she wasn't at all prepared for this moment. She'd convinced herself that her father would like him, but would he?

"Let me talk to him first, and then I'll bring him inside and introduce you two. I think it'd be better if I tell him what's happened—"

"Why are you upset? Will he be angry to find me here?"

"Not if you're dressed. But he's a father. I'm his little girl."

"Understood."

She pulled up the covers and then, glancing at the bed, realized how it would look. She took one of the pillows and a quilt and carried them to the living room, where she made a second bed on the ground.

He'd followed her into the living room, brow lifting quizzically. "My bed, I take it?"

"Yes." She shot him a desperate look. "Do you mind?"

"Am I really to sleep there?"

"If you'd prefer, *I* can sleep there—"

"Don't be foolish. I love sleeping on the floor."

"You don't mean that."

"True. But for you, I'd do anything." And then he pulled her into his arms and kissed her hard, the kiss hot and possessive. When he lifted his head, his blue gaze scorched her with its heat. "And I do mean that."

He released her and Josephine slipped out of the cottage and ran down to the beach where her father was anchoring the boat. He was just reaching for the second line when he saw her. "Perfect timing," her father called.

She took the line from him and attached it to the mooring buried deep in the sand. He jumped out to give her a hand.

"You're back early," she said as he finished attaching the heavy chain through the iron loop.

"I was worried about you. I couldn't reach you on the radio."

"It broke a few days after you left."

"And you couldn't fix it?"

"I dropped it, smashing too many parts."

"I bought a new one, just in case."

"Smart thinking." She pushed her hair back from her face, feeling ridiculously nervous. She wasn't used to feeling this way, not around her father. "How was your trip? Everything go all right?"

"Everything went well. Had some good news while at the university. Picked up some more grant money, which is always nice."

"Money pays bills."

"Also necessary when restocking supplies." He waded

back into the water and climbed into the boat and began dragging boxes and crates forward. "How have things been here? Anything exciting?"

She darted a glance toward the stone house. "Actually, yes. Far more exciting than usual." She took a quick breath. "We have a visitor."

Her dad stopped in his tracks, slowly straightening. "A what?"

"A visitor." She smiled brightly. "It's quite the story, too. You see, he went overboard and I saved him." She gulped more air, needing courage. "He was injured in the accident. He's lost his memory. Can't remember anything, not his name or where he's from."

"He's been alone with you this entire time?"

"Not the entire time. Just a week or so."

"A week or so." He paused, his weathered forehead creasing even more deeply. "Here? On the island?"

"Yes."

"Where is he now?"

"Inside the house. I asked him to stay there while I told you about him. I knew it'd be a shock. It was a shock to me—" she broke off as her dad jumped over the side of the boat and started for the house. "What are you doing?"

"Going to tell this fellow to pack up—"

"Pack what?" she cried, running to catch up with him. "He went overboard. He has nothing!"

"Great. It'll make it that much easier to ferry him to Antreas and hand him over to officials there."

"What are you talking about?"

"You know nothing about this man. He could be dangerous."

"If he was dangerous, wouldn't I know it by now?"

"I'll be the judge of that."

"Dad, stop. Listen." She grabbed his coat sleeve, tugged on it hard, stopping him. "He has *amnesia*."

"Which would make him all the more unpredictable. You're lucky he hasn't hurt you—"

"Why would I hurt her when she saved my life?" Alexander said, his deep voice catching them both by surprise. He approached her father and extended a hand. "I'm grateful for your daughter's bravery, Professor Robb."

Her father warily shook his hand. "I understand you've had an accident."

"I did."

Her father stepped back, still studying him, his expression shuttered. His closed expression worried her. Her father was a professor—his career had been filled with young people, students—and he was usually affable, friendly. He wasn't now. What was wrong?

"Let's get the supplies in," her father said, turning to her. "While you put away the food, I'll set up the radio."

"Can I help?" Alexander asked.

"No, but thank you," her father said.

"Then I'll give you some time to catch up."

In the cottage, Josephine kept glancing at her father as she unpacked the groceries and various supplies needed for life on Khronos. Her father worked on the radio, attaching it to the solar panels that would maintain a constant charge. Normally he'd talk to her while he worked. This morning he was silent.

She folded her arms and faced him. "You're upset."

"Do you know who he is?" he asked. "This shipwrecked man of yours?"

"No. But he's obviously European, and wealthy. It was a huge yacht, incredibly luxurious."

Finished with the radio, her father went to his backpack and retrieved his computer and a pile of newspapers. "He's a prince from the kingdom of Aargau. And he's been missing for over a week."

She laughed. "A prince?"

Her father didn't smile. His expression was stony.

"A *prince*?" she repeated, her throat suddenly scratchy.

"Yes."

"You're sure?"

Her father flung down the stack of newspapers. "It's in all the news, in papers from all over the world. Everyone is looking for him. It's been in the headlines daily. At first he was merely missing, but they have now begun to worry he's not going to be found—at least not found alive. All the more tragic as he's supposed to be getting married in just a few weeks."

He was getting married?

No…

No.

"Maybe it's a different person. Maybe—" she broke off as her gaze fell on the top newspaper, the headline paired with a photo. The bold headline read "Prince Alexander Feared Dead," and while she didn't recognize the name, she recognized the face in the photo.

It *was* him.

And his name was Alexander.

Alexander. She said the name silently, rolling it over in her mind, before looking back down at the photo. Her mystery man, her beloved stranger, wasn't a rich Italian but a Mediterranean prince. Thirty-four-year-old Prince Alexander Julius Alberici, who was engaged to marry Princess Danielle Roulet at the end of this month.

Her father returned to the radio, adjusting the signal. "I'm going to call the Greek authorities," he said. "They'll in turn alert the authorities in Aargau. I imagine they'll send help right away, probably a helicopter."

She crossed the floor to the open window, where she stood facing the sea. She couldn't see Alexander, not from where she stood, but she knew he was out there, probably in the sheltered cove.

"Do you have to call today?" she asked quietly, her back to her father, her gaze still on the bay. "Can you wait until the morning? Give us this last day."

"That would be cruel. His family thinks he's dead."

She nodded, swallowing hard around the lump filling her throat. She didn't want to be cruel, but she would miss him. Terribly.

"Can you at least wait until I'm gone?" she asked, glancing over her shoulder to where her father sat at the table with the radio.

"I'm going to call soon," her father answered.

She fought the salty sting of tears and forced back the lump making it difficult to swallow.

It was ending so quickly. She'd thought she'd have at least two more days before her father returned, but instead he was here and taking control, and she was grateful he was doing the right thing, the proper thing, but she wasn't ready to say goodbye to Alexander.

She didn't want to be here when they came for him. She couldn't imagine parting, never mind surrounded by strangers who didn't understand what the past week had been like.

It had been heaven on earth.

She'd never been so happy in her entire life.

And yet he wasn't hers. He was never meant to be hers. What they'd shared here on Khronos was a mistake—no, she wouldn't call it that, but a fluke, something that hadn't been meant to be. And while the time they'd shared couldn't be taken from them, there was no future for them. It was unlikely their paths would ever cross again.

"I don't want to be here when they come for him," she said quietly, her gaze meeting her father's before shifting away. "May I have your permission to take the boat to Antreas? I haven't been off Khronos in ages. It'll be good for me to get out and do something."

"You don't want to see him off?"

"You know how I am about goodbyes. I find them painful."

"Won't the prince be offended?"

"It will be better for him if people don't know he was here alone with me. It will be better if help comes and they find you."

"The truth will get out. It always does."

"But that won't be my problem then. He'll be home in Aargau with his family and his fiancée." The words stuck in her throat. She managed a tight smile. "And at least this way I'll have some dignity. Goodbyes always hurt too much."

"You've been this way ever since you lost your mom—"

"I don't want to talk about her. Let me gather a few things quickly as I'd like to leave soon. I'll take the boat to Antreas for the night and return by noon tomorrow."

"It's too far on your own."

"It's a straight shot north. I'll be fine, and I've done it before." She managed another small, brittle smile. "And when I return tomorrow, all will be well, and life will return to normal."

CHAPTER FIVE

ALEXANDER RETURNED FROM his swim to discover Josephine had left, and she'd gone without a word to him. She'd gone without a goodbye.

Her father attempted a weak explanation, which only made Alexander grit his teeth. It was a battle to hide his shock and disappointment.

"She didn't know how to say goodbye," Professor Robb added. "She doesn't like to cry."

"And why would she cry?" Alexander retorted stiffly.

The professor pushed a set of newspapers across the rough-hewn table, giving him a glimpse of headline after headline.

"Aargau's Prince Alex Missing"
"Tragedy on Yacht in Aegean Sea"
"Royal Prince Feared Dead"

"She knows who I am," Alexander said.

Professor Robb nodded. "But so do you, don't you?"

"I started remembering pieces a few days ago, but it wasn't until yesterday that I remembered my name and who I was."

"You didn't tell her."

Alexander didn't reply. "When will she return?"

"After you're gone."

"And when will that be?"

"I suspect help will be arriving later this afternoon."

The professor was right.

A helicopter from Aargau's Royal Navy arrived within hours, a medic on board in case Alexander needed care, but after a quick exam, he was cleared to fly, and they left Khronos.

Alexander didn't speak the entire flight to Aargau, nor did he speak as the Mercedes whisked him from the helipad to the palace. It was just a fifteen-minute drive and he stared out the window seeing, but not seeing, the streets of Roche, Aargau's capital city, home for the past one hundred sixty-five years to the royal Alberici family.

His family.

As the chauffeur drove him, with cars driven by security ahead and behind him, he wondered why he didn't feel relief that he was home.

He wondered why sights that were familiar didn't fill him with any comfort or pleasure.

Instead he felt only an oppressive sense of dread. He knew his father was ill—he remembered that clearly—but there was something missing in his memories, something that didn't explain the dread that felt like a lead weight in his gut.

Perhaps it was because he didn't remember his time on the yacht. Perhaps it was because he feared questions about the trip and his injury and his questionable memory. He didn't want to alarm his mother by letting her know that there were things he didn't remember. He needed to protect her from more stress. The past nine days couldn't have been easy for her.

Arriving at the palace, the gates opened for the parade of black Mercedes and then closed behind them. The palace was surrounded by thick walls dating back to the fifteenth century, and portions of that early fortress remained: a chapel, a tower, a prison dungeon. Newer buildings had risen around the medieval architecture, sometimes incorporating them, sometimes ignoring them. The Alberici family lived in the eighteenth-century palace, and guards and staff filled some of the other buildings. Years ago Alexander had claimed the tower as his own, converting each floor into rooms of his own. He had a private gym on the ground floor and an office one floor above that. His private library was on the third floor, with access to a guest suite on the fourth. The stairwell between the fourth and fifth floors led to the roof and the parapet where antique cannons remained.

When he needed to be home for long periods, he'd retreat to the tower guest suite, sleeping there to give himself some much-needed privacy. No one entered the tower without his permission, and he limited access when he was in residence to his own butler and valet.

His butler and valet were on the palace front steps as the motorcade drew to a stop, and they ushered him to his suite of rooms in the palace, where he showered, shaved and dressed.

"Are you well, Your Highness?" his valet asked after giving Alexander's coat a tug, adjusting the fit over his shoulders.

"Yes, thank you," Alexander answered.

"You have quite a cut on your head, sir."

"It's nothing."

"The doctor has seen you?"

"A navy doctor checked me out on the way here."

"Very good, sir."

And then Alexander was off, leaving his suite for that of his parents' rooms.

The meeting with his mother and father was brief. His father was in a chair, his eyes closed, when Alexander entered the room. His mother, Serena, was sitting in a chair nearby, embroidering. She'd taken up embroidery a few years ago and now it was rare to see her in private without a needle and thread in her hands.

Seeing that his father was sleeping, he paused at his mother's chair, stooping to kiss her forehead. At fifty-five she was slim and elegant and until recently had looked far younger than her years, but his father's change of health had unfairly aged her. "Hello, Mother."

She reached up to pat his cheek and tears filled her eyes. "Alexander," she said, the quiver in her voice betraying the stress of the past few weeks.

He glanced to his father's chair. His father looked shockingly thin, his complexion gray. "How is he?"

Her shoulders shrugged. "He's—"

"Tired of worrying about you, you thankless scoundrel," his father answered, his voice hoarse and thin.

Alexander smiled faintly. His father wasn't joking, either. He'd been a disappointment to his father ever since he was a boy and had refused to hunt and shoot animals and whip his horse and do any number of things that a male should do to prove his dominance. "You can stop worrying then. I'm back, safe and sound," Alexander said lightly.

"It crossed my mind that you were deliberately staying away, enjoying our discomfort."

"No, never." He glanced down at his mother, his expression softening. "I'd never want to distress Mother. Now, you, you're a different matter." His lips were curved, his tone dry and slightly mocking because that was how he and his father communicated. With biting sarcasm and stinging disdain.

"Ha, I knew it." His father struggled to sit up in his chair and Alexander went to his aid but his father brushed him away. "I'm not so frail that I can't sit up in my own chair."

"Never doubted your strength, sir."

His father cleared his throat and then coughed and coughed. And coughed some more. It was a long time before he could speak. "Your cousin," he rasped, eyes watering, voice quavering. "He's been quite anxious about your return. Damian's been checking in a half-dozen times a day."

"Hoping to inherit, I'm sure."

His father looked at him hard from beneath dark brows. "He has always respected the crown, unlike you."

"I was a boy when I said those things. Don't you think it's time to forgive?"

"I forgave you, but I won't forget."

Alexander held back the words he wanted to say. There was no point in defending himself, no point in arguing his case. It would change nothing. "I would have it no other way, Father."

"Princess Danielle's family has also been in touch daily. Have you spoken yet with her?" His mother asked, diverting the attention. "She's been frantic."

"Does she do *frantic*? I've only ever known her to be the epitome of calm."

"Not frantic as in frenzied, but concerned," his mother conceded. "Which is why we like her so much. She won't embarrass you. She won't embarrass us."

"A perfect wife," he murmured.

And yet his mother heard, her dark blond eyebrows rising. "I thought you liked her."

"And I do," Alexander answered. "She's a perfectly lovely princess."

"Faultless," Serena added.

"Right." He gave her a slight bow and then another in the direction of his father, and he was off. The great homecoming was over.

Alexander's close friends were warmer in their greetings. They descended on him, gathering in his large suite in Alberici Palace, exclaiming over his tan, offering fierce hugs and pats on the back. These were men who'd grown up with him and gone to university with him and served in the Royal Navy with him, and they were damn glad to see him home.

"We were desperate," Gerard said as they all took seats

in Alexander's living room. "Once we discovered you were gone, we notified the palace immediately, and they sent planes and helicopters, and the Greek Air Force and Navy joined in the search, but there was no sign of you. We honestly feared the worst."

"When did you realize I was missing?" Alexander asked, the only one not to sit.

Gerard grimaced. "When you didn't come out for breakfast, and then lunch, I knew something was wrong. I ended up breaking your door down."

"Well, I broke it down," Rocco corrected. "Gerard was trying but not very successfully."

Everyone laughed, but the laughter died to an uncomfortable silence.

"Have you talked to her yet?" Marc asked after a moment. "She's been really upset."

"Danielle?"

"No, Claudia," Marc answered. "I hate playing the big-brother card, but it seems that you owe her an apology."

"Not now," Gerard murmured. "He's only just returned. This isn't the time."

"Why not now?" Marc retorted. "Better to handle this now without Damian here, don't you think?"

Alexander glanced from Marc to Gerard to Rocco. There were undercurrents he couldn't read. Things had happened that he didn't understand. He still had no memory of the trip and yet clearly he needed his memories. "What is this about Damian? And where is he?"

His three friends all glanced at each other before Gerard, the diplomat, answered. "It's been a difficult ten days for him. You and he had that…falling-out…on the ship. And then you went missing. He's been juggling shock and grief—"

"About what?" Alexander interrupted, frustration sharpening his voice.

"Damian said you'd consumed more liquor than we knew. Maybe it was true," Rocco said bluntly.

"And not to play big brother again, but Claudia wasn't yours anymore, Alberici," Marc added. "You broke up with her, not the other way around. You should have left her alone."

The gathering abruptly ended. Alexander asked Gerard to remain behind. He and Gerard had been roommates at the Naval Academy and then had served together all three years in the Royal Navy, and there was no one Alexander trusted more. Gerard was a vault. The man knew how to serve, protect, and keep a secret.

"I need you to tell me what you remember of that last night," Alexander said after the other two had gone.

"What's happened?" Gerard asked quietly. "Something has, hasn't it?"

"Other than the fact that I'm being accused of hitting on my ex-girlfriend and fueling a feud with my cousin?"

"None of that took place?"

"I don't believe so."

"But you don't know."

"I'd like to look at the footage from the yacht's security camera."

"I already requested it."

"And?"

"There is none."

"What?"

"There is no footage, that end of the ship was never equipped with security cameras."

Unbelievable. Alexander closed his eyes and held his breath, containing his disappointment. He'd been counting on footage helping him piece together the mystery of what happened on the boat, and why.

"So what do you remember of that last night?" Alexander said, when he could trust himself to speak calmly.

"You were having a drink with us and said you'd be right back, but you never returned."

"What time did I excuse myself?"

"It was after dinner, so maybe ten. Annaliese said it might have been a little earlier. Gigi thought it was a bit later. But ten is a safe bet." Gerard watched Alexander pace the length of the room and the tense silence stretched. After several minutes passed, he said, "You're worrying me, Alex. You are the most detail-oriented person I know. Nothing escapes your attention. Why all the questions? What's happened?"

"I don't know," Alexander said simply, facing his friend. "I've told no one this, but I trust you, and I need your help. I have no memory of that night at all. It's all a blank, and I was hoping you could help me clear up some of the mystery."

Gerard's jaw dropped. "So you don't know how you ended up in the water?"

"I don't remember anything from the trip." He hesitated. "But it's worse than that. For an entire week, I had no memory at all. For a week I didn't know who I was. I didn't know my name."

"How did you manage?"

"I was rescued by a girl on an island. She saved my life and took care of me."

"That's a story."

"It was like a story," he agreed. "The Prince and the Mermaid."

"There is a story like that by Hans Christian Andersen."

"Does it end happily?"

"For the prince."

"And the mermaid?"

"She sacrifices herself for him and turns to sea foam."

"I don't think I'd like that story."

Gerard's brow creased. "I'm worried about you, Alex. If Damian knew this, it could be quite bad for you."

"I know." Alexander sighed and dragged a hand through his hair. "I need the missing pieces. I need my memory. And I definitely need the security footage from the yacht."

Josephine was sure that once she returned to Khronos, life would be fine. Prince Alexander would be gone and she'd be able to focus on her work again.

She expected some sadness and knew she'd miss his company, but she'd lost her mother and lived, and so she'd survive Alexander's departure just fine. The tears she cried at night into her pillow were just part of the process of letting him go. And she would let him go. The intense memories would eventually fade, and over time she'd think of him less and less until one day she could remember him with something other than pain.

It was a good plan, and it might have worked out that way if she hadn't discovered she was pregnant two weeks after his departure for Aargau.

Josephine had suspected within days of Alexander leaving Khronos that she *could* be pregnant, but she'd told herself she was being dramatic, letting her imagination run away with her, which was why she waited almost two weeks to take an over-the-counter pregnancy test that she bought in Athens when she was there with her father for a foundation meeting.

She'd waited until she was alone to buy the test, and then in her hotel room she followed the steps and told herself everything would be fine, that she didn't need to panic or worry—

And then came the immediate positive result.

She *was* pregnant.

And Josephine sat on the side of the bathtub, holding the stick, thinking that she'd known. She'd known because her body felt different. Her breasts were fuller and more sensitive, and she felt nauseous and fatigued.

She couldn't even pretend to be shocked. They'd made love a half-dozen times and they hadn't taken precautions. Yes, he'd withdrawn, but it wasn't true birth control. It was far from foolproof. She didn't know why they hadn't discussed it more. She didn't know why it hadn't been a more urgent issue. It was stupid. She'd behaved irrationally. She'd behaved as if she was the one with amnesia, not he.

And she wasn't just pregnant, but pregnant with the child of one of the most fascinating, wealthy royal families in the world.

Josephine felt sick. Heartsick. Disgusted with herself, disgusted by her lapse in judgment.

If she went to her father she knew what he would say. He would say she had three options: terminate the pregnancy and tell no one, keep the child and tell no one, or keep the child but tell Alexander because he had a right to know.

It took little or no thought to eliminate option one: she wasn't going to end the pregnancy. That wasn't an option, not for her. She tried to imagine raising Alexander's child in secret, and that wasn't a viable option, either. It wasn't right or fair, not to him or their child. But how could she just show up at the Alberici palace in Roche and demand an audience? Never mind just a week before Alexander's wedding to Princess Danielle?

Stomach churning, she waited for her father to return from his meeting. "I need to reach Prince Alexander," she told him. "I need to speak with him about a matter of some…urgency."

Her father eyed her in silence for a long minute. "You're pregnant, aren't you?"

She nodded.

"Well, that explains the food poisoning. It wasn't food poisoning at all."

"I had hoped."

"So had I." He sighed and shook his head. "This is going to change your life. It will never be the same."

"You don't think I'll be a good mother?"

"It's not that simple. I'm not a monarchist, and I don't know all the laws in Aargau, but this isn't just any baby. You're carrying the future king's heir."

"Maybe I shouldn't tell him."

"You are as honest as they come, Josephine. You'd never keep the truth from him, or a child from his father. You wouldn't be able to live with yourself. So contact the palace security—I have a number, they left it with me when they came for him—but don't expect this meeting of yours to be easy. Your news could change everything."

The return to Khronos was so different from his departure two and a half weeks earlier. When he left, he hadn't thought he'd see Josephine again and he'd been livid with her, seething the entire trip to Roche. At the time, he didn't know what had upset him more—the fact that she'd left Khronos without telling him, or that she'd left the island without him telling her who he was.

He'd known that day, and every day since, that he should have told her his memory had returned. He'd been painfully aware that he should have handled things differently.

And now he was to see her again. She'd sent word through his security that there was an urgent private matter, and she'd asked his security how she should best deliver this urgent, sensitive information.

He'd known at once why she was reaching out. It was the only reason she would reach out.

Alexander requested the helicopter and flight crew for the following morning and now they were traveling above the blue-green water. Soon they'd be touching down on Khronos. He wondered if she had any idea he was on his way or that if her news was as he expected, then he'd be taking her back to Aargau with him. Today.

Helicopters were impossibly noisy, their turning blades impossibly distinctive. Josephine emerged from the small house, her pen still in her hand as she shielded her eyes to look up into the sky. The huge helicopter was flying low and coming directly toward her.

Her heart fell even as her stomach lurched, not a good combination when she was already nauseous.

Her father stepped out from the house, as well. His brow creased as he took in the helicopter dropping even lower. "He must have gotten your message," her father said.

She swallowed hard, her legs suddenly weak. "Maybe it's someone else."

"It's the same helicopter that came before. If he is any man at all, he'll be inside it and eager to speak with you."

Josephine wanted to throw up. She put a hand to her middle to slow the churning sensation that made her feel so sick. "You sound pleased."

"I'll be pleased if he comes in person to sort this out with you." He glanced at her, his expression suddenly critical. "Perhaps you'd like to change and comb your hair."

"Why? Because he's a prince?"

"No, because he's the man you love."

Josephine refused to change out of her yellow checked sundress, but she did run a brush through her hair and then pulled it back into a smooth ponytail, and then she took a seat at the table in the house and waited.

It wasn't long before she heard his footsteps outside and then his rap on the door that was already open.

She rose, hating how nervous she felt. "*Prince* Alexander Alberici," she said, accenting the word *Prince*. It wasn't polite, but then, she didn't feel polite. How could she when she was suddenly blisteringly angry?

"May I come in?" he said formally, still standing on her threshold.

"You know the house. You know your way around."

He entered, stooping slightly to clear the low doorway and then straightening once he was inside. His gaze swept the stone walls and rugged beams running across the ceiling. "Nothing's changed," he said.

"It's been this way for a hundred years. I expect it'll remain this way for another hundred."

He crossed the floor, glancing right and then left. "Your father?"

"Is at his desk in the foundation office." She struggled to contain her temper. "So no, there is no one here. It's just you and me. We won't be overheard."

"I wasn't worried about that. I wanted to be polite and pay my respects."

"How kind of you."

"You are angry."

"I am." She hadn't even realized just how deeply upset she was until he stepped through her door looking even more handsome than she remembered. He'd been beautiful to her in her father's faded chambray work shirts and linen shorts, but now in elegant trousers, dark shirt, and dark tailored blazer, he looked powerful. Magnetic. He was a man of position and wealth. And he knew it, too.

"You didn't have to reach out to me," he said, slowly walking around the central room, studying everything as if he'd never seen it before.

She hated his slow, lazy perusal because she was sure it wasn't lazy at all. He was doing his best to remember details. Or perhaps he was checking details against his memory. Either way, he had no right to be so relaxed, so indolent, in her home.

Her arms crossed over her chest, fingers curling into

small, tight fists. "Does Princess Danielle know you're here?"

"We're not married yet."

"What does that even mean?"

"She doesn't get access to my personal schedule."

"Does she even know about me?"

"The palace hasn't released any information about you." He gave her a considering glance. "Unless you'd like the palace to release information?"

She shot him a furious look, giving him the full measure of her wrath. "When did your memory return?" She asked, her voice flat, hard. "At what point on Khronos did you know who you were?"

"The day before your father returned."

She stared at him, clearly struggling. "You should have told me."

"Yes."

"Why didn't you?"

"Because at that point I wasn't ready to lose you."

Her mouth tightened; her jaws ground together. She was not going to cry. She would not allow herself to show any weakness or emotion at all. "You mean you weren't ready to stop having sex."

His black eyebrow lifted. "Is that what we were doing? Having sex?"

"Unprotected sex. And there were…are…consequences."

"I suspected that was why you reached out to the palace."

"You're not shocked?"

"As you said, there are consequences."

"You sound so cavalier," she gritted out. "You must have a plan in mind. A suggestion for managing this *complication*."

"Are you enjoying yourself?"

"No. I'm sick and heartsick and I should have heard

the truth from you. I should have heard the truth, if you knew it."

"Agreed. I was wrong. I am truly sorry."

His apology caught her off guard and she felt herself sag, so she sat down in the chair at the table, her hands balling in her lap.

He crossed the floor, approaching her, so tall that she had to tip her head back to look him in the eye.

"I didn't tell you," he added, "because I was determined to find a way to save us."

"Save us?" She made a soft, hoarse sound of protest. "How? You were engaged to someone else. Your wedding was weeks away. You weren't free to be with me. You weren't free to make love to me."

He crouched in front of her, his hands on her knees. "I can't change what happened when I didn't have my memory—"

"No, but that doesn't mean I don't regret it." She pushed his hands off her knees, feeling burned. "All of it."

"No."

"*Yes.* I hate that week we spent together. I hate that I fe—" She broke off, swallowing hard, smashing the words that had nearly escaped her lips. *I fell in love with you.* But she couldn't love him. Not anymore. She'd smash her feelings now, just as she'd suppressed the words. What had happened was history. The past was behind them. The only thing to do now was move forward without him. Somehow.

"Have you seen a doctor?" he asked.

She shook her head.

"Then how do you know?"

"I took a test in Athens yesterday, and I took it because I've never been late, and my body is different. Everything feels different. I'm violently ill, sometimes in the morning, sometimes at night. The only time I seem to be okay is in the afternoon and early evening." She fell silent for a moment before drawing a breath for courage. "I wouldn't have reached out to you if I wasn't certain. I am pregnant. And I intend to keep the baby. I don't need anything from you—"

"Of course you do. It's my child, too."

"I'm not asking for support. I'm not asking for—"

"Anything, yes, I know. But it doesn't work that way, *cara*. You are carrying my child, my heir. You might not ask for anything, but that doesn't mean you don't get everything."

She blinked, not understanding. "I'm sorry. I don't follow. What is everything?"

"Marriage. My home. My kingdom."

"But I don't want any of those—"

"I knew you'd say that. I was actually counting on you saying that. You didn't sleep with me to become pregnant. You didn't make love to me for any ulterior motive. You are not one of those women that try to entrap a man."

"Maybe it's time for you to go. You know the truth. I've kept nothing from you—"

"We need you to see a doctor. We need to be sure."

"I am sure."

"Yes, but I can't end my engagement to Danielle without proof. It wouldn't be fair to her."

"I don't want you to end your engagement to her. You're engaged to her. You must marry her—"

"I can't, not if you're carrying my child."

Her lips parted but no sound came out.

"The babe you're carrying is Aargau's future king or queen." Alexander rose. "I shall go look for your father and let him know you'll be returning to Roche with me."

He was so very different from her Alexander. But then, on the other hand, he wasn't. He'd always been rather imperious, if not downright commanding. She'd known from the moment he'd first spoken to her that he was a man familiar with authority and accustomed to being obeyed. But that didn't mean she had to fall in with his plans. She'd fallen in love with a man, not a prince, and she wanted the man, not the prince. "No, I'm not going."

His mouth tightened. Creases fanned from his eyes. He looked as if he was hanging on to his patience by a thread. "I'll explain to your father—"

"No need to look for me, I'm here." Her father stepped through the doorway. "I've heard most of what's been said. And I agree with Prince Alexander. You should see a doctor. You should be certain. Feelings are not facts, and what you both need now are facts. Having clear facts will help you make the right decisions."

CHAPTER SIX

SUNLIGHT PIERCED THE TALL, narrow windows of the tower suite. Holding her breath, Josephine watched the light pattern the smooth stone floor, focusing on where the blue-gray fieldstone disappeared beneath the pale ivory-knotted fringe of the burgundy and peach antique carpet.

If she stayed very still and very calm, she could lose herself in the streaks of golden light.

If she stayed very still and very calm, she could almost believe she hadn't been locked for days in a high tower without any connection to the outside world.

And then, since she *was* pretending, she could pretend her room, with its high vaulted ceiling, lovely, narrow leaded windows, and imposing four-poster bed in the middle of the floor, was a luxurious historic hotel room, and she was a guest at this stunning five-hundred-year-old castle, making her much envied by those who loved luxury travel. She would also pretend that the man who'd locked her here, the man she'd fallen in love with, was a handsome, kind prince instead of a cold, heartless one.

Unfortunately, Josephine wasn't good at sustaining the pretend game. It wasn't that she didn't have an imagination, but being the daughter of two scientists, she was more practical than impractical and loathed everything about her tower, and the man who'd locked her here.

Jo sat up straighter as she heard the scrape of the key turning in the lock. She fought a momentary panic because once the door opened, she couldn't play her games of pretend. It was so much harder to manage her emotions with Alexander in the room.

Four weeks ago Josephine wouldn't have believed any

of this was possible. But then, four weeks ago she hadn't known who Alexander was.

Four weeks ago, neither had he.

Now she wished she'd never told him she was pregnant. She'd thought she was doing the right thing, the honest and fair thing. But Josephine regretted her decisions with her whole heart as Alexander was neither honest nor fair, as it was his decision to put her here in this tower suite. It was his decision to lock the door. It was his decision to cut her off from communication with the world, but locking her away wouldn't help his cause. If he imagined that a few days of solitary confinement would weaken her resolve, he was painfully mistaken. She'd spent weeks, *months*, alone on Khronos while her father was off teaching. She wasn't afraid to be alone, and she wasn't easily intimidated.

But she was beginning to realize that her upbringing, so isolated from society, had not prepared her for dealing with complex relationships, and she suddenly doubted herself. She'd always thought she was a good judge of character, but apparently she wasn't. It seemed that she knew too much about science and too little about human beings. Which was why she'd told Alexander on arriving in Aargau that she'd include him in their child's life, even share parental responsibilities with him—because that was the fair thing to do—but he'd refused to even consider co-parenting. Their baby would live with him in the palace. Their baby required both mother and father, and they'd do it together. Married. And that would never ever happen. She'd never agree to marrying him, not after he'd revealed his true colors.

The door swung open and Prince Alexander Julius Alberici stood on the threshold, tall, broad shouldered, and impeccably groomed. His thick black hair was ruthlessly combed back, hiding the fact that it had an inclination to curl. His blue eyes focused on her with that laser focus that always made her feel as if he could see straight through her.

She sat up taller, her own shoulders squaring, chin lifting defiantly. She'd been told on first arriving in Roche that she should curtsy before him, and she'd laughed. *Laughed.* "I'd sooner have a lobotomy," she'd snapped.

Prince Alexander had heard and his lips had tightened.

His mouth—which she'd once thought so lovely—tightened now, but she no longer cared. Right now she didn't care what he thought, and right now she didn't care what he did, as long as he let her return to Khronos. It felt as if every good and tender feeling had been smashed, and it was his fault. He'd done this to her. To *them.*

"Can I help you?" she asked coolly.

Alexander entered the tower bedroom, unsurprised to find her where he'd last seen her, in the middle of her bed with a pile of books around her, her expression hard and shuttered. Her sketchbook was open next to her, a charcoal pencil against white paper, but the page was blank.

"How are you this morning?" he asked, stepping into the room, the door closing and locking behind him.

He saw her head turn, her honey hair scraped back from her face, pulled into a severe knot at her nape. Her green gaze focused on the door, her lips compressing with displeasure as the lock scraped closed. He knew she hated being locked in, and he hated locking her in. But he wasn't about to run the risk of her leaving Aargau in the dark of night, not when she was pregnant with his child.

"I am as tired of this as you," he said flatly, approaching the bed. "I just want a resolution. I want us to move forward."

Her head jerked up, eyes flashing with contempt. Even with her hair drawn back and not a bit of makeup to enhance her features, she was strikingly beautiful. He'd wondered when he first returned from Greece if he'd imagined her and her breathtaking beauty. He hadn't. If anything, she was more ethereal, and even lovelier than he'd remembered.

But her delicate beauty belied her strength. Josephine was livid, and she was not about to be strong-armed into marriage. "I don't like this any more than you," he added. "Marry me so we can be done with this. We were friends once—"

"*Not* friends."

"On Khronos you told me you loved me, Josephine. You said the words."

Color flooded her cheeks, making her eyes brighter. "I had no idea you weren't free. I had no idea you were…*you*."

"Neither did I."

"For your information, I liked the other you better, the one with amnesia. The one that didn't know his name, because at least he knew how to be kind. What you're doing now is unforgivable. You can't lock women in towers. It's medieval. Machiavellian." Her chin lifted, her gaze locking with his. "Even *you* must know that it's not done."

"I'm not happy about this, *bella*. I would prefer you to have a normal guest suite. I would prefer to be able to introduce you to my family and friends—"

"And your fiancée, Princess Danielle Roulet? What about her? Or have you not given her any thought or consideration?"

"You know I ended my engagement to her the moment we had confirmation of your pregnancy." He leaned against one of the enormous wooden posters on the antique bed. "There is nothing standing in the way of our marriage now."

"Nothing but my objections, but apparently that doesn't signify in your world. You're a prince, and I'm just an ordinary American girl."

"Who will one day be queen."

"I don't want to be queen. I'm not marrying you."

"Josephine, I'm trying to make this work—"

"Locking me in a tower is not making it work, Alexander!"

"You shouldn't have tried to run away."

"I wasn't running away. I was simply leaving the castle."

"With the intention to take a ferry to Italy and then disappear into Europe." He gave her a sympathetic look. "Next time, don't admit so much to a taxi driver, especially when he's a member of palace security."

"I did think it strange that you had a taxi just waiting outside."

"He wasn't there for you, if that's any consolation."

"It's not."

"Can we agree that you're not going to run away anymore? Because if you can give me your word—"

"I'm not sure I can, Alexander. I'm sorry."

"I am, too, because the baby you carry is my heir and thus the heir to the Aargau throne, which gives you two choices—marry me, or grant me sole custody of our child."

He saw her lips press and pain shadow her eyes. "You know I'd never give up my child. You're not giving me a choice."

"Most women would jump at the opportunity to become Aargau's queen."

"I'm not one of them."

"You're offended because it's not a romantic proposal."

"I'm offended because you're arrogant and rude, and baffled by what you call a proposal. You've flung the word *marriage* at me as if I'm a dog being dangled a bone. But the bone, Your Highness, isn't remotely appealing."

Alexander was torn between amusement and outrage. He wondered what his old self would have thought of her response. He'd been told by his friends that his old self lacked a sense of humor. That was interesting because sometimes Josephine made him want to laugh. Or shake her. Or make fierce, hot love to her.

"I'm phrasing things badly," he said. "But we have a wedding to plan, *cara*. We can't keep arguing and wasting time. We have to marry soon. It's essential we avoid scandal."

"You mean it's essential to *you*. I don't care about the scandal."

"That's because you live on an uninhabited rock, apart from society. The rest of us, I'm afraid, are not so lucky."

"You're not serious."

"About the marriage, or being determined to avoid scandal?"

"Both."

"We don't do scandals in Aargau. There has never been a divorce in the Alberici family."

"Just unhappily married, is that it?"

"My parents and grandparents and great-grandparents all knew better then to air dirty laundry. If there is strife, it's dealt with privately, behind closed doors. As we are doing now."

"So women are routinely locked in chambers and towers here?"

"You failed to mention the dungeons."

"I suppose if you have a historic castle, one should use all the rooms."

His lips twisted faintly. She amused him, and yet their current situation was anything but laughable. The palace was in an uproar. His father wasn't speaking to him. His mother was quietly frantic. The public couldn't understand what had happened to their prince.

"I want out of this room," Josephine said clearly, firmly.

"And I want you out of this room. I'd like it to become my retreat again. It used to be one of my favorite rooms, but holding you hostage here has diminished my pleasure in it."

"Poor Prince Alexander. How you suffer!"

He had to smash the laughter. "You are in such a foul mood. Perhaps I should kiss you—"

"No!" She scooted back on the bed. "You come near me and I'll throw every book I have at your head. And I've a good arm. Believe me."

"I do. That's why I want to move forward. It's why I want to introduce you to my kingdom and my people, but I can't do that until we've come to an understanding."

"We can raise our child together without being married." She paused, her winged eyebrows arching even higher. "Or resorting to locking me away as if I'm a dangerous criminal. You must know your strong-arm tactics only make me dislike you and mistrust you more."

"Trust goes both ways."

"Absolutely, and when have I ever let you down? Or betrayed you in any way?"

"You left me on Khronos. You disappeared without a word. And then you tried to run away from here after we saw the doctor. Josephine, I accept that I haven't been the model prince, but you have a poor track record when it comes to staying in place."

"Fine. Next time I'll put up a few signs to advertise that I'm leaving so there won't be any mixed signals," she flashed, hiding how much he continued to hurt her. She told herself she didn't care about him anymore, but if that was true, why did his every word wound? Why did he have such power over her? Worse, how could this be the man she'd loved so passionately on Khronos? He was nothing but cold and hard and calculating. How had she not seen his true nature before?

"Give me your word that you will not run, and I'll move you from the tower to a proper suite in the palace. Better yet, accept my proposal and let us plan the wedding together so that our baby will be born without any shame or scandal surrounding his or her birth."

If only it were that easy, she thought, drawing her knees to her chest and wrapping her arms around her legs, trying to anchor herself, craving safety and stability. Ever since she'd arrived in Roche, she'd felt rootless. Lost. She desperately missed her life on Khronos, needing her work to give her days structure and purpose. "I want to return to Khronos," she whispered. "I want to go home."

"Not until after the baby is born, but then yes, you could go for a visit."

"A visit," she said, her voice trembling.

He said nothing and she glanced around the room, taking in the thick stone walls, the narrow windows, the heavy beamed ceiling. "You're punishing me."

"That's not fair."

"I was a virgin when I met you and now I'm pregnant. Doesn't seem fair at all."

"You wanted to be with me."

"Because I thought you were free. I thought you cared about me."

"I do care about you, which is why I'm marrying *you*, not Danielle."

"You're only marrying me because I'm pregnant!"

"Do you want me to deny it? No, it's true. I'm marrying you because you're carrying my child, but that doesn't invalidate my offer—"

"Oh, it does. It most certainly does, *Your Highness*."

He sighed. "You're being childish."

"You're being hideous."

"We can't go back, Josephine. We can only go forward."

"And we will," she agreed huskily, "but not together. We might have created a baby together, but that doesn't mean we must punish ourselves for eternity—"

"Marriage is not hell."

"So says the man who had a girlfriend *and* a fiancée."

"I broke up with my girlfriend months before my engagement was announced."

"But you were privately engaged to the princess, weren't you?"

"We've had an understanding for years, yes, but Danielle also dated. She had relationships—"

"That still changes nothing. I'm not about to have my heart broken by a man who only cares for himself."

"But why would it be broken if you don't care for me? This isn't a love marriage, Josephine. It's a business deal, an arrangement to protect our child, who will inherit the Alberici wealth and title."

She blinked, hard. "So I don't matter."

His sigh was deep, heavy. "Of course you matter."

Her head dipped, her gaze dropped. "Please leave."

"It's time to put our child first. Stop with the selfishness—"

"*Me?* Selfish? Clearly, you don't remember Khronos or what happened there. But I do. And I was never selfish, never unkind, not toward you."

He left her then, and as the door closed behind him, she put her head down on her knees and fought tears.

She was exhausted and nauseous and sick of emotion. She wasn't used to feeling this much, and certainly not used to so little physical activity. For a girl who'd grown up outside, so close to nature that she felt she was an extension of the mountains and sea, being cooped up in a tower, in a castle, in a city, was a terrible punishment indeed.

Alexander descended the tower staircase to his office on the second floor, aware that Josephine wasn't wrong. He was different here. He had to be different here. On Khronos he'd been just a man. In Aargau he was the future king. He'd rather enjoyed being just a man. There had been freedom, and an ease he didn't know in his world here.

Aimee, his secretary, was at her desk when he entered the room and she glanced up at him, a troubled crease between her brows. "Her Highness has requested you join her in her rooms immediately." Aimee glanced at her watch. "That was nearly an hour ago. Her staff has followed up with me twice since, worried I haven't passed on the message."

"You knew where I was."

She gave a faint smile. "Yes, but you said not to bother you, and so I didn't."

Alexander crossed the Alberici castle grounds, heading for the pale yellow eighteenth-century palace that travel guidebooks always falsely claimed had been inspired by the architecture of Versailles but in reality drew its inspiration from the Royal Palace at Caserta, which was just fifty years older and much closer geographically.

Alexander climbed the grand pink and yellow marble staircase to the second floor and headed back down the long corridor to the set of rooms that were his mother's. There was no need for him to knock as her butler opened the door, announcing him.

Queen Serena waved him to a chair near hers. "You kept me waiting long enough," she said as he sat down and stretched out his legs.

"I came to you the moment I was free."

"I'm hearing things, worrying things." She gave him a long look. "Do you have any news for me? News that would ease some of my anxiety, because your father grows weaker. He slept most of today. We're running short on time, particularly if you hope to have him present at your wedding. Or perhaps you intend to marry after he's gone?" His mother's tone was cool and distant. But then, it was the tone he knew best. She was beautiful and regal, elegant and refined, always cognizant of her power and responsibility as the queen of Aargau.

"Of course I want him there."

"Then the wedding needs to be sooner, not later."

"I understand."

"Then what is the problem, Alexander?"

"Josephine isn't…ready…to marry."

"Excuse me? She's carrying your child, the heir to the kingdom."

"I understand."

"The longer you wait, the more difficult it becomes from a PR standpoint. You understand that, don't you? We're trying to do damage control, Alexander, and all we need is a small, private service in the palace chapel—"

"Unless she wants the formal service in the cathedral."

"We don't have time to plan a formal wedding, and she doesn't need a big, formal wedding. Your father is very unhappy that she's trapped you."

"*I* trapped *her*, not the other way around."

"You're a prince. She is no one."

He knew his mother well enough to know that she wasn't trying to be cruel or rude, just honest. "She didn't care that I was a prince, and she is most definitely someone."

The queen sat back in her chair, her jaw dropping slightly. "You *love* her."

"I want her, yes. But love? I don't know about that. I was once teased for being so emotional. Now I'm criticized for not having feelings. Having feelings would make all of this easier."

"I didn't have…feelings when I married your father. But they developed over time. Yours will develop, too." Her head tilted. She studied him intently. "Are you completely recovered from your accident?"

"Why do you ask?"

"You haven't been the same since you returned home. You are less…you."

He gave her a half bow. "Apologies. I shall try to be more...me."

"I don't appreciate the sarcasm, Alexander. It's very tense here, not simply because your father slips away from us a little more every day, but King Marcel Roulet is livid that his daughter has been profoundly embarrassed just a week before her wedding. And I've just been informed that you are keeping your American locked in your tower—"

"I did lock her in the first night. But she hasn't been locked in since."

"But she believes she's locked in."

He shrugged. "She has a tendency to run away. I need her to remain."

Her eyebrow lifted. "This is not how we conduct our affairs, nor is this how an Alberici royal handles his fiancée. Less drama, more efficiency, please. Put the ring on her finger. Give me a wedding date. We'll have a party this weekend—"

"Too soon."

"She could be *showing* by the next, Alexander."

"Then make it a week from now."

"An engagement party on a Wednesday?"

"Or Tuesday. We'll keep it small and intimate, for our closest friends and family only."

"Fine. But we'll need a portrait of the two of you to give the media." Her glance narrowed. "I don't suppose we can take your official engagement portrait and photoshop Danielle out and put your new girl in her place?"

"Was that a joke, Mother?"

Her lips curved faintly. "I was not always Queen Serena, Alexander. I, too, was once a young girl with a sense of humor and a hunger for adventure."

Josephine crossed to the window of her tower room, stepping up on the footstool she'd positioned beneath it, needing the extra height to look out the leaded glass. It was late afternoon, but due to the summer solstice a week ago, the sun was still high in the sky, shining brightly on the thick, gray slate roofs of the various castle buildings and then, farther out, the high, majestic stone walls that surrounded the castle itself.

She rested her chin on her fist, staring out, taking in Roche, Aargau's capital city famous for its medieval architecture and charming, narrow cobbled streets. She might have liked Roche, but after days of confinement she felt suffocated by all the walls and slate and cobbled stone. Her jaw tensed as her gaze went to the glimpse of sea beyond the city streets, the dark blue water calling to her, reminding her of Khronos.

A scrape sounded at the door, and the lock turned. She nearly fell off the stool as the door swung open and she took a sudden step back, misjudging the distance to the floor and needing to grab the wall to keep from falling down.

"Careful," a crisp, low feminine voice said from the doorway. "That's a good way to hurt yourself."

Josephine stiffened, surprised that it wasn't Alexander as he was the only one who'd been to visit her since she arrived, and yet she knew immediately who had come, having seen photos of her in magazines. "Queen Serena," she said faintly, letting go of the wall.

The slender blonde queen approached. "I haven't thwarted your escape plans, have I?"

Josephine thought she heard a hint of amusement in the older woman's voice. "I don't have Rapunzel's hair," she answered. "And even if I did, the window is a little narrow."

Serena stopped before her, her back straight, her bearing regal. In her icy-blue dress with the ropes of pearls, she looked every inch a queen. "I'm sorry I haven't been to see you sooner. I'm afraid our hospitality isn't what it should be."

"Does your son routinely lock his women up?"

"No, you're the first." She grimaced. "I'd like to say that it's a sign of his affection but you and I both know his behavior is inexcusable. One doesn't lock up beautiful young women in towers anymore. It's positively medieval."

"That's what I told him."

"Machiavellian."

"I said the very same thing."

"What are you going to do?"

"I don't know."

"What do you want to do?"

"Leave."

"What is keeping you here then?"

"Besides the locked door? The need to protect the baby." Josephine's chin lifted. "And not because he or she is an heir, but because he or she is my child."

"And Alexander's."

"I don't want Alexander, though. I realize he's your son, and you love him—"

"He's a man. Men are notoriously thickheaded and thin-skinned, but they have their uses and virtues."

Josephine wasn't sure how to take that last bit. She felt her shoulders tense, and she clasped her hands tightly. "I used to care for him very much, before he was—" she glanced around the room, and her hand followed in a sweeping gesture "—this."

"He's afraid of losing you."

"No, he's afraid of losing his heir, not me."

"If you truly believe that, you don't know my son."

Josephine's lips compressed and she held her tongue, not wanting to argue with the queen, because of course she'd take Alexander's side. She was his mother.

"But he won't lose his heir," Serena added after a moment. "You're not a woman who'd keep a child from his father, so there is something else driving him and making him act like a Neanderthal. Men usually only resort to caveman tactics when cornered and desperate." She glanced from Josephine to the bed, still piled high with books. "You're a scientist. Don't let your emotions cloud your brain. I understand you have a very good brain, so use it. Put my son on notice. Make him earn your favor."

"That will never happen."

"Fine. Then make him earn your trust, but do *something* so that you feel properly empowered and can respect yourself, if not him."

Josephine frowned. "You don't think I respect myself?"

"I think you know what you need to do, but your pride is keeping you from making the right decisions."

"Your solution is for me to marry Alexander."

"I have no solutions, but I do have a preference, and that is for my grandchild to grow up in a stable, loving home."

Josephine looked at the queen for a long, tense moment. "What happens now? When you leave, do you just lock me back in?"

"No. I have no patience for locked doors, secrets, or games."

"So I could leave now with you if I wanted."

Serena's fair head tipped. "Is that what you truly want? To leave here now?"

"I want Alexander to stop intimidating me."

"Then isn't it time to stand your ground?"

The queen walked out, and true to her word, after she left the door remained open, wide-open. Josephine waited a minute, and then another, and another, wondering when one of the palace security would come and close the door, locking it.

But no one came.

Josephine hesitated a long moment and then crossed the threshold, leaving her suite for the tower stairs. For another minute she stood at the top of the circular staircase listening. She heard voices coming from below, and then something was being moved or dragged, something heavy.

Josephine carefully went down the stairs to the next floor. The door was wide-open and it looked like a library, a very handsome library with vast bookshelves that rose all the way to the ceiling. Two men in uniform were carrying chairs while a woman ironed the creases from a heavy brocade cloth covering a table that had been placed in the center of the room.

She didn't know if she made a sound or if one of them felt her there, because suddenly they were all nodding and murmuring polite greetings while continuing with their work.

As if she hadn't just been locked away upstairs for days.

As if it was perfectly acceptable for her to wander around the tower.

She continued down the next flight of stairs, wondering if she'd now be stopped, wondering when she'd be told to return to her room, but she passed staff and no one said anything to her or expressed surprise that she was roaming the tower. She peeked into the room on the second floor and discovered an office suite. It was surprisingly sleek and modern, with computers and big screens and stylish leather chairs and lots of steel and plates of glass set into the wall, filling the spaces where a cannon or some other weapon must have once been.

A pretty young woman sat at one of the sleek ebony desks in the corner typing away on a computer. She looked up and nodded at Josephine before continuing with her work.

Everything seemed so ordinary and yet at the same time, everything was extraordinary.

Josephine cleared her throat. "His Highness, Prince Alexander," she said, her voice not entirely steady.

The young woman looked up again, smiling politely,

professionally. "His Highness has arranged for dinner at nine in the library. That is on the third floor, one level up."

"Thank you." And yet still she hesitated, chewing on her lip, trying to process what she was hearing and seeing. It seemed she'd been given freedom. Was this the queen's doing? Or had Alexander changed his mind?

Josephine walked down the last set of stairs to the first floor. She pushed open the cloudy glass door and entered a huge private gym. There were free weights and weight machines, a treadmill, a stationary bike, and another piece of equipment she'd never seen before, and behind all that was a stone wall covered with brown, gray, and dark green bumps.

She looked at the wall hard, trying to understand what the bumps were before walking toward it, letting her fingers trail over a light gray wedge jutting out from the tower wall at her shoulder height.

"It's a climbing wall," Alexander said, behind her.

She turned around to find him standing not far behind her. He was wearing charcoal-colored shorts and a white T-shirt, and his bronzed skin was flushed, his black hair damp. She couldn't help noticing the way his thin T-shirt clung to the planes of his broad chest and the curve of his sinewy biceps.

"I didn't realize you were here. I'm sorry I interrupted your workout," she said.

"I'd stepped out for a moment to take a call," he answered, lifting the hem of his T-shirt to wipe his jaw, revealing his hard, flat abdomen with his chiseled abs. "But you're not interrupting. I'm just about finished."

She heard the words but couldn't focus on them, suddenly transfixed by the glimpse of his chest, reminded of how that lean, hard torso had felt against her. Her gaze dropped to his hips just before he dropped his shirt, covering himself, but she remembered him there, too, and how his body had given her such pleasure.

Josephine swallowed hard and averted her gaze, but it was too late. Heat rushed through her and she felt tingly and exposed, even as a deep craving hit her, making her ache for the feel and weight of him. "It's an impressive gym," she said hoarsely.

"You're welcome to use it anytime."

She didn't want the gym, though. She wanted him. And the unbidden thought made her loathe herself because she shouldn't be so weak. She shouldn't still want him, not after everything that had transpired. "Your mother came to see me just a little bit ago," she said, struggling to distract herself. "Was that how my door was left unlocked?"

"It's been unlocked for the past two days."

"It hasn't."

"It has."

"But that scraping sound—the lock turning…"

"It's just the hardware. It's old. It should be replaced."

"You let me think I was locked in."

"I did."

"That's horrible. You should be ashamed."

"I am."

"You don't sound it. If anything, you seem rather pleased with yourself."

"I'm pleased to see you."

Her lip compressed and she glanced away, but not before her gaze swept over him, focusing on his midsection, seeing yet again that lovely hard torso in her mind's eye.

She'd been fascinated by him before they'd ever met. She'd watched him on the beach, interested in only him. She'd filled her sketchbook with his likeness.

He was her weakness.

And yet she felt increasingly vulnerable, and not at all safe. "I'm afraid this isn't going to work," she said, her voice low and husky. "And I don't know how to make it work since I no longer trust you."

"I'll earn your trust back."

"I don't think—"

"You have to give it a chance, Josephine."

"It will take time."

"Yes, it will. Unfortunately, it's the one thing we're short on, and so I ask you to trust me that the trust will grow."

"Alexander."

"We need to marry soon—as in right away. As it is the baby will be born early, and we can fudge a few weeks, but every day it will become harder to hide the facts of his or her conception. I can handle gossip. I'm accustomed to slights and insults, but I don't want there to be excessive speculation about our child's birth. Nothing should mar his or her future. Life is hard enough without being born under a cloud of doubt."

Finally, he'd said something she agreed with. Life was hard, and no child should have to grow up with any stigma or gossip surrounding him or her. "Do you even like children?" she asked.

"What a strange question."

"I think it's a fair question. You had never mentioned them before."

"Before? You mean on Khronos when I didn't know my name or where I came from or even my native tongue?"

She squirmed inwardly, thinking he'd made a fair point. "You never asked me how I felt about becoming a mother. You never asked me my feelings on anything."

"I'm sorry."

She shot him a narrowed glance. "So my bedroom door will remain unlocked?"

"Yes."

"You're giving me my freedom back?"

"Freedom to explore the palace grounds, yes."

"But not beyond?"

"You may leave to explore Roche provided you have ample security. But I warn you, it won't be the same as before. The people know you're here—"

"How?"

"I'm followed constantly, *cara*. When I leave these castle walls, I'm followed and photographed and everything I do and eat and buy is documented. Which is why I've kept you here, on the inside. I'm trying to buy you time, giving you a chance to mentally adjust to the changes taking place."

She was silent a long moment. "I don't have very much control anymore, do I?"

"No."

"Or very many options."

"Unfortunately, no."

"What options do I have? What am I allowed to decide?"

"The time of day you'd like to be married. The choice of venue for the ceremony—the chapel here, within the palace grounds, or the Gothic cathedral on Roche's historic square."

He added in the same flat, unemotional voice, "You can choose the type of reception we will have. You have absolute control over the wedding details, large and small. You can decide where we will honeymoon—"

"I don't want a honeymoon."

"You don't think it would be good for us to get away and have some time alone?"

"I've had time alone with you. And look at me now."

A possessive heat flickered in his blue gaze and the edge of his mouth lifted in a sensual curl. "I'd like a week with you where you don't have to cook or wait on me. I'd like to do nothing but keep you in bed all day."

She felt the curl of his lip as darts of sensation raced from the tips of her breasts through her belly to between her thighs. "I think we did that, too."

"There are so many things I want to do with you—"

"No, thank you."

"You'd enjoy it."

"Just like I enjoyed being locked in your tower?"

He considered her words. "Bondage is a form of foreplay. I find the idea of tying you up, or maybe handcuffing you to the bed, very erotic. I think you would, too."

Her pulse leaped. Heat stormed her cheeks. "You clearly don't know me, not if you think I'd enjoy being handcuffed or tied up."

"You don't know that until we try."

She'd never imagined such a thing, and yet she could see herself naked, tied to her bed, waiting for him. Waiting on him. It was shocking and yet thrilling. A frisson of raw desire, spiked by nervous excitement, shivered up and down her spine. "You are being blatantly sexual," she murmured huskily.

His gaze slowly roved her face, lingering on her lips. "You like me blatantly sexual."

"You made me sexual."

His broad shoulders shrugged. "Chemistry has never been our problem. We work. We make sense. Why? I don't know. You're the scientist. You tell me."

Her breath caught in her throat as heat and awareness surged through her. It had been almost three weeks since they'd been intimate and yet her body remembered him and ached for him to hold her down and make her his again. She could remember his lips at her neck and the roughness of his chest against her breasts and the thickness of his hard, hot shaft entering and filling her. When he was with her, in her, she felt unbearably good… She felt complete.

And part of her desperately wanted him again. She wanted his warmth and the sensation of being his, and only his, but another part of her knew he wasn't good for her. Her desire made her dependent. Her desire clouded her thinking. She struggled to remember why they were at odds, needing to create distance, needing a form of defense. "But it's changed," she said breathlessly. "We did have chemistry, but that was before, back when we were on Khronos. When I felt safe with you. I don't anymore."

"You will again."

"So I can go out? I can resume normal living?"

He took so long to answer that she dreaded the answer. "It won't ever be the normal you knew before," he said at length, "but yes, you can go out, and yes, you can go shopping, or out for a meal. But it will be choreographed at our end. Palace security will want to know the details so they can have a plan, create a route, and ensure your outing will be as stress free as they can make it."

"My normal isn't shopping and restaurants. My normal is home. My work. The beach."

"You will have work. It will just be different—"

"Is that supposed to appease me?"

"No. I'm being honest. I think it's better if we lay all the cards on the table. The truth is you will have a new life here, and you will have a new normal, and I promise that I will do everything in my power to help you settle in so that you can be happy, eventually."

A new life here.

A new normal.

Be happy...eventually.

The words echoed in her head. She raised a hand to her face, fingertips pressing against her forehead where pain throbbed. She didn't want a new normal, and she didn't want a new home, but none of that seemed to matter, and honestly, she had no one to blame but herself. She'd lost her head on Khronos. She'd thrown caution to the wind. They'd made love a dozen times. Risks had consequences and the consequence was that they'd created a new life.

She dropped her hand, looked up at him. "Does anyone even know about me?"

"They know you rescued me after my…accident. They know you saved my life, and they believe you're here to be thanked by my parents."

She frowned as a troubling thought came to her. "What about the pregnancy? Does anyone know about that?"

"No. It's a closely guarded secret. Only four people know you are pregnant: our parents and the doctor who performed the ultrasound, and I'm determined that no one else know, not until we choose to make an announcement, most likely once you are well into your second trimester."

"Who is *we*? The palace, or you and me?"

"It will be up to us, I promise."

Up to us. *Us.*

"Don't you think I should meet both of your parents before I say yes?" she asked, taking a deep breath. "I realize your father is the king, but he will be the grandfather of my child. I want to be sure he approves of…me." *Us.*

Alexander hesitated. "My father can be difficult."

"Is that your way of saying I should lower my expectations?"

He smiled crookedly. "You're quite good at subtext."

CHAPTER SEVEN

THEY WERE TO have dinner in his tower library that night. Alexander had given his staff instructions to set a proper table and provide a proper meal with a proper dessert, and since he had a few minutes before dinner, he stopped by his father's room.

The king's butler opened the door to Alexander. "He's awake," the butler said. "But he's not in the best of tempers."

"Thank you," Alexander replied, grateful, as forewarned was forearmed.

King Bruno was in bed already, and he watched Alexander approach his bed from beneath heavy lids. "You've cleaned up. Who are you trying to impress tonight?"

"I'm having dinner with Josephine."

The king's jaw tightened, his expression closing. When his father said nothing else, Alexander added, "I intend to present her to you tomorrow, Father."

"I'd prefer not."

"I'm aware of that, but she doesn't need to be, and then after I introduce you, I'm moving her into the palace. It will be a short meeting. You won't have to do much—just nod and I'll whisk her out and it will be over."

"I heard that you and Damian had a falling-out. I hope it's not true."

His father had always been more interested in Damian than him. "We're fine."

"Why hasn't he come around, then?"

"I wondered the same thing."

"He's always been very loyal to me."

"Just as I have, Father."

But Bruno had no response to that, choosing to close his eyes, ending the conversation.

In the tower library, iron-and-glass wall sconces had been lit so that the room glowed with red and gold light. A ruby brocade cloth covered the round dining table and the stemware had ruby-colored crystal stems. The walls of books added to the richness, and Josephine found herself relaxing as they were presented with their second course.

"You will meet my father tomorrow before lunch," Alexander said. "I cannot predict how he will behave."

"You have a difficult relationship?"

"It's been tense since I was a very young boy."

"Is he that hard to please?"

"He's quite pleased with my mother."

"How have you disappointed him?"

"I'm too cerebral. He would have preferred a son more like my cousin, Damian. Damian is physical, shrewd, and aggressive. My father admires a man who will lay down the law and command."

"How are you not commanding?"

Alexander smiled, and then his smile faded. "Josephine, we might never be who we were on Khronos, but that doesn't mean we can't be happy and that we can't create a strong and loving family for this child and any others we choose to have."

"Would you want more?"

"I would like more."

"Because you need an heir and a spare?"

"Because I was an only child and was often lonely. I would love my son or daughter to have siblings, brothers and sisters to play with. Why grow up in a castle if you have no one to chase you up and down stairwells, or play hide-and-seek with in the dungeon?"

She swallowed hard, unaccountably moved by his words. "Your nannies didn't play with you?"

"How can a nanny ever be a substitute for a brother? Nannies don't whisper secrets and share dreams."

Josephine hated the lump filling her throat. She didn't want to care for him; she didn't want to feel connected, and yet his words made her heart ache. She understood better than he knew. She had grown up alone and lonely. She had grown up wishing for a playmate, someone to talk to late at night, someone to wake up with in the morning, someone who would go on an adventure with her. Instead, she'd spent her life entertaining herself. She'd spent her childhood trying to pretend she didn't need anyone.

"You want our child but you don't want me," she said after a moment. "I think that is the most difficult part for me. And maybe it sounds selfish—"

"But I do want you. I want you very much. I locked you here, trapping you in my home, to keep you from leaving."

"To keep your unborn child here."

"To keep *you* here, Josephine." He signaled for the table steward to leave, and once the door closed, leaving the two of them alone, he said, "I still don't have all of my memory. It hasn't completely returned," he added. "It's incomplete, and there are areas of my life that still have…blanks. I know things because people have told me things, but I have no memory of them."

"Such as?"

"The trip with my friends on the yacht."

"Is that all?"

"The first day or two on Khronos."

"You were recovering from an injury. I'm not surprised you're having difficulty with those memories."

"But I was on the yacht for a week before the accident. That's essentially nine days I don't remember, plus the week where I had amnesia."

"What do the doctors say?"

"I haven't told them."

"Why not?"

"Because I'm worried it would get back to my mother, and she has enough to deal with at the moment."

"Is there more I don't know?"

"My father is dying," he said bluntly. "He has lung cancer. It's stage four now. The radiation and chemotherapy have stopped. There is no more prolonging his life. The only thing that can be done is to try to make him as comfortable as possible—and that's not working."

"And this is why you keep saying we're running out of time. Because you literally are running out of time."

He nodded. "I want my father there when we marry… if humanly possible."

"But why didn't you just tell me? I would have better understood the pressure and urgency."

"Because this is how families like mine operate. We're royals. We maintain facades. We keep up appearances. We're not supposed to have problems. We're not supposed to struggle. And to accomplish that, we suppress anything that is remotely problematic—"

"Like emotions?"

His lips curved wryly. "Indeed, emotions are terribly dangerous."

"I think living without emotions is dangerous."

"Says the woman who loves volcanoes and lava."

"Don't forget plumes of ash."

"How could I?" He hesitated, gathering his thoughts. "We don't do *dramatic* here. And we don't have volatility in the palace. It's all very contained and controlled."

"That's dreadful."

He hesitated. "It can be."

"So who knows about your father?"

"Just a handful of us. Those who must know."

"Rather like my pregnancy."

"But that will be good news, just as our wedding will be good news. I know my mother is hoping our happy news will help soften the public's grief when they learn of my father's cancer."

Josephine swallowed hard, her mouth going dry. "That's a lot of pressure."

"I've grown up in a fishbowl. You're being thrown into it. But I have faith in you. You're a strong swimmer."

His gaze held hers, and there was something in his eyes, as well as the gruffness in his tone, that made her feel tender. She pressed her hand to her chest, pushing against her heart. "Thank goodness I like the water."

He rose and left his chair, and once standing next to her, he reached into his coat and withdrew a small velvet box. As he lifted the lid, he knelt at her side. "Josephine, would you do me the honor of marrying me and becoming my wife and future queen?"

She looked from the huge ring in the box—a massive square-cut emerald surrounded by layers of diamonds—up into his face. He was so very handsome and yet so very aloof. In Khronos he'd been relaxed and physical, and she suspected that in bed he'd be just as sensual here, but she worried that there was no room for emotion. She wondered if he'd ever loved a woman. She wondered if he'd ever love her.

His mouth tugged into a reluctant smile. "I'd hope you would say yes."

She flushed. "Yes, it is a yes. I'm sorry."

"Don't be sorry. Just give me your hand."

Mortified, she held her hand out to him and he slid the ornate ring on her fourth finger. It was loose and slid sideways. She shifted it around, struck by the weight of it.

"We'll get it sized tomorrow," he said, rising.

Josephine couldn't look away from the immense emerald. "It's beautiful."

"It's an Alberici family heirloom, from the early nineteenth century."

She balled her hand to keep the ring from slipping sideways again. "Your world is overwhelming."

"Trust me, I understand."

"I never wanted to be a princess…not ever, not even as a young girl playing make-believe. I loved fables, not fairy tales. I identified with animals, not villagers."

"I never wanted to be a prince," he said, taking his seat at the table again. "As a boy I rebelled against my birth. I didn't want to be nobility. I didn't want to be privileged. My father thrashed me for being ungrateful and undeserving of my position, and I learned never to voice my concerns or objections again."

"It must have been quite a thrashing to have permanently silenced you."

"The thrashing wasn't that bad, but being sent away from home was. Although I imagine it would have happened sooner or later."

"Do you remember it still?"

"The conversation with my father, or the punishment?"

"Both, I suppose."

Alexander leaned back in his chair. "I remember the conversation because I felt very pleased with myself. Rather righteous, if you will. You see, from a young age I'd been uncomfortable with royal protocol, almost cringing when government officials and the public bowed to me, thinking I'd done nothing to earn their loyalty and deference. I didn't think it fair that I was simply born with advantages. It wasn't egalitarian."

"Oh, dear, I can see that being problematic if your father was as old-fashioned as you say."

"Mmm. How dare I be a populist?"

"And you, his only child."

"An embarrassment to the Alberici name." Alexander smiled wryly. "I'm sure I didn't help things by pointing out to my father that the monarchy was a huge expense for the people of Aargau, costing over two hundred million euros a year to support the monarchy here, and yes, a portion comes from the Alberici estate, but didn't an equal portion come from the Aargau government, which was really from the taxes the people pay?"

"You didn't."

"I did."

"And then what happened?"

"Thrashed, sent to my room without food or water for the night, and then the very next day I was packed up and shipped off to a military academy where the staff was told to turn me into a proper man."

"I would think that was an invitation for abuse."

"For someone raised outside society, you understand it very well."

"I read a lot."

He reached across the table to fill her glass with more sparkling water. "I remained at the academy until I was seventeen, then served three years in the Royal Navy and was finally allowed to attend university at twenty. I escaped Europe for four years in New Haven, Connecticut, where I studied philosophy, economics, and environmental science before returning to Europe to earn a graduate degree from Cambridge in land economy, a field that combined environment, law, and economics."

"That's why your English is so good."

"I confess, I liked living overseas and loved my time in America. You have a freedom we don't have here. It's probably why I took a job in Paris after my graduate degree. I wasn't ready to come back to Aargau and be Prince Alexander. I liked being one of the people."

"You don't think you can be one of the people as your country's king?"

"Not the way I was raised."

"Then when it's your turn, do it differently so that our son or daughter can embrace a future in which he or she has the opportunity to be happy."

"I would encourage a career, then."

"Your father didn't have one?"

"From the age of eighteen he has been king."

"He has done his duty, then."

"Yes."

"And when it is your turn, you will do your duty, too."

The meeting with his father was short and rather brusque, but Alexander admired Josephine's calm and gracious manner even under fire. His father spoke barely a dozen words to her, but at least those words included curt approval granting them permission to marry.

Queen Serena didn't speak until the end, but once her husband had given his blessing for the marriage, she rose and gave both Alexander and Josephine a kiss on the cheek. "Congratulations," she murmured. "And welcome to the family," she added to Josephine.

The meeting lasted barely five minutes and they were done, exiting the room with Josephine's hand tucked into the crook of his arm. Her hand was trembling. He'd had no idea she was nervous until then.

He glanced down at her bent head as the doors to his father's room closed behind them. Her thick, light brown hair with the streaks of blond had been pulled back in a stylish twist. She was wearing a simple navy dress paired with navy heels. Small pearl drop earrings dangled from her earlobes. "You look very elegant," he said quietly, trying to distract her from the hollow ring of their footsteps on the marble floor. "Have I seen this dress before?"

She reached up and touched the matching strand of pearls at her neck. "No." Worry darkened her green eyes. "Your mother sent the dress, shoes, and jewelry to me this morning. She said I was probably wishing I had something chic for my presentation and hoped the dress and shoes would help me feel suitably prepared."

He was surprised, but then again not. His mother excelled at soothing and smoothing tension. And yet she was no pushover. His mother was probably the strongest woman he knew. "I wish I had thought of that. You do need a new wardrobe. And an assistant. I will have a team meet with you after lunch."

"I don't need an assistant or a new wardrobe, and I have this dress now in case I need to see your father again."

He stopped on the bottom marble stair. "I don't think you realize what is about to happen. Our engagement is being announced this afternoon. We will soon become the focus of the press and a great deal of speculation, particularly when we announce the wedding is just a week from Saturday."

"Nine days from now?"

"It's not a lot of time, no, which is why we'll have a little preparty next week, either Tuesday or Wednesday, to celebrate our good news—"

"Is that really necessary?"

"We must do something or people will find it odd that I've kept you locked away—"

He broke off as she arched a brow. He laughed softly. "You will never let me forget I locked you up, will you?"

"Absolutely not. You're terrifying. I should call you Bluebeard."

He smiled and kissed her, and then again, his lips lingering against her mouth. She shivered against him, her hands pressed to his chest. "You're too good at this," she murmured. "You make me almost want to be locked up with you."

"I knew it," he said. "Now, where are my handcuffs?"

"Easy does it, Your Highness. We're not even married yet."

"True, and speaking of marriage, I think it'd be wise to make some decisions so my mother won't worry."

"Can't we just make some decisions now and tell her?"

"Do you know what you want?"

"Small wedding, only our immediate family—yours, and my father. I'd like it to be a quick service, if possible, so that it's not too much for King Bruno. Afterward cake and a toast with our parents and then, later, a private romantic dinner for just you and me."

"That's not a very proper royal wedding."

"We both know I'm not a proper royal bride."

CHAPTER EIGHT

WHEN ALEXANDER HAD said that the palace would begin the wedding preparations immediately and that Josephine's days would quickly become tightly scheduled, he hadn't been exaggerating. She'd expected some appointments and anticipated some meetings, but her entire life was taken over. She also quickly discovered that future princesses lived anything but private lives.

Within an hour of the engagement being announced, she was surrounded by staff. There were women at her side who were assistants managing her schedule, with others managing her wardrobe, while others had tasks she didn't yet understand.

It only took a few days of constant companionship to make her miss her tower bedroom, which was far from the bustle of the palace. She missed her view of the sea, which reminded her of Khronos, her father, and the work that had been such a passion for so many years.

She also struggled with the sheer number of women who surrounded her now, women who all had corrections for her. They coached her on how to walk, how to carry herself, how to speak. How to hold her knife and fork. How to lift a glass. How to place a teacup. How to sit. How to rise. How not to cross her legs. How to hold her head. How to smile. How not to smile. And how never, ever to laugh.

The hours of daily instruction were meant to help her. The instruction was meant to help shape her into a proper princess. But all the lessons in etiquette and deportment, all the correction of her grammar, all the jabs at her posture simply made her feel pathetically inadequate. Every moment of her life had become a teachable moment, and for someone who'd been homeschooled and who had done her learning through stacks of books, the very vocal, critical coaching was an excruciating reminder that she was a problem. A *mistake.*

More than once she overheard her ladies murmuring about the difficulty in shaping her into a lady before the party on Tuesday, where she'd be presented to various members of the aristocracy, family friends, and a selection of Aargau's Parliament.

In addition to the lessons, there were fittings and more fittings, and she was tired of standing still, being measured and draped and discussed as if she were a headless mannequin.

In the last four days she'd been pricked with more pins than she cared to remember. She noticed there were no trousers for her and nothing remotely slouchy or comfortable being made. Everything was expertly tailored: scooped necklines, snug belts, skirts with demure hemlines. But the fabrics were gorgeous and every finished item was beyond luxurious.

Alexander appeared at her room one afternoon, interrupting a meeting with Lady Adina, who was again going over the guest list for Tuesday's party with her, ensuring that Josephine was indeed familiar with all the names and the correct titles.

No one had heard him enter, and Josephine didn't know how long he'd been standing there, observing them at her writing table. "Hello," she said breathlessly, happy to see him and grateful for the interruption. "Do you need me?"

"No. Not if you're busy."

"We're not that busy," she said, rising, thinking he looked ridiculously handsome in crisp olive trousers and a starched white shirt, the sleeves rolled up on his bronzed forearms. His shirt hugged his shoulders and molded to his chest and narrow waist. Just looking at him she could see why she'd thrown caution to the wind and fallen for him so hard. "And I feel like I haven't seen you in ages."

"I know, and now I'm heading to Paris but I should be back tomorrow."

She looked up quickly, hopeful. "Could I go with you? I've never been to Paris and I'd love to see something new—"

"I wish you could, but last-minute trips are expensive, even without the additional rooms and security we'd need since we're not yet married." He reached for her hand. "Come, walk with me in the picture gallery. I don't think I've taken you there yet, have I?"

"No," she said quietly, feeling flattened.

His fingers laced more fully with hers. He gave her hand a slight squeeze. They walked silently from the room and down the hall. It wasn't until they'd reached the staircase and gone up a floor and then entered a long corridor filled with enormous oil paintings that Alexander stopped walking and faced her.

"I am going to Paris to see one of my friends, Phillipe," he said quietly. "Phillipe was on the yacht with me, and he's leaving for an extended trip to Buenos Aires and I want to catch him before he goes."

"He hasn't tried to see you or reach out to you?"

"He's close with Damian, my cousin. And the fight on the yacht, it was between Damian and me. I think Phillipe has avoided me to avoid having to take sides."

She was silent a moment in order to process what he was saying. "The fight on the yacht... It was between you and your cousin?"

"Yes."

His expression was so grim that she was almost afraid to ask anything else. But she'd been there, on the beach, when he'd gone overboard, and she'd been the one to rescue him. She'd seen the wound on his head. She knew firsthand the damage inflicted. "This is the cousin your father wanted you to be more like."

"We were raised almost like brothers."

"But he was the one that hit you?"

"Apparently in self-defense."

"What? How?"

"I don't know. That's the problem. I only know what I've been told. If only I could remember, but I can't, and so I'm dependent on the memories of those who were there."

"Have you asked to see the footage from the security cameras? The ship must have them. Everyone has them—"

"It was the first thing I asked for on returning home. But it seems there were no cameras at that end of the ship. It was one of the few places that lacked surveillance."

"Strange, don't you think?"

"From what I've learned, I was the aggressor that night. If what is being said is true, my behavior is inexcusable."

"What are they saying you did?"

He shook his head. "I'd rather not."

"And I'd rather hear it from you than from someone else."

"Fair enough." Alexander moved away from her toward the wall of framed portraits, but he didn't seem to be looking at any of the canvases. "It's all rather complicated, as I'm telling you what Gerard told me took place."

"So Gerard was there? He saw it happen?"

"No, this is what Damian told Gerard."

"I don't find that very reassuring."

Alexander shot her a pensive glance. "According to Damian, he noticed I was missing, and then he noticed Claudia—"

"Who is Claudia?"

"His girlfriend." Alexander swallowed. "And my ex-girlfriend."

Josephine's eyebrows arched but she held her tongue.

"So he went looking for us," Alexander continued, "and found us on the deck off her room. We were having an argument." His jaw tightened. "I had my hands on her. I was threatening her, shaking her, choking her. Damian intervened and rescued her, taking Claudia to get medical care and leaving me alone on her deck."

"How did you go overboard?"

"I don't know."

"No one came to confront you? No one came to kick you out of her room?"

"Gerard came to find me. He said her room was empty."

"Did he then go to your room?"

"Yes, and the door was locked, so he left me alone." Alexander fell silent. "Everyone assumed I'd gone to bed to sleep it off. But when I didn't emerge from the cabin by early afternoon the next day, my friends forced open my door to check and discovered I was gone."

"That's why they never sounded the alarm."

"And why no one knew where to look for me. By early afternoon the yacht had covered a great distance." He drew a breath and forced himself to continue. "What worries me is the fight. The fact that I was shaking her or angry with her. I don't know why I'd be upset. I've never been bothered by her seeing Damian. How could I be? I was the one who ended it with her."

"You think Damian is making all of this up?"

"But why? What purpose would it serve?"

"So you believe him, then? You shook Claudia and choked her, and then you somehow, all on your own, fell off the yacht?"

"People do stupid things when they drink, and I have been told I was drinking heavily that night."

"I'm sorry but none of this makes sense. I've never seen you drink to excess."

"I did, when I was younger, back in my university days. And I had a reputation for being a bit of a hothead when I drank, but that was years ago. Ten years ago. I don't drink like that anymore."

"Tell me about Claudia."

He shot Josephine a sharp glance. "Why?"

"I've never heard you mention her until now and I find it interesting that your ex-girlfriend was on your bachelor trip."

"As my cousin's girlfriend."

"But wasn't that awkward?"

"Claudia is also the younger sister of Marc, one of my best friends. She's been part of my circle forever, which was why I began dating her in the beginning. She knew my world. She understood the rules of my world. She was… convenient."

Josephine didn't know whether she was more shocked, angered, or puzzled. Worse, Alexander's story didn't line up. It wasn't logical. "What were Claudia's injuries?" she asked. "Did the medic on board take photographs? Did she have bruises? Have you spoken to her?"

"Marc, her brother, has told me to stay away from her."

"Is Marc close friends with Damian, too?"

"We met Marc our first year in the military academy. We've been friends with him ever since."

"And Phillipe?" she asked, suppressing a heavy sigh. "How does he fit in?"

"He was another friend from the academy."

"You trust them all? Every last one of them?"

Alexander looked away. He said nothing. His silence ate at her.

She pressed her hands together, fingers interlacing. She was afraid for him. Afraid for both of them. "I'm not trying to play Devil's advocate, Alexander, but something isn't right. I'm worried you've been set up."

He glanced at her, his expression almost bleak. "But what if I did do it?"

She'd been hurt and angry when she'd first arrived in Aargau and locked in the tower, but deep down, she'd always known who he was and what he was. And that was honorable. "I don't believe it. And neither should you."

Alexander's trip to Paris was a waste of time and money. When Alexander arrived at Phillipe's apartment, he discovered Damian was already there. The three of them had dinner together, and on the surface everything was cordial, but conversation was superficial at best. During the meal, they all avoided speaking of the trip. They avoided discussing Alexander's wedding. They actually only spoke of football and the new exclusive VIP club that had just opened up in Paris.

Alexander regretted the trip. He wished he'd remained in Roche with Josephine, and then it crossed his mind that he didn't have to stay. He could leave now and return home tonight. He could return now.

Alexander acted on impulse and rose. "Thank you for dinner, but I should get back. Phillipe, enjoy Buenos Aires. It's a favorite city of mine." He nodded at Damian. "I expect I'll see you back in Roche soon."

"I've been waiting for an invitation to the wedding."

"We're keeping it small and private."

"And the party Tuesday? No invitation for that one, either?"

"I was going to give it to you in person when you came to see me at the palace. You haven't come by. You haven't phoned."

"I was waiting on an apology."

"Ah, I see. Good to know." Alexander tipped his head and started for the door.

Damian was on his feet and he followed. "You need to

get help, Alex, and if you won't do it on your own, I'll make sure you do. I'll speak to your father. I'll go to Parliament. I'll take it to the media."

Alexander turned around. "Why make it public? What do you hope to accomplish?"

"You'll no longer be able to avoid the truth—that you're not well, and potentially unfit to rule in your current condition."

Alexander regarded his cousin a long moment and then nodded. "Good to know." And then he walked out, grateful for the car waiting for him downstairs and the private jet that could fly him home tonight.

Josephine hated being at the palace without Alexander. She felt trapped and bullied, although she suspected Alexander wouldn't understand because he'd grown up here and he'd been raised to conform. But it wasn't just the constant critical company that wore on her; it was her boring, uninspiring routine. She could only hope that once the wedding was over she'd be given more space, as well as more control over her day. Until then, she'd have to stand at windows, looking out, waiting for Alexander to find her and make her feel safe and wanted again. He was the only reason she was here in Aargau. Her hand went to her belly and she cradled it protectively. Well, Alexander and this one. Her baby.

In the beginning she'd been nervous about the pregnancy, but now she was excited, and determined to be a great mother. Josephine had been raised by a single father, and while he'd loved her, he'd never quite managed to be both mother and father. As a little girl, she'd desperately missed her mother, and that ache for a mother had never gone away. Even now, maybe particularly now due to the pregnancy, Josephine longed for a mother to talk to her, give her advice, and reassure her. Fathers were good at many things, but they didn't carry the baby, and they didn't deliver the baby, or nurse, or do any of those other things, and what Jo needed now was a strong maternal figure to help her adjust…or even some knowledgeable girlfriends would do. She hoped that later Queen Serena could maybe become that figure, but until then, Josephine would continue being her own best friend.

On Sunday afternoon, Alexander walked the castle parapet with the stunning views of Roche's medieval walled town against the brilliant blue of the sea. Damian's words haunted him. He'd returned from Paris in the middle of the night, and it had taken him hours to fall asleep, deeply troubled by the tense meal as well as perplexed by Damian's threats.

This wasn't the Damian Alexander knew. This Damian was bitter, with a score to settle.

Was it really about Claudia? Or was there something else that had happened, something that Alexander couldn't remember?

He closed his eyes and drew a deep breath, and in his mind's eye he saw Josephine, lovely, warm, smiling.

He was glad she wasn't Danielle—sleekly sophisticated and coolly polished—and he didn't want anyone to try to make her into something she wasn't, because he liked her the way she was. He liked everything about her. She was the woman he wanted, and she'd be a good queen even if she hadn't been raised in his world. Maybe she'd be a better queen because she hadn't.

He wished he'd taken her to Paris yesterday. He wished they had more time together, just the two of them. Maybe he should steal her from the palace and take her for a drive. They could run away for a couple of hours, just the two of them. They could escape in one of his cars, perhaps one of the convertibles, and drive, the wind in their hair, the open road before them.

Alexander stopped pacing, the idea cementing. He knew where he'd take her, too. It would be an hour drive, but it was a beautiful one, across the middle of the country, through picturesque villages, all the way to the country's highest point, Mount Bravura. But if they were to do it, he'd need to put the plan in motion now.

Alexander made a call to Julio Costa, the owner of the restaurant, and then went in search of Josephine. His valet was the one who told him to look in the tower guest suite.

When his valet saw his surprise, he smiled faintly. "Miss Robb likes it there," he said. "Everyone knows it's her favorite place to go when she needs a break from her ladies."

This drew Alexander short. "Are her ladies difficult?"

"I think they're excessively preoccupied with rules and protocol."

Alexander left the palace for the tower and climbed to the fourth floor. When he entered the tower bedroom he found Josephine standing on a stool before the tall, narrow window. She was barefoot and her chin was propped in her hand, her elbow resting on the thick stone ledge.

"What are you thinking about?" he asked.

Alexander's voice caught her by surprise. She jumped a little as she glanced over her shoulder at him. "Nothing much," she answered.

"Your *nothing much* is always something."

The corners of her lips lifted. She turned back to the window and gestured to the horizon. "I was thinking the ocean from here looks more green than blue, and those puffy white clouds, cumulus clouds, are casting moving shadows on the water, making the sea look as if it's filled with a fleet of ships, all at full sail. I was imagining the adventures those brave voyagers would have."

"You make me want to be one of those brave voyagers."

"But then who'd be king? This kingdom has but one heir, which is you."

A half-dozen different responses came to mind and in the end he chose none of them. “I should have taken you with me last night. I didn’t enjoy Paris without you.”

“How did it go with Phillipe?”

“Not well.” He hesitated. “Damian was there.”

One of her winged eyebrows arched higher. “You didn’t expect to see him, did you?”

“No. And it was an awkward meal. I left early.”

“And your cousin? How was he?”

“Baffling,” Alexander said after a long moment. “I don’t understand it. I don’t understand him.” And then he shrugged impatiently. “Let’s not discuss him anymore. He ruined my night. I won’t allow him to ruin today, and I’m organizing something fun for us for dinner tonight. It will be just the two of us. We’ll leave here at six. Our reservation is for seven.”

Josephine studied him a long moment, trying to read his expression because he wasn’t smiling and yet there was this curious light in his eyes. He looked tired but also eager, and she suddenly pictured him as a boy and thought how lovely he must have been. He wouldn’t have been one of those who hurt things and broke things. No, he would have been smart and thoughtful and kind. “I’m looking forward to it,” she said, and she meant it.

“Good.”

“How should I dress? Do I need one of my formal dresses that require the spandex girdle beneath?”

“That sounds horrendous.”

“It feels horrendous.”

“Then no, please don’t wear one. Be comfortable. Choose a dress that makes you happy.”

Josephine went through her wardrobe and in the end chose a ruby-red silk dress that was sleeveless, fitted through the waist, and featured a stunning bright pink flower on the full skirt. The neckline plunged, showing off her tan and her curves, making her feel gorgeous and feminine.

After saying good-night to her staff, she hurried downstairs, where Alexander was waiting by the front door for her. He smiled as she came down the steps. "You look stunning."

Pleasure filled her. She felt stunning tonight. "And you're very dashing in your…um…trousers and…shirt."

He laughed, the sound low and husky and unbearably sexy as the butler opened the front door for them. "I'm rather boring—is that it?"

"Actually, no. You're anything but boring," she said as they stepped outside. Her attention was immediately drawn to the hunter green convertible sports car parked in the drive. It was low and sleek with a handsome cream interior. It was also a two-seater, which meant no room for a driver. "Is that for us?"

"It is. Do you approve?"

"Very much so. But where will your security go?"

"Security will be behind us, but they're to be discreet and give us some room."

"I love it, but I think I might need a shawl for the way home. Let me run back up. I won't be long."

"I can have someone fetch you something—"

"No need. I won't be but a moment." Josephine went back inside and up the marble staircase.

She'd just opened the door to the suite when she heard one of her ladies say, "They said Damian found them together on the yacht, in her room, in her bed. He confronted them and things turned ugly. It's why Damian has been forbidden from coming here."

Josephine froze, unable to make herself move.

"Not surprised about the love triangle. There has always been some friction between those two," someone said.

"It doesn't help that the king has always favored Damian over his own son."

"And Claudia? Where is Claudia now?"

"Paris, I believe."

Josephine felt sick. Her legs shook. She put a hand to the wall, trying to steady herself. Was it true, what her ladies-in-waiting were saying? Had Alexander gone to Paris not to see Phillipe but to see Claudia?

Was it possible that Alexander wasn't who she thought he was?

Closing her eyes, she pictured him downstairs waiting for her next to the sleek sports car, handsome, smiling.

She pictured him as he was when he came to her in the tower…

She remembered how he'd pulled her aside to talk to her in the picture gallery…

Had he been lying to her all those times? Had he been twisting the truth, pretending to be someone he wasn't?

She didn't think so. Maybe she was crazy, but she trusted him. She did.

Josephine drew a breath and pushed the door all the way open, silencing the conversation as she stepped into her sitting room. She ignored the startled glances—as well as the fact that the ladies were sitting in her sitting room—and continued on to her bedroom.

Adina jumped up. "Did you forget something?" she asked, following Josephine into the bedroom.

Josephine counted to ten as she went through her wraps and then selected a charcoal-gray pashmina and draped it over her arm. "I have it now," she said, turning around and heading back out. She didn't pause until she reached the door to the corridor, and then she glanced back at the three women. "If you're going to gossip, please do not do it in my rooms. Good night."

For the first twenty minutes of the drive, Josephine was

quiet, replaying the conversation she'd heard in her room, wondering if she should tell him. She didn't want to spoil the night, and it would certainly spoil the night. She chewed on the inside of her lip, wishing she hadn't gone back to her room, thinking she would be so much happier right now if she'd never heard any of that.

Alexander shifted and glanced at her. "Is my driving making you nervous?"

"No. Just thinking about something I heard earlier. It was disturbing."

"Want to tell me?"

"No." She swallowed around the lump in her throat. "I'm just upset on your behalf."

He shifted again and braked, pulling off on the side of the road. Alexander faced her. "Tell me, *cara*. We're in this together. Let's do this together."

"People are talking," she said quietly after a moment. "Staff. They're saying you…" She closed her eyes, shook her head. "I can't say it. I can't. And I don't believe it, so it doesn't matter."

"But it does matter because clearly it's upset you."

She opened her eyes. "They're saying on the yacht, Damian found you…in bed…with Claudia."

"What?"

"And that's why Damian is angry."

"No."

"And Claudia is in… Paris." She looked at him. "Tell me it's just a coincidence. Tell me you didn't go to Paris to see her—"

"Absolutely not. I didn't even know she was in Paris. Furthermore, we weren't in bed together. I can promise you that. And yes, I know I have memory issues, but there has been nothing between Claudia and me since I ended the relationship, and I haven't wanted to be with her. I might not remember the trip, but I know me, and I wouldn't start something with her again, not when she's involved with my cousin. I hate even discussing Claudia with you, but you must believe me—"

"I do." She reached out, her fingers light on his cheekbone and then his jaw. "I do. I'm just disgusted by the gossip. I'm disgusted that people in the palace would speak that way about you."

"Damian grew up in the palace. His father, Aldo, was my father's twin. I think Damian has always struggled with the fact that my father was born two minutes before his father, making my father the future king and me the heir instead of the other way around."

"Damian resents you."

"I think Damian is envious, yes."

"That explains a great deal," she murmured, leaning forward to kiss him. "But let's not let Damian and his green-eyed jealousy ruin our evening, because I'm so happy being out with you. Let's just savor our night."

"I couldn't agree more."

Now outside the city, they turned off the main highway onto a narrower rural road, and for the next half hour they threaded their way through the countryside filled with farms and little stone houses with charming shutters and window boxes.

Josephine thought it looked like a blend of Provence and Tuscany. "It's so picturesque," she said as they slowed for a shepherd and his flock of sheep, the fluffy creatures slowly crossing the road just ahead of them and then deciding they no longer wanted to cross the road but instead mill about, taking over the road.

"We might be a while," Alexander said, shifting into Neutral.

"I'm enjoying myself immensely," she replied, delighted by the herd's inability to decide if they'd all cross together or one at a time. She entertained Alexander with a sheep-by-sheep accounting, describing the wayward members of the flock, giving them all personalities, including the shepherd, whose quiet resignation coupled with his inability to direct his flock only served to make the sheep more ambivalent about crossing the road in the first place.

"He is not a very good shepherd," Alexander muttered, as five minutes turned to ten.

"Not terribly passionate about his work," she agreed, "but he's giving me the best show."

"He's also going to make us late for dinner."

She glanced at him. "Is that going to be a problem?"

"No. It's Sunday, and Julio is opening the restaurant specially for us."

"I've never had anyone open anything for me."

"Well, you will now. In just five days you'll be Princess Josephine Alberici."

The sun was just setting by the time they pulled in front of the restaurant, with its exterior of local wood and stone. The restaurant owner, Julio, warmly welcomed them before escorting them inside to a table in an alcove with windows all around. The view from the restaurant, which happened to be perched on the edge of a cliff, was nothing short of glorious.

"We're up so high," Josephine said.

"It's Mount Bravura, the highest peak in Aargau and Aargau's only volcano, although extinct now."

"No wonder I like it so much!"

They drifted into easy conversation, interrupted only by the waiter when he took their order and then returned later with their first course. Time passed quickly, and Josephine was surprised when she sat back and glanced out the window and found it was pitch-dark and that the restaurant itself was empty save them and the owner. "It must be late," she said. "All the staff has gone."

"Even Julio?"

"No, he's still here. He's setting the tables for tomorrow."

"I'm sure he'd have no problem kicking me out when he's ready to go home."

She frowned, skeptical. "Even though you are Prince Alexander Alberici?"

He laughed lowly. "Okay, Julio would probably never kick me out, but he's thrilled we're here. Tomorrow he'll share the news with everyone and he'll get a great deal of press out of this. His bookings will double, triple overnight."

"Well, that does make me feel a little better, but I still wouldn't mind stepping out for fresh air."

"Because you're tired or because you want Julio to be able to close his restaurant and go home for the night?"

"You know me so well," she murmured, thinking Alexander had the loveliest blue eyes and his smile created these grooves on either side of his lips. Lightly she brushed a fingertip across his mouth, wanting more than a light kiss. She missed the heat between them. She missed the tension and electric sensation.

He rose and held her chair for her. They left the restaurant for the patio with its breathtaking view. It was only up here, so high, that Josephine got a sense of the island and its size. Lights twinkled far away—the capital of Roche, Josephine thought—with other lights dotting the coast. Waves crested with white reflected the moonlight.

"This was just what I needed," she said with a sigh. "It almost feels like we're on Khronos. It's just you and me."

"You miss Khronos."

"I think I always will. I had so much freedom, and I miss the water everywhere." She darted a look up at him. "And I miss having it be just you and me."

He leaned against the railing and drew her to him, his hands low on her back. "You have no idea how much I've missed you. I want to feel you and love you. It's been too long."

Love her, Josephine repeated silently, even as her heart did a painful double beat. She knew he didn't mean love, *real* love, but still, it was heady hearing the words and knowing he desired her—and at least desire was something. Maybe desire could be enough. Maybe she could be satisfied with being wanted. Maybe she didn't need to be loved. Or maybe her love for him would be enough for both of them.

She stared deep into his eyes, flooded with so many intense emotions, emotions that were stronger than she'd ever felt before, and then, sure of her feelings, she leaned closer, leaning into him, and pressed her lips to his. "It has been too long," she whispered against his mouth. "I need you to love me."

He kissed her back, his hand cupping the back of her head, drawing her against him so that her breasts pressed against his hard chest and her mouth was his for the taking.

The kiss was fierce and hot, his tongue parting her lips, sweeping her mouth before tangling with her tongue, teasing it, teasing her.

She felt as if the kiss was just the beginning of something huge and wonderful and she mimicked the way he kissed her, sucking on the tip of his tongue, drawing on it hard. He groaned against her mouth, his hands sliding down her back to grip her hips and grind her against his hard length.

Her arms wrapped around his neck, her fingers twining in the dark strands of hair at his nape. She tugged at them even as he shifted her hips, drawing her over him again, making her feel his heat and hunger. Sensation flooded her. Emotion flooded her. She'd desired him on Khronos, but it was so much more intense now, her feelings making the need and sensation so much more powerful.

His tongue played her mouth in a rhythmic stabbing that mimicked how the thick head of his shaft pressed up between her thighs. He'd found her breast with one hand and was kneading the peaked nipple, making her whimper and shudder, and if it weren't for the fact that security was just around the corner and Julio was somewhere inside the restaurant, she would have begged him to take her here and now, as the delicate silk of her dress gave her little protection. But then, she wanted no protection. She wanted him, all of him, forever.

He lifted his head. "I'd have my way with you right here if I didn't think it'd make Julio feel awkward."

She laughed and blushed. "I was just thinking the same thing. Can we go back home and be together?"

"Absolutely."

They returned to the palace and he led her to his room. They made love twice, and she spent the rest of the night barely sleeping because she didn't want to forget how good she felt in his arms, in his bed.

CHAPTER NINE

TUESDAY, WITH ITS cocktail party of important people and influential guests, had finally arrived, and Josephine's team spent hours preparing her, giving her a complete makeover. The hairdresser, makeup artist, and stylist fussed over her for nearly two hours but now she was dressed and waiting for Alexander to collect her.

Josephine did a little twirl before her mirror, absolutely thrilled with her dress. The sleeveless gown featured a dramatic V neckline, with a soft cloud of a skirt shimmering with gorgeous gold embroidery. The skirt floated around her legs as she walked and she was wearing glittering chandelier earrings from the Alberici vault. With her hair pinned up, she definitely looked older and more sophisticated.

Alexander arrived exactly on time to escort her to the ballroom, and when he entered her room she expected him to smile and compliment her because it's what he usually did, but tonight he kept his distance and stared at her, jaw flexed, gaze shuttered. Her ladies-in-waiting noticed, too, and they fell silent. The silence grew, making Josephine uncomfortable.

"Something's wrong," Josephine said quietly. "Is it the dress? Would you like me to change?"

"The dress is beautiful."

"Then what is it?"

"I'm having a difficult time understanding why you look so different. I don't understand what has been done to you. You don't look like you."

She remembered the hours of tortured hairstyling and makeup application and lifted a hand self-consciously to her nape, which was exposed tonight, with all her hair coiled and pinned tightly on top. "It might be this style," she said. "It's structured."

"Too structured. It doesn't suit you. You are too pretty to look like an old lady." He approached her and reached out to tip up her chin, examining her makeup. "You're wearing quite a lot, aren't you?"

"The eyeliner is rather heavy, and the lipstick is dark," she said faintly.

"Why didn't you stop them?"

"I was told they'd been instructed to polish me, remove the hard edges."

"There were no hard edges. You're lovely as you are."

His words made her eyes sting and it was all she could do to keep tears from welling up. She glanced at the women in the corner who were hanging on every word and she gave them a faint smile before looking up at Alexander. "Please don't be disappointed. They've been working very hard to prepare me for tonight—"

"You are not a rock," he gritted out, interrupting her. "You do not require polishing or refinement, and if this is what they're telling you, then I will throw them all out, every last one of them, because I like you, and I want you to look like you. I want your mouth to look like your mouth. I want to be able to kiss your lips—" And then suddenly his head dropped and his mouth slanted over hers, and he was kissing her with hunger and passion, as if they were alone.

By the time he lifted his head, ending the kiss, her head was spinning and her senses swam with the erotic pleasure of his kiss. She loved his mouth on hers. She loved the feel of him and the smell of him and the way he made her feel every single time he touched her.

For a moment she just stared up at him, dazed, and then he reached up and began tugging the pins out of her hair one by one. "The public will like you," he growled, his deep voice humming through her. "The public will love you. You don't need to be someone you're not, and you most definitely do not need to be a puppet on a string." He kept pulling out pins until her thick hair fell over her shoulders in long, loose waves. "This is better," he said, combing his fingers through the waves. "This is you, and how I like to see you."

He turned and faced the ladies in the corner. "Do not put her hair up unless Josephine asks for it to be up. Do not apply more makeup than she is comfortable with. Ask her what she wants—do not tell her. Am I clear?"

Josephine was simultaneously awed and horrified. "They will not like me better for that," she whispered, trying not to smile as she wiped away the lipstick staining his mouth.

He turned his head and kissed her palm. "Maybe not, *bella*, but I will."

They were only a few minutes late arriving for the party in the ballroom, and while Alexander had assured her it was an intimate gathering, the fact that they were going to the ballroom spoke volumes.

As the doors opened to admit them, Josephine's breath caught in her throat, and her fingers tightened on his arm as she was immediately dazzled by the splendor of the grand ballroom. Her appreciative gaze swept the space, trying to process everything she was seeing even as people began bowing to Alexander. Immense chandeliers ran the length of the high ceiling, each dripping with glittering crystals, reflecting shimmering light across the elegant baroque ballroom, enhancing the gold and white scheme where gilt-framed mirrors lined the walls.

"Confidence," Alexander murmured at her side.

She eased her grip on his arm and forced a smile, trying to block out the sheer number of people filling the room. There were so many people here, and they were all staring. "This is not a small party," she whispered as his hand slipped to her lower back.

"It's fewer than three hundred," he answered under his breath. "Larger than I hoped but small compared to the usual number we host for formal gatherings." He began introducing her to people, a couple here and a couple there.

She nodded, smiled, and spoke when required, but the entire time she was most conscious of *him*. His warmth filled her and his fragrance teased her nose. Even though she was uneasy with the sheer number of people present, she felt safe with him, reassured by him at her side. There was something in his touch that made her skin come alive. She loved it. She hated it. He was never supposed to be hers, and yet here she was, being introduced to his court as his bride-to-be.

"You're doing well," he murmured when they had a moment to themselves. "You're quite impressive actually. You'll be the princess they adore, and before long their queen."

She glanced up, her gaze meeting his, his irises almost lavender blue in the glittering light. She wanted to tell him she loved him. She wanted him to know how much she cared about him and that she didn't need the public to love her, as long as he did.

Later, as they mingled, she found herself watching him, and she knew he was also watching her. She could feel his gaze on her, and he made her feel so many things—taut, edgy, physical, desirable.

Tonight, everything in her felt sensitive and alive, especially when he looked at her, as he did just now, his lids lowered and his lovely mouth lifted just so, and she felt that half smile all the way through her, the awareness making her skin warm and her body tingle and ache.

Tonight she felt unbearably feminine, all curves and softness. Her breasts. Her waist. Her hips. Her thighs.

She loved everything about him. She loved the way he moved, she loved watching his hands, loved the width of his shoulders. She watched his eyes, the focus, the intensity, the hint of amusement lurking there in the light blue gaze.

Perhaps she wasn't a mistake.

Perhaps she was the right bride.

The party was a success. Photographs of Prince Alexander and his beautiful young fiancée, Josephine Robb, filled the papers, and Josephine could tell from the smiles of the staff that everyone was pleased.

Josephine was pleased, not because the party was a success but because the party was over. She couldn't wait to escape the palace the next afternoon, retreating almost immediately after lunch for the tower bedroom where she could be alone with her favorite view of the water.

She waved at Alexander's secretary, Aimee, on the second floor as she hurried up the stairwell, and then she peeked through the open door to the library and saw Alexander there in a chair reading a thick sheath of papers. She nearly spoke to him but then thought better of it because he was lost in thought, and she raced on up, feeling immeasurably lighter and happier.

The formal party was over. The wedding was coming on Saturday, and then soon the spotlight should be off her, and she and Alexander could develop their own routine and their own life together.

She couldn't wait for them to be a proper family, and she wondered where they'd raise the baby. She was trying to imagine the nursery when she moved too quickly, misjudging the distance between the stone steps. Josephine flung her arm out to brace her fall but it was too late to stop herself, and she screamed as she fell, crying out again as she slammed onto the stairs, the impact knocking the air out of her.

For a moment she lay dazed, and then she pushed herself up into a sitting position. She flexed her hands, tested her legs. Nothing seemed broken. She ached though, with pain in her torso and a wrenched back.

"What happened?" Alexander demanded, charging up the stairs, coming to her side.

"I fell," she answered, trying not to wince, not wanting to alarm him. "I was distracted and lost in thought and my feet ended up going faster than the rest of me."

"You could have been seriously hurt," he said.

"I know. But I wasn't." She allowed him to help her to her feet but she frowned at the twinge in her belly.

"What's wrong?" he asked.

She forced a smile, hiding her pain, thinking now wasn't the time to be melodramatic. She'd just taken a fall, and by most standards it was a very small fall. She hadn't even gone down more than five or so stairs. Everything was fine. She was certain everything was fine. "Just a bit stiff from falling. Your stairs are hard," she added lightly, trying to tease him to ease the tension.

"You shouldn't be coming up here. It's a very old staircase, the steps far too narrow and steep. My mother mentioned they were dangerous years ago—"

"I've never fallen before, and next time I'll go more slowly. I promise."

"There won't be a next time. The tower is off-limits."

"Stop it! You're being ridiculous. I'm fine. Look at me—" She broke off to wiggle her fingers and flex an ankle. "No cuts. Nothing is broken."

"I'm taking you back to your suite in the palace."

"You don't need to take me anywhere, Alexander. I can walk just fine."

"I'll feel better if I see you there."

"Fine."

He held her hand as they started down, and she could tell by the firm clasp of his fingers that he was trying hard not to lift her up and carry her the rest of the way. She was touched by his concern. It was a little heavy-handed, but he'd always been protective.

She was just about to thank him for his assistance when she felt another twinge in her abdomen, sharper, much sharper than before. Startled, she paused on the step and suddenly she had to look at Alexander. Suddenly she needed to hear from him that everything was okay.

"Something is wrong," he said roughly. "Don't tell me everything is fine."

"It's pinching on the inside. It's getting stronger."

"Where?"

She put her hand on her still-flat belly. "Here," she whispered, cupping her womb. "Where the baby is."

He muttered an oath and swung her into his arms. "Let's get you to your room and we'll call the doctor from there."

She was in bed when the doctor arrived, but she'd been to the bathroom twice because she'd noticed she'd begun spotting. She was trying to contain her panic as she added pads to her panties, trying to tell herself that this was just a little blip and everything would be fine.

But as the doctor drew out the fetal Doppler to listen for a heartbeat, her eyes burned and then filled with tears because she could see from Alexander's tense expression just how concerned he was.

They were all quiet as the doctor listened. An hour ago she'd been so happy, almost elated that everything she wanted was finally coming together. But now Alexander stood just behind the doctor, silent, watching and waiting.

When the doctor put the Doppler away and made a call for someone at the hospital to bring over an ultrasound, her heart fell.

"You don't hear anything, do you?" she said, her throat constricting.

"You're still quite early. It can be difficult listening for a heartbeat with a Doppler. The ultrasound will allow me to have a better view, and we'll be able to see the heart beat."

Alexander was thanking him but Josephine closed her eyes and turned her face away, unable to let them see her fear because something was wrong. She felt it. She knew it. From the cramping to the bleeding to the doctor's non-expression, the professional kindness intended to mask concern.

The nurse arrived with the equipment in just thirty minutes but the doctor's silence as he studied the ultrasound image crushed her. She knew.

She knew.

"There is no heartbeat," he said quietly. "I am so sorry."

For a moment she couldn't breathe. For a moment she felt as if she'd just vanish into thin air.

There was no heartbeat.

The little life inside her was gone.

She shook her head, and then again, unable to look at the doctor or Alexander. This time when she turned to face the wall, she stayed that way, even after the doctor and his nurse had gone.

She gripped her hands into fists, trying to keep from screaming. This was her fault. All her fault.

"Josephine," Alexander said, putting a hand on her shoulder.

She shrugged him off. "Don't say anything."

"I know what you're thinking," he said. "I know what you're saying to yourself, and it was such a little mistake, such a simple thing."

"Please go. Please leave." She squeezed her eyes shut, fighting the scalding tears.

"The doctor wants us to go into his office for the procedure he mentioned—"

"I don't want to do it."

"I know, and I don't want you to be put through it, either, but he believes it will be better for you, less risk of an infection."

"Alexander, no."

"I hate this, too, *cara*, but we need to keep you well. We need to do what's best for you now."

The procedure on Wednesday night was horrendous, and Josephine slept in on Thursday, having cried herself to sleep the night before.

She didn't want breakfast Thursday morning, and she didn't want to get up, too spent, worn-out, wrung out, cried out. Queen Serena came by her room just before noon to tell her how deeply sorry she was, and shared that she understood Josephine's grief because she had miscarried, too, and that Josephine should feel free to come to her anytime, for anything.

Josephine got through the short visit without breaking down, but once Serena had gone, she curled into a ball and cried again. The last six weeks had been a gigantic roller coaster and this last drop was too much, too frightening, too heartbreaking.

Worse, there was no reason for Alexander to marry her anymore. He was only marrying her because of the baby, but now that there was no baby he was free.

She'd freed him. That was good, right? Still crying, she threw back her covers and got out of bed. She should go. That's what she should do. She should just go and put this whole nightmare behind her.

Josephine was in the middle of packing the few things she'd brought with her when Alexander entered her room. From his expression, she knew that someone from her staff had alerted him that Josephine was preparing to leave.

"What are you doing?" he asked quietly, taking in the clothes she'd put in the pile to leave at the palace and the sarong and blouse and swimsuit she would take back to Greece with her.

She wiped tears away. "I want to see my father. I want to be in my house again."

"Your father is on his way here for the wedding."

"We're not getting married now," she said, folding another simple blouse. "There is no reason for him to come."

He crossed the room and closed the door that divided the bedroom from the sitting room where her staff had collected. "You can't run away every time there is a problem," he said tersely, facing her. "You have to be stronger than your fear."

"I think there is some confusion here. I'm not afraid. I'm just no longer necessary, which is why I'm choosing to return home."

"Not necessary? You're my fiancée. My intended. My betrothed. We've announced it to the world. We've celebrated it in style. We have a wedding in two days."

"It's a small wedding, a very private wedding. It's not going to be difficult to cancel it."

"I don't understand. I know you're upset about the miscarriage, but why are you doing this to us?"

"Because there is no *us*!" she cried, balling up a T-shirt and smashing it against her knees. "There has never been an *us*. This—" she gestured to him, and then herself "—this has never been about you and me. It's only been about the baby, and the baby is no more."

"You are my fiancée. We're marrying in two days."

"Why? You don't need me. You don't want me. You were only marrying me because I was pregnant, and I'm not pregnant anymore. You're free. Go! Find Danielle. Or find a new princess. Find someone who wants to be your princess. I never wanted the job." She rose and stepped over the clothes, wishing she could fling the doors open and escape, but there was no escape here, and there would be no escape, not until she was on her own island, in her own world.

"I am not going to break off our engagement." His voice was hard, every word sharp and brittle. "I cannot put my father through the humiliation of another broken engagement. It would kill him—"

"He's going to die anyway!"

"How dare you?" He took an enraged step toward her and then stopped himself. "How dare you disrespect him—"

"I'm not trying to disrespect him, Alexander." Her voice broke. "I'm trying to save us from disaster. You don't love me. You desire me. You've sexualized me. But there is nothing else for me... There is no real relationship. I'm to be in your bed, and at your side for important appearances, but what else is there for me? Why should I stay? Give me one good reason to stay!" She was almost trembling with emotion, trembling with the need to hear him say he loved her and wanted her above all else—not because she was pregnant and not because this was duty but because he couldn't live without her. He didn't want to live without her.

"Because you made a promise," he ground out, jaw flexed, blue gaze icy. "My father has given us permission, and we have announced our wedding, and I will not disappoint my father again. I refuse to disappoint my father. I will not."

They weren't the words she needed. Her eyes burned, filling with tears. "So you'll trap me and disappoint me."

"You benefit, *cara*, you benefit beautifully from this arrangement."

"No."

"And there will be children. You will be pregnant again soon—"

"I knew you were not a terribly sensitive man, but your lack of empathy at the moment is astonishing."

"My lack of empathy? My father is dying—"

"And my child just died." Her voice broke and she reached up to knock away the tears, hating them and hating him. He had no idea how much he was hurting her. He had no idea how every word he said wounded. "And I appreciate that your father is a king and I am but an ordinary woman, an American at that, but can you please allow me to grieve for what I have lost? Or are you too self-absorbed with duty and your tortured relationship with your father to allow me time to mourn and heal?"

She'd finally effectively silenced him.

He stood there stiffly, features granite hard, no emotion anywhere on his handsome face.

She should have felt a thrill of victory because she knew that finally something she'd said had penetrated his thick skull and the even thicker wall he kept around his emotions. But she hated that it was the miscarriage that should do it. How much better if he'd actually loved her. How much better if he'd been willing to fight for her.

Alexander saw the pain in Josephine's eyes and her pain unnerved him. She was so open and so vulnerable and he could see what she was feeling—even feel what she was feeling—but the sheer intensity of so much emotion made him shut down and pull even further away.

Emotions had always been problematic for him, but his father's death was even more challenging because this was his last chance to get it right. This was Alexander's last chance to try to make amends with a father who had never wanted or needed him. If there ever was a time to be the son Bruno had wanted and needed, it was now. "I am not indifferent," he said lowly, his voice rough to his own ears. "I am more disappointed than I can say—"

"I don't believe you."

He gave her a slight bow. "I'm sorry."

Her eyes welled with tears. "Let me go."

"No." *Never.*

"You don't need me—"

"But I do." *Always.*

"Those are just words!"

But words didn't come easily to him, either.

What he longed to do was take her in his arms. He wanted to hold her and comfort her, but his own control was being tested. He was battling to keep it all together. He hated what was happening to them, and yet there were bigger things than their own personal drama.

"We will get through this," he added quietly. "I promise."

"You disappoint me," she whispered, averting her face.

He flinched but said nothing.

She blinked hard, adding, "I kept thinking we had a shot at making a marriage work. I thought that there was something real between us. But I was wrong. There is no *us* in your world—there is just you. It's your world, your title, your future…not mine. It was never mine."

She was wrong. There was an *us*, but he didn't have the energy to argue, and so he stopped focusing on Josephine's words, unable to take them in. He'd been mocked for his feelings as a boy. He'd been brutalized in the boarding school by other boys because he'd dared to care…to hurt.

In the navy, he'd been drilled to be tough. Feelings, once again, had been shameful. They made a man weak when he needed to be clearheaded and logical and strong.

So no, he wouldn't feel her pain, and no, he wouldn't let her words register because it would do no good. Her pain and disappointment would change nothing.

His father was dying.

The country would need a new king.

His mother would be widowed and displaced.

Alexander needed to do now what he'd been raised to do. Shoulder the weight of Aargau. Do right by the crown. Honor his father's memory and name.

He didn't know why he'd been on the yacht near Khronos, and he didn't know what had happened on that yacht or why she'd been there to save him, but it had happened and they were now here, and everything was about to change.

Josephine might not like what was happening, but she'd rise to the occasion. He knew she would. Just as he'd known she'd do the right thing by their child.

Josephine understood honor. And in her own way, she understood responsibility and duty. She'd be an excellent queen one day. He just wished the path could be less painful.

"You can return to Khronos after the wedding," he said. "You can take some time once we're married. I will speak with the security—"

"No. Not after. There is no after—"

"Josephine, stop for a moment. Think carefully, please. Look at the bigger picture, if you can."

"You mean you and what you want?" she flashed bitterly.

He ground his teeth together. She didn't understand that he was trying to do the right thing now, which was give his father peace of mind so King Bruno could let go of this life and the pain racking his body. Because his father wouldn't let go, not if he believed the family was in crisis.

His gut hurt. His throat felt thick. Alexander forced the words out because they were not easy to speak. "My father is a fighter. My father has lived his life for his country and his duty. But he's in constant pain, terrible pain, and he's ready to go. The only thing he lives for now is seeing us married. But if that doesn't happen, he'll try to cling to life, which will only increase his suffering. We must protect him from pain. He mustn't think we are in crisis. He needs us to be strong, *cara*. I need you to be strong. I am sorry I've hurt you, and I'm sorry to have disappointed you, but consider him. Consider my mother. They need us to show courage and leadership now. They need to know the monarchy isn't in crisis and that you and I are unified and committed to Aargau."

She stood utterly still, chin lifted, eyes shimmering with tears. She stared at him so long he could see the pulse beating at her throat and the faint quiver of her lips.

Anger blazed in her eyes. Hurt created shadows, too.

"I wish you'd never come to Khronos," she said at last, her voice hoarse. "I wish I'd never seen your yacht anchored in the cove or watched you and your friends on my beach. I wish I had amnesia. I wish I could blank out the entire thing so I didn't have to remember it, either."

He winced inwardly. They were sharp words and they pricked, like shards of glass scraping across his skin.

"I thank God every day because you are what I woke to," he answered gruffly. "I thank God that you were there, grateful that you are here. We will get through this. We are a strong family, and you are part of us now. There is no crisis here. You are hurt and upset, but you belong here. You belong with me. There is no running away. We are out of options and out of time. We will do what needs to be done. You and me, together."

She looked away, her pale throat working, her eyes blinking as she tried to contain her emotions. She'd been through a great deal in the past twenty-four hours, but they couldn't give up now. His father needed peace. The wedding would go ahead as planned, and eventually all would be well. Storms passed, skies cleared. Josephine would get pregnant again, and there would be a royal heir; Alexander didn't doubt it, which was why he could walk out of her room and go to his father's side and assure him all was well and they were looking forward to the wedding on Saturday.

CHAPTER TEN

HE DIDN'T WANT the truth, and he didn't want her emotions. He didn't want her to feel.

So she wouldn't feel. And she wouldn't care about him any longer. She'd do her duty. She'd marry him and stand at his side and fulfill the obligation, and then she'd leave.

She'd return to Khronos and stay there, not for a visit but until her father took a new position with the foundation and was sent elsewhere. She'd go where he went and continue assisting his work. She'd lose herself in the work, and the idea of going somewhere pleased her. She imagined a return to Washington State, or possibly Peru, or maybe even to Mount Etna in Sicily because she'd never feel the same about Khronos. Alexander had ruined it for her.

On Saturday morning Josephine was numb as her staff dressed her. The wedding was a late-morning service, designed to accommodate King Bruno as he was at his best in the morning and wouldn't be too groggy from the heavy-duty pain medicines he took at noon.

Josephine's gown looked like something from a fairy tale. She was reminded of Cinderella at the ball, except her dress was white, with a big tulle skirt, a sweetheart neckline, and an impossibly long train. Her long sleeves were sheer and her lace veil was attached to a delicate tiara, the veil as long as her dramatic train.

The hairstylist curled her hair and left it down in long, loose curls, and the makeup artist took forty minutes trying to cover Josephine's pallor and make her look fresh and dewy instead of heartbroken.

Her ladies escorted her down the stairs to the palace front steps where a special carriage waited. Her father stood next to the carriage in his formal wear looking nervous, and yet his expression cleared as he caught sight of her. "You look so lovely, Josephine," he said, reaching for her hands and giving them a squeeze. "And so very much like your mother. I wish she could be here to see you. She'd be so proud."

Josephine was glad now she hadn't told him about losing the baby, or her anger, or the fact that she'd soon be returning to Khronos. She'd give him this moment. He deserved the moment. "I think Mama is here," Josephine whispered.

Her father wasn't a sentimental man, but his eyes glistened. "She wanted the best for you, but I'm sure she never imagined you here, about to become a princess."

Josephine couldn't answer and was grateful when the royal page opened the carriage door, and her father assisted her up the steps. Her ladies lifted her skirt and long lace veil, and then they were seated together and the door closed. The carriage was off.

The ride to the cathedral on the square should have been short but crowds had lined the sides of the street, hundreds of people, no, thousands, coming out to witness Josephine dressed to marry their prince. They cheered for her, time and again, and she blinked repeatedly, fighting tears, touched by the cheers and the shouts of *Princess Josephine! Princess Josephine!* not expecting such a welcome.

The cheers and nerves all became a blur once she reached the cathedral. Her ladies were there again, somehow making it to the square before the carriage, and once again they straightened her dress and veil and handed her flowers from the carriage, flowers she had somehow missed before.

The walk down the cathedral aisle was endless. Sunlight poured through the tall, arched stained glass windows. The soaring ceiling provided the perfect acoustics for the organ. She knew the classical piece being played. It was Mozart. Her mother loved classical music. The thought gave her comfort as she approached the altar. She spotted Alexander there at the very front, standing next to the robed priest. He was dressed in his Royal Navy uniform, the jacket black, the thick shoulders covered with ropes of gold. He had medals across his chest, and with his black hair combed severely back, he looked tall and powerful, virile and handsome.

Part of her thrilled that he was hers, and another part couldn't forgive him for not loving her. Today should have been joyous, not a duty to be borne.

Reaching his side, her father placed her hand in Alexander's and then stepped back to take his place in the front pew.

She felt Alexander's gaze bore into her but she wouldn't look at him. She just wanted to get the service over and the formalities completed so she could take this gorgeous fairy-tale dress off and remove the delicate, sparkling diamond tiara—a tiara she'd been told was worth millions of euros—because although she was marrying Alexander, she hadn't grown up on fairy tales and she no longer wanted to be his princess.

The drive back to the palace was stiff but not quiet as the crowd chanted their approval, the cheers like thunder as Alexander traveled in the carriage with Josephine.

She lifted her hand and waved to the crowds, smiling when she spotted a sign with her name, but she never once looked at him.

He told himself he didn't mind, but he did. He actually minded a great deal. And so he focused on other things, turning from Josephine's elegant profile, and how beautiful she looked in her lovely gown, to nod and wave to the crowd.

He'd done what he needed to do today. He'd married,

and one day in the future there would be another baby, the heir, and his father could return to his room and his bed, and take his medicine, and escape his pain.

"I think we will save the cake and champagne for later this afternoon," he said as the coach passed through the palace gates. "Let my father rest and my mother relax, and then we'll meet before dinner and have a toast before your father goes home."

She turned her head then and looked him in the eye. "Yes, Your Highness."

"Josephine."

"You got what you wanted, Alexander. Your father can rest easy now. But please don't expect me to celebrate."

Josephine had just finished changing into a slim skirt and elegant blouse—her new official royal uniform, it seemed—when a knock sounded on her door. It was one of her ladies, and she was in tears.

"He's gone," she choked. "King Bruno is dead."

That day there was no celebratory cake or champagne. Indeed, the entire wedding was eclipsed by the death of Aargau's beloved king. The shocked public immediately went into mourning.

Josephine herself didn't know what to feel. On one hand, she was glad the king was no longer suffering, but she felt for Serena and for Alexander. They had been expecting his death but not quite so soon.

Perhaps it was better it had happened so suddenly.

Perhaps it was best that it had happened today as it shifted the focus from the newlywed couple to the funeral for the late king.

Josephine's father returned to Khronos and Josephine kept to her rooms, or when she did go out, she walked the safe paths on the castle grounds, going from the rose garden to the orangery and then through the vegetable garden and the orchard.

Alexander did not come to her, and she did not seek him out.

His mother, though, was another matter, and Josephine took to spending a half hour in the queen's chamber every afternoon after her garden walk, either reading or attempting to do some needlework. She was terrible at needlework but her efforts seemed to please Serena, and so she tried. Serena would have tea served and the two of them would pretend to eat one of the cakes that accompanied the tea tray. During their time together, Serena did not mention her son and Josephine did not bring him up. Sometimes Serena would say something about the funeral plans—the funeral now just days away—and Josephine would nod and listen, because Serena seemed to need that.

Josephine needed someone to talk to as well, but the ladies surrounding her were employees, staff members, not friends. It would have helped to have a friend in the palace. Someone Josephine trusted, someone Josephine could ask for advice, because clearly Alexander had no need of her, not anymore. He was much in demand, busy planning funerals and coronations. Why did he need her now? He didn't. She resolved that the day after the funeral, she'd go. She wouldn't make a fuss. She'd slip away. It was the best way to handle the goodbye since they weren't exactly her strength and Alexander wouldn't pursue her. Alexander no longer needed her.

Alexander was in his tower office at his desk when his secretary approached, letting him know that he had a visitor.

"It's Claudia," his secretary said. "I've taken her upstairs to the library. I thought it better than in the palace."

"Thank you," he said, rising and heading for the stairs.

Claudia was pacing the library when he entered. "I wasn't sure you'd see me."

"Why wouldn't I?"

"You've avoided all of us since the trip."

"Gerard told me you'd left Roche for a while." He hesitated. "Someone else said you've been in Paris."

"I've been in Zurich, not Paris." She looked at him hard. "I thought I'd hear from you, though. I was sure I would. I even left my number with your secretary in case you wanted to speak to me. But when you didn't, I began to worry."

He arched a brow. "Worry about what?"

Her relief gave way to wariness. "You don't remember the fight on the trip, do you?"

"Why would you say that?"

Claudia sat down in one of the winged chairs. "Because I keep thinking, if you remembered what happened, you would have taken action. But you've done nothing, at least not as far as I can see, and I've been on tenterhooks waiting for you to reach out to me."

When he said nothing, she added, "I'm not trying to cause a problem, but I keep thinking, something's not right. This just isn't like you."

He drew a slow breath, telling himself not to react. "What should I have done?"

Her brow creased. "Then? Or now?"

Alexander hated not remembering; he hated the blank spots in his memory. "Both."

"I think this is the wrong place to start the conversation. I think we need to back up and I need to say that you weren't rough with me. You were never rough with me in any way, at any time. You do know that, don't you?"

He clasped his hands tightly behind his back, not trusting himself to speak. Why was Claudia here? What did she want? Was this a trick? Was she going to ask for money?

"I don't know what game Damian is playing with you,

Alex, but you weren't drinking that night, and you didn't hurt me." Her voice broke. "*He* did. You saved me. You found us on my balcony and you tried to help me and he clubbed you with the lantern." She gasped for air. "I ran away terrified, and I've been terrified every day since."

Alexander didn't even realize he'd been holding his breath until little spots danced before his eyes. He exhaled roughly. "Why?" he ground out.

"Because I thought he'd killed you, and I was so afraid he'd kill me. And then when you were found, I was afraid he'd try to silence me. I've been hiding from him. Hiding from everyone, but I can't live like this. I can't avoid him forever."

"Why were you two fighting that night?"

"He thought I was flirting with you. He can't stand it if I speak to you or look at you. He's so jealous of you. You must know that. You have everything he ever wanted—"

"He was always like a brother to me. Growing up, he was always saving me from the worst fights."

"That's not true, either. He was behind those fights and behind those beatings. He always arrived after you were beat up and bloody, didn't he?" Her voice quavered. "Did you ever wonder how he always just happened to be there when you were getting the snot kicked out of you? It was because he paid the other boys to beat you up. He paid them so that he could come and look like the hero when actually all they'd done was what he longed to do—hurt you."

"What do you want from me? Money? A couple hundred thousand euros? What is it, Claudia?"

"I just want to be safe. That's why I'm leaving. I have my own money, and friends in Vancouver, but I needed you to know the truth. I couldn't just go and have you think that you are any way responsible for what happened on that trip."

"I'm not a monster, then," he said under his breath, but Claudia had heard him.

"A monster, Alex? Never. You've always been my hero!"

Aimee saw Claudia out and Alexander paced his room for a moment, trying to process everything he'd just learned.

He hadn't hurt Claudia. He hadn't betrayed anyone. He hadn't failed anyone—with the exception of Josephine, then.

He swallowed hard at that thought because he had failed her, and she was the one who deserved his love and loyalty the most.

Alexander returned to the palace to find Josephine, but when he reached her room, she was gone. One of her ladies said that Josephine might be in the garden as she liked the garden, especially in the latter part of the afternoon. He hadn't known that. He thought he should have known it.

He walked through the rose garden and then the orangery, ending up in the kitchen garden where he found her sitting on a bench beneath a peach tree.

She looked up at him without a smile. She looked at him as if he were a stranger. His gut tightened. They'd become strangers since the wedding.

"Can I help you with something?" she asked coolly, formally.

He wanted to kiss her, touch her, love her, make her his again. Instead he stood there stiffly, aware of the staff probably watching, aware of the security cameras in every corner. He wanted her desperately, but life in the palace was not for intimacy. It was a stifling world, filled with rules and formalities and never-ending protocol.

"I wanted to tell you," he said gruffly, "that Claudia came to see me this afternoon." He frowned, uncertain how to explain everything Claudia had told him. "She said she suspected I didn't remember what happened on the yacht and thought I should know."

"What happened on the yacht?"

"There was a fight, but it was between Damian and Claudia."

"So why were you the one in the water?"

"Claudia said I intervened, saving her from Damian when he became physical." He felt Josephine's gaze bore through him. Did she doubt him? Or did she doubt Claudia? He wished he knew. "Damian grabbed a lantern and struck me with it. Claudia ran away, afraid, and she's said nothing about the incident because she's afraid Damian might turn on her."

"That must be a relief for you to know."

Alexander hesitated, flashing back to how they were on Khronos. How simple life had been and how happy he'd felt with her. Happy and free. She'd been happy, too.

He struggled with the words. "I also just want to tell you I'm sorry. I'm sorry for dragging you into all of this. I'm sorry for forcing you into a marriage you clearly didn't want—"

"Good. You should be sorry," she said, rising. "You did force me into this marriage, and yes, you can be incredibly selfish, but I'm not surprised you went to Claudia's aid. It's what you would do. You understand responsibility. You never fail to do your duty." And then she walked past him, her skirt brushing him as she headed back to her suite.

Josephine entered her bedroom and carefully closed the bedroom door. She lay on her bed trembling. She had no fight left in her, no fight at all. It was time for her to go. Time to leave. Thank goodness King Bruno's funeral was in the morning. She'd pack tonight and be ready to go as soon as they returned from the service.

The funeral was held in the same cathedral as their wedding. The cathedral was packed with kings and princes, and political leaders from all over the world. The service was long, with prayers and songs from the choir, and two speakers—Alexander and his cousin Damian.

Alexander spoke first and was eloquent about his father's virtues and his passion for his country, while Damian spoke of his uncle Bruno's vigor and strength and reminisced about the trips they'd taken, the sporting matches they'd played, and how close they'd been, more like father and son than uncle and nephew.

Josephine could see Alexander's jaw tighten and his fist clench as Damian spoke. She found herself watching Alexander's hand and the way his fingers curled and then unfurled. She kept her gaze fixed on Alexander's hand because it was far better than seeing the pain in his face.

Two hours later, Josephine gave her suite of rooms a last glance before lifting her small suitcase and heading for the corridor.

She'd written Alexander a note and she intended to put it on his bed. But as she approached his suite, she heard voices, and she hesitated outside the door to his living room, not wanting to interrupt.

But one of the voices grew louder, the tone menacing. "You think because your father is gone I won't tell the Parliament what you've done? You think I'm going to protect you when you're a violent, unpredictable man, not fit to lead this country or wear the crown?"

Josephine shivered a little, recognizing the voice as belonging to Damian. But that's not why she shivered. She shivered because she was remembering the yacht and the voices she'd heard the night she'd saved him.

It was the same voice. The same anger. The same delivery, the same inflection.

It was Damian who'd fought with Alexander. Damian who'd struck him.

Fear swamped her, not fear for herself but fear for Alexander, and just like that night on the beach, she couldn't move. She couldn't leave him.

She slowly twisted the doorknob and opened the door just enough to get a look inside. Alexander was sitting in a chair, calm and composed, while Damian paced back and forth.

"I will tell them everything," Damian said. "I will destroy you. I will make sure everyone knows who you really are, and when I'm finished, you will be finished because no one will believe you or trust you, not when they find out you have mental problems and lapses in your memory—"

"Whatever are you talking about?" Josephine interrupted, pushing the door open and entering with a faint smile. "You sound almost…crazy, Damian. I'm surprised because you gave the most moving tribute to King Bruno earlier. Was it all an act? Or is this an act now?"

Alexander was immediately on his feet. "Josephine," he said, a warning in his voice.

She walked toward Damian. "Please explain something," she said, still smiling. "Why do you think people will believe you? What makes you think they won't believe him?"

"Because he's brain damaged. He's lost his memory—"

"Yes, he lost it. But it's back. He's told me everything. I know everything. Shall I fill you in?"

"Josephine," Alexander growled.

She ignored him again, her arms crossed over her chest. "You despise him because he's the heir and you're not. During your trip, you were seething with jealousy because Alexander would soon be king. Not you. Never you. Not as long as he lived. And so you provoked him, hurting Claudia, knowing Alexander would go to her aid. Once Alexander was where you wanted him, you took a lantern—very handy, I might add—and bashed him over the head, and then while he was reeling, you pushed him overboard."

She stood now just in front of him and she practically

vibrated with fury. "You thought you'd gotten away with it, too," she added. "You thought you were going to be Aargau's next king. But then Alexander returned, and you lost your big opportunity. You must have been devastated. I can only imagine your pain. I almost—*almost*—feel sorry for you."

Damian stared down at her for long moments before he stepped back and barked a laugh. "That was good. I almost believed you. But you have no proof, he doesn't remember—"

"But he does. He told me everything. How else do you think I know?"

Damian stopped laughing. He glanced from her to Alexander and back. "If he knew, why hasn't he said something? Done something? It's because he's still brain damaged—"

"I'm not brain damaged," Alexander said mildly. "I object to that. But Josephine is right. I told her everything, and she has told her staff everything, and they in turn told security." He walked to Josephine's side and slipped his arm around her waist, holding her tight. "The palace guard has been instructed to arrest you should they find you anywhere near the palace or any member of the royal family again."

"You're lying. You're bluffing," Damian choked, furious. "You can't arrest me because you had no proof, and you'll never have any—"

"The palace guard is here, Your Highness," a voice said from the doorway.

They all turned as Gerard entered with the palace security. "We've heard everything and there is more than enough evidence to convict you," Gerard said shortly.

"But I did nothing! This is all hearsay!" Damian cried.

Gerard shrugged. "I was able to recover the missing security footage. It's all on camera. Every word Josephine said was true."

"But there was no security camera," Damian protested. "I know. I checked her room and balcony carefully."

Silence followed. Gerard gestured for the guards to take him. Panicked, Damien put his hands out. "Wait. I'll leave. I'll leave Roche. I won't come back. I promise—"

"Not just Roche, but Aargau," Alexander said flatly. "You're not welcome here, and should you be found trying to enter Aargau, you will be arrested and charged with crimes against the state. Understood?"

It had been a very long, difficult day, but Alexander was finally alone with Josephine in his bedroom, which was just where he wanted her.

"You saved me twice," he said, sitting down in a chair near the bed and then pulling her onto his lap.

He noticed she'd allowed him to draw her down, but her posture remained ramrod straight. She was still upset. He didn't blame her, but he was also beyond proud of her, and in awe. She was a marvel, a heroine, and she was his.

His hand skimmed over her hair, stroking from the top down. "How am I to live without you?" He didn't give her a chance to answer. "I'm afraid it's impossible, which is why I can't let you go."

Her chin tipped, nose lifting. "You can't make me stay. I'm done being ordered about."

He checked his smile. "Well, then, I'll just have to lock you back in the tower."

She turned her head sharply and glared at him. "Have you learned nothing these past few weeks?"

He lifted one of her long silky curls. "I did. I just told you. You weren't listening. I can't live without you."

"You'll be fine. You're not in danger anymore."

He stroked another curl and then wrapped it around his finger. "Not true. I'm in danger of losing you and it'll break my heart, and what kind of king would I be with a damaged brain and a broken heart?"

She smothered a laugh but he felt her back heave and the inelegant snort made him smile. It felt good to smile. It felt good to have her with him like this. He'd missed her so much.

"You'll be fine without me," she said huskily. "You'll find another princess—"

"Never. You're the only princess I want and the only woman I love." He turned her head toward him. "I love you, Josephine, I do, and I know I don't deserve you, but I'm asking for a second chance. Let me make things right. Let me prove to you how much I love you and how sorry I am for hurting you—"

"You did hurt me."

"I know I did. I wasn't sensitive about the miscarriage, and I shouldn't have forced you to marry me. I should have let you go home and grieve and come back when you were ready."

She said nothing and he gave her hair another stroke.

"I'm not being honest," he said after a moment. "I'm sorry for what I did, but the truth is I'd do it all over again if I thought I might lose you. I didn't let you go home because I was afraid you wouldn't come back. I demanded you marry me because I couldn't imagine living without you. From the time I was on Khronos, I wanted you, and not just for a few days but forever. There is no one else for me, *cara*, only you."

He tipped her chin up and kissed her lightly. "Tell me we can make this work. Tell me you'll give me another chance. You don't have to love me. You don't have to forgive me. Just promise you'll give me time to get it right, because that has been the one thing we have never had enough of...time. It's always been against us. It's always running out. I need time with you, Josephine, time to prove to you that I can make you happy, and make you feel safe—"

"You do," she whispered, interrupting him. "And you have." She blinked, chasing away tears. "I love you," she added simply. "I have loved you from the moment I saw you on my beach. I was meant to rescue you, just as I was meant to love you. Sometimes I think the only reason I was put on this earth was to be there when you needed me."

"If that's the case, know now that I will always need you, and I will always love you, and I will always want you at my side. We belong together. You, me, and the children we will have."

Her eyes filled with tears. "Do you think we'll be able to have another baby? I want to start a family with you."

He clasped her face and kissed her fiercely. "We will," he murmured a long time later. "I promise we will. Just as I promise you my love and my heart forever."

CHAPTER ELEVEN

THEY WAITED UNTIL the period of mourning was over to take a much-needed honeymoon, and then after the honeymoon there was the coronation with all the pomp and circumstance the crowning of Aargau's new king required.

But finally, thankfully, the guests were gone, and the fuss was over, and life was settling into a pleasant routine at the palace. Alexander would be busy during the days, but he was all hers at night, and they made love with an unending passion and hunger.

But after two months of palace walls and palace views, Josephine longed for a change, and she mentioned to Alexander that she hoped they could sneak away for a few days, or even a day, and do something adventurous and new just the two of them.

She didn't think he was listening, but the next morning while she was having breakfast he strolled into her room and told her that they'd be leaving within the hour.

"What should I wear?" she asked.

"Something comfortable, and bring a sweater or a jacket just in case it gets cold."

Their driver ferried them to the dock, where a boat was waiting. Josephine glanced nervously at the boat. "Where are we going?"

"It will take us thirty minutes by boat. At this time it's the only way to get there."

"What are the conditions like today?"

"It'll be a little bumpy, but I'll make sure we take it slow."

She nodded and stepped into the speedboat and told herself she wouldn't get seasick and hoped it was true. "Are you going to tell me anything else?" she asked, taking a seat and watching Alexander take one across from her.

"In a bit," he answered. "But for now, just try to relax and enjoy the adventure." He gave her a faint smile. "You like adventures, and freedom. Remember?"

"I do," she agreed cautiously, even as her stomach lurched. She'd been queasier lately, her morning coffee no longer the treat it had once been. And as the speedboat raced across the water, bouncing on some of the bigger waves, sending up a mist of sea spray, she clung to her seat praying she wouldn't throw up.

This was probably not the best adventure when she wasn't feeling well, but Alexander looked so happy that she didn't want to ruin his pleasure.

"Where are we going?" she asked, as the minutes slid by and the boat kept bouncing and she kept swallowing hard.

"There is a bit of rock ahead, nothing too grand. It's barren and remote. But I thought you might like it. I thought you might need a place of your own, a place off the grid with plenty of sun and quiet beaches." His voice had dropped and he gave her a crooked, rather tender smile. "A place where you can be a mermaid and raise our children away from society, noise, and rules and regulations."

Her eyes suddenly stung. Did he know? Did he suspect? She hadn't said anything yet, but she had seen the doctor and he'd confirmed her suspicions. He'd even done an ultrasound and let her watch the tiny, steady, strong heartbeat.

"You're describing paradise," she said softly.

"I wouldn't call it paradise, but it is yours, all yours. I'm giving you your very own island."

The speedboat was slowing and yet the wind tangled her hair, and she struggled to push back wild, damp strands from her salt-sticky face. "An island of my own?"

"It's there, ahead of us. Just keep watching the horizon."

She watched and her gaze narrowed as she waited for

something to appear. He told her a little more about the island that lay off the coast of Aargau. It was rocky and barren and good for nothing, but it did have a small beach and a tiny little cove, neither of which were used by the public since they had been owned for the past 160 years by the Alberici family.

"So you have been here before?" she asked, leaning forward, thinking she could see a small lump of land in the distance, but not sure.

He shook his head. "I was there once as a boy. My father and Uncle Aldo took Damian and me there for a fishing trip. It wasn't a success, though, and we never returned."

"So you have bad memories of the place?"

"I don't know if they were bad, but they weren't good enough to make me want to return. But it's different now. We're going together."

Yes, it was land ahead of them. It appeared to be a small hill rising from the sea. The island wasn't very big, but then again, it wasn't quite as small as she'd imagined, either. She could see little green from where she sat, and she suspected it was, as he said, nearly all rock.

The motorboat slowed yet again as they approached the shore. The purplish-blue water lightened, turning a shimmering aquamarine as they arrived at the cove, capped by an ivory crescent of sand. The sides of the cove were rocky and relatively high, but the beach was lovely, with its generous swathe of pale ivory sand.

Their boat's driver steered them as close to the shore as he could before turning off the motor. Alexander jumped out of the boat, waded into the surf, and held his arms up to Josephine. "Come, Queen, I'll keep you from getting wet."

"I like the water, remember?"

"Yes, you have gills and fins, I believe."

She laughed as he lifted her from the boat and carried

her through the rushing surf to relatively dry, packed sand. Once there, he put her on her feet and together they faced the boat and the view of the sea.

Open water everywhere.

Gorgeous blue sky, a turquoise sea, pale rocks standing sentry at the mouth of the cove, and nothing and no one else for miles until you reached the mainland.

"It's perfect," she said, nodding. "I love it. Is there any place to pitch a tent? Because this is most definitely off grid."

"I thought of that, too. Let me show you what is here and we can see if you think it has potential."

He took her hand and led her toward the back of the beach where it butted against the rocky cliff, and there at the back was a little path carved from the boulders, which actually tunneled back through the rocks.

Josephine felt like she was on a grand adventure as they walked up the path through the small tunnel. She reached out and touched the wall. It was surprisingly smooth. Her lips quirked, wondering at the feat of nature required to make such a tunnel out of what was most likely volcanic rock, and then they emerged into the light, and they'd come to a protected clearing. But it wasn't a true clearing at all as right in the middle sat a small stone house virtually identical to the one she'd called home on Khronos. Josephine's jaw dropped and she looked from the cottage to Alexander and back again.

Same stone. Same shape. Same placement of windows and doors.

She walked quickly to the house, and as she crossed the threshold she felt a jolt of recognition—rough-hewn beams across the ceiling, a big stone hearth dominating the center room, and two bedrooms, although as she inspected both, she discovered that the master bedroom was the one at the front, where Jo's had been, and the one at the back had been divided into two, with a cradle and bunk beds, as if anticipating quite a brood.

"This is my house," she said, doing a slow circle, trying to take it all in.

"I had it copied as closely as I could," he said, arms folded across his chest, a faint smile curving his lips. "The contractor and builders wanted to add more amenities but I refused. I told them it was meant to be rustic and an escape from civilization as we know it."

"You gave me my home back," she whispered, her voice breaking.

"With all the solar-efficient technology we could find," he said, exiting the house and heading to the back where a pretty trellis concealed a tidy grid of solar panels, tubing, and equipment. "Solar power for heating and electricity. Solar-powered communication. Enough energy to run your own little lab of computers as well, if you should so desire. And last but not least, your own desalination system for as much fresh water as you, and your future garden, desire."

She shook her head, incredibly touched and overwhelmed by the thought and effort that had gone into creating this world for her.

From the beach, this was a deserted island, and yet tucked behind the safety of the rocks was a little house ready for her to come play house. "You make me feel like Marie Antoinette with her little farm."

"The Hameau de la Reine," he said, blue eyes creasing as he smiled. "The thought crossed my mind, too, but it's not quite so extravagant. We left out the farm, the mill, the Temple of Love, the belvedere, and the grotto."

"Tell me you didn't import all those stones for the house."

"No. Thankfully the island has an abundance of stone, and we were able to use all local stone, cutting them here, which made it far easier physically, as well as more affordable."

"And yet this is still extremely costly."

"Can I not give my bride a wedding gift?"

"Will your people want my head?"

"My people are your people, and they will want you and our children happy." He drew her into his arms, kissing her, oh, so slowly and tenderly, and when he raised his head, his blue eyes were bright and warm and filled with conviction and love. "You will have more children, *cara*. It will all work out. It might just take time—"

"I know," she interrupted, standing on tiptoe to kiss him back. "And it will work out, always, as long as you and I are together and we stick together. Friends, lovers, partners." She felt the secret rise in her, the joy overwhelming. "Parents."

"Yes, we will be parents," he agreed firmly, sounding like the man who'd served his country in the Royal Navy.

"In just six months," she said, kissing him again. "And next week, we can find out the sex, if you want. Or we can both go and just look at the ultrasound and watch the baby's lovely little heart."

Alexander's jaw worked and he blinked hard, clearing the sheen gathering there. "A baby."

"Our baby."

"You've seen the doctor?"

She nodded. "I have, and I've seen the ultrasound and everything looks good. There should be no problems. I just can't go racing up and down steep stairs."

He glanced toward the water. "Or riding in bumpy speedboats. Why didn't you tell me?"

"The boat ride was fine. Trust me. And I was going to tell you this weekend. I had a special reveal planned, but this was actually so much better."

"I'm calling for the helicopter to take us home."

"Alexander."

"I'm taking no chances."

"Alexander!" she protested, laughing.

"I'm taking no chances at all. I love you, Josephine. I love you more than you'll ever know."

* * * * *

UNTOUCHED QUEEN BY ROYAL COMMAND

KELLY HUNTER

PROLOGUE

Augustus

THEY WEREN'T SUPPOSED to be in this part of the palace. Fourteen-year-old Augustus, Crown Prince of Arun, had been looking for the round room with the domed glass roof for at least six years. He could see that roof from the helicopter every time they flew in or out, but he'd never been able to find the room and no adult had ever been willing to help him out.

His father said that those quarters had been mothballed over a hundred years ago.

His mother said it was out of bounds because the roof was unsafe.

Didn't stop him and his sister looking for it, even if they never had much luck. It was like a treasure hunt.

They wouldn't have found it this time either, without the help of a map.

The floor was made of moon-coloured marble, and so too were the columns and archways surrounding the central room. The remaining furniture had been covered with dusty drapes that had probably once been white. Above all, it felt warm in a way that the main castle living areas were never warm.

'Why do we not live in *this* part of the palace?' asked his sister from somewhere not far behind him. She'd taken to opening every door of every room that circled the main area. 'These look like bedrooms. I could live here.'

'You want fifty bedrooms all to yourself?'

'I want to curl up like a cat in the sunlight. Show me one other place in the palace where you can do that.'

'Mother would kill you if you took to lounging about in the sun. You'd lose your milky-white complexion.'

'Augustus, I don't *have* a milky-white complexion—no matter what our mother might want. I have black hair, black eyes and olive skin—just like you and Father do. My skin likes the sun. It *needs* the sun, it *craves* the sun. Oh, wow.' She'd disappeared through another marble archway and her voice echoed faintly. 'Indoor pool.'

'What?' He backtracked and headed for the archway, bumping into his sister, who was backing up fast.

'Something rustled in the corner,' she muttered by way of explanation.

'Still want to live here?' He couldn't decide whether the hole in the ground was big enough to be called a pool or small enough to be called a bath. All he knew was that he'd never seen mosaic floor tiles with such elaborate patterns before, and he'd never seen exactly that shade of blue.

'I still want to look around,' his sister offered. 'But you can go first.'

He rolled his eyes, even as pride demanded he take the lead. He'd been born to rule a country one day, after all. A rustling sound would not defeat him. He swaggered past his sister and turned to the right. There was a sink for washing hands carved into the wall beside the archway, and taps that gleamed with a dull silver glow. He reached for one and, with some effort, got it to turn but there was no water. Not a gurgle, a splutter or even the clank of old pipes.

'What is this place? What are all these stone benches and alcoves for?' his sister asked as she followed him into the room. She kept a wary eye on the shadowy corners but eventually turned her attention to other parts of the room.

It was an old map of the palace that had guided them here. That and a history teacher who preferred giving his two royal students books to read so that he could then nap his way through afternoon lessons. Their loss. And sometimes their freedom. If they got caught in here, he could probably even spin it that they were continuing their history lesson hands-on.

'Maybe it was built for a company of warrior knights who slept in the rooms and came here to bathe. They could have practised sword-fighting in the round room,' his sister suggested.

'Maybe.'

Kings had ruled from this palace stronghold for centuries. It was why the place looked so formidable from the outside and had relatively few creature comforts on the inside, no matter how many generations of royals had tried to make it more liveable. There was something about it that resisted softening. Except for in here. There was something soft and strangely beautiful about this part of the palace. Augustus plucked at a scrap of golden silk hanging from a peg on a wall and watched it fall in rotting pieces to the floor. 'Did knights wear embroidered silk bathrobes?'

His sister glanced over and gasped. 'Did you just destroy that?'

'No, I moved it. Time destroyed it.' Rational argument was his friend.

'Can I have some?'

Without waiting for permission, she scooped the rotting cloth from the floor, bunched it in her hand and began to rub at a nearby tile.

'It's going to take a little more than that to get this place clean.'

'I just want to see the pictures,' his sister grumbled, and then, 'Oh.' She stopped cleaning.

He looked, and…oh. 'Congratulations. You found the ancient tile porn.'

'It's *art*, you moron.'

'Uh-huh.'

'I wish we could see better in here,' his sister said.

'For that we would need electricity. Or burning torches for all the holders in the walls.' He closed his eyes and a picture came to mind, clear as day. Not knights and warriors living in this part of the palace and bathing in this room, but women, bound in service to the reigning King.

Augustus had never read about any of his ancestors having a harem, but then, as their eighty-year-old history teacher was fond of telling them, not all facts made it into their history books. 'So, bedrooms, communal bathing room, big gathering room…what else?'

There were more rooms leading from the centre dome. An ancient kitchen, storage rooms with bare shelves, larger rooms with fireplaces, smaller rooms with candle stubs still sitting in carved-out hollows in the walls. They found chests of drawers and sideboards beneath heavy canvas cloth, long mirrors that his sister swore made her look thinner, and even an old hairbrush.

'I don't think people even know this stuff is here,' Moriana said as she put the brush gently back into place. 'I don't know *why* they're ignoring it. Some of it's really old. Museum-old. The back of this brush looks like ivory, inlaid with silver, and it's just been abandoned. Maybe we should bring the history prof down here. He'd have a ball.'

'No.' His voice came out sharper than he meant it to. 'This is a private place. He doesn't get to come here.'

Moriana glanced at him warily but made no comment as they left the side room they'd been exploring.

All doorways and arches led back to the main room. It was like a mini town square—or town circle. He looked up at the almost magical glass ceiling. 'Maybe our forefathers studied the stars from here. Mapped them.' Perhaps he could come back one night and do the same. And if he took another look at those naked people tiles in the room with the empty pool, so be it. Even future kings had to get their information from somewhere. 'Maybe they hung a big telescope from the ropes up there and moved it around. Maybe if they climbed the stairs over there…' He gestured towards the stairs that ran halfway up the wall and ended in a stone landing with not a railing in sight. 'Maybe they had pulleys and ropes that shifted stuff. Maybe this was a place for astronomers.'

'Augustus, that's a circus trapeze.'

'You think they kept a circus in here?'

'I think this is a harem.'

So much for his innocent little sister not guessing

what this place had once been. 'I'm going up the stairs. Coming?'

Moriana followed him. She didn't always agree with him but she could always be counted on to be there for him at the pointy end of things. It didn't help that their mother praised Augustus to the skies for his sharp mind and impeccable self-control, and never failed to criticise Moriana's emotional excesses. As far as Augustus could tell, he was just as fiery as his sister, maybe more so. He was just better at turning hot temper into icy, impenetrable regard.

A king must always put the needs of his people before his own desires.

His father's words. Words to live by. Words to rule by.

A king must never lose control.

Words to *be* ruled by, whether he wanted to be ruled by them or not.

They made it to the ledge and he made his sister sit rather than stand. He sat too, his back to the wall as he looked up to the roof and then down at the intricately patterned marble floor.

'I feel like a bird in a cage,' said Moriana. 'Wonder what the women who once lived here felt like?'

'Sounds about right.' He wasn't a woman but he knew what being trapped by duty felt like.

'We could practise our archery from up here.' Moriana made fists out in front of her and drew back one arm as if pulling back an imaginary arrow. 'Set up targets down below. *Pffft.* Practise our aim.'

'Bloodthirsty. I like it.' Bottled-up anger had to go somewhere. He could use this place at other times too. Get away from the eyes that watched and judged his every move. 'Swear to me you won't tell anyone that we've been here.'

'I swear.' Her eyes gleamed.

'And that you won't come here by yourself.'

'Why not? You're going to.'

Sometimes his sister was a mind-reader.

'What are you going to do here all by yourself?' she wanted to know.

Roar. Weep. Let everything out that he felt compelled to keep in. 'Don't you ever want to be some place where no one's watching and judging your every move? Sit in the sun if you want to sit in the sun. Lose your temper and finally say all those things you want to say, even if no one's listening. Especially because no one's listening.' Strip back the layers of caution and restraint he clothed himself in and see what was underneath. Even if it was all selfish and ugly and wrong. 'I need somewhere to go where I'm free to be myself. This could be that place.'

His sister brought her knees to her chest and wrapped her arms around her legs. The gaze she turned on him was troubled. 'We shouldn't have to hide our real selves from everyone, Augustus. I know we're figureheads but surely we can let *some* people see what's underneath.'

'Yeah, well.' He thought back to the hour-long lecture on selfishness he'd received for daring to tell his father that he didn't want to attend yet another state funeral for a king he'd never met. 'You're not me.'

Sera

Sera wasn't supposed to leave the house when her mother's guest was visiting. Stay in the back room, keep quiet, don't ever be seen. Those were the rules and seven-year-old Sera knew better than to break them. Three times a week, maybe four, the visitor would come to her mother's front door and afterwards there might be food for the table and wine for her mother, although these days there was more wine and less food. Her mother was sick and the wine was like medicine, and her sweet, soft-spoken mother smelled sour now and the visitor never stayed long.

Sera's stomach grumbled as she went to the door between the living room and the rest of the once grand house and put her ear to it. If she got to the bakery before closing time there might be a loaf of bread left and the baker would give it to her for half price, and a sweet bun to go with it. The bread wasn't always fresh but the sweet treat was always free and once there'd even been eggs. The baker always said, 'And wish your mother a good day from me'. Her mother always smiled and said the baker was a Good Man.

Her mother had gone to school with him and they'd played together as children, long before her mother had gone away to learn and train and become something more.

Sera didn't know what her mother meant by *more*; all she knew was that there weren't many things left in their house to sell and her mother was sick all the time now and didn't laugh any more unless there was wine and then she would laugh at nothing at all. Whatever her mother had once been: a dancer, a lady, someone who could make Sera's nightmares go away at the touch of her hand...she wasn't that same person any more.

Every kid in the neighbourhood knew what she was now, including Sera.

Her mother was a whore.

There was no noise coming from the other room. No talking, no laughter, no…other. Surely the visitor would be gone by now? The light was fading outside. The baker would close his shop soon and there would be no chance of bread at all.

She heard a thud, as if someone had bumped into furniture, followed by the tinkle of breaking glass. Her mother had dropped wine glasses before and it was Sera's job to pick up the pieces and try to make her mother sit down instead of dancing around and leaving sticky bloody footprints on the old wooden floor, and all the time telling Sera she was such a good, good girl.

Some of those footprints were still there. Stuck in the wood with no rugs to cover them.

The rugs had all been sold.

No sound at all as Sera inched the door open and put her eye to the crack, and her mother was kneeling and picking up glass, and most importantly she was alone. Sera pushed the door open and was halfway across the room before she saw the other person standing in front of the stone-cold fireplace. She stopped, frozen. Not the man but still a visitor: a woman dressed in fine clothes and it was hard to look away from her. She reminded Sera of what her mother had once been: all smooth and beautiful lines, with clear eyes and a smile that made her feel warm.

Sera looked towards her mother for direction now that the rule had been broken, not daring to speak, not daring to move, even though there was still glass on the floor that her mother had missed.

'We don't need you,' her mother said, standing up and then looking away. 'Go home.'

Home *where*?

'My neighbour's girl,' her mother told the visitor. 'She cleans here.'

'Then you'd best let her do it.'

'I can do it.' Her mother stared coldly at the other woman before turning back to Sera. 'Go. Come back tomorrow.'

'Wait,' said the visitor, and Sera stood, torn, while the visitor came closer and put a gentle hand to Sera's face and turned it towards the light. 'She's yours.'

'No, I—'

'Don't lie. She's yours.'

Her mother said nothing.

'You broke the rules,' the older woman said.

Sera whispered, 'I'm sorry…'

At the same time her mother said, 'I fell in *love*.'

And then her mother laughed harshly and it turned into a sob, and the older woman straightened and turned towards the sound.

'You didn't have to leave,' the older woman said gently. 'There are ways—'

'No.'

'You're one of us. We would have taken care of you.'

Her mother shook her head. No and no. 'Ended us both.'

'*Hidden* you both,' said the older woman. 'Do you really think you're the first courtesan to ever fall in love and beget a child?'

Sera bent to the task of picking up glass shards from the floor, trying to make herself as small as she could, trying to make them forget she was there so she could hear them talk more, never mind that she didn't understand what half the words meant.

'How did you find us?' her mother asked.

'Serendipity.' Another word Sera didn't know. 'I was passing through the town and stopped at the bakery for a sourdough loaf,' the older woman said with a faint smile. 'Mainly because in all the world there's none as good as the ones they make there. The baker's boy remembered me. He's the baker now, as I expect you know, and he mentioned you. We talked. I mean you no harm. I want to help.'

'You can't. I'm beyond help now.'

'Then let me help your daughter.'

'How? By training her to serve and love others and never ask for anything in return? I will *never* choose that life for my daughter.'

'You liked it well enough once.'

'I was a fool.'

'And are you still a fool? What do you think will happen to the child once you poison your body with drink and starve yourself to death? Who will care for her, put a roof over her head and food in her mouth, educate her and give her a sense of self-worth?'

Mama looked close to crying. 'Not you.'

'I don't see many choices left to you.' The woman glanced around the room. 'Unless I'm mistaken, you've already sold everything of value. Any jewellery left?'

'No.' Sera could hardly hear her mother's answer.

'Does the house belong to you?'

'No.'

'How long have you been ill?'

'A year. Maybe more. I'm not—it's not—catching. It's cancer.'

The older woman bowed her head. 'And how much longer do you think you can last, selling your favours to the lowest bidder? How long before he looks towards the girl and wants her instead of you? Yuna, please. I can give you a home again. *Treatment* if there's treatment to be had. Comfort and clothing befitting your status and hers. Complete discretion when it comes to *whose* child she is—don't think I don't know.'

'He won't want her.'

'You're right, he won't. But I do. The Order of the Kite will always look after its own. From the fiercest hawk to the fallen sparrow. How can you not know this?'

A tear slipped beneath her mother's closed lashes. 'I thought I'd be better off away from it all. For a while it was good. It can be good again.'

'Do you really believe that?' The older woman crossed to her mother and took hold of her hands. 'Let me help you.'

'Promise me she won't be trained as a courtesan,' her mother begged. 'Lianthe, *please*.'

'I promise to give her the same choice I gave you.'

'You'll dazzle her.'

'You'll counter that.' The older woman drew Sera's mother towards the couch, not letting go of her hands, even after they were both seated. Sera edged closer, scared of letting the hem of the woman's gown get in the puddle of wine on the floor, and loving the sweet, clean smell that surrounded her. The woman smiled. 'Leave it, child. Come, let me look at you.'

Sera withstood the other woman's gaze for as long as she could. *Stand tall, chin up, don't fidget.* Her mother's words ringing in her mind. *No need to look like a street urchin.*

Fidget, fidget, beneath the woman's quiet gaze.

'My name's Lianthe,' the woman said finally. 'And I want you and your mother to come to my home in the mountains so that I can take care of you both until your mother is well again. Would you like that?'

'Would there be visitors for Mama?'

'What kind of visitors?'

'The man.'

Her mother and the lady shared a long glance.

'He would not visit. I would be taking you too far away for that.'

'Would there be wine for her?' Because wine was important. 'Wine's like medicine.'

'Then there will be wine until we find better medicine. Tell me, child, are you hungry?'

So, so hungry but she'd learned long ago that sometimes it was better to say nothing than to give the wrong answer. Her stomach grumbled the answer for her anyway.

'When did you last eat?' the lady asked next.

Same question. Trick question. 'Would you like some tea?' Sera asked anxiously. There was tea in the cupboard and Mama always offered visitors a drink. Tea was a warm drink. She knew how to make it and what cups to use. There was a tray. 'I could bring you some tea.'

The lady looked towards her mother as if she'd done something wrong. Something far worse than forgetting to lock the door or not turn off the bedroom lamp at night. 'Yuna, what are you doing? You're already training her in the ways of self-sacrifice and denial. It's too soon for that. You know it is.'

Another tear slipped silently down her mother's face. Lianthe's gaze hardened.

'And now she looks to you for guidance and approval. Yuna, you *must* see what you're doing here. This isn't freedom. This isn't childhood as it's meant to be lived. This is abuse and, of all the things we taught you, no member of the Order ever taught you that.'

'He's not to know,' her mother said raggedly. 'He's not to take her.'

'He will never know. This I promise.'

'She's not to be sent anywhere near him.'

'You have my word.'

'She gets to choose. If she doesn't want to be a companion, you set her up to succeed elsewhere.'

'Agreed.'

'Sera?' Her mother asked her name as a question but Sera stayed quiet and paid attention because she didn't yet know what the question was. 'Should we go to the mountains with the Lady Lianthe? Would you like that?'

Away from here and the baker who was a Good Man and the kids who called her names and the men who looked at her with eyes that burned hot and hungry. Away from the fear that her mother would one day go to sleep on a belly full of wine and never wake up. 'Would there be food? And someone to take care of us?'

Her mother buried her face in her hands.

'Yes, there will be food and people who will care for you both,' the Lady Lianthe said. 'Sera. Is that your name?'

Sera nodded.

'Pretty name.' The woman's smile wrapped around her like a blanket. 'Pretty girl.'

CHAPTER ONE

SHE WAS A gift from her people to the King of Arun. An unwanted gift if the King's expression spoke true, but one he couldn't refuse. Not without breaking the laws of his country and severing seven centuries of tradition between his people and hers. Sera observed him through a veil of lashes and the protection afforded by her hooded travelling cloak. He could not refuse her.

Although he seemed to be considering it.

She was a courtesan, born, bred and shaped for the King's entertainment. Pledged into service at the age of seven in return for the finest food, shelter and an education second to none. Chosen for the beauty she possessed and the quickness of her mind. Taught to serve, to soothe, and how to dance, fight and dress. One for every King of Arun and only one. A possession to be treasured.

She stood before him, ready to serve. She wasn't unwilling. She'd already received far more from the bargain than she'd ever given and if it was time to pay up, so be it.

He was a handsome man if a tall, lean frame, firm lips, a stern jaw and wayward dark hair appealed—which it did. He had a reputation for fair and thoughtful leadership.

She definitely wasn't unwilling.

He looked relaxed as his gaze swept over her party. Two warriors stood to attention either side of her and another watched her back. The Lady Lianthe, elder spokeswoman for the High Reaches, preceded her. A party of five—with her in the centre, protected—they faced the Arunian King, who stood beside a tall leather chair in a room too cold and bleak for general living.

The old courtier who had guided them to the reception room finally spoke. 'Your Majesty, the Lady Lianthe, elder stateswoman of the High Reaches. And party.'

He knew who they were for they'd applied for this audience days ago. His office had been sent a copy of the accord. Sera wondered whether he'd spent the past two days poring over old diaries and history books in an effort to understand what none of his forefathers had seen fit to teach him.

He had a softness for women, this King, for all that he had taken no wife. He'd held his mother in high regard when she was alive, although she'd been dead now for many years. He held his recently married sister, Queen Consort of Liesendaach, in high esteem still. His name had been linked to several eligible women, although nothing had ever come of it.

'So it's time,' he said, and Sera almost smiled. She'd studied his speeches and knew that voice well. The cultured baritone weight of it and the occasional icy edge that could burn deeper than flame. There was no ice in it yet.

Lianthe rose from her curtsey and inclined her head. 'Your Majesty, as per the accord afforded our people by the Crown in the year thirteen twelve—'

'I don't want her.'

Lianthe's composure never wavered. They'd practised for this moment and every variation of it. At the King's interruption, the elder stateswoman merely started again. 'As per the accord, and in the event the King of Arun remains unmarried into his majority, the people of the High Reaches shall provide unto him a concubine of noble birth—'

'I cannot accept.'

'A concubine of noble birth, charged with attending the King's needs and demands until such time as he acquires a wife and produces an heir. Thereafter, and at the King's discretion—'

'She cannot stay here.' Finally, the ice had entered his voice. Not that it would do him any good. The people of the High Reaches had a duty to fulfil.

'Thereafter, and at the King's discretion, she shall be released from service, gifted her weight in gold and returned to her people.'

There it was, the accord read in full, a concubine presented and a duty discharged. Sera watched, from within the shadows her travelling hood afforded her, as Lianthe clasped her bony hands in front of her and tried to look less irritated and more accommodating.

'The accord stands, Your Majesty,' Lianthe reminded him quietly. 'It has never been dissolved.'

The King's black gaze swept from the older woman to rest broodingly on Sera's cloaked form. She could feel the weight of his regard and the displeasure in it. 'Lady Lianthe, with all due respect to the people of the High Reaches, I have no intention of being bound by this arrangement. Concubines have no place here. Not in this day and age.'

'With all due respect, you know nothing of concubines.' Fact and reprimand all rolled into one. 'By all means petition the court, your parliament and the church. Many have tried. All have failed. We can wait. Meanwhile, we all do what we must. Your Majesty, it is my duty and honour to present to you the Lady Sera Boreas, daughter of Yuna, Courtesan of the High Reaches and valued member of the Order of the Kite. Our gift to you.' Lianthe paused delicately. 'In your time of need.'

Sera hid her smile and sank to the floor in a curtsey, her head lowered and her cloak pooling around her like a black stain. Lianthe was not amused by their welcome, that much was clear to anyone with ears. This new King knew nothing of the role Sera might occupy if given the chance. What she could do for him. How best he might harness her skills. He didn't want her.

More fool him.

He didn't bid her to rise so she stayed down until he did. Cold, this grey stone hall with its too-righteous King. Pettiness did not become him.

'Up,' he said finally and Sera risked a glance at Lianthe as she rose. The older woman's eyes flashed silver and her lips thinned.

'Your Majesty, you appear to be mistaking the Lady Sera for a pet.'

'Probably because you insist on giving her away as if she is one,' he countered drily. 'I've read the housing requirements traditionally afforded the concubines of the north. I do hope you can supply your own eunuchs. I'm afraid I don't have any to hand.' His gaze swept over the warriors of the High Reaches and they stared back, eyes hard and unmoving. 'No eunuchs accompany you at the moment, I'd wager,' he said quietly.

He wasn't wrong. 'I can make do without if you can, Your Majesty.' Sera let warm amusement coat her voice. 'However, I do look forward to occupying the living quarters traditionally offered the concubines from the north. I've read a lot about the space.'

'Is there a face to match that honeyed voice?' he asked, after a pause that spanned a measured breath or four.

She raised her hands and pushed her travelling hood from her face. His eyes narrowed. Reluctant amusement teased at his lips. 'You might want to lead with that face, next time,' he said.

Sera had not been chosen for her plainness of form. 'As long as it pleases you, Your Majesty.'

'I'm sure it pleases everyone.' There might just be a sense of humour in there somewhere. 'Lady Sera, how exactly do you expect to be of use to me?'

'It depends what you need.'

'I need you gone.'

'Ah.' The man was decidedly single-minded. Sera inclined her head in tacit agreement. 'In that case you need a wife, Your Majesty. Would you like me to find you one?'

Augustus, King of Arun, was no stranger to the machinations of women, but he'd never—in all his years—encountered women like these. One cloaked in a rich, regal red, her beauty still a force to be reckoned with, never mind her elder status. The other cloaked in deepest black from the neck down, her every feature perfect and her eyes a clear and bitter grey. Neither woman seemed at all perturbed by his displeasure or by the words spilling from their lips.

He was used to having people around who did his bidding, but he called them employees, not servants, and there were rules and guidelines governing what he expected of them and what they could expect from him.

There were no clear rules for this.

He and his aides had spent the last two days in the palace record rooms, scouring the stacks for anything that mentioned the concubines of the High Reaches and the laws governing them. So far, he'd found plenty of information about their grace, beauty and unrivalled manners. So far, he'd found nothing to help him get rid of them.

A concubine of the High Reaches was a gift to be unwrapped with the care one might afford a poisoned chalice, one of his ancestor Kings had written. Not exactly reassuring.

'These living quarters you've read about…' He shook his head and allowed a frown. 'They've been mothballed for over a hundred and twenty years.' As children, he and his sister had been fascinated by the huge round room with the ribbed glass ceiling. Right up until his mother had caught them in there one day, staging a mock aerial war on a dozen vicious pumpkins. She'd had that place locked down so fast and put a guard detail on the passageway into it and that had been the end of his secret retreat. 'There's no modern heating, no electricity, and the water that used to run into the pools there has long since been diverted. The space is not fit for use.'

'The people of the High Reaches are not without resources,' said the elder stateswoman regally. 'It would be our honour to restore the living area to its former glory.'

They had an answer for everything. 'Don't get too comfortable,' he warned and looked towards his executive secretary. 'Let all bear witness that the terms of the accord have been satisfied. Let it also be recorded that my intention is to see the Lady Sera honourably discharged from her duty as quickly as possible. I'll find my own wife in my own good time and have no need of a concubine.' He was only thirty. Wasn't as if he was *that* remiss when it came to begetting an heir and securing the throne. His sister could rule if it ever came to that. Her children could rule, although her husband, Theo, would doubtless object. Neighbouring Liesendaach needed an heir too, perhaps even more so than Arun did. He nodded towards his secretary. 'Show them the hospitality they've requested.'

If the abandoned round room didn't make them flinch, nothing would.

The guards bowed and the women curtseyed, all of it effortlessly choreographed as they turned and swept from the room, leaving only silence behind. Silence and the lingering scent of violets.

Sera waited just outside the door for Lianthe to fall into step with her. Two guards and their guide up ahead and another guard behind them, a familiar routine in an unfamiliar place.

'That could have gone better,' Sera murmured.

'Insolent whelp,' said the older woman with enough bite to make the stone walls crumble.

'Me?'

'Him. No wonder he isn't wed.'

The King's secretary coughed, up ahead.

'Yes, it's extremely damp down here,' offered Lianthe. 'Although I dare say the rats enjoy it.'

'We're taking a short cut, milady. Largely unused,' the man offered. 'As for the rooms issued for the Lady Sera's use, I know not what to say. You'll find no comfort there. The palace has many other suites available for guests. You have but to ask for different quarters and they'll be provided.'

He opened a door and there was sunshine and a small walled courtyard stuffed with large pots of neatly kept kitchen herbs. Whoever tended this garden knew what they were about. Another door on the other side of the little courtyard plunged them into dankness once more before the corridor widened enough to allow for half a dozen people to walk comfortably side by side. At the end of the corridor stood a pair of huge doors wrought in black wood with iron hinges. Two thick wooden beams barred the door closed.

The old guide stood aside and looked to the High Reaches guards. 'Well? What are you waiting for?'

'*Very* welcoming,' murmured Sera as the guards pushed against the bindings and ancient wood and metal groaned. 'Perhaps some plinths and flowers either side might brighten this entrance hall? Discreet lighting. Scented roses.'

With another strangled cough from their guide, the bars slid to the side and the doors were pushed open. A soaring glass-domed space the size of a cathedral apse greeted them, encircled by grey marble columns and shadowy alcoves. What furniture remained lay shrouded beneath dust sheets and if rugs had once graced the vast expanse of grey stone floor they certainly weren't in evidence now. Dust motes danced in the air at the disturbance from the opening of the doors, and was that a dovecote in one of the alcoves or a postbox for fifty? Another alcove contained the bathing pool, empty but for dirt, but the plumbing had worked once and would work again—it was her job to see to it. There were faded frescoes on the walls and a second floor with a cloistered walkway that looked down on the central area. Chandeliers still hung in place, struggling to shine beneath decades of dust. There was even a circus trapeze roped carelessly to a tiny balcony set one floor above the rest. Illustrations in the journals of the courtesans of old had not done the place justice.

'Well, now.' Sera sent a fleeting smile in Lianthe's direction. 'Nothing like a challenge.'

The older woman nodded and turned to their guide. 'Can you offer us cleaners?' The man looked unsure. 'No? Then we shall invite our own, and tradespeople too. I suppose we should thank the monarchy for preserving the space in all its historical glory. At least there are no rats.'

'And I think I know why.' Sera stared up at the domed glass ceiling to where several lumpy shapes sat, nestled into the framework. 'Are they owls?'

Lianthe looked up and smiled. 'Why, yes. A good omen, don't you think? Would you like to keep them?'

'Depends on the rats.' Call her difficult but if the rats were gone Sera was all for providing alternative living space—and hunting options—for the raptors. 'We may need the assistance of a falconer. I don't suppose King Augustus keeps one of those any more either?'

'No, Lady Sera. But King Casimir of Byzenmaach does,' said their guide.

'Ah, yes.' Lianthe nodded. 'The falconers of Byzenmaach are men of legend and steeped in the old ways. Tomas-the-Tongue-Tied is head falconer there these days is he not? How is the boy?'

'Grown, milady, although still somewhat tongue-tied,' said the old guide and won a rare smile from Lianthe. 'But ever devoted to his winged beasts. If you need him here, we can get him here.'

'Wonderful,' said Sera. Eyes on the prize, or, in this case, the speedy removal of hunting birds from her future living quarters. 'Let's aim for that. Unless by "Don't get too comfortable" King Augustus meant for me to sleep with the wildlife? Perhaps I should go back and ask.'

'You must definitely ask,' said Lianthe.

It was decided. Sera shed her travelling cloak and watched the old courtier blink and then raise his hand as if to shade his eyes from the glare. Granted her dainty six-inch heels were a burnt orange colour and her slimline ankle-length trousers were only one shade darker, but her tunic was a meek ivory chiffon and the gold metal bustier beneath it covered far more than usual and ran all the way up and around her neck.

'Something wrong?' she asked the old guide.

'Headache,' he said, and touched two fingers to his temple.

'I know massage techniques for that,' she began. 'Very effective. Would you like me to—'

'*No*, milady. No! You just…' He waved his arm in the air ineffectually. 'Go and see Augustus. The King. King Augustus.'

'I know who you mean,' she said gently, sharing a concerned glance with Lianthe. 'Are you quite well? I'd offer you a seat if I could find one. Or a drink. Would you like me to call for water?'

'No, milady. I'm quite recovered.'

But he still looked painfully pinched and long-suffering. 'Is it the jewels? Because the bustier isn't quite my normal attire. It's part of the courtesan's chest.'

'It certainly seems that way, milady. I must confess, I wasn't expecting the bejewelled wrist and ankle cuffs either.'

Ah. 'Well, they are very beautiful. And surprisingly light given all the bronze and amber inlays and gold filigree. There are chains to go with them,' she said.

'Of course there are.' The man's fingers went to massage his temple again.

'Will I find the King in the same place we left him?' asked Sera, because sometimes it paid to be practical.

'He may be back in his office by now. Two doors to the left of the room you met him in. The outer area houses the secretary's desk. The secretary's not there because that would be me and I am here. The inner room is his, and the door to it may or may not be open. Either way, knock.'

Sera found the King exactly where the old courtier said he would be; the door through to his office was open and she paused to check her posture before knocking gently on the door frame. He lifted his gaze from the papers on the big black table in front of him and blinked. And blinked again.

She curtseyed again, all but kissing the floor, because this man was her King and protocol demanded it.

'Up,' he said, with a slight tinge of weariness. 'What is it?'

Not *Come in*, so she stayed in the doorway. 'I want to invite Tomas the Byzenmaach falconer to call on me.'

'Tired of me already?' He arched an eyebrow, even as he studied her intently, starting with her shoes and seeming to get stuck in the general vicinity of her chest. The golden bustier was quite arresting but not the most comfortable item of clothing she owned. 'That was quick.'

'I need him here so he can remove the raptors from my quarters.'

'Raptors as in dinosaurs? Because it's been that kind of day.'

'Raptors as in owls.'

'I'm almost disappointed,' he said, and there was humour in him, sharp and slippery. 'What is that you're wearing, exactly? Apart from the clothes. Which I appreciate, by the way. Clothes are useful. You'll get cold here if you don't wear more of them.'

'You mean the jewellery? Your secretary seemed very taken by it as well. It's ceremonial, for the most part, although practical too.'

'Practical?'

'D-rings and everything.' She held up one wrist and showed him the loop and then pointed to another where the bustier came together at the back of her neck. 'So do I have your permission to call in the falconer?'

'Is this a plea for different living quarters? Because I'm being as clear as I can be here. I don't want to give you *any* quarters, but, given that I *must*, you are welcome to more suitable living arrangements than the ones you have requested. I would not deny you that.'

'It's not a plea for new quarters.' He tested her patience, this King with the giant stick up his rear. 'And, yes, you're being very clear. Perhaps I should be equally clear.' Save herself a few meetings with him in the process. 'I want your permission to clean and ready my living quarters for use. I will call in experts, when necessary. I will see the courtesan's lodgings restored and it will cost you and the palace nothing. I will take all care to preserve the history of the rooms—more care than you or your people would. I will submit names, on a daily basis, of each and every craftsperson or cleaning person that I bring in. By your leave, and provided I have free rein to do so, I can have those rooms fit to live in within a week. Do I have your permission?'

'You argue like a politician. All fine words, sketchy rationale and promises you'll never keep.'

'I'll keep this promise, Your Majesty. Consider this a test if you need a reason to say yes.'

'And when you leave again? What happens to all these home improvements then?'

'I expect the next courtesan will benefit from them.'

'Sera.' He spoke quietly but with an authority that ran bone-deep, and it got to her in a way the authority of her teachers never had. 'There's not going to be another courtesan delivered to a King of Arun. This I promise.'

'Then turn the place into a museum,' she snapped, defiant in the face of extinction. 'You don't value me. I get it. You don't need my help, you don't want my help, and you don't understand the *backing* you've just been blessed with. So be it. Meanwhile, we're both bound by tradition and moreover I have dues to pay. Do I have your permission to engage the help I need to make my living quarters habitable?'

'And here I thought courtesans were meant to be compliant.'

'I am compliant.' She could be so meekly compliant

his head would spin. 'I can be whatever you want me to be. All I need is direction.'

His face did not betray his thoughts. Not by the flicker of an eye or the twitching of a muscle.

'You have my permission to make your living quarters habitable,' he said finally. 'And Sera?'

She waited.

'Don't ever walk the halls of my palace in your ancient slave uniform again.'

The King's secretary had gone by the time Sera arrived back in the quarters she'd claimed as her own. She held her head high as she entered, never mind that the chill in the air and the ice in the King's eyes had turned her skin to gooseflesh. She wouldn't cry, she never had—not even at her mother's funeral—but the gigantic task of readying this space for use and earning Augustus of Arun's trust, and, yes, finding him a wife, was daunting enough to make her smile falter and her shoulders droop as she stared around at her new home.

Lianthe and the guards had already begun pulling covers off the furnishings and for that she would be grateful. She wasn't alone in this. Other people had faith in her abilities.

'I've already sent for cleaning equipment and linens,' Lianthe said when she saw her. 'Did you find him again?'

'I did.'

'And?'

'He's a funny guy. He's also hard as nails underneath, doesn't like not getting his own way and he's going to be hell on my sense of self-worth.'

'We knew this wasn't going to be an easy sell. I'm

sure you'll come to a greater understanding of each other eventually.'

'I'm glad someone's sure,' she murmured.

'And what did he have to say about securing a falconer to help get rid of our feathered friends?'

'Oh, that?' She'd forgotten about that. 'He said yes.'

CHAPTER TWO

SIX DAYS LATER, Augustus was no closer to a solution when it came to removing his unwanted gift from the palace. He'd kept his distance, stuck to his routine and tried to stay immune to the whispers of the staff as word got around that the palace's pleasure rooms were being refurbished. Ladies Sera and Lianthe had engaged cleaning staff and craftspeople to help with the repairs. Stonemasons had been brought in. Electricity had been restored. Structural engineers had been and gone, proclaiming the glass-domed roof still fit for purpose, with only minor repair required.

Tomas the falconer had come for the owls and brought King Casimir of Byzenmaach's sister Claudia with him. Apparently Sera and Claudia had gone to school together. Sera had prepared a lavish dinner for them that had gone on for hours. They'd caught up on each other's lives. Swapped stories. Augustus had been invited.

He hadn't attended.

Whispers turned into rumours, each one more fanciful than the rest.

The Lady Sera was a sorceress, a witch, an enchantress and his apparent downfall. Her eyes were, variously, the softest dove-grey and as kind as an angel's or as bleak as the winter sky and hard as stone. She and her guards danced with swords beneath the dome, and splattered reflected sunlight across the walls with uncanny precision, so the cleaners said. She'd had the trapeze taken down only to replace it with another, and this time the trapeze fluttered with silks that fell to the floor, his secretary told him.

Silks she climbed up and down as if they were steps.

Yesterday, a convoy of heavily guarded trucks had arrived from the north and requested entry, sending palace security into a spin and Augustus into a rare temper. *Don't get too comfortable*, he'd said. He would find a way to undo this, he'd said. They *knew* he was working on it. They had no need for deliveries full of priceless artworks only ever revealed when a courtesan of the High Reaches was in residence at the palace.

Even the palace *walls* were buzzing.

Augustus's father, former King and still an advisor to the throne, had been no help. He'd been married with two young children by the time he'd reached thirty and no courtesan of the High Reaches had ever come to him. There was no *precedent* for getting rid of one that didn't directly relate to the rules of the accord. A courtesan, once bestowed, could be removed once a wife and heir had been secured and not before. She could be sent elsewhere at the King's bidding but would still retain full ownership...no, not ownership, access...full access to her quarters in the palace.

She had the right to refuse entrance to all but him. She had the right to entertain there but the guest list had to be approved by him. He'd asked for more details when it came to Sera Boreas's background and education and an information file had landed on his desk this morning. She'd studied philosophy, politics and economics at Oxford. She'd taken music lessons in St Petersburg. Dance lessons with members of the National Ballet company of China. Learned martial arts from the monks of the High Reaches. Her origins were shrouded in mystery. Her mother had kept the company of high ranking politicians and dignitaries the world over. Her mother had been a companion, a facilitator, often providing neutral ground where those from opposing political persuasions could meet. Lianthe of the High Reaches might just be her grandmother but that had yet to be verified. The more he read, the less real she became to him.

For all her contacts and endless qualifications, he still didn't know what she *did* except in the vaguest terms.

In the last year alone, and as the youngest representative of the Order of the Kite, she'd graced the dining tables of dozens of world leaders and people of influence. Her reach was truly astonishing.

And he was currently keeping her in the equivalent of his basement.

He needed to talk with her at the very least.

And damn but he needed another woman's opinion.

And then his intercom flashed.

'Your sister's on the phone,' his well-worn secretary said.

'Put her through,' he murmured. Problem solved.

'Augustus, I know you're pining for me, but did you seriously buy a cat?'

'I—what?' Not exactly where his head had been at. Augustus scowled, and not just because his sister's recent marriage had left his palace without a social organiser and him with no clue as to how to find a replacement equally dedicated to the role. 'Who told you that? Theo?'

'He told me I needed to phone you because he'd heard rumours you were all lonely and had acquired a pet. He also mentioned something about a cat. Is it fluffy? Does it pounce? Has it conquered cucumbers yet?'

Theo, King of Liesendaach and neighbouring monarch, was Moriana's new husband. Theo, King of sly manoeuvres, knew exactly what kind of cat Augustus had bought. 'Moriana, let's get something clear. I am not a lonely cat king. I bought a catamaran. An ocean-going, racing catamaran.'

'Ah,' she said. 'Figures. In that case, I have no idea why Theo was so insistent I phone you this morning. We've just returned from visiting Cas and Ana in the Byzenmaach mountains and, by the way, I will *never* tire of the views from that stronghold. More to the point, I got on well with Cas's new bride and his newfound daughter. There's hope for me yet. They did ask me why they hadn't received an invite to your Winter Solstice ball. Strangely, I haven't received my invitation yet either. I left very comprehensive instructions.'

Moriana was the Queen of Checklists. He had no doubt there would be a binder full of colour-coded instructions sitting on a table somewhere. 'Why isn't Marguerite on top of this?' his sister scolded.

'She didn't work out.'

Silence from his sister, the kind of silence that meant she was valiantly trying to keep her opinions to herself. He gave it three, two, one…

'Augustus, you can't keep firing social secretaries after they've been in the role for two weeks!'

'I can if they're selling palace information to the press,' he said grimly.

'Oh.'

'Yes. Oh. There's a new assistant starting Monday. Meanwhile, what do you know about the Order of the Kite?'

'You mean the courtesans?'

'So you do know something about them.'

'I know they existed centuries ago. They were kept in our round room. Like pets.' Moriana paused, and Augustus waited for her to put Theo's comment about him having a pet together with his question and come up with a clue, but she didn't. 'There are some costumes in the collection here that were reputedly worn by them.' Moriana was warming to her theme. 'Gorgeous things. I wouldn't call them gowns exactly—more like adventurous bedwear. The leather one came with a collection of whips.'

'Whips.' No guesses needed as to how some of those courtesans of old acquired their exalted levels of influence. Augustus put two fingers to his temple and closed his eyes, a habit he'd picked up from his secretary, or maybe the old man had picked it up from him. 'So what else do you know about them? Anything from this day and age?'

'These days they're the stuff of legend. There's a children's book in the nursery about them, assuming it's still there. Seven-year-old girl, clever and pretty, gets ripped from the arms of her unloving family and taken to a palace in the sky to learn how to dance and fight and be a spy. Then she meets a King from the Lower

Reaches and spies for him and he falls in love with her and they live happily ever after. Ignore the bit where she poisons his barren wife. You should never believe everything you read.'

'Does this book have a name?'

'*The King's Assassin.* It was one of my favourites. Why?'

No one had ever read it to *him*. 'I currently have the Lady Sera Boreas, daughter of Yuna, Order of the Kite, staying in the round room. She arrived last week, as a *gift* from the people of the High Reaches.'

Silence from Moriana the Red, whose temper, once roused, was also the stuff of legend, and then, 'Say that again?'

'There is a courtesan here in the palace and at my service. Yesterday, six truckloads of priceless antiquities turned up. They belong to the Order of the Kite and can only be seen when a courtesan is in residence here. *Now* do I have your attention?'

'Did you say *priceless antiquities*?'

'*Focus*, Moriana. There is a pet concubine in the round room. No—did you just squeal? Don't squeal. Invite her to stay with you. Keep her. Show her the whips. No! Don't show her the whips. I take that back. But find out what she's doing here. Can you do that?'

'Does she have books?' his sister asked. 'I bet she has history books with her as well. Do you know what this means?'

It probably meant Moriana was about to try and organise an exhibition of antiquities native to courtesans. 'It means I have a problem that I don't know how to solve yet. What exactly am I supposed to do with this woman?'

'Is she beautiful? They were reputedly all rare beauties.'

'That bit's true.'

'Is she smart?'

'I would say so, yes. Also cunning and completely unfathomable.' Keeping her distance and rousing his curiosity, making her presence felt all the more keenly by the simple act of staying out of his way. 'I need you to come here and see what she wants. Befriend her. Gain her confidence. Tell me what she wants.'

'I can be there in a week.'

'I meant today,' he countered.

'Can't. I have a luncheon at twelve, a charity meeting at two, hospital tour at three and then I'm having a private dinner with my beloved husband who I've barely seen all week.'

'Absence makes the heart grow fonder. I'll send the helicopter for you.'

'Or you could talk to her yourself and find out exactly what this woman can do for you. Can she act as a social secretary, for example? Can she organise the Winter Solstice ball? Courtesans of old were muses, strategists, women of great influence. Think Madame de Pompadour or Theodora from the Byzantine empire. She might be one of those. Give her something to do. Apart from you, obviously.'

'She is not doing me,' he ground out.

'Has she offered?'

She'd arrived wearing a collar and manacles, amongst other things. She'd called herself a courtesan and then she'd ignored him. 'Who the hell knows?'

'Do you—okay, you know what? Never mind, because there are some things sisters simply shouldn't know. Give her the Winter Solstice ball to oversee. I'm serious. Put her to work. See if she truly wants to be of use to you.'

'I'd rather she left.'

'But why? You need a social secretary who wants to do a good job and isn't inclined to sell us out. Talk to her. See what she wants from her role and from you. Your goals might align.'

'What if she doesn't want to be here at all?'

'Then you'll work together to find a way out of this. But not before I've seen all the art and persuaded her to let us photograph and document it, where possible. I can't wait to see it.'

Augustus sighed. Theo really was a bad influence on his sister, who'd once dutifully dedicated herself to serving the Arunian monarchy. These days she shone a light on the already glittering Liesendaach crown and Augustus sorely missed her attention. He did need someone to replace his sister. Someone with a personal stake in taking on the role and making it their own. A wife… he'd been thinking of it. Not doing anything about it, mind, but thinking that soon he would start looking in earnest. Meanwhile, he had a…courtesan…at his disposal. Whatever that meant. Maybe they could renegotiate her job description.

'All right.' There was nothing else for it. 'I'll talk to her.'

It took until mid-afternoon before Augustus made his way to the round room in search of the elusive Sera of the High Reaches. Ignoring her presence and hoping she'd miraculously go away wasn't working for him. Answers on how best to get rid of her were not forthcoming. Moriana thought she might be of use to him and he trusted his sister's judgement in most things. Sera's CV would make any power broker salivate. To have those kind of contacts at his disposal...

And yet he wasn't the type to share power and he didn't trust her motivations one little bit.

So here he was, foul of temper and distinctly lacking in patience as he stood at the closed doors to the round room and eyed the profusion of damask roses and soft greenery with distaste, even as the scent of them conjured memories of cloistered gardens and all things feminine. His mother had enjoyed overseeing the floral arrangements throughout the palace, but she'd not have allowed this flat-out challenge to grim austerity. This tease to stop and sniff and feast the eyes on such unrepentantly fleeting beauty.

With one last scathing glare, Augustus stood firm against the temptation to lean forward and let the scent of the roses envelop him. Instead, he pulled the dangling cord that would announce his arrival at the doors. He heard the faint chime of bells and then nothing. Ten seconds later, he reached for the cord again, and then the door opened and the roses were forgotten.

Never mind the creamy skin and the perfection of her lips, the delicate curve of her cheekbones, the raven-black hair that fell in a thick plait to her waist or those eyes that glistened dove-grey. Today his courtesan wore low-slung loose trousers and a cropped fitted top that clung to her curves like a greedy lover's hand. She was lean and lithe in all the right places, and generously voluptuous in others.

It was a body designed to bring a man to his knees and keep him there for eternity.

She stepped back and dropped her gaze demurely, even as she opened the door wider and sank to the floor in a curtsey, and he might have felt a heel for causing such an action except that she moved like a dancer, fluid and graceful, and he wanted to watch her do it all over again.

'Don't do that.' It was a curt reminder, mostly to himself, that she shouldn't be on her knees in front of him. It gave him too many ideas, all of them sexual.

'My mistake.' She rose as gracefully as she'd gone down in the first place. 'Welcome, Your Majesty. Please forgive my appearance. I wasn't expecting company.'

'What were you doing?' Her skin glowed with a faint sheen of exertion.

'Forms,' she said. 'Martial arts patterns.'

'Don't stop on my account.'

'I can do them any time,' she murmured. 'I'd rather have company.'

He looked around, taking in the now spotless round room, its stone walls and floors covered in tapestries and carpets, oil paintings and silver-edged mirrors. A huge round sofa had been placed in the centre of the room, beneath the domed glass ceiling. The seats faced inwards and there were openings at all four points of the compass. 'Where is everyone?'

'The tradespeople and artisans have gone and the Lady Lianthe with them. My guards are currently in a meeting with your guards about how best to utilise their services, given that standing outside a door that no one ever knocks on is a waste of their time and expertise. The maids have been and gone. There is only me.'

Holding her own in a round room built for hundreds

to gather in and bedrooms enough for fifty. 'It's you I've come to see.'

She turned her back on him and led him towards the sofa at the centre of the room. It was leather and studded and looked comfortably soft with age. Pillows and throws had been placed on it at intervals, and the circular floor tapestry framed by the sofa had a stained-glass quality about it, with different scenes to look at depending on where a person sat. 'What is that?'

'On the floor?'

He nodded.

'It's a communication device. Each scene depicts an action: a need or desire, if you will. In older times a visitor to this place—or even another courtesan—would approach this area and in choosing where to sit would telegraph their needs. Those needs would be seen to.'

'Just like that?'

'So they say.'

'And is that the way it's going to work for me?'

'Why don't you sit somewhere and see?'

'Maybe I will.' Maybe he wouldn't. Better all round if he didn't engage, no matter how fascinating the history she brought with her. 'I've been trying to get rid of you.'

'I know that, Your Majesty.' She glanced towards the tapestry. 'Take your time looking at it. Even if you don't plan to use it as directed it's an amazing piece of artistry. I'll make tea.'

He watched as she walked away from him, tracking every curve as if it would somehow allow him to see inside her skin. Only once she had withdrawn from sight did he turn his attention back to the mood-gauging tapestry on the floor in front of him. He'd never seen such a thing.

Some of the panels were easy enough to figure out. There was an orgy scene, with bodies entwined in the throes of ecstasy. A gentler scene in which a man reclined while a woman read to him. Another scene depicted people eating from a table covered in delicacies. A bathing scene. A sword-fighting scene. Another showing a reclining man being entertained by dancers holding fans. A dozen men and women stood around a table, deep in sombre discussion. A sleeping couple filled another panel. With every step another mood or need satisfied. A man lashed to a wooden X, his back a mass of welts as he writhed beneath the whip. A beautiful woman holding that whip, her expression one of complete control and focus. Punishment delivered, but not in anger, and the man on the cross looked…grateful.

His courtesan had returned with tea; he could hear her off to one side and see her in his peripheral vision.

'You do all this?' he asked, keeping his gaze fixed on the whipping scene. 'Put a man to the lash and strip the guilt from his soul before putting him back together again?' The next scene showed the same woman tending the man's wounds.

'I've been trained to, yes.' She approached from his left and held out a porcelain cup filled with pale amber tea. 'Will you sit?'

He took the tea and let his fingers brush hers. She stilled, and so did he.

He didn't believe in instant attraction. He'd never been a slave to his body's baser demands. But if one tiny touch could send this much heat and awareness coursing through him, imagine what she could do with full body contact?

'It's a trap,' he said at last.

'How so?' Her gaze was steady, her features as smooth as marble.

He gestured towards the depictions of service laid out before him, and it was all very tempting, except that beneath the surface pleasures lay a darker truth altogether. Mind, body and soul. She wasn't here to serve. She was here to own him. 'What wife could ever compete if I had this at my disposal? Where else would I go but here, where every whim would be served up to me on a gilded plate? By the time I'd satisfied every corrupt thought lying dormant in my soul it would be too late for either of us to escape. I'd *own* you, in ways you've never dreamed of. And you'd own me.'

'Well, that's one interpretation,' she said. 'There are others.'

'Tell me some others.'

'Ignore the sexual element and take advantage of my political prowess instead. Arun is a stabilising force in this region. Many would like to keep it that way, including those I answer to. Including you.'

'Am I not doing that already?' Because he thought he was.

'Your plans to unify water resources across four neighbouring nations haven't gone unnoticed. This region will grow to become a power bloc—provided you can hold it together.'

He had Theo, Casimir and Valentine right there with him, a shared vision for their region. 'I can hold it together.'

'Indeed, we think so,' she said. 'But who will explain your ambitions to a wider world that might fear such a power shift?'

'And I suppose you can help me there.'

She couldn't fail to pick up on the sarcasm in his voice but she paid no heed to it. 'The Order of the Kite has contacts you don't yet have. I can make introductions, facilitate communication channels that you will then keep open when I leave.'

'And what's in it for you?'

A tiny smile graced her lips. 'World peace?'

'You're a saint,' he said. 'But I still want to know—what's in it for you personally? I don't understand why a modern-minded woman with your kind of looks and education would choose such a role. I don't know what your angle is. Do you want to marry a man of power and gain power and status through him? What happens after me? Do they send you onto the next visionary King in need? And the next after that?'

'I only need to do this once,' she replied quietly. 'I serve you until you release me, at which point my debt will have been repaid. Then I'm free to choose my own way.'

'What debt?'

'The Order cared for my mother through a long and arduous decline and she died with peace and dignity. They saved me from a life in the gutter.'

'And how old were you when this happened?'

'Does that matter? Others turned away from us. They didn't.'

'It matters.'

A small frown appeared between her eyes. 'I was seven.'

Seven years old and taken and trained and made to

feel beholden to her rescuers. 'So basically you've had no choice but to do what they ask of you.'

'Have you ever had a choice but to serve the monarchy?' she asked, and he glared at her. 'I think not. We are not so different, you and I. You were born into service. In a way, so was I.'

Except that for her it wasn't a lifetime commitment. 'I'm releasing you from your duty. Soon as I can.'

She nodded. 'I'd like that. But at least make use of me first.'

His gaze slid to that cursed wheel of desire on the floor.

'You don't have to take advantage of all that's on offer.' She barely knew him and already she was reading him like a book. That didn't happen to Augustus. Ever. 'But you could take advantage of some of it without surrendering your mortal soul.'

'There's an opening on my staff for a social secretary. I need someone to organise a ball and other smaller events.' He handed the teacup back to her, still full. Not a drop had passed his lips. 'Can we start with that?'

Sera nodded as she set the tea aside. 'Of course.'

'I think fixed boundaries between us would be best. Meanwhile, is there something I can do to make your stay here more comfortable? Anything you need that you haven't already seen to?' She wasn't a sorceress. He wasn't a lovesick fool, but he could still offer common courtesy.

'If you and I are to be observing fixed boundaries, there is something I'd like to discuss.'

He waited.

It was the first time he'd ever seen her looking nervous.

'Am I free to seek sexual satisfaction elsewhere?'

Continued silence was often a tactic he used to force the other person to speak. This time, pure shock stilled his lips.

Sera of the High Reaches squared her delicate shoulders and fixed him with pleading kitten eyes. 'I've never truly been intimate with another person. That was reserved for you. I'd be lying if I said I wasn't looking forward to it. And seeing you're not of a mind to…'

He wasn't a complete stranger to women becoming impatient for sexual experience. His sister, dear Lord, had been quite adamant about partying up a storm at one point. But not under his roof, and she'd never actually gone through with it. Theo had seen to that, with Augustus's full blessing. Now this.

'You're a *virgin* courtesan?'

'Yes. Do you seriously think they would send someone *used*?'

'Oh, pardon my ignorance. Forgive me that I assumed some small measure of *experience* from a trained *courtesan*!' Never mind the beast in his belly that flicked a scaly tail and roared because she'd been kept pure so that *he* could be her teacher. It wasn't *right* for him to want that, and it certainly wasn't right that she'd had no say in her own sexual enlightenment.

He had a courtesan. A virgin courtesan. Standing there beneath the dome, her midriff bare, hair pulled back and no make-up on her face. 'Do you have someone in mind to be intimate with?'

He had the sudden reckless desire to strangle them.

'I had you in mind,' she said as her gaze briefly dropped to his lips. 'I do know what to do in theory.'

'Theory isn't *doing*. What if I wanted to use you roughly? Tie you down, take away all your control and self-respect and make you beg for release? Take away your ability to reason? Take every slight ever dealt me and transfer them to your flesh? Did your illustrious tutors ever teach you how to deal with sadistic madmen?'

She had no answer for him.

'You know *nothing*,' he challenged.

Her first kiss was his if he wanted it, not to mention the second. All of it. He headed for the door before he lost his mind and took what she offered so freely. He had his hand on the door before something made him look back. She'd fallen to a curtsey facing him and the door, her body placed right in the centre of that cursed carpet depicting every sin and pleasure known to man.

'Get up.' He didn't want this. He didn't dare take it. 'Come here.'

He waited until she stood before him, her eyes betraying uncertainty as he leaned down until their lips almost touched. 'Lord knows I didn't ask for you, but you've come here labelled as *my* courtesan and I will cut the hand off anyone who touches you. No kissing. No sex. No flirting with any of my employees. Are we clear?'

'Clear. Very clear,' she whispered with a tell-tale tremor in her voice. He was scaring her.

And then he got caught in the whirling vortex of her expressive grey eyes, and maybe he wasn't scaring her at all. Because that look right there looked a whole lot like surrender.

'Do the work I ask of you,' he grated. 'Put me in contact with the power brokers you think I need to cultivate. Find me a suitable wife if you can.' He could claim those perfect lips if he wanted to, tease the bow of the upper one with the tip of his tongue, slide in easy and experienced and lay her mouth to waste. She wasn't unwilling. She definitely wasn't unwilling.

'Above all...don't tempt me.'

Sera shut the door behind him and leaned against it, still reeling beneath the weight of his words and that brief brush of his lips against hers. It had barely qualified as a kiss but she could still feel the burn of his palm against her chin and the rough stroke of his thumb against her cheekbone. His breath caressing her lips and the swift charge of desire when their eyes caught and held.

She'd wanted him to kiss her properly. Lay claim or lay to waste; either would have been acceptable. She slid to the floor, both hands between her legs, pressing down hard against the feelings he'd ignited inside her. She was so ready for a physical awakening. All the theory in the world and exploration with her own hands could only get her so far. She wanted *his* hands where her hands were, driving her higher until she broke all over him.

It wouldn't have to be all give on her part and all take on his, even if she did want to read and respond to every nuanced muscle twitch he made. She *had* been trained to please, no matter what he might think. The physical arrangement between courtesan and King didn't have to be the bad thing he was making it out to be. Did it?

Closing her eyes, she pressed up into her hand, seeking release, sharp and swift, as she allowed herself to imagine his kiss. Not the tease he'd left her with.

A proper kiss.

She ran her tongue over the spot where his lips had just been and came moments later, imagining it.

CHAPTER THREE

IT TOOK SERA two days to organise the midwinter ball. The guest list had already been prepared by Moriana, formerly of Arun and now Queen Consort to the King of Liesendaach. Her Royal Highness Moriana had returned Sera's call promptly and approved the additional guests Sera had put forward for the express purpose of finding Augustus a wife. Invitations had gone out. The palace staff were happy for someone—anyone—to take the helm and direct the preparations. The ball was an annual event and they were well trained and competent.

After that, there was a dinner for twelve to organise, and then an informal supper for thirty in one of the smaller palace libraries. Moriana had phoned Sera about the library event guest list several times already and once to discuss what books would go on display in the library given the handful of historians on the guest list. Moriana had asked if there were any books belonging to the courtesans of the High Reaches that Sera could put on display.

At that, Sera had hesitated. Some books could be displayed without controversy, but not all. The journals of the courtesans of old were fascinating, but they weren't for public viewing.

Augustus had not been back. No other visitors had called on her and her guards had been incorporated into the regular ranks of the palace, although she still met with them for morning exercise. They met in the horse yard behind the stables, where the sawdust on the ground was sweet and soft. They'd thought it out of the way enough that they wouldn't bother anyone. Three days in and already they had a growing audience for the martial arts patterns they completed in unison and the sparring that came afterwards. Give it another week and the requests for lessons would start. She could see the hunger for more in the eyes of those watching. The curiosity, reluctant admiration, and sometimes the heat.

Always the heat.

Aware of the restlessness riding her, Sera pushed her body hard during morning exercise, as comfortable as she could be with the hot eyes of the crowd, the sun weak and watery and a chill in the air that reminded her of the mountains.

When she met the ground for the third time because of inattention, Ari, the guardsman who'd put her there, stepped back and disengaged from their sparring. She wasn't easy to take down, and this time the kick to her sternum would have broken bones if she hadn't deflected the blow at the last minute. Ari had expected far better from her. She wasn't concentrating.

She lay there, eyes closed and reluctant to take a breath because when she did it was going to hurt. She felt rather than saw someone crouch down beside her and, quick as a snake, she clamped her hand around their wrist as they went to touch her torso.

'Easy.'

She opened her eyes to slits and studied the forearm

she'd captured. It was tanned and corded with muscle, the hand looked strong and the fingernails blunt. She looked for a face to match the hand but the sun was directly in her line of sight. It wouldn't be Ari or Tun; they knew better than to offer to help her up. It might be someone from the audience who didn't understand the limits she lived by.

She moved just enough to let the man's body block the sun, the better to see his face.

Augustus.

She took in a breath and pain didn't slice at her. She eased into a sitting position and didn't pass out. Good news.

'You went down pretty hard,' he said gruffly.

'My own fault,' she murmured, and let go of his arm. He had the right to touch her. She could not refuse.

He stood and held out his hand and slowly, carefully, she put her hand in his and let him help her up.

His hand was more calloused than she'd been expecting from a man who did no physical work. Her hand looked tiny clasped in his. His dark eyes showed no emotion.

'Why are you here?' she asked.

'I live here. And when rumour reaches me that half my security force is turning up on their days off to watch the northerners beat the living daylights out of each other I get curious.'

Fair enough. She took back her hand and spared a glance for her guards. Only two were here with her; the third was on duty. Neither stepped forward, although Ari's fingers flickered a message that hopefully only she could read. Had he injured her?

No.

A silent conversation, meant to set her guardsman at ease.

He didn't seem convinced.

'What may we do for you, Your Majesty?'

'Find somewhere else to practise, for starters. You have half my men-at-arms gagging for a glimpse of you. The other half have already seen you fight and now have a new erotic fantasy to be going on with.'

He wasn't being fair. 'Sawdust is soft and the floors in my quarters are too hard for serious sparring. Where else might we practise? We are also open to teaching those of your court who wish to learn the forms and uses they might be put to. Ari is a master. Tun a champion who will soon retreat to the mountains for his final year of meditation before he too becomes a high practitioner of the art.'

'What grade do you hold?'

'I hold my own.'

'You didn't today.'

'I lost focus. If there's some other place you'd rather we practise we'll take it, Your Majesty. We practise daily, together and alone. It's not just exercise. It's a way of life for those who guard the temples of the High Reaches. It's contact and communication. Learning how to read a person's movements. It's non-sexual. Instructional. There's no harm in it,' she said in the face of his continued silence.

He gave Tun and Ari a glare far sharper than any knife. 'Then why are you hurt?'

'I'm wiser in the face of Ari's takedown. It won't happen again.'

'What did the older one say to you with his sign language?'

She hadn't thought he'd been in any position to see that. 'He wanted to know if I was injured.'

'He could have asked.'

'You were there and seeing to me. Discretion was best.'

'Tell them not to use sign language again in front of my men. It breeds suspicion and there's already far too much of that around here because of you and the old ways you've brought with you.'

It was true; the people here continued to see her as *other*. 'People fear what they don't understand.'

'They also fear rare beauty, overt displays of power and influence and those who never stay down, even when beaten. Especially when beaten. Tone it down, Sera, or I'll shut you in your room full of temptation and beautiful things and leave you there.'

'I'm never going to please you, am I? You give me functions to organise and I organise them. I come meekly when called. I've stacked the midwinter ball full of accomplished single women for you to meet. I've set up introductions with people of influence. What else do you want?'

'I want sweet dreams,' he grated. 'I'd prefer them not to be about you. My sister has just flown in. She says she's already been in contact with you by phone. She wants to meet you.'

Sera wasn't ready for guests, sweaty and aching as she was. She wanted to ask more about his dreams. 'I'll need half an hour before I'm properly presentable.'

'You don't have it,' he said, and opened a half-hidden door in the castle wall. 'After you.'

She had sawdust in her hair and on her sleeve and down the leg of her loose cotton trousers. 'Are you always this petty?' she asked, and watched his eyes narrow.

'It's an impromptu visit and my sister schedules herself so tightly that she never has much time,' he countered. 'Believe me, I like spontaneity less than you do but she's here now and you look fine as you are. Through this door and keep walking for a minute or two. After you.'

She stepped inside and kept to a brisk pace. The corridor was narrow but well lit. The next door he bade her to walk through opened into a large sitting room with a wall full of windows overlooking palace gardens. An elegant woman in a tangerine sundress rose from a chair as they entered. Sera took note of her poise and careful smile before dropping to the floor in a curtsey, suddenly light-headed at the piercing pain coming from somewhere near her ribs. Maybe she had taken some damage after all.

'Moriana, meet Lady Sera, Courtesan of the High Reaches,' Augustus said from somewhere beside her. 'Sera, get up.'

'Augustus, she's not a hound,' Moriana protested.

'If I don't tell her to get up she stays down.' Augustus scowled as he bent forward and curled his hand around her upper arm and drew her to her feet. 'You *are* injured. Don't lie to me again.'

'I'm okay.' If he would stop looking at her as if she were a stain on his shoe she might feel less dizzy and disoriented.

'Have I caught you at a bad time?' his elegant, well-mannered sister asked as Sera swayed and tried to find her centre and her balance. Augustus's hand tightened vicelike around her arm. 'I hope Augustus hasn't had you cleaning out the stables.'

'No, Your Highness.'

'I found her engaged in hand-to-hand combat with two of her guards.'

'For exercise,' Sera stressed.

'Find another form of exercise.' His eyes burned black.

'I've been doing martial arts for fifteen years. If you tell me to give it up I will because I'm duty bound to obey you, so here's a thought. Don't ask me to.'

The quiet clearing of a throat reminded Sera that they weren't alone and she bowed her head in shame. She wasn't presentable or amiable enough for guests. 'I can do better,' she offered quietly, and it was a blanket statement that covered a multitude of sins. 'I will do better.'

'Oh, for f—I'm trying to *protect* you.' He turned to his sister. 'She's here. She's all yours. I have other things to do. If she collapses, leave her where she falls.'

'Augustus!'

Sera watched from beneath lowered lashes as Augustus stalked from the room, leaving thick silence behind him and no even ground to stand on.

'Well, that was…unexpected,' the King's sister said with no little bemusement. 'What *have* you done with my courteous, by-the-book brother?'

'Barely anything.' And wasn't that the truth. 'He doesn't want me here, Your Highness. That's all.' It underscored their every interaction.

'And how old are you?' Augustus's sister asked next.

'Twenty-three.'

'You look about sixteen. Maybe that's what's bothering him.'

Sera couldn't say.

'Are you here of your own free will?'

'I am.' Perhaps this woman, out of everyone here, would understand. 'I undertake my role willingly and with honour.'

'I'm glad to hear it. But it's been over a hundred years since this court has seen a courtesan of the High Reaches. We are, as a rule, a suspicious lot and fiercely independent. How can you serve my brother? What is it you bring?'

'Political backing and access to people of influence. You saw the additions to the most recent guest list for the library evening?'

'A diplomat, a peacekeeper and a historian from well beyond our northern borders. Not people we usually deal with.'

'Yet their voices are heard elsewhere, where others have concerns over the grand water plans for this region. What better way to begin conversation than with a casual evening of books, fine food and access to one of the monarchs at the heart of those plans?'

'Are you saying that my brother can't find his own way through the political mire?'

'I'm saying that the Order of the Kite has influence far beyond Arun's reckoning, and beyond Liesendaach's too, never mind your husband's dealings. Should your brother ever ask for access to people who can aid him in his vision, he shall receive.'

'And has he asked?'

'No.' There was the not so small matter of his pride, not to mention his innate suspicion. Trust did not come easily to the royals of Arun. 'There's also the issue of your country needing an heir to the throne.'

'I fail to see how a courtesan can help with that.'

'And yet courtesans throughout the centuries have brokered marriages and more. Something is holding your brother back from making a commitment. Once we understand what it is we can address the issue and find someone who can give him what he needs. I can encourage him to explore or even simply to voice those… needs…in a safe and confidential environment.'

The elegant Queen Consort suddenly looked supremely uncomfortable. 'What makes you think my brother has particular needs?'

'The fact that he's not yet married, perhaps?' There was no delicate way to put this. 'Look, everyone explores their inner desires given the right opportunity. My job is to give the man a non-judgemental space to do it in. Some of the preferences of former Kings of Arun have been quite specific.'

Moriana blinked. 'Do I really want to know?'

'There are journals, milady. As a direct member of Arun's royal family, you have the right to view them.'

'May I see them now?'

'Of course. I have some in my quarters.'

'The rumours surrounding your quarters are quite… elaborate.'

'The rumours are true. Would you like to take tea with me there? Your brother has yet to put a cup of mine to his lips but I assure you there's no poison involved. That would be counterproductive.'

'You do know that I can't tell whether you're joking or not?'

Sera smiled. The King's sister stared.

'I'm beginning to realise the extent of my brother's problem,' Moriana said drily. 'Yes, I'd like to see the journals and what you've done with the round room. I'll cancel the rest of my morning engagements.'

'Wonderful.' Sera thought about curtseying again, but the memory of the pain involved gave her pause. She turned and headed for the door instead, opening it for her companion.

'So you've been working with Augustus and his assistant. Have you met our head of household staff yet?'

Sera nodded. 'And the chefs, function waiting staff, and the head gardener.'

'Have you met my father?'

'Only briefly, Your Highness. He came to view the work of the stonemasons. He didn't stay long.

'He tends to leave things to Augustus these days. Do you have family?' Moriana asked.

'No, Your Highness. My mother died in my early teens and I have no brothers or sisters.'

'And your father?'

Sera paused. 'He is unknown to me.'

'It's just…the accord says you are of noble bloodlines.'

'My mother's ancestry,' said Sera. 'The Order traces its bloodlines through the female.'

'How unusual,' murmured the other woman. 'And when you leave here, once Augustus marries and gives the country an heir, what will you do? More courtesan work? Or do you get to become something else then?'

'There are many forks in my road. Some of them lead to high places and some of them don't. I have contacts the world over and a good education. The opportunities available to me after I've discharged my duty here are truly limitless.'

They'd reached the round room doors. Sera opened

them and stood back to allow Moriana to enter. Augustus had not cared for the artwork on display or the comforts on offer; he'd barely glanced at them. Perhaps his sister would show more interest.

Moriana stepped inside, her gaze instantly drawn upward towards the sunlit glass dome. 'It's still stunning, that roof. But the sun doesn't always shine in Arun. I grew up here and I should know. Are you warm enough in here?'

'There's oil heating in the side rooms and alcoves for when the sun doesn't shine and warm the stone in the central dome. It's enough.'

'And far too big for just one person,' murmured Moriana. 'In times of old, how many others would have attended you here?'

'Dozens, Your Highness. But the Lady Lianthe will visit on occasion. And others might also venture here, with your brother's permission. Friends and tutors, other members of the Order.'

'How many members of the Order are there?'

'That I couldn't say. But I'll show you where the journals are. By your leave, I'll make myself presentable while you look at them.' Sera was very aware of the sweat on her skin and the sawdust still clinging to her trousers.

Moriana nodded. 'Shall I ring for tea?'

'I don't ring for service, Your High—'

'Call me Moriana.'

'I don't ring for service, Lady Moriana. I'm the one who serves.'

'Then we shall both serve ourselves,' said Moriana easily. 'You get clean; I'll make the tea. Shall I sit in the middle of the room once I've explored the art on the walls and discovered your journals? Is that appropriate?'

'Of course. The journals are in the glass case in the library alcove. They can't leave here, nor can they be copied. You'll understand why once you begin to read them. Of the other books in the library, I've left some on the table that might be suitable to place on display in the palace reading rooms and libraries. I haven't forgotten your earlier request.'

A visitor, finally, and an important one. Sera shed her clothes and combed out her hair. Not as swiftly as she would have liked, but it couldn't be helped given the state of her ribs. Nothing broken, no, but there was bruising already and had she been alone she'd have iced the area. As it was, she took a soft cotton scarf and wrapped her torso tightly and wished for painkillers. Maybe she'd find some later, but right now she had Moriana of Liesendaach to make welcome.

Sera chose a simple linen tunic and stretchy leggings to wear over her makeshift bandage. Loose enough to hide the torso wrap, embroidered enough to show her respect. She wound her hair into a bun, slipped her feet into backless high heeled sandals and swiftly applied eyeliner, mascara and soft, moist lipstick.

By the time Sera returned, almost ten minutes later, Moriana was standing at the edge of the floor tapestry that had so captivated Augustus, a fragile porcelain cup in her hand.

'This is quite something,' she said as Sera approached. 'Does it tell a story?'

'It's a request wheel, my Lady Moriana. You arrive and sit where you will, according to need, and I will see to that need.'

Moriana froze, her cup of tea halfway to her lips.

'Your brother doesn't like it,' Sera added. 'I think he found the whipping scene somewhat confronting.'

'Uh-huh,' his well-spoken sister said with a blush. 'So he's supposed to come in and choose his…'

'Fix,' suggested Sera. 'Yes. Having said that, he's been here exactly once and refused a seat. Perhaps he just needs to get used to it. It saves quite a lot of time.'

'Uh-huh.' No more tea for Lady Moriana. She returned her cup to the saucer she held in her other hand and walked a slow, rapt circle around the tapestry. 'There's an orgy scene.'

'Yes. If you don't mind me saying so, you Arunians do seem a little repressed.'

Moriana smiled faintly. 'Perhaps. Do you have a favourite scene?'

'I like reading aloud to people.' She'd learned that particular skill while tending to the children of the High Reaches. 'I like spirited intellectual debate and reasoned argument, so I quite like the conversation scenes too. As for the sex scenes…' Chances were she'd like those too if she ever got a chance to indulge in them. 'Each to his own, no?'

Moriana hadn't yet fled the room screaming. This was a good thing. 'What's the one with the people standing around the table covered with maps?'

'Strategy sessions for weighty subjects like war and succession. There is a book to accompany the carpet. I've set it aside for your brother, assuming he ever wants to see it.'

'I could take it to him when I leave here,' Moriana offered. 'It might be better presented to him as a curious artefact rather than a working guide to your services.'

Sera nodded. 'Please do. Would you like to sit?'

'This…circle…works for me too?'

'Of course.'

'So if I wanted to sit and discuss my brother's marriage options with you, which panel would I choose?'

'You might choose the panel with the maps. Strategy session,' Sera offered. 'I'd get my computer and take a seat within that area also and we'd discuss options. I'd provide refreshments. More tea or cold drinks, stuffed dates or something savoury. We'd plot and plan and consider what we already know when it comes to the monarchy's needs and preferences. We'd come up with a list I would then consult whenever I have to plan another function or dinner and I would make sure to get the women on that list in front of him.'

Moriana sat where suggested and the world did not end. She took a deep breath and then looked up at Sera with a smile. 'I love stuffed dates.'

'Tell me…' Sera was wholly prepared to woo the King's sister to within an inch of her life. 'Do you like them dipped in chocolate?'

CHAPTER FOUR

IT WAS A TRAP. Even as Augustus stood at the door to Sera's quarters at half eight the following evening and pulled on the bell to signal his presence, he knew he should have stayed away or at the very least had her brought to his office earlier in the day. He wanted to talk about this list of potential brides she and Moriana had cooked up between them. The first three on the list would be presented to him at the Winter Solstice ball, Moriana had said. Sera would not be present.

What good was a matchmaker if she wasn't even going to be present?

The door in front of him opened, and this time the menace from the High Reaches stood ready to serve him. He'd told her he was coming. He'd given her a time frame and ample opportunity to get ready for him. Nothing was going to happen except conversation. Moriana had navigated that blasted courtesan's carpet wheel successfully enough, and there was even a training manual to go with it. He'd browsed through it during his lunch break.

He was getting more used to the physical effect Sera of the High Reaches seemed to have on him. Eyes soft and inviting, lips curved in welcome. Her over-tunic a flowing drape of gossamer moss-coloured silk, then underneath a plum-coloured bodice and straight skirt that finished an inch or so below the tunic. Her hair had been pulled back into a high ponytail yet still reached her waist. Delicate silver fans with tassels fell from her ears and swung gently as she moved. Matching tassels fell from the place where she'd gathered her hair. Her make-up was subtle rather than overwhelming.

She was breathtaking.

Wordlessly, she invited him to enter and he did.

'May I take your jacket?' she asked. He thought *Why not?* and let her ease it from his shoulders and hang it on a wooden clothes dummy in the alcove beside the door. She closed the door behind him and studied his face intently. 'I haven't curtseyed,' she said.

And for that he was grateful. Every time she did she fed a demon that demanded he take advantage of her willingness to grant him anything he wanted. 'How are your ribs?'

'Perfectly fine, thank you.'

There was a new table in the round room. A small round table with room enough for three people to sit around comfortably or four people at a squeeze. There was a new sofa as well, although the round one and the cursed floor tapestry still took pride of place. This new sofa had been placed against a wall. A stack of reading books sat next to it and two wing-back leather library chairs had been positioned to either side. The carpet in between looked thick and plush and was a deep and solid red. She saw him looking at the set-up and extended a graceful arm in its direction.

'I took the liberty of setting up another seating area. Your sister thought it might encourage more visitors, or, at the very least, make them less suspicious once they got here.'

His sister was a genius when it came to putting people at ease.

'You must miss her,' Sera said next.

'We all do.' He'd once thought Moriana neurotic and highly strung. He'd thought his palace would run just as smoothly without her incessant attention to detail. It hadn't. A fact which had surprised him and approximately no one else in the palace. 'My sister used to manage the monarchy's social obligations. There can be two or sometimes even three social functions a day here. And then there are the balls and state dinners. She left comprehensive instructions for every event, but even so I miss her judgement when it comes to who to seat where and what alliances are to be encouraged. It's all in her head, and in mine, and neither of us have time to download a lifetime's worth of observations into someone else's brain. Especially when that someone is just as likely to go to the press with tasty gossip at the first opportunity.' He was tired and irritable and what was it about this woman that had him spilling confidences like an overwrought teenager?

Moving on.

Moriana had sat in the strategy section yesterday morning, she'd told him. It had worked for her. It would work for him. He strode to the central sofa and sat in the area with the people and the table and the maps. Strategy session.

Sera smiled at him, really smiled, as if he'd made her happy, and—oh, *crap*.

Could he order her not to smile at him like that?

'Would you like water, wine, coffee or tea?' she asked.

'None of it. Go get the list of potential wives you and my sister cooked up between you and then take a seat. I have some amendments to make.' He hoped he sounded rigidly officious rather than downright surly but he didn't like his chances. Neither option was a good example of confident, competent leadership.

'I'll get my computer,' she said, and when she came back she sat beside him easy as you please and earnest in her role as matchmaker. For his part, he found himself moving closer, well and truly enmeshed by her delicate perfume and perfect profile and the little fan earrings that brushed the skin of her neck.

All of it was captivating and it took all the willpower he had to turn his attention to the database full of potential brides. A database full of not just names but lineages, occupations, hobbies and… 'Is that a character assessment column?'

'Subjective, of course, and predominantly based on their public personas. They may be quite different underneath. We can adjust it as we go. It would be helpful if you could give me some indication as to what you admire most in a woman,' she said. 'Do you want someone with a calm disposition or are you after more fire than that? Someone fun-loving and easy-going or someone more highly strung and demanding? A pliable companion or someone you might on occasion have to work to placate?'

'Meekness bores me. Theatrics annoy me. And stupidity is an unpardonable sin.'

Sera's fingers flew across the keyboard and several

names disappeared. 'Any hair, eye or skin colour preferences?'

'None.' He hadn't known he had a preference for grey eyes, raven-dark hair and skin the colour of pale rose petals until a few days ago. Hopefully his current obsession would be short-lived.

'Will you entertain marriage to a woman whose religion is different to yours?' she asked.

'No. She would have to convert.' The demands of the Crown overrode all else in that regard.

More names disappeared from the list.

'Would you like a virgin?' she asked.

'Are you serious?'

Her fingers paused over the keyboard. 'Ah…yes? Historically—'

'Let's keep it modern day.'

'The question stands,' she offered quietly. 'Some things are best left to those who enjoy initiating others. Do you want a virgin or would you prefer someone who brings adequate experience to sexual matters?'

'It's not important!' Said no scaly possessive alpha beast ever.

'Okay.' Another pause. 'Thank you for answering.'

'You're blushing,' he told her darkly. 'All virgin brides aside, how can you possibly think yourself ready to do some of the things in these pictures when you've never been touched?'

His virgin courtesan. The idea was ridiculous.

Beyond ridiculous.

No wonder it kept him awake at night.

'Bodies can be prepared in advance for just about anything. It's the endorphins.' Sera stared at the screen, delicate colour still filling her cheeks. 'More specifically, increased levels of oxytocin can act as a natural pain inhibitor. Additionally, minds can be manipulated to respond with pleasure to dominance, submission or many other…things.'

All of a sudden the idea of a virgin concubine wasn't ridiculous at all, and it was burning hot in this room built for pleasure. 'So you think you're ready for anything?'

'I hope I am. To be otherwise would be unacceptable. Disgraceful.'

'On what planet is not being ready to partake in an orgy or whip a man bloody disgraceful?' She had a flawless knack for rousing his temper. 'Dammit, Sera. I have no idea who you're answering to!'

'I answer to you.'

'The hell you do! Otherwise you'd be gone from here, as requested! Do you even understand the Pandora's box of problems you bring with you? That I'm trying to *work* through while keeping you protected?'

'I don't need protecting.'

'You say you're innocent. The innocent *always* need protecting.' He stood abruptly and stepped away from temptation before he did something unforgivable. 'Read out the remaining names,' he ordered, and she did, her voice becoming steadier as she went. He had her remove several more names from the list, because he'd met those women before and they weren't for him. He found himself circling the sofa, and then moving further afield, looking at other tapestries and sculptures, other furniture sent to grace a courtesan's workplace.

Over and over, his feet returned him to the centre of the room where she sat, his gaze drawn to the pleasure wheel at her feet. Where would a virgin trained as a courtesan even want to start when it came to serving someone sexually?

Finally the names stopped coming and his reason for being there ended.

'It would help if you could give me some additional ideas of what you're looking for in a wife,' she said.

Good question, but he didn't really have an answer for himself, let alone one he'd ever voiced to anyone else. He was so used to *not* voicing his innermost thoughts. 'Why? So you can sell a list of my private wants and needs to the highest bidder?'

'I would never do that. No courtesan of the High Reaches would ever betray your confidence. Above all else, it is the rule that governs us.'

He wanted to believe her. And really, what would it matter if people knew what he was looking for in a wife? The basics, at any rate.

'Resilience is important,' he offered, and wondered why it was easier to talk to her than just about anyone. 'There's no point choosing a wife who'll crumble beneath the pressures and constrictions placed on her. She'll be bound by duty to Crown and country. She'll have to cope with extensive press coverage wherever she goes. I want her at the centre of things, right by my side, and she needs to be stubborn and curious, observant, intuitive and good with people she barely knows.'

Now that he'd started, he didn't know how to stop confiding in her, because he *had* thought about this. He'd thought about this long and hard and it was good to finally say some of it out loud. 'Above all I want to know what's going to keep her at my side when the going gets tough. Because it will. My mother loved my father above all else and he loved her. This country benefitted greatly from their love match. My sister loves Theo and he loves her. Liesendaach wins. Sometimes I doubt I have the capacity to *be* in love with another person in that same way. And yet I can see the benefits. The strength in it. I'm not against it.'

Too much.

Too much revealed.

He turned away to study yet another tapestry that hung on a nearby wall. She had no comment for him other than the tapping of computer keys.

'Okay,' she said finally. 'And, forgive me the intrusion, but do you find sex satisfactory?'

'What are you now? My virgin sex therapist?'

'Do you need one?'

He barked a laugh. Better than a growl for this confidante with a sharply honed wit. 'I get by.'

'Some of your ancestors have preferred men. They've required wives who could accommodate those preferences. Turn a blind eye at times.'

'I prefer women.' Truth.

'What of fidelity?' she asked. 'Will you practise it?'

'Yes.'

'Do you require fidelity from your wife?'

'Yes.' Surely she knew this already? He'd already banned her from taking her kisses elsewhere and had almost punished her guard the other morning for daring to spar with her. 'I don't share.'

More typing and no comment whatsoever.

'I'm thirty years old. I prefer women to men. I've never been in love. And I thought I had more time in which to marry before the courtesans of old descended from a mystical mountain to help me do my duty,' he offered curtly. 'I can find my own wife, regardless of what you, your Order or my sister might think. The only reason I'm here is because I refuse to let you conspire behind my back. You may as well conspire with me. It'll go much faster if we work together on this.'

'Yes, I know,' she offered quietly.

'I also want to be able to explain your role here without calling into question my sanity, my morals or yours. From here on in when you're dealing with my staff or handling guest lists you'll be known as Lady Sera Boreas, Executive Function Manager for the Royal Palace of Arun. You'll answer to me or my executive secretary. You will oversee the functions in person but not be in attendance as a guest. I want you in corporate clothing. Smart suits, modest jewellery, tidy hair. No shackles or manacles, no golden bustiers, no six-inch heels while you're on duty in public.'

'And in private?'

'I can't tell you what to do once you're in the privacy of your own quarters.'

'Actually, you ca—'

'Don't say those words.'

It occurred to him that he was already telling her what to do in the privacy of her quarters, and he smiled without humour. It was an impossible situation and he saw no way out of it other than to make her leave or turn her into a respectable employee of the palace. He waved his hand around the room. 'All that you've brought to my palace works against me in the wider world. The rebirth of these quarters is all my staff can talk about. Word has spread. King Augustus of Arun keeps a courtesan hidden in a round room, built like a birdcage. He's been bewitched, his needs are dark, he's not a modern-day king. You're a sorceress, a temptress, a creature of myth. That's what they're saying about you, me and this situation. It's time to take control of this narrative.'

'You want to reframe me.'

He nodded. 'Minimise the mystery. Modernise the mythology. I need you to arrange for one piece of art to be displayed in the palace's grand entrance hall. I want notes to accompany it, emphasising its historical significance. I want a dozen books from your collection showcased in the state library, several pieces of art or treasures of historical significance in circulation throughout our galleries. I want a narrative built around the Order of the Kite that starts with it being supportive, historically complex, non-political, culturally significant and ends with the information about your current non-sexual role in my administration. I want you to give history talks in university lecture halls and libraries. I want you to be the guest of honour as each treasure on display is unveiled. I want you to talk about the Order of old and then I want you to talk about the roles women have traditionally played in government, the roles open to them today and your own education.'

'Your Majesty, the Order does *not* seek publicity.'

'Then they shouldn't have sent you here.' His gaze clashed with hers, storm clouds meeting a bleak black sea. 'I'm asking you to be a modern-day woman for a modern-day audience. One who embraces the history and power of your Order and can competently explain your presence here. One who shines a favourable light on us both. Do it or I'll do it for you.'

Augustus shoved his hands in his pockets and turned away. Looking at her never ended well. He always grew resentful of his body's instinctive response and his brain lost its way. 'You're not stupid, Sera. Philosophy, politics and economics—those are your degree subjects and you only ever earned distinction marks or higher. If you want power here I'm challenging you to take it openly. Carve out a place for yourself that the public will accept. That *I* can accept.' He spared a glance for the pleasure wheel. 'Because there are too many elements here that I *dare* not accept.'

'Your Majesty—'

He wanted to hear her say his name. Not *Your Majesty* or *milord* or *sire*. Only his mother and sometimes his sister had managed to make his name sound anything more than an unwieldy mouthful. They'd laced it with affection and love. Exasperation too, for his cool and calculating deliberations. His father didn't call him by name all that often. His father called him *Son* and it was a reminder of his role in the continuation of their line more than anything.

He wanted to hear her say his name but there was no picture in the carpet for that. 'The only words I want to hear out of your mouth are "I accept your challenge and this amazing opportunity to become a relevant member of your court".'

Silence filled the room as he looked up to the soaring ceiling, anywhere but at the woman seated somewhere to his left. There were other ways he could deal with this. Send her away on a quest, take his case to parliament and the high courts and dissolve the accord and make an enemy of a secret Order with tentacles everywhere. The way he'd outlined—dealing openly with a modern interpretation of her position here—was by far the best. But he needed her co-operation.

'I accept your challenge.'

He closed his eyes as her soft words slid through him

and with them came relief. 'Your owls have returned,' he said by way of acknowledgement. 'Two of them. Are they inside or out?'

'In. But I don't think they've returned. I think these ones were merely absent when Tomas came for the rest. I'm glad they were both away and not just one of them. I think they're a mated pair.'

'Do you know what kind they are?'

'Tomas tells me they're Great Horned Owls. I sent him photos. Lianthe would say it's a good omen.'

'And what do you say?'

'As long as they stay up there and I stay down here, I say we can probably come to some kind of mutual living arrangement. The bathing pool was filled today.' It was a change of topic, a change of voice—lighter now, with a faint undercurrent of enthusiasm. He risked a backwards glance and found her standing and somehow changed. More hopeful, perhaps. More relaxed. 'It really has been a pleasure to see this place come alive again. It's been over a hundred and twenty years since anyone's lived here. Don't you find that just a little bit fascinating?'

Memory conjured up the marble pool room, with fancy tiles, private alcoves and exposed stone benches. He did want to see the transformation; there was no denying it. 'Show me.'

The dirty grey colours he remembered now glowed ivory, each marble vein shining beneath layers of polish. Sera flicked a switch and lit the area, contemporary lighting, all of it, but it felt as if flame flickered and shadows danced.

'What are the alcoves full of pillows for?' he asked.

'Massage, body treatments, sex. There's a steam

room here too. I know you'll not use any of it but we went with authenticity. This was its function.'

She had such an easy way of saying *sex*. As if it was nothing. Just another function of the body. He'd never found it so, endorphins or otherwise. Sex was revealing, and he far preferred to keep his own counsel. 'And the main pool is heated?'

'To three degrees above body temperature. Three hundred years ago your forebears and mine used fire to heat the pool. Yesterday, engineers from the High Reaches laid solar strips to the framework of the dome. This part of your palace now powers itself, and then some.'

Her face had lit up and her pleasure at the improvements seemed real.

He'd agreed to modifications to the rooms Sera occupied. He hadn't specifically agreed to *any* of this. Under the guise of honouring tradition, it felt as if the power here had been quite deftly wrested from his grasp.

She watched him from the shadows while he struggled with what to do with her in private as well as in public.

'Would you like to bathe?' she asked at last—she had to know he wanted more than that. She'd been taught to read people, had she not? Surely she could see the tension and the want in him and not just for warm water. He wanted what the cursed pleasure wheel had told him he could have. He wanted her hands on him, undressing him, washing his hair as he reclined. All those things the bathing picture showed and more, while the light from the wall sconces threw puppet shadows on the walls.

'I shouldn't.'

'Seems a shame to let it go to waste.'

'Don't tempt me.'

'Sometimes a bath can be just a bath.'

'Say my name.' He needed to hear it fall from those perfect lips.

She looked at him, as if trying to read his mood and good luck with that.

'That was an order.'

'Augustus.'

She made it sound like welcome and desire all rolled into one and he tried not to curse as he shoved his hand through his hair and tried to make sense of both his demands and his resistance. 'Did they make you practise that?'

They had. Sera knew better than many how to modulate her voice to convey different feelings. But the breathlessness in her voice this time was all hers. She gestured towards a stack of towels and potions, trying to get back on track. 'Augustus, would you like to bathe? The pool is ready and I've had lessons in how to make the experience a relaxing one. I could wash your hair. Oils to soothe, invigorate and everything in between. What is your mood?'

'You mean you can't tell?'

'You're hard to read.' She hadn't been expecting the way forward for her that he'd proposed. A public image to craft and shape. A role beyond those already identified by the tapestry. And nothing but strict hands-off in private. It was the keeping-distance-in-private request she would have the most trouble with. 'Or you could bathe alone and I can go and read a book in another room. This pool is for *your* use, Augustus. In any way you see fit.'

She turned away, left him to his thoughts, and approached a small side table groaning with essential oils and liquid soaps. She reached for the sandalwood, bergamot and orange and mixed them in a hand bowl, taking her time. 'I find ritual soothing,' she murmured, still not looking at him as she took the bowl to the water's edge and poured the fragrant oil mix into it, rinsing the bowl three times before setting it aside and rising. 'But if you prefer less ritual and more distance, perhaps you might cast me in the role of pool attendant. I can pile towels by the side of the pool and leave you to it.'

She didn't want to shatter the fragile peace they'd created this evening. She wanted it to continue.

'What does the ritual involve?' he rasped.

'I would remove your clothes, provide your soap, wash your hair, towel you dry, moisturise your skin and dress you again. It can take up to an hour of your time.'

'And what's in it for you?'

'Ritual soothes me. And also…'

'Also what?'

'You're not going to like it.' He wasn't going to *accept* it. 'I want to serve here, the way I've been trained to serve. It doesn't have to be sexual. It doesn't have to be complicated. You could find refuge and relaxation here if you wanted to.'

'Do it.'

His words didn't come from a place of acceptance. They came at her twisted and wrapped in loathing. Not a good start but at least she had permission to try to bathe him properly.

She ventured closer, until she was standing in front of him. Undressing a man wasn't a hard thing to do. There was an order to the releasing of buttons and the removal of clothes. She knew what to do. Only her trembling fingertips betrayed her as she reached for one of his wrists, turned his forearm towards her and fumbled with the tiny cufflink there. She bit her lip, intent on her task, and wondered if the crazy throb of the pulse point at his wrist was for her.

She slowed her breathing and got on with her task, undoing first one cufflink and then the other. She stepped in closer as she undid his tie, and his eyes never left her face and hers never left his. Buttons, so many buttons on his shirt, tracking a path down his chest, the last of them hidden beneath his trousers as she pulled the shirt free and dealt with them too. Buttons and knuckles and air that had suddenly grown too thin for breathing.

'This isn't going to end well,' he rasped.

'Relax. I'm a professional.' She pushed the front of his shirt aside and slid her hands up and over his shoulders, taking his shirt with her. By the time she'd smoothed her hands down his arms the shirt was on the floor.

She knelt at his feet, removing his shoes and socks and running her hands up his legs and over his thighs as if soothing a savage beast. She kept her hands on him as she undid his trousers, slid her hands beneath his waistband and down over his buttocks, taking the fabric with her, all the way down his legs. 'Put your hand on my shoulder or my head for balance,' she said, as she lifted first one foot from the puddle of his trousers and then the next.

His boxers were stretched tight over his manhood, plumper now than it had been moments ago but not yet at full stretch. If she removed his underwear in the same manner she'd removed his trousers she was going to get an eyeful.

And then she leaned in, her hands high on his thighs, and breathed him in.

Hours of video instruction had done nothing to prepare Sera for the impact of the man standing before her. The heat coming from his skin and the scent of him. The glittering black eyes and his complete attention.

She didn't know where or how he exercised but he did, his body lean and his belly ridged with muscle. He had body hair but not a lot. His manhood looked thick beneath the thin stretch of cotton, and she wondered if her mouth would fit around it. Not just thick but long as well. The stretch for her mouth and throat would be considerable.

He took a ragged breath and stepped away from her touch and shed his boxers. He was beautiful naked. He was beautiful everywhere.

'I'll take that bath now.' His voice whispered over her, making promises not kept by his retreating body. She felt the loss of his regard as he stepped into the water and submerged himself completely. The bathing rituals went unobserved as she knelt on a cushion and waited for him to need something more from her, hands clasped in her lap, back straight, head bowed. Still and silent until needed. Ritual.

She watched from beneath her lashes as he selected soap and started washing, his touch far rougher than hers would have been. She watched him rinse off, water running in rivulets down the hard planes of his chest, dripping from his elbows as he pushed dark tendrils of hair away from his face. He caught her watching him and stilled. Did he want to get out now? Should she anticipate his need for a towel? Would he accept one from her hand? Bathing rituals shot to hell by him, leaving her untethered and wanting.

'Sera.'

Surely she could look her fill now that he'd called her name. She lifted her head.

'Will you wash my hair?'

Finally, something she had previous experience with. She almost fell over herself in her haste to fetch the water jug and shampoo selection. Ritual, as he watched her prepare the edge of the pool and gesture for him to lie back with his head in the shallow dip. She leaned over and filled the jug, wetting his hair all over again, her hand firm on his forehead to prevent water trickling down his face.

She opted for a firmer touch than the one she'd used on the children of the High Reaches, massaging his scalp once the conditioner had gone on and drawing from him a groan that made her smile her relief.

'Harder,' he rasped, so she increased the pressure from her fingertips and leaned into it. With his eyes closed she could study his profile more closely. Inevitably, her gaze moved on from his lips to his chest, then his stomach and onto lower depths. His legs were slightly parted. His manhood looked erect.

When she finally turned her attention back to his face, he was watching her through narrowed eyes.

Hot-faced, she filled the water jug again and began to rinse his hair.

He let her finish, he gave her that, and then he was underwater again, and again, and then standing and heading for the steps.

To ogle his sharply defined muscles and the proud

jut of his arousal or pick up a towel and have it ready for him? Sera knew what she ought to be doing. She'd trained for this.

By the time she reached the side of the pool and handed him a towel and he'd taken it and wiped his face and dropped it and stood naked before her, she met his gaze unflinchingly. He had nothing to be ashamed of.

Neither did she.

'If you could kiss me in one place and one place only, where would you kiss?' he demanded.

She'd seen so much sex in the guise of instruction. She knew the psychology and physiology behind each and every action, but knowing wasn't doing and she'd never done any of it. His lips beckoned, the fierce cut of his cheekbones. The curve of his shoulder appealed, the water droplet sliding down his neck—she could lap it up and find the pulse point.

But his hand moved to curl around his erection and it drew her gaze like a lodestone. More than anything else, she wanted to know more of *that*. For some reason, kissing his lips seemed like more of an intrusion than kissing him *there*.

He looked so good naked and wanting, almost vibrating with tension as he waited for her to choose which part of him to kiss. He might not even allow it. Maybe all he wanted to know was her preference so he could destroy her with wanting and never having any of it.

She dropped to her knees and his eyes flared a heated warning.

'Really?' he rasped.

'I want to know what it's like,' she replied. 'Do you?'

'I already know.'

She kept her gaze on his face, willing him to let her have this. 'I want to know too.'

'Brave,' he rasped. 'Did they teach you how to do this?'

'Yes.' With toys and tutorials but it was nothing compared to the soft warmth of his shaft as she leaned forward and placed her moist and parted lips against the most sensitive area just beneath the tip.

She tongued him carefully and he tasted of nothing but water. Not until she ran her tongue across the slit did she get a sense of his essence. The skin was slick and smooth. His hiss was hopefully one of pleasure. She knew not to use her teeth. She sucked, ever so gently, and received a fresh burst of flavour for her efforts.

'That's it,' he murmured. 'How much can you take?'

All of it. She closed her eyes and opened her throat and took him deep, down to where her lips met his testicles and she had to breathe through her nose. His hand came to cover her head, not pushing, just keeping her there, then he slowly withdrew until only the tip of him touched her lips.

'Breathe,' he ordered, even as his hand reversed its pressure and he drew her back down onto him. 'Again.'

She lost herself in the rhythm of his slow and measured thrusts.

'Put your hands on me,' he said, and she did, first his thighs while her thumbs brushed the swell of his balls, and then more boldly while he simultaneously thrusted and cursed.

'Look at me,' he ordered on his next withdrawal and she opened her eyes while he searched her face as if studying a puzzle he had no answer for. 'You like this,' he muttered finally. 'Heaven help us both.'

Yes, she liked it. The careful thrusting, his innate gentleness and iron control. The satisfaction that came of knowing that she was the cause of his arousal. She knew how to finish a man, theoretically. Suck and swallow, throat muscles working him over, but when she tried he withdrew so fast and roughly he left her blinking up at him. What had she done? Or not done? 'I'm sorry, I—'

'Don't apologise,' he said, but she still felt as if she'd failed and he must have seen some of that thought written on her face, because he groaned and hauled her up and into his arms and crashed his mouth down over hers, hard and hungry, all power and unrestrained passion, and she responded in kind because this kiss was better than anything she'd ever felt.

He groaned into her mouth and she swallowed it down and opened for more. He tilted her head and consumed her and she fisted her hand in his hair and worked her lips down his neck, nipping and sucking, because she could do that to him here, and skating the edge of violence suited her, suited them both.

She had too many clothes on and he had none. They were ignoring so many steps in the sex-making process. Or maybe they weren't.

'Take me in hand,' he muttered. 'Touch me.' He lifted her bodily and she curled her legs around him. He put her back to a column and rocked against her as his mouth claimed hers again.

He came with layers of silk clothing still between them, grinding down hard against her core and tipping her over into orgasm moments after his own release, strong hands to her buttocks, wet hair at odds with the harsh heat of his breath and the still scorching feel of his mouth on hers. She'd always known about the fire deep down inside her. It was the reason they'd chosen her.

She'd suspected from the beginning that there was a matching fire in him.

After a dozen more harsh breaths, both his and hers, he set her gently on her feet and turned away, not looking at her once as he found his clothes, put them on. He didn't speak, didn't look her way as he headed for the main room and swiftly strode towards the door. He didn't speak as he opened it and let himself out. He left, that was all.

And then the emptiness crashed down on her.

CHAPTER FIVE

AUGUSTUS, RULER OF ARUN, had always kept himself tightly under control. Born to inherit his father's throne, raised to think before he spoke, to weigh and qualify every action. His sister had been the unruly one, governed by her emotions, and only careful tutelage and cultivation of a serene public persona had ever contained her. For Augustus it had been easy. Not for him the pitfalls of adolescent crushes or fierce bursts of anger. He was the cool-headed one, the old soul, the stuffy one. No unexpected or unplanned behaviour from Augustus of Arun. He knew what he had to do at all times and he did it, all childhood resistance to his lot in life long since diminished.

So what the ever-loving hell had just happened in there?

Because he'd never done that before in his life. Taken his own pleasure and given nothing back in return. Leave a woman, *any woman*, let alone a virgin, leaning against a wall for support, her clothes stained and her eyes blown wide with shock, her lips…

Her lips…

What she'd done with them.

He could write an incoherent ode to them.

What had he done? Where was all his rigid moral certainty now?

No one should be made to serve the way she had been groomed to serve him. Even kings needed barriers. Free rein and ultimate power was never a good combination. That was how despots were created.

He hadn't even given her pleasure.

Augustus stopped to lean against the cold stone of the corridor wall. He closed his eyes and bowed his head and tried to make sense of what he'd done. He was attracted to Sera—had been from the moment he'd laid eyes on her. He'd wanted to set her free from the duty bestowed on her and he'd tried. He'd combed every old text and obscure law journal he could find for ways to release her. It was the honourable thing to do. So far, so good. And while that was still happening he'd allowed her to settle into those dusty old quarters and revive a tradition long dead, and legitimise it with artwork and furnishings, and he'd left her alone to get on with it. He'd given her a secretarial role to be going on with because he'd needed a social organiser and she'd needed to serve.

He'd let her draw up a list of potential brides, not because he wanted to get married but because if he did marry she would surely go away. A stupid reason to marry but he needed to marry sooner or later and he wasn't complaining.

He'd behaved.

Right up until he hadn't.

He'd left her standing there, wide-eyed and mute, her mouth a wreck and her body trembling.

He heard a slight sound, a shuffle, and opened his eyes and met the shadowy gaze of one of her guards, half hidden in a recess. The man wanted him to know he was there, that much was obvious. Would he check on Sera once Augustus had gone? Would he comfort her and curse his King?

When had all reason and rational good sense deserted him?

Augustus pushed away from the wall and turned back towards the double doors that kept people out and Sera in. He rang the bell and stared at the flowers and waited.

Nothing happened.

He rang the bell again, and this time, after several more impatient seconds, a peephole opened and he moved to stand in front of it.

She opened the door to him in silence, a towel wrapped around her otherwise wet and naked body.

Washing the stench of him away, he thought grimly, and his heart clenched.

'Your Majesty,' she said, and her voice was huskier than it had been earlier, and he certainly knew why.

'You know my name.'

Only she didn't say it.

'May I come in?'

She stood aside and opened the door and glanced behind him and so did Augustus. The guard stood there watching them, fully visible now, arms crossed in front of his chest and his eyes sharp. Augustus didn't know what she did—more of that silent communication business—but the guard nodded slightly and faded from view.

'You told him you had everything under control?' he asked.

'Yes.'

'Is that what you really think?'

'I think you're conflicted.'

'I think I'm a monster,' he said.

'Because you gave me what I asked for?'

'You didn't ask for that.' She looked at him sharply and then glanced towards the big circular sofa. 'I don't want to sit at your cursed wheel,' he muttered. 'You were bathing. Do you need to continue with that?' She might as well be clean. God knew no amount of water was going to wash him clean of this sin.

With the grace of a dancer and no inhibitions whatsoever, she walked towards the pool and shed her towel before stepping lightly into the water, deeper and deeper still, until she was shoulders deep and her hair billowed about her like tendrils of ink.

'I'm sorry.' She'd never know how much. 'The way I treated you earlier was unacceptable.'

She watched him pace and then reached for the soap. 'You fear passion,' she said.

'No.'

She raised an elegant eyebrow.

'I lost control. I took without thinking. I hurt you.' The way she'd taken him in her mouth, letting him push deeper than he'd ever pushed before—all animal instinct. 'I can hear the damage in your voice.'

She looked at him, her thoughts her own, and then swam to a tap and turned it on and pushed her face beneath it and opened her mouth and drank. He wanted to look away from the innocent abandon in even that small act. The open mouth and the eyes that never stopped watching him, cataloguing every tiny twitch—or so he imagined. She swallowed and so did he, remembering, and the deep ache of desire that should have been sated sputtered to life again.

She swallowed more and then turned the tap off and cleared her throat. 'How do I sound now?'

A little less rough. 'Your lips are still swollen.' The make-up was off but the lush redness remained.

'I can't tell.' She was at the side of the pool again, closest to him, all graceful hands and arms, breasts with the nipples puckered up tight, but she wasn't self-conscious—not one little bit—and he looked away and kept right on pacing, wondering why he'd turned around and come back because he was unravelling all over again.

'Have you finished bathing?' she asked solemnly.

He'd finished undressing in front of her, full-stop. At least one of them should be clothed at all times. It was his new motto when dealing with her. 'I didn't—'

She waited for him to continue.

'You didn't—'

She was still waiting for him to finish a damn sentence.

'First times should involve satisfaction for all concerned,' he muttered finally. 'I should have made it so. I can still show you what it can be like.'

'By taking control?'

'Yes.' By taking control and keeping it and pasting over the last twenty minutes with something infinitely more palatable.

'You do realise that my satisfaction isn't the goal here?' she asked, and that, more than anything else in this crazy set-up, made his temper spike.

'Because your teachers say so? Because you're here to serve and my satisfaction comes before yours? Because you don't deserve a first kiss that's gentle and respectful? Because, believe me, Sera of the High Reaches, everyone deserves that.'

'It wasn't gentle, true.' She was getting out of the bath now and walking towards him, water caressing her skin. 'But my self-respect is intact, even if yours is not.' She tilted her head back to look at him. 'Your ego is bruised because you think I didn't like your taste or touch? I can assure you I did.'

How could she have?

Her eyes seemed to soften as she stared at him. 'Would you like to try again?' she invited softly. 'Bolster your ego, dilute your guilt—whatever it is that brought you back here to apologise? Because you can kiss me again if you like.'

It wasn't *about* him. 'What would *you* like? From me?'

'Right now?'

'Right now.' Because he'd do it. 'This isn't about me.'

'Do you really believe that?' She picked up a towel and patted her face and wrapped it around her small frame and tucked it in. She pushed her hair to one side and combed through it with her fingers before wrapping slender fists around the dark mass and stripping the water from it in one smooth movement. 'I'd like to kiss you again,' she said at last. 'I'd like for you to kiss me, gently and respectfully, whatever it is you think I need, and we'll see how that goes. I might like it more than our earlier kisses. I might not. I'll let you know.'

She would like it more. She had to—for his sanity. He didn't know what he'd do if she liked it greedy and rough, because that wasn't him. He wasn't drawn to explore the darker sides of desire, those places where control bled away and chaos slipped in. Regardless of whether she was willing to accommodate him.

One kiss, and this time he'd do right by her, ease in

slow with the barest touch of his lips against hers. Plenty of room for her sigh and his relief as her eyes fluttered closed as he slanted his head and fitted his lips more firmly against hers. Waiting rather than demanding her compliance, and there it was, the tip of her tongue skating along the edge of his upper lip, and he was careful, so careful to follow her cues and keep his hands to himself. Easy, never mind the want that pushed up from those places he always kept hidden. Sweet, because first kisses should be savoured, not driven into someone with the force of a fist.

He pulled back slowly, letting the space between their lips grow, watching her face come back into focus, pale and perfect, and her eyes open to regard him steadily.

'Better?' he asked and she smiled ever so slightly.

'Different.'

He could do better. Another kiss, this time with the reins less tightly held. Letting slip, just a little, to allow for a response that wasn't so carefully composed. She responded beautifully, so willing to follow where he led, so open to whatever he wanted to bestow. Enough to make a blush light her cheeks and her eyes look unfocused. Enough to risk his thumb against her lips when his mouth wasn't there, smoothing them, learning them, setting everything back in order because he couldn't have it any other way. 'Better?'

'Is this what you want from a wife? Someone who'll never truly know your heart because you're too busy hiding beneath all that delicious self-control?'

'Don't push me.' Even as he pressed her bottom lip lightly against her teeth. Not hurting her, no. And yet. 'Rule number one of the Arunian monarchs: don't ever lose control.'

'And what's rule number two?'

'An eye for an eye.'

He dropped to his knees in front of her and tugged the towel from her body. He pressed his lips to a bead of water that sat at the junction of her perfectly toned thighs. She gasped, and it was all the encouragement he needed. Hands sliding up her thighs to part them. The taste of her sweet on his tongue, and just like that he was ravenous again, licking and striking, flicking and sucking, listening and responding to every sound and twitch she gifted him with. He was good at this.

And she was so utterly, gloriously responsive.

Virgin.

A virgin he should have left alone or, failing that, someone whose pleasure should have very definitely come before his own. His shaft twitched, only this time he ignored it. He'd taken his pleasure. Now it was her turn.

Her fingers came up to guide his head with more force than expected. But then, this slip of a woman knew exactly how to wield swords and knives and even sharper words.

A ragged curse that felt like an endearment. A trembling 'oh' when he redoubled his efforts.

He wanted her to say his name again as she came.

Words that seemed lost beneath her quiet gasps and his growls when he grew greedy and still couldn't get enough.

She came on his tongue, tense and trembling, and he could swear he felt the ripples of her body beneath his hand, and he should have withdrawn then, done and done, but there was always one more taste he had to have, even if he did avoid her most sensitive areas, and then she was dropping to her knees to face him and her hands were on his shoulders, and she said, 'Kiss me again and mean it, Augustus,' and his name on her lips was like a promise, so he did as she asked and knew himself for lost.

'Don't,' he whispered, when he finally found the will to pull away from her. 'Don't tempt me.'

This time, when he left, he made it all the way back to his quarters before shedding his clothes and stepping beneath a scalding shower in a futile effort to cleanse his soul.

Don't make me lose control.

Physical activity was the only thing that prevented Augustus from climbing the walls in the days that followed. He swam until he either had to get out of the pool or drown, he ran on the treadmill in his private gym until he bent double and emptied his stomach. He put his recently purchased catamaran through its paces until he found its tipping point and it still didn't take the edge off.

He tried burying himself in work, which worked until his put-upon secretary demanded an assistant.

He went on a date with a perfectly eligible woman who was charming and accomplished and didn't challenge his self-control one little bit. He hated every awkward, stilted moment of it.

He visited Theo's cousin Benedict to look at horseflesh and met the long-term mistress of Theo's father, who just so happened to own the horses they were looking at, and he'd stood in the stables and wanted to ask her what it was like to own the heart of a king but never to hold his hand in public. In the end he didn't ask because he didn't have the right to pry and he probably wouldn't have liked the answer anyway.

Benedict, after spending half a day with him, dropped all pretence of pleasantries the minute they left the stables and brought out the bolt-cutters in an attempt to prise Augustus open.

'What on earth is wrong with you?' he demanded bluntly. 'I've seen junkies desperate for their next fix in better shape than you.'

And Benedict would know. Even though he'd settled down and returned to the family fold after his father's death, there wasn't much Benedict of Liesendaach didn't know about the darker side of sex, drugs and reckless self-indulgence.

'I'm not on drugs.' He'd never followed that road.

'And yet you're radiating barely concealed angst all over my calm. Are you having an existential crisis? You'd be surprised how many people invite me to tea and then proceed to come undone. As if I give a damn.' Benedict was eyeing him speculatively. 'Although for you I might show minor concern. I owe your sister a favour. She gave me my cousin back.'

'Whatever debt you think you owe Moriana, leave me out of it.' He didn't need saving or fixing or whatever else Benedict thought he was doing. He just wanted a distraction from the woman in his birdcage who was messing with his head. The woman who this morning had put a tapestry illustrating one of his ancestors feasting in the round room on show in the main entry hall. The accompanying plaque named every nobleman in the picture, the names of every courtesan and the date. On a plinth beside the tapestry sat an open recipe book, written in a language of old. Beside it, she'd offered a printed translation of *Feast Number Six for Midwinter Dining.*

Augustus scowled afresh. Sera of the High Reaches was doing exactly what he'd told her to do and, what was more, she was doing it well.

'No sexual identity crisis?'

What the hell was it with these questions lately? 'I'm male. I'm straight. I sincerely don't know what else to say to that question.'

'Not a problem,' said Benedict blithely. 'But if that *had* been your problem I would have helped. I take my role seriously when it comes to being a guiding light for same sex relationships of the royal variety.'

'You buried yourself in vice, became estranged from your family and then downplayed your most important romantic relationship for years.'

'And now I'm back. Like I said: guiding light. I'm a veritable lighthouse.'

Augustus snorted.

'Besides, there are other existential crises to be had,' continued Benedict. 'No unexpected desire to be tied, gagged and at someone's mercy?'

'No.'

'Bootlicking, public sex, voyeurism…'

'I worry about you occasionally,' said Augustus.

'I'm worried for you right now, in spite of my self-proclaimed indifference. It appears I'm getting soft.'

'Worry about something else.'

'I hear you have a courtesan in residence. Moriana thinks it's wonderful. A revelation, rich in art, history and cultural significance. Which, while I embrace your sister's enthusiasm for all things cultural, rather seems to be missing the point. You have a woman who has been trained to indulge your every sexual whim living in your birdcage. How's that working out for you?'

Trust Benedict to get straight to the sexual point.

'The Lady Sera has now retired from her former role as courtesan and has taken on an events management and PR position.'

Benedict had his head down and his hands in his pockets as they headed for the car that would take them on to future engagements, but at this he looked up. 'No special services at all?'

'She's finding me a wife.'

When Benedict laughed, he did it body, heart and soul. He was laughing now, near bent double, and all Augustus could do was scowl.

'That's the worst idea you've ever had,' offered Benedict when his amusement no longer threatened his ability to talk.

'Thank you for your enduring support. Moriana's helping her.'

'Good heavens, you're serious.'

'When am I not?'

'Says he who threatened Theo with a procession of elephants after he proposed to your sister.'

'I reiterate—when am I not serious?' Elephants too had been part of Arun's lore of old. His courtesan could probably tell him all about them. 'I need a wife in order to make the courtesan in the birdcage go away. I also need an heir and Arun could use a Queen. They seem like good enough reasons to make marrying a priority.'

'I understand your need for a wife. I even understand your desire to canvass other royal opinions as part of your decision-making process. But why's the courtesan helping you choose one?'

'She's not helping me choose, she's simply helping to organise the parade of eligible women.'

'Giving her ample opportunity to manipulate the parade itself,' Benedict offered with a hefty helping of sarcasm.

'If I don't like what I see I can always look elsewhere.' Augustus was famously picky when it came to choosing women to keep company with. 'It's not as if I haven't already looked. I need to broaden my horizons. This is one way to do it.'

'Are you intending to bed your former courtesan while you wait for your potential Queen to amble by?'

'No.' But his brain conjured the image of Sera on her knees before him and then another one of her naked beneath him, a writhing, pleading mess as he sent her soaring, those expressive grey eyes blind to everything but the feel of him. 'That would be potentially off-putting to said future wife.'

'Tempting, though.'

'Very,' he admitted through gritted teeth.

Benedict smirked. 'I see your dilemma. Fewer scruples would help.'

'A king leads by example. Sera of the High Reaches needs to leave my employment in the same state in which she entered it.'

'Right. And meanwhile you…'

'Go slowly round the twist, yes.'

Sera knew Augustus was avoiding her and, frankly, that suited her just fine. Courtesans weren't meant to blush at the memory of a man's mouth on her. She wasn't supposed to crave Augustus's attention the way she did. Anything would do. A touch, a glance, the merest shred of his attention. Anything to feed the bubbling cauldron of emotion he'd awakened in her. The desperate need to satisfy his desires and hers. The things they could *do*, and *feel*. They could be fearless together…

She read texts on controlling sexual situations, because that was his way, was it not? She read texts on how best to stay safe while surrendering control. She did everything he asked of her. Put artwork from the High Reaches on display in his palace and the libraries and galleries of Arun. Arranged speaking engagements for herself and spent hours crafting speeches to fit various target audiences. She set about reinventing her role here and part of her relished the challenge even as another part mourned the loss of tradition. She purchased clothes more suitable to a corporate banker than a courtesan, and when the Winter Solstice ball came along she attended it as the events co-ordinator, dressed fully in nondescript black. Black boots, black trousers, fitted black blazer and her black hair pulled back in a high ponytail. Communication pack at her waist and an earphone in her ear, she was quite clearly working the event and not there as a guest.

It didn't stop people—mostly men—from staring at her regardless or luring her to their side under the guise of making a complaint and then asking for her phone number or simply asking her what she was doing later. No finesse, but most accepted her polite brush-offs with equal civility. Those who pressed their suit met Ari and Tun. Augustus might have requested her presence here tonight but he hadn't been stupid enough to leave her unprotected.

Small mercies.

Just because he had no desire for a courtesan, didn't

mean others were equally restrained. Augustus had relinquished his claim on her in the most public way possible—by putting her to work, very visibly, in another role. Others were singularly inclined to pick her up where he'd left off.

It made it extremely difficult for her to competently do her job.

When Augustus's long-suffering secretary caught her eye and wordlessly directed her to the service doors, Sera made her way towards them. He met her there, his face impassive.

'The King respectfully requests that from this point onwards you leave all requests for your personal attention for either me or your guards to deal with,' he began.

'With pleasure.'

'He also requests that you stop deliberately attracting attention.'

Deliberately attracting attention? 'Are my black clothes not modest enough?'

The older man hitched his shoulders in a wordless gesture signifying who knew what.

'Shall I overcome years of comportment training and walk with a slouch?'

Another shrug. 'I'm just the messenger.'

'Then you can tell the King that this is no more and no less attention than I ever receive. People look and people want. There is no "off" switch. The relationship between King and courtesan is often mutually beneficial in that once he stakes his claim the unwanted attention afforded a courtesan will *stop*. Of course, *this* King is far too enlightened to understand that the course of action he insists I follow has consequences he knows nothing about.'

'I'll let him know,' the older man said, and strode off.

The next time a guest beckoned her forward, she sent Ari to deal with him.

The next time the King's secretary approached she summoned her gentlest smile.

'The King suggests you supervise the event from the upper west balcony,' he said. 'From behind the lights.'

'Of course.' There were two ways to reach the suggested balcony. By the servants' entrance or by the central staircase. She chose the stairs. Head held high and the six-inch heels of her boots very much on show, she made her way straight up the middle with Tun and Ari falling into place on either side of her and two steps behind. She didn't bother looking back.

She knew damn well she had almost everyone's attention. Including Augustus's.

He found her two hours later, after the remains of the meal had been cleared away and guests had gravitated towards the dance floor, some to dance, some to stand and mingle at the edges. He'd mingled too, for as long as his patience would allow, and then he'd slipped away through a side door and taken the back way to the balcony. She had her back to him as one of her guards opened the door so he could enter. The second guard appraised him coolly before apparently making some kind of decision and silently taking his leave and closing the balcony door behind them and plunging them into near darkness.

'Why are you up here when you should be down there?' she asked without even turning around.

Why indeed? 'How did you know it was me?'

'Ari gave us privacy. There's only one person in this

palace he'd do that for without waiting for my command.' She turned to face him. 'Your Majesty.'

He didn't make the mistake of thinking Sera's guards were under his control. According to his Head of Security, they were compliant to a point. Co-operating when they could, fitting unobtrusively into whatever protection detail was in place. Beyond that, they were hers. 'Lucky me.'

Her shuttered glance mocked him.

'Would you prefer I call him back in?' she offered, dry as dust.

'No. The evening didn't go quite to plan, as far as you were concerned.'

'Didn't it?' She sounded wholly unconcerned. 'I thought it went well. You mingled. Ate well. Met the women you wanted to meet. I gather Katerina DeLitt is a pleasant enough conversationalist.'

'She is.' One of his sister's additions to the potential brides list. A noblewoman with strong trade connections. 'She's titled, well-read, entertaining and perfectly pleasing to the eye. And yet no one here this evening seemed to be able to see past you.'

'It happens.'

'Why?' His knew his voice sounded tight with frustration. 'You were supposed to blend in as an employee, shatter the myth of the courtesans of old. Instead you—'

'Instead I what?' He really should have taken note of the sharp note in her voice. He hadn't grown up with a temperamental sister for nothing. 'Did I not dress appropriately and make sure the evening ran smoothly? Was I not available to troubleshoot guest issues as they arose? Did I not do what you asked of me?'

'You drew too much attention.'

She leaned back against the balcony and crossed her arms in front of her, wholly unconcerned by the low balustrade and the significant drop to the floor below. 'I've been drawing that kind of attention since childhood. They say I have too much presence, that my beauty serves to make others insecure. Some people want to tear me down before I've ever said a word to them. Others would own me for their own ego enhancement. I don't blend in. I never have. My beauty will always be both celebrated and demonised, sometimes both at once, because beauty is power, and never more dangerous than in the hands of someone who knows how to use it.' She cocked her head to one side, her face in shadows and the spotlights behind her shining out across the ballroom below. 'You want me to craft a new persona while I live beneath your roof and I have no objection to doing so. But the response of others to power such as mine is always going to be part of it. *Your* response to me is always going to be part of it. So what's it to be? Are you here to work with me? Ask me to set up another meeting for you with the pleasant enough Katerina DeLitt? Perhaps you'd also like to tell me to make a note to never invite Peter Saville and Ricardo Anguissey to the same event again lest their wives and everyone else discover that they're in each other's pants? Or are you here to condemn me because my mere presence makes others behave badly?'

He'd been about to do that last one. He hadn't liked the attention his guests had bestowed on his new events co-ordinator. The predatory nature of some of it. His instinctive desire to protect her from it. He'd wanted to claim her, to own her, to tear into anyone who dared covet her. Berate her for using the same stairs dozens of his other employees had used throughout the evening.

He wanted to step away from the door and look into her face, the better to try and interpret her every thought. He wanted to see her eyes darken with desire not hurt, and then he wanted to turn her around to face the ballroom and tell her that none of the people down there mattered; only his elemental desire to claim her mattered. And then he would step up behind her, open her trousers and bring her to quivering arousal with his fingers while his mouth ravaged hers and smothered her soft gasps of completion. She'd let him.

He knew damn well she'd let him.

And the next time he saw her she'd have drawn up a new list of candidates eligible to become his Queen—women with a knack for surrendering to exhibitionism or possessiveness or whatever this was that he wanted from her.

From *her*, not them.

'Is my Minister for Trade really having an affair with our Liesendaach Ambassador?' he said instead. 'I'll have to tell Theo.'

'You're assuming he doesn't already know.'

Augustus lowered his head and bit down a snort. She had a point. 'In that case, I'll ask my sister why I shouldn't simply send Liesendaach's diplomatic representative home and get them to send a new one.'

She smiled ever so slightly, and dropped her arms to her sides and then curled her hands around the railing behind her. 'That would be one way of opening dialogue about the conflict of many interests, yes.'

He liked seeing her less defensive when she looked at him. 'What else did you see?'

'Your Transport Minister's wife is pregnant and not coping well with the demands of his job and her first trimester sickness. One of the Cordova twins of Liesendaach will be going home this evening with your Horse Master, although I'm not sure which one. And Prince Benedict of Liesendaach enjoys winding you up more than you can possibly imagine. If he wasn't so enamoured of his partner I'd think him desperate for your attention.'

'Benedict enjoys cultivating other people's low opinion of him. It prevents them from noticing how ruthlessly cunning he is until it's too late. At which point he usually has enough dirt on them to make them beholden to him for life. Never underestimate him.'

'I like him already,' she murmured.

'He collects art. I'm sure he'd like to see some of the treasures that now reside in the round room.' Benedict would go nuts over the tapestry wheel on the floor. 'You might want to be careful about where he wants to sit on that round sofa of yours. Because he'll doubtless want to sit in every damn section, just to see what happens.'

She smiled and for a moment his breath caught in his throat. It didn't matter what they'd just been talking about because that smile was one he hadn't seen before—openly conspiratorial and at the same time unguarded. As if gossiping about guests and trusting her to deal with Benedict however she saw fit made her happy.

He looked away, trying desperately not to be one of those men who looked at her and wanted her for all the wrong reasons. Nor did he want to be among the masses who became putty in her hands with just one smile. He wanted to do right by this woman who'd been placed in his care regardless of whether he wanted her there or not. Set her up to succeed. Give her a way out of the lifestyle she'd had thrust upon her when she was seven years old.

No judgement. No slaking his desires. Just common human decency. 'Make sure Katerina DeLitt is invited to the next palace function, along with the next set of candidates,' he said gruffly. 'I like her.'

And then he left.

CHAPTER SIX

THREE DAYS LATER Sera stepped naked into the bathing pool and kept going until every part of her was underwater from the neck down. The pool had been getting warmer by the day and now it ran hot, day in and day out. No one used it but her. Augustus had declined, ever since that first time. Her guards declined the use of it—even if they knew she'd be out all day giving a talk at one gallery or another or being interviewed by journalists or overseeing this function or that. Augustus kept her busy and if he wasn't in residence, his secretary kept her busy. TV show hosts loved her because the cameras loved her face and she could string two words together.

She was compliant, carving out a place for herself in his world that had nothing to do with the sexual aspects of a courtesan's role and everything to do with social outreach and celebration of history and letting people get a behind-the-scenes glimpse of the day-to-day running of the palace.

She was an ambassador. Making connections, building a web, consolidating power that didn't belong to her, and the role suited her to perfection. She was good at it.

Augustus was managing her, piling on the work, keeping her so busy in her dual roles of palace PR and events management that there was barely time for thought, and far too little time for herself.

This morning she'd requested of his secretary that down time be built into her weekly schedule and that if she was obliged to work weekends she wanted the following Tuesday kept free for her own use.

'Finally,' she thought she'd heard the old man mutter beneath his breath, and then he'd pulled a file drawer open and moments later handed her a bunch of papers on workplace rights. 'Read these, sign these, hand them back in and I can most assuredly do something about that, Lady Sera. Not everyone here is willing to work like a dog for no apparent reason.'

She'd read through the employment conditions, signed them and handed them back in and now had every full Tuesday, Wednesday and Thursday morning off.

Much to Augustus's displeasure.

Sera ducked beneath the water, wetting her hair and holding her breath until the need to breathe forced her to rise.

Tomorrow was Tuesday, her first full day off, and Ari had invited her to spar with him during tomorrow's six a.m. lesson. She hadn't sparred with anyone since Ari had dropped her to the ground and Augustus had helped her back up. She'd taken on a tutor's role instead, helping those who'd taken up the invitation to practise the forms, and she enjoyed her role, but maybe tomorrow she *would* spar with Ari again.

Take back some of her own identity.

If Augustus objected she would tell him she was a tutor now and call it a demonstration.

As for the charities she'd been working for so tirelessly, maybe it was time to invest some of her own identity into that too.

And see what good and noble King Augustus would do.

'What do you mean she wants to take a courtesan's clothing collection on the road, starting with viewings at city brothels?'

Augustus knew he was glaring at his personal secretary but the idea was preposterous. He was doing everything in his power to *remove* her courtesan status. He was trying, above all, to render her role here respectable. The very *least* she could do was appreciate it.

'Lady Sera's guards put forward the security arrangement plans this morning,' his secretary informed him placidly. 'There's a fifty-page report justifying the social benefits involved, including collaboration with community welfare groups and backing from your police commissioner and city mayor. Two of the brothels are extremely prestigious. Others are less so. I have it on good advice that several are for...acquired tastes. They're all registered and legal.'

Silence was one response to situations out of his control. It wasn't the only response available to him. 'Get her in here. Now.'

'Lady Sera's schedule for the day puts her at the state library attending a history lecture until one. This afternoon she'll be overseeing the botanists' picnic on the lawn surrounding the royal glasshouses.'

Roses. Good grief. Roses and social welfare. Just what he needed.

'Ask the Lady Sera if she's available for dinner this

evening. Put us in the blue dining room with several dishes for sharing, a small selection of sweets and let us serve ourselves.' It wasn't an unusual request, although it was one he usually reserved for family.

'Does next week's costume tour have your approval?' His secretary reminded him of the matter in hand.

'No. Have you read the proposal?'

'It makes for interesting reading. I particularly enjoyed Chapter Two.'

'Fifty pages, you say?'

'With references, footnotes and a reading list,' the older man said, handing it over. 'She's also written you a report outlining new initiatives for education reform, particularly with regard to non-academic children. She confirms a substantial donation from the temples of the High Reaches to set up a pilot project. You want to see that proposal too?'

'Give it over.' He didn't have time for this. He truly didn't.

'Additionally, Lady Sera has been restructuring the fund-raising portfolio related to education. The one your grandmother, mother and Moriana have toiled over for generations.'

'What for? What part of "It's a good one" doesn't she understand?'

'I'll leave that for you to judge. I'll warn you though, she's already engaged your sister's co-operation and they're looking at some quite sweeping reforms.'

'They'll still have to go through me.' He wasn't looking forward to being the voice of reason. He could already name a dozen education initiatives that Moriana had wanted to support that had been shut down by various committees full of education experts. 'Let's dig deeper into Sera's background and education qualifications. Personal history too. I want no surprises when it comes to what kind of reforms she's likely to advance.'

'You have a dossier on her.'

'I have a CV. I want to expedite that full investigative report I ordered. Whatever has been collected, get them to send it.'

The older man nodded.

'As for education reform—'

'It's been on your agenda for the last six months,' the older man offered drily. 'You keep shuffling it to the bottom of your pile while you concentrate on regional water plans. I gave the portfolio to Lady Sera a week ago on a whim. So if you want to blame somebody for that particular report, blame me.'

'I will.' Augustus looked at the folder in his hand and scowled.

'Children are our future,' the older man said serenely. 'I so look forward to yours.'

'Alas, that will require a wife.' And, at last glance, he still didn't have one in mind.

He already gave careful consideration to the charities and initiatives he supported.

'Will you be requiring casual dress for dinner this evening or something more formal?' his secretary asked.

'Casual.' Even if the image of Sera in a formal evening gown made him momentarily lose focus. What would a courtesan of the High Reaches regard as formal clothing? What would she regard as casual? He hadn't forgotten the collar and the manacles she'd worn upon her arrival. 'Definitely casual.'

* * *

Sera arrived at the door to the blue dining room at precisely thirty seconds past seven. The door was open and Augustus was already within. She entered and he looked up, a dark-haired devil with classically handsome features and black eyes that knew how to drill deep.

She pushed back the hood of her travelling cloak and met those eyes with polite composure, before dropping to a curtsey and rising again before he could tell her to get up. He could add *Doesn't take orders* to her list of sins. There were bigger sins.

'You wear a travelling cloak to walk down a corridor?' Augustus asked as she reached for the tie at her neck and stepped aside so that Ari could wheel a covered rack of clothes into the room and set it to one side. She waited until Ari had stationed himself outside the door before closing it behind him and turning to face her host.

'You ordered me never to appear in front of your court wearing the clothing of my profession,' she reminded him gently. 'Remember?'

The cloak came off. Her tunic was sheer and the bodice beneath it was more beautiful and intricate than he had ever seen before. Fitted trousers, high heels, no jewellery but for the pearls in her hair. Modesty for the most part, enticement if anyone was so inclined. She draped the cloak over the back of a nearby chair and turned to face him again.

'You call that casual dress?' he asked.

'Yes. Also, you're wearing a hand-tailored suit, a fifty-thousand-dollar vintage watch, and the only concession you've made to dressing casually is that the top button of your shirt's undone and you've loosened your tie.' She arched an elegant eyebrow. 'Did you expect me to wear shorts?'

'I'm pretty sure the watch wasn't worth fifty thousand when my grandfather bought it,' he offered mildly. 'But point taken. You look lovely.' She always did, no matter what she wore.

He ought to be used to it by now.

'I know your interest in historical gowns and clothing is limited,' she said, turning towards the clothes rack. 'But I took the liberty of bringing a few along for show and tell. They'll form part of the costume collection I'd like to take on the road to various places, should you give the go-ahead.'

Which sounded all well and good, but he'd read the proposal—all fifty pages of it and the appendices—and by *various places* she meant brothels.

Augustus would have reprimanded her for being so blatantly obvious about her political agenda, only she'd turned her back on him and his attention had been firmly caught and held by the dazzling dragon-shaped embroidery that wove through the material at her back, leaving pockets of nothing but creamy skin showing through the delicate gaps. Shimmery scales collected from heaven only knew what kind of beast highlighted various dips and curves, and as for those forest-green stilettoes that matched one of the dragon's main colours, how did she even balance on those things?

'Would you like a drink?' he asked, rather than engage with the topic she'd introduced. He was no novice when it came to directing conversation where he wanted it. Or keeping people off-balance, if he wanted to.

Movement was good. Movement meant he could

leave the dragon at her back behind. The sideboard was stacked with a selection of beverages. 'Wine?'

'Thank you.' Sera smiled, her movements quick and effortless as she removed one particular gown from the rack and twirled it around on its hanger, the better to make the skirt flare. 'Take this gown, for example.'

'No. Sera, you're not taking it anywhere.'

Her eyes turned stormy. 'You haven't heard me out.'

'Red or white?'

'White.'

He poured some into a wine glass and took it to her and their fingers touched.

Her gaze met his and the outside world as he knew it skidded to a halt as a kaleidoscope of memories flashed through his brain. Sera on her knees in front of him, swallowing him down. Sera rising naked from the bathing pool and wringing water from her hair. Sera pushing back the hood of her travelling cloak. Sera, all too tempting, no matter what she said or did.

Perfect posture, regal bearing. He wondered if it came naturally to her or whether it had been drummed into her by her elders, the way Moriana's had been ground into her. The way cool analysis and never letting anyone get close enough to truly know him had been drummed into him.

'Is there a reason you don't trust me to do a good job with this?' she asked. 'Have I not been pitch-perfect in my presentation of the courtesans of old so far?'

'You have.' He had to give her that. 'Different audience.'

'You mean you'd rather not put me in front of an audience that might actually *benefit* from their profession being acknowledged and treated with respect?'

'You can reach them without prioritising them. You already are.'

'But I want to prioritise them.'

'Why?'

'You've never lived at the edge of poverty and violence and hopelessness, have you?' She waved a careless hand in his direction. 'No need to answer; I know you haven't. But I have. And every day I thank my looks and my luck and the training someone saw fit to grace me with that I'm not still there.'

'I can't imagine you there.' He just couldn't.

'My mother was once a courtesan to a high-born man. She loved him, and in many ways that precipitated her downfall because I don't believe he ever loved her at all. He just wanted her at his beck and call. He certainly didn't want me to ever draw breath. My mother fled, but his reach was long. She tried to start over, but he always found her. She hid, and once I was born she hid us both, over and over again, always moving, always one step ahead. The houses got smaller. The cupboards got barer. Her sponsors meaner.'

He didn't like this history she was telling him, but he listened while she paced.

'I don't remember all that much of the very early years but, by the time I was seven, my mother was lost in the bottle and dying of cancer and I was so skinny and malnourished that I couldn't even sit at a table and eat the first meal Lianthe ever put in front of me. I ate a quarter of it, and even that was too much for me. To this day I still prefer to snack rather than sit down to a three-course meal.' She spared a glance for the dinner table. 'I trust it's simply an eating preference by now but it was born of necessity.'

'Why are you telling me this?' About the food. Her mother and the bottle.

'You ask me why I proposed the costume tour of the brothels and this is part of it. It's personal for me. This lavish, glittering history of the Kings' courtesans is their history too, and you have no idea what simple acknowledgement can mean to those who are outcast. Those who live on the fringes of society and who are so often overlooked. I'm already reaching out and talking to your noble art curators and librarians about the history of courtesans—at your request. Why *not* reach out to the people who identify with that history the most?'

She was warming to her theme and he couldn't take his eyes off the glittering, shimmering dragon which writhed on her back.

'Education and learning. Physical and mental health. Those are causes the Arunian royal family has supported for centuries.' Irony tinged her voice. 'Causes you continue to endorse and pour money and resources into. My costume tour proposal should have made sense to you. I designed it to fit within your broader mission statements.'

Too smart by half. Too bold with her plans. And defiantly, unapologetically idealistic. He wondered if he'd ever been like that when it came to what causes to support. He rather thought not. 'It fits to a point,' he said carefully. 'I applaud your...passion for outreach.'

'No, you don't. You'd rather bury it. Turn me into a perfect puppet who performs whatever tasks you deem suitable for someone like me.'

'What I'd rather do is protect you,' he argued. 'Keep the press off your back and your reputation spotless by only giving you certain roles to play. If I send you to brothels the press will draw comparisons to what you do here, for me. They'll dig up your history, make front page news out of you.'

'So? I'm not ashamed of my pathway through life. I am who I am. You think you're protecting me—you're not. You think that by carving away at the unsavoury parts of me you're reshaping me into something better. You're not. All you're doing is carving me up.'

Sera's hands trembled as she cupped her wine glass and brought it to her lips. She made a good show of wetting those lips but he'd bet his kingdom on the fact that she didn't swallow so much as a drop. He strode to the sideboard, poured her a glass of water and exchanged it for the wine before she could protest.

'Why say yes to wine when you don't even drink?' he snapped.

She took the water and drank it down, not stopping until she'd finished, and then set the glass on the table. 'Is that a no to taking the costumes on tour throughout your city brothels?'

'Yes, it's a no. You're not doing it. It's a bad idea.'

She looked strangely shattered as she collected her cloak and fastened it around her neck. 'As always, I am bound to your will and will abide by your command. Now, if you'll excuse me, I'll take my leave.'

'Sera.' Her compliance should have pleased him. Instead, it left him strangely bereft. 'You could stay and eat.'

Not that she ate in the same way he did, apparently. She'd already told him that.

'And talk about what?' she asked coolly. 'Adding perfection to the list of things you require in a wife? No supporting those lost causes, right? No acknowledging the seething, need-ridden underbelly of humanity from that pedestal she'll be standing on, right? Consider it done.'

'I didn't say that.' She could get under his skin faster than any woman he'd ever known. Call up a temper he took a great deal of care to conceal. He still had her glass of wine in his hand. The temptation to drink it was strong. His fingers tightened on the stem. That tiny insignificant tell did not go unnoticed by his courtesan.

'Go on.' She drew closer and closer still until her breath fanned his ear and the scent of tea roses teased his nose. 'Throw it.'

'Why would I do that?' He set the glass on the table gently, never mind that the temptation to hurl it at the nearest wall was strong. 'I'm not a savage.'

'I guess they carved that out of you as a child.' She drew closer and closer still until her lips touched his ear. He shuddered and not with disgust. She didn't miss that tell either. 'Who needs passion? Who needs compassion? Not a king.'

'There's nothing wrong with cool calculation,' he argued. It was what he'd been raised to believe. 'Passion's overrated.'

'If you truly believe that, I pity you.' Her hand snaked up to fist in his hair and he made no move to stop her. 'You should have just thrown the glass.'

'The world might have ended if I had.'

'It wouldn't have.'

The kiss, when she dragged his head down and lifted her lips to his, was searingly hot and decidedly angry. It brought him to full and throbbing hardness in the space of thirty seconds. If this was punishment for his refusal to accommodate her wishes, he'd take it. If it was a thirst she couldn't control, he'd slake it. If this was her way of trying to make him change his mind, good luck with that.

She drew back all too soon as far as he was concerned, but he wasn't the one running this little power play; she was. He'd figure out what that kiss meant soon enough.

'You're a good king, Augustus. No one can deny it.' She let go of his hair, took a breath, stepped back. 'I hope one day you get to be human too.'

He waited until she and her dragon and her rack full of courtesans' clothing had left the room. He shut the door behind her and counted to ten, and then ten again, before striding across to the table and draining her wine glass.

He let anger, frustration for all the things he could not do, and aching desire for all the things he could not have fill him. He flung the wine glass at the fireplace, where it smashed into glittering pieces.

And the world did not end.

The following day didn't begin well for Augustus of Arun. He'd slept poorly and risen with the sun. He'd gone to the kitchen to find his own breakfast, only to overhear two of his catering staff talking about how Sera's guards had put on a fighting display with long sticks yesterday morning, apparently, and the hits had come thick and fast and left everyone who watched in awe. They fought in the covered stable area these days, not because he'd given his tacit approval but because of the sawdust on the ground and the space and relative privacy it afforded them. Augustus wondered if they fought there because any gathered crowd could melt away into the shadows fast if they were discovered.

He grabbed a bread roll straight from the oven, ripped it open and cut the end from a length of resting roast beef, and knew for a fact that he wouldn't have got away with either action had he still been a child.

He cut through the back door and headed for the stables. He found the crowd easily enough and it looked like a regular martial arts lesson to him, with Ari leading and Tun and Sera helping the trainees with the movements. Sera still practised the forms with her guards on a daily basis, so he'd been informed, but she hadn't sparred since that day he'd hauled her off the ground.

Two men standing in front of him sent him startled looks and shuffled to the side but he shook his head and gestured for them to stay where they were. He didn't want to be noticed this morning. He just wanted to watch.

When Ari told the class they would be doing the form one last time from start to finish, Sera and Tun fell into step with him, making it look effortless. And when that was done and everyone had bowed and the class had been dismissed, Ari and Sera moved over to a canvas holdall and unzipped it and rolled it out along the ground—it was like no holdall he'd ever seen. More like a portable armoury.

Ari selected two wickedly curved short swords with black handle grips, while Sera selected similar, only her grips were red. They sat in her hands as if they'd been made for her. Maybe they had. The form they practised next had its origins in the one they'd practised in class, that much he could see, the lines of their bodies extended by glittering curved knives.

They made it look as if they'd been born holding knives and cutting patterns in the air.

And then Sera said something to Ari and he frowned, and she smiled back at him sharp and sure and broke from her pattern and moved to face him, not quite head-on, a little to one side. They bowed to each other, plenty of space between them. Tun came to stand between them as a referee would in a boxing ring. At his word he stepped back and they began to fight.

If anyone thought they'd hold back because of the lethal weapons in their hands, they thought wrong.

The fighting was fast and vicious, with Sera on the attack and Ari defending, and Augustus felt his breath lodge somewhere in his throat. Ari was bigger, stronger and his reach was longer and still Sera came at him, even when he began to strike back. The clash of swords rang in his ears, broken only by the occasional murmur from those watching.

He thought about stopping the fight. Demonstration. Whatever it was, he thought about stopping it, but there was no way he wanted to break their concentration. Absolute focus and unearthly skill was all that stood between them and a potentially fatal blow.

And then, between one moment and the next, Ari was on his back on the ground and Sera was on top of him, the curve of one blade at his neck and the other poised to take his upraised hand off at the wrist.

The man in front of Augustus swore silently beneath his breath, and Augustus knew that by lunchtime the palace would be buzzing with the news that the courtesan of the High Reaches was some kind of mystical warrior in addition to being the Devil's temptress.

Surely she'd been sitting on the fallen sword master for far too long.

He watched her roll off and to her feet as if she'd heard him. Tun clapped once and she and Ari moved close for quick smiles and quiet conversation as they released their fighting grips on the blades and began to examine the edges of them. All in a day's work. Nothing unusual about what they'd just demonstrated.

Who were these people?

She saw him out of the corner of her eye and started to walk towards him. People melted away as if sensing conflict. All except for her guards, who stayed right where they were, neither courting conflict nor avoiding it.

'Is that your way of blowing off steam?' he asked.

'It works.'

He'd been thinking about her words from last night. Her scorn for his cool calculation and his need to control what he could. 'You want to know what I see when you're out there passionately blowing off steam?' He didn't wait for an answer. 'Absolute control.' His gaze skipped towards Ari. 'And lives utterly dedicated to the quest for it.'

'Why are you here?' she asked next.

'I've been thinking about what you said last night and all the things I didn't say. The personal things that might have helped you understand my reluctance to have you reach out to a bunch of brothels.'

She waited for him to speak, and he didn't want to, he really didn't, but she'd shown him her heart last night and her passion and maybe they would understand each other a little better if she knew his.

'When I was fifteen I had my first kiss. She was a stable girl, several years older than me, and she'd been lobbying for that kiss for at least three years. It was pretty chaste, as far as kisses went, but she sold her story to the papers that afternoon and we all read about it at breakfast the following morning.'

The lecture his father had given him still had the power to make him wince.

'The woman I finally lost my virginity to was an older woman as well—a woman with enough money and power and sheer front to withstand the hounding of the press for months. Just long enough for me to feel safe in her arms. And then she turned around and finally granted that press interview and laid me bare.

'She called me an accomplished lover—and I was by then—and then added that I could also be a little too passionately intense for some tastes. She told them she envied me my brilliant mind and in the same breath warned of sweeping social and economic reforms once I took the throne. I'd made the mistake of talking to her about the causes I was passionate about, you see. I'd talked big bold plans that didn't have a hope of seeing the light of day—not then. Not without years of careful planning. The press called me an ignorant, idealistic fool and I was—I was a fool to think I could confide in her or trust her. She praised my protective nature, especially when it came to those I consider family, and then casually mentioned how rigidly impenetrable I could be when it came to letting other people in.'

None of it true. All of it true.

'Which was quite the complaint because, as far as I was concerned, I *had* let her in. Like a fool.'

Sera opened her mouth to speak but he put his hand up to stop her.

'And now you, a courtesan sent here specifically to serve me, wants to go into the brothels and talk job descriptions, and they're going to have questions art curators and librarians would never dare ask you. Questions about me and what I want and need and think and who's to say you won't expose me?'

'I would never do that.' She drew herself up and still didn't manage to reach his shoulder. Bare feet. A face flushed with exercise. 'I am a courtesan of the High Reaches. Confidentiality is the key to our *existence*, and beyond that…' She shook her head. 'Augustus, I will never betray your confidences. Not sexual, emotional or intellectual. You have my word. My oath. That's what you *get* when you get me. A safe space in which to simply be human.'

'I want to believe you.' He looked away from those earnest grey eyes. Experience suggested he shouldn't.

'I can't make that decision for you,' she offered quietly.

He nodded. He'd think on it. 'There was another reason I came out here this morning,' he said, while in the distance a stablehand worked on a horse's hoof with a file.

'What is it?'

He couldn't even bring himself to look at her while he was saying it. 'I love the way you move.' It was as simple and as complicated as that. 'I envy the fierce blend of passion and control you bring to everything you do and it's never more evident than when you're out there, facing an opponent. It's beautiful.'

It was the first thought he'd shared in years without analysing the pros and cons of doing so.

And it was met with complete and utter silence.

He glanced back, just in time to see a softly startled smile cross her face.

'I…thank you,' she said.

And the world did not end.

'What do you want done with the costume tour proposal?' Augustus's secretary asked him two hours later.

Augustus ran a hand across his face and memories flashed before him. Sera with a blade in each hand and total concentration on her face. Sera with a dragon on her back and her face alight with pleasure. Sera, who never failed to stand out, no matter what kind of company she was in, and who had yet to set a foot wrong in public.

Sera as a child, with a plate full of food in front of her that she could not eat. A plate that was only there in the first place because someone had *seen* her plight rather than turn away from an outcast child struggling for existence.

Sera's proposal to reach out to her sisters in service had healthcare and educational elements, but first and foremost it was about acknowledging their existence.

She could have been one of them. *Was* one of them, for all her finery and expensive education, and he'd never met a woman more accomplished.

Her mother had been one of them. A broken one.

This was no soulless, rudderless outreach programme. Sera had this one covered. He could trust her not to make this all about him. Couldn't he?

He dropped his hand and searched his heart and not his head.

'Green-light it,' he said.

CHAPTER SEVEN

THE INAUGURAL COURTESAN costumes tour, starting at a seedy but legal downtown brothel and finishing at the National Art gallery of Arun, received some of the best press Augustus had ever seen. It brought together six health and education outreach programmes already in place and cemented Arun's reputation as a progressive nation with the welfare and education of *all* its people at heart. Far from damaging his personal reputation, he was being hailed as a saviour. A man that any woman, courtesan or not, would be proud to have in their corner. He'd even accompanied Sera on one of the tours, to watch her in action and lend his support, and there'd been not one single, solitary crack about him partaking of her sexual services.

It was a God-given miracle.

Suffice to say, the fund-raising dinner he was currently attending suffered a little in comparison, even if Sera had organised it. The dinner helped raise funds for cancer research and had been on his social calendar for the past seven years running. He was seated next to Katerina DeLitt at his request and the lady was well aware of it. To her credit, she was socially adept and inclusive of the others around them. She had a charming smile and the kind of effortless poise he was used to. She had yet to hold his attention for long but maybe that was his fault for having Sera oversee the event.

Sera, with her tailored black suit and sky-high stilettos. Sera, with her hair coiled tightly into a bun at the nape of her neck and a face practically devoid of make-up. She didn't need make-up. She was quite beautiful enough.

He'd corner her afterwards for a crowd report and she'd tell him whom was currently at war with whom and other minor matters of interest. Her powers of observation kept his sharp too. Being able to one-up her in the observation stakes was wholly satisfying. Not to mention hard to do.

'She's very beautiful,' said Katerina DeLitt from somewhere beside him.

'Excuse me?'

Could be his attention had been somewhere it shouldn't be, but he trusted Katerina DeLitt's manners to prevail and doubted she would repeat such a confronting statement.

'Lady Sera Boreas. She's very beautiful.'

'Ah.' Guess he was wrong. He eyed the woman seated to his left with renewed interest. She smiled wryly, diamond earrings dangling as she tilted her head the better to observe him.

'And talented too, assuming even half the things I hear about her are true,' she said next.

He knew full well he should steer the conversation elsewhere. Hard to court one woman when seemingly fixated on another. He could talk about the weather. The charity. Or horses—he had a fleeting memory of Katerina talking animatedly about horses.

Or he could succumb to curiosity. 'What kind of things do you hear?'

Katerina shrugged. 'She has great skill with knives, she can dance like a dream. She has a mind trained towards observation and is bound to you in ways no one can quite explain. You were forced by ancient laws to open your home to her. You can't get rid of her until you find a future wife and take steps to secure the throne. Even then, you might not let her go.'

'Sounds about right.' Katerina's information was good. 'Although I will let her go.'

'They say she has your ear, among other things. That she is your muse.'

Augustus frowned.

'Your Majesty, if I may be bold—and that does seem to be the best way to deal with you—what is it you want from me, when your attention is so obviously elsewhere?'

He appreciated her bluntness and returned it in full. 'I need a wife who will give me children and occupy the role of Queen Consort with all due diligence. Your name came up and I enjoy your company. I'm getting to know you.'

'I see. And what of love?' Katerina asked drily.

'Love can grow.'

'Your Ma—'

'Call me Augustus,' he interrupted.

'Augustus.' She said it nicely but not the way Sera did. 'Your Majesty, I know it's not fashionable, but let us be even more frank. As honoured as I am to have your attention, I'm in no hurry to put my heart on the line for you, knowing what else is available to you at any given time.'

'Meaning?'

She inclined her head towards Sera.

'That is not an option,' he grated. 'Sera will leave once the terms of the accord have been satisfied. She may well leave before that if I can find a workaround.'

'But will your chosen Queen Consort ever be able to take her place? I have my doubts. Ask yourself this, my King in need of a Queen. When you walked in here this evening, who was the first person you looked for? Who did you *keep* looking for until she appeared?' Katerina smiled again, and it was a gentle smile, without malice. 'Be honest. Because it surely wasn't me.'

Another event, another debrief afterwards. That was the routine Sera and Augustus fell into over the weeks that followed. Sometimes they talked in his office and sometimes they used a small parlour in the west wing that he favoured, and sometimes, if he'd been held up after the event, he came to her quarters and sat within her sofa circle, always requesting a strategy session. Sera didn't mind it. She took quiet satisfaction in her ability to be of use to him, and if he kept his hands and his kisses carefully to himself while in her presence, so be it.

She didn't want to think about her growing need for his attention. The way her body craved his touch and her mind constantly circled back to him and what he was doing, how he was feeling. Whether he'd ever touch her again with the sole purpose of giving and taking pleasure.

She didn't want to admit she might be falling for him.

Nothing good had ever come of a courtesan falling for a king.

Tonight, Augustus's behaviour was different in that he stood staring at the request wheel at his feet for a good long while before turning to look at her. She'd been expecting him—maybe—and had changed out of her workwear into casual trousers and her customary tunic top. Nothing too sheer or revealing. No jewellery or make-up embellishment. The only concession she'd made to vanity was to let her hair down after she'd showered and not put it back up before opening her door to him. She liked the way he looked at it. The way he jammed his hands in his pockets as if to stop himself from reaching out to touch it.

The sexual attraction between them hadn't gone away, for all their business-based interactions. It simmered between them, thick and syrupy. Every glance, every pause, a study in denial.

For both of them.

'You know what I really want tonight?' he asked, and her brain helpfully supplied the perfect answer.

Me! You want me! Please take me!

'A toasted cheese sandwich.'

Or—or she could feed him. He wasn't even looking at her. 'That can be arranged,' she offered hospitably. 'Anything else?'

Me! Pick me!

'I wouldn't mind if it came with a glass of wine and some background music that I don't have to listen to as if it's the finest thing I've ever heard.'

'You didn't like the music gala this evening?'

'I liked it well enough but I was tired. Maintaining the fiction that I wanted to be there took more effort than usual.'

An honest response that painted him in a less than

perfect light. A rare occurrence for this man who'd been trained from childhood to never show weakness or reveal any thoughts that could be used against him.

'Sit. Please.' She had music, food, and an excellent cellar full of wine on hand. 'I can feed you.' Cross off another scene on the pleasure wheel as done. It wasn't the sex scene she craved, granted, but it was progress.

'We can call for food,' he said.

'No!' Just…no. 'Does it matter who prepares it? I have a fully stocked kitchen. Why not let me put supper together?'

'You don't have to. That's not your role.'

'Always so hung up on roles.' He had no idea how much it pleased her when she was able to put her training to use and serve him. It wasn't a hardship. It was her pleasure. 'Many people take great pride and pleasure in being able to put food on the table and invite others to share it. It happens I'm one of them. Sit. Please.'

Please.

Sera didn't wait to see if he did her bidding, but when she returned he was sitting on the sofa in a different place to usual and the picture at his feet was that of people sharing a meal.

The wine she returned with was the best in the cellar and she knelt at his feet to pour it, faltering only when she went to hand it to him and found him watching her with hooded eyes that burned with a hunger that had nothing to do with food.

But he took it from her with a quiet, 'Thank you,' and if his fingertips touched hers, well, he'd said he was tired and it wasn't exactly light in here tonight with the moon behind a sky full of clouds. It wasn't warm in here either, beneath the glass dome, but he didn't seem to notice. Sera wanted to pretend that the tremble in her fingers as she released the wine was because of the cold, but self-deception had never been her friend. She'd shivered at the merest touch of his hand.

He said nothing more as she rose and turned some music on, soft and soothing.

He had his eyes closed and his head resting against the back of the sofa when she returned with the food. She'd brought extra: a small plate of honeyed pastries and a bowl of nuts. Sliced melon. Not a lot. Not a feast to make a person groan at the thought of eating it all.

'I hope some of that's for you too,' he murmured.

'It is.'

'Don't kneel at my feet, Sera. It might be what the picture shows and your courtesan training demands but I couldn't stand it.'

More weakness from him tonight, and he was deliberately letting her see it. She didn't know what to do with it. How to process it. So she sat and helped herself to some melon and then a glass of wine and sipped.

'You don't drink.' He was watching her, eyes still half closed.

'It's not that I don't drink at all. Sometimes when the vintage is very fine, I do.' She lifted her glass to the light and hid behind the poise the Order had instilled in her. Her relationship with alcohol was complicated. There was the way her mother had abused it. The way it lowered inhibitions and let devils in, false confidence in. But there were other things about it that deserved consideration. 'I learned about wine as part of my training. If you were to ask me to rank different areas of study, I'd put my study of wines and winemaking somewhere near the top, mainly because it's proven surprisingly useful. Everything from making small-talk with the high-flying wine aficionados of the world to tweaking wine selections for different charity functions so that the chefs are happy, the drinkers are happy and the hosts are not paying a fortune for it.'

He smiled and she wished he wouldn't, because it made her glow on the inside. Such a whore for his attention.

'And is there a wine to go with toasted cheese sandwiches?'

'There is, and we're drinking it.'

His smile widened. The glow inside her ignited and morphed into an open fire surrounded by a hearth.

In a family room.

'How are the owls?' he asked as he reached for a sandwich.

'They have names now,' she told him, taking on the mantle of conversation while he ate. 'Tomas and Claudia had lunch with me on Wednesday and we chose names then. I did notify your secretary Claudia was coming, and Tomas with her. I always ask permission to have visitors and provide details.' No exceptions.

Augustus shrugged, seemingly unconcerned. 'Some details stop at my secretary, especially if they're of no concern. How is Claudia?'

'She misses the freedom she had in the mountains.'

'Is that why she spends so much time with the falconer?'

'There could be another reason for that.' Augustus raised an eyebrow and this time it was Sera's turn to shrug. Far be it for her to lay Claudia's heart bare, although she had a fair idea where it lay. 'So, the smaller of the two owls is the male. His name is Orion. His larger companion is Ara, his mate, and he indulges her shamelessly. Their enemies are other owls of the same species and the occasional falcon. They're very adaptable and tend not to make their own nests, preferring instead to use nests abandoned by others, or make do with a man-made structure. Orion will fly down and perch on the trapeze on occasion, the better to see what I'm up to. He then reports back to Ara, who likes to pretend my activities are beneath her notice.'

'But they're not?'

'I've seen her watching me. She's more interested than she lets on.'

He'd finished the sandwich and was washing it down with wine. He looked more closely at the label on the bottle and then back at her.

'From the cellars of the Order of the Kite,' she said in answer to his question. 'They have quite the collection.'

'So I see. I know so little about this Order of yours. I have historians researching it, of course, but there are no experts to be found. Not amongst anyone I can get hold of.'

'What would you like to know?'

He snorted softly. 'Start at the beginning.'

'Of the history of the Order? It's over two thousand years old and began as a way for women in positions of power, or women close to men in positions of power, to connect and share journeys. They created a mountain retreat, a place of learning. Alliances were forged. Daughters were positioned for particular roles within the world order of the day. Was a particular ruling court strong in trade but weak when it came to the comforts of its people? Who, from the pool of women available, was best placed to effect change? Occasionally, a ruler would reach out and request someone with particular connections and skills. If the Order could accommodate them, and it was perceived as being in their best interest to do so, they would.'

'Did the women of the Order ever have individual agendas or did they serve a higher cause?'

'I'm sure many have had their own agendas over the years. Politics is everywhere, and the Order is not immune. But on the whole I'd say the quest for balance, peace and prosperity guides all our members. I think of us as a benevolent force rather than a disruptive one.'

'I hate to break it to you, Sera, but taking up residence here in my palace and worming your way into my life and my thoughts…it's disruptive.'

'Am I not helping?' Pain lanced through her chest and she clamped her lips shut on a barrage of protest.

'In some ways you are. In other ways you're not helping at all.'

She didn't know what to say to that, and he didn't seem inclined to elaborate. Instead, he leaned back with his head against the back of the sofa and stared at the stars as if they had failed him.

'I was fourteen when I finally found this room,' he offered quietly. 'I'd been looking for it for years. I could see the dome from the sky, but the passageway to get here was boarded up and the room was out of bounds. Forgotten, until Moriana and I found it again and made it our own.' He pointed with his wine glass towards the platform halfway up the wall. 'We used to sit up there and shoot arrows into pumpkins down below. We damaged so many arrows when they struck stone instead of the target. I don't think we had a straight arrow left between us by the end of it all. I know we damaged the walls and the floors but I didn't care. Told myself I was striking back at the source of my discontent. The palace. The Crown. The expectations that rode me like a second skin. *Be worthy. Don't fail. Perform.* I was the Crown Prince—I had to perform. Everywhere except for here. There was no judgement here. I could curse and roar and take risks I could never take elsewhere. When I was in here, I could fly.'

Suspicion bloomed swiftly. 'You used the trapeze?'

'It's just a swing,' he offered mildly.

No safety net, half-rotted rope. No training. Dear God. 'And the adrenaline rush the first time you used it?'

'Pretty big.' He snorted softly. 'I thought this room would no longer feel like sanctuary once you claimed it. Figured if I stayed away my problem with you would go away, only I keep turning up at your door and you keep welcoming me in, offering me anything. You've no idea how much I want to claim you, and to hell with self-restraint and leading by example and kings not having courtesans in this day and age.'

'You could.' Her hands shook with the force of her need as she set her wine on the small side table. 'You could do that.'

'I'd make it so good for you.' He had a voice tailored for sin and seduction and lips that beckoned, even when his words were cruel. 'Treat you like a queen.'

'I don't want to be a queen,' she said, but he was drawing closer and she wasn't moving away.

'We all do things we don't particularly want to do.' He brushed his lips against hers and she opened for him instinctively, her tongue coming out to meet his. He slid a gentle hand beneath her hair and cupped the back of her neck, his thumb brushing the skin just behind her ear as he tilted her head where he wanted it and claimed her lips once more. Her eyes fluttered closed.

It was a kiss to get lost in.

When they broke it several years later, he rested his forehead against hers and drew a ragged breath. He ran his hand across her shoulder and down her arm to tangle her fingers in his. 'Last chance to tell me you don't want my hands on you, Sera. Because this is going to complicate things.'

'I want this.' She'd never for one moment not wanted this, from the moment she'd laid eyes on him. 'I crave this,' she whispered, and took the initiative and straddled him, a knee either side of his hips, and slid her hand from his the better to bury both of her hands in his hair. 'I can make it good for you too. So good.'

His shirt had to go. Hers too, and he helped her with that, in between a dozen deep and drugging kisses. Breathing was overrated. His tongue curled around her puckered nipple was not overrated, and then he closed his mouth around it and sucked and she nearly came from that alone. His hands dug into the globes of her behind as he ground up against her, and she gave herself over to sensation and arched into the hardness of his erection and let her head fall back and her hands guide his head towards her other breast.

A soft grunt punched out of her, and he groaned and his hands tightened on her.

Moments later, she was on her back and seeing stars, real ones shining through the glass-domed roof, and Augustus was lifting her legs and removing her shoes and stripping her naked.

She'd been taught what to do, how to please, but she was too caught up in sensation to do any of it.

He started with kisses and gifted them everywhere. The tender curve of her shoulder, the hollow of her armpit and the curve of her breast. Her ribs, the jut of her hip. And then he lifted her leg and started again at her instep and worked his way up. The back of her knee—who knew that would be a go-to zone for squirming? The flesh of her inner thigh. Higher. Black eyes glittering as bold fingers paved the way for his mouth.

She was gone the minute his lips closed over her and his tongue flicked. Whatever this was had been weeks in the making. Every fight, every glance, every moment of pregnant silence between them had been a stroke towards this, and it was wingless flight and fall without a safety net and utterly overwhelming.

It still wasn't enough.

'I need—'

'I know what you need,' he growled. 'And I need a condom.'

'I'm protected.' She opened hazy, glazed grey eyes and caught his face between both hands. 'But there's physical protection to hand if you want to be sure. Be sure.'

She slid out beneath him and crawled naked towards the orgy picture of the pleasure wheel offerings, reaching down to push at something that snapped open, a formerly hidden drawer at the very bottom of that part of the sofa. 'What size?'

What *size*? His brain struggled for clarity until she held up several packets.

'Not that one, not that one, probably this one,' she

said, reaching down and plucking a packet from a well-ordered tray. 'You seem rather well formed.'

'You seem rather well stocked.'

He had to laugh. He had to stalk, and push her down on her stomach and start kissing her all over again, even as he reached for the packet in her hand. He hadn't kissed his way down her back yet and that was an oversight he aimed to correct. She was so responsive, so very ready to melt into his touch and give herself over to him. And his need to take was so very big.

He took his time, calling on every bit of the control that had been drilled into him since birth. *Don't lose it. Don't let go. See to the other person's need first because that was service and above all a king served his people. Don't be greedy or entitled.*

Give.

So he gave and gave but she gave it all back and they fed off each other and when he finally breached her, slow and sure, it felt like sliding his soul home.

He stilled, murmuring nonsense against her lips, and she surrendered, eyes never leaving his face as she asked for more.

He took her to the edge, time and time again.

And then he ruthlessly tipped her over the ledge and followed and gave her everything.

CHAPTER EIGHT

'DOES IT HURT?'

Sera couldn't believe how gentle Augustus was being as he bathed her, every stroke of the wash cloth a caress, the water soothing on her skin and the lowlights in the sconces making shadows dance on the walls. He'd been born to care for people, this King, even if he did it from behind self-imposed walls. Get behind the walls of the man and he was overwhelmingly responsive to passion and possession and taking overwhelmingly good care of the woman in his arms.

'It doesn't hurt,' she assured him as he dragged the wash cloth slowly over her centre folds. She'd been a virgin, yes, but her life to date had been an active one and penetration hadn't hurt her the way she'd been warned it might. If the lover was careless or in too much of a hurry.

Augustus had been neither.

'I liked it very much,' she offered and thought to win a smile from him, but he didn't smile.

'Guess you're in the right profession, then.'

Her smile faltered. 'I guess so.'

'Sera—'

But she didn't want to hear what that roughened, sex-soaked voice had to say next. Didn't want to spoil this night with politics or reality or the sure knowledge that she was never going to get to keep this man on a permanent basis. She told herself she didn't want to keep him. That what he'd given her was enough. That she could still walk away from him with her heart intact.

She tried to believe it.

She put her finger to his mouth to silence him, and when he put his hand to her wrist and drew her finger away, she replaced it with her mouth. 'There's more we could do,' she whispered against his lips. He'd been tender with her but she knew there was more. The fingers at her wrist tightened. 'You know there's more you could teach me.'

'Eager.'

'I've been waiting a long time.'

'For me?' This time when he caressed her folds the wash cloth was gone. 'Or for sex?'

'All of it. I didn't expect to want you as much as I do. I could kiss you for hours.' No one had ever told her she'd feel like this. 'Soft and gentle.' Because he had been so very, very gentle with her. Taking care of her pleasure before his own. Reining himself in. 'Or not. Let's try not.'

He claimed her lips with his in a punishing kiss that she returned in full measure. Slick-scraping and filthy, it sent a lightning arc straight through her. And the passion grew.

With a rough fist in his wet hair, she dragged his lips from hers. 'You've seen me dance with swords. You know I'm not going to break.' She knew where she was going with this and it was like stepping off a ledge with a trapeze swing in hand and no knowledge at all of where they might land. 'You know we're not going to be able to have this for ever, but we do have tonight and I want you inside me again, cursing me because you've never had it so good. Ride me till you scream. Or I scream. Take me apart and put me back together again with a piece of you in me.' He was on board with every loaded word, if his glittering, hooded gaze and his iron-hard erection was any indication. 'So do me a favour and this time don't hold back.'

He carried her, wet and wanting, to an alcove filled with pillows and throw rugs and all manner of oils and unguents.

And this time he didn't hold back.

CHAPTER NINE

AUGUSTUS STRODE INTO his office in a mood that ran blacker than usual. He'd woken alone in Sera's quarters, with a breakfast tray beside him and a blanket draped over his nakedness. They'd finally made it to her bed during the night. Sleep had overtaken him at some point after that. There'd been a note on the pillow next to his head. *Exercising*, was all the note said. A morning ritual for his courtesan of the High Reaches. No matter what.

He'd left a similar note on the pillow requesting her company mid-morning. He had a lunch date he couldn't get out of. With Katerina DeLitt.

He stalked to the coffee corner in the outer office and poured a cup for himself in silence. Lukewarm coffee was his friend.

His secretary cleared his throat and Augustus spared him a glance and there was something off in the older man's gaze—but how could he know?

Granted, the man knew practically everything, but still…

Did he have *I lost my mind and my heart last night* written on his forehead?

'Morning,' he muttered.

'You're late,' the older man said.

Augustus nodded. Instead of taking a quick morning shower, he'd lingered in that damned bathing pool of Sera's, working the kinks out of his body and hoping she'd turn up. She hadn't.

The older man handed him a file and Augustus took it. 'What's this?'

'The investigative report on Lady Sera's mother arrived last night, hand-delivered.'

'Sounds ominous.'

'My investigator judged the information to be of extreme sensitivity so he went old school, helped by the fact that he's seventy years old and *is* old school. The report is hand-written; no digital copies exist and he cleaned up as he went.'

'Meaning?'

'Meaning no one's ever going to find that information again unless they read the file you're holding. You've paid handsomely for the information and that service, by the way. Enough to send an old military-hero-turned-investigator into welcome retirement.'

'I live to serve.' Augustus took the folder from the other man with a frown. He dealt with classified information on a daily basis. He'd never read a hand-written report before. 'Is the information really that sensitive?'

'I doubt it'll start a war. I suspect it'd come as a shock to some of the people involved. Perhaps not all.'

'Be cryptic, then. What do I have on at eleven? Can we clear some space for a meeting with Sera?'

'Another costume tour of the brothels? Circus arts for children? Tortoise races?'

Augustus allowed himself a smile. 'Not yet. And I'm going to need more coffee. Double shot. Hot.'

He went to his office and shut the door behind him,

slapped the file down on his desk. His desk was big, black and imposing and his chair was fit for a king and significantly more comfortable. The room was cold, his sister was always complaining of it, but he found it stopped people from lingering overlong and the less they lingered, the more work he got done.

The first half hour of his day was always dedicated to reading. Daily reports sat waiting for him in a tidy pile, arranged in order of importance. He could have read them on his computer just as easily, but there was something about the ritual of paper copies and the pile getting smaller as he worked his way through them that appealed to him. There was an end to that pile of papers, whereas digital news was never-ending. Even if he was deluding himself, he liked to think that his workload had an end-point.

Sera's mother had loved a man, an abusive man, and had a child by him. Sera had already told him this. But she'd never mentioned names, and if he was contemplating marriage to her—which, God help him, he was—he wanted no surprises.

Sera didn't know what to expect when she walked into Augustus's office at exactly eleven a.m. She'd left him sleeping soundly in her quarters because she hadn't known how to deal with him after a night like the one they'd just shared. She still didn't know how to deal with him. But she crossed the cold room and took a seat in the chair placed strategically on the opposite side of his gleaming black desk and tried not to fidget beneath his impenetrable black-eyed gaze.

Gone was his openness of last night and the defencelessness he'd exposed in his sleep. The tousled hair and the boneless weight of his body in her bed. The long, dark lashes fanning delicately over the skin beneath his eyes. He'd been beautiful in his sleep. Softer and more boyish and she'd looked her fill in case she never got to see it again. Some of the things they'd done last night… Skin to skin with heaven in between.

She'd asked for it. She had asked for it. And she had received. 'Morning.'

He quirked a brow and returned her greeting and asked if she wanted some coffee.

She didn't. 'You wanted to see me?'

'For several reasons, not all of them concerning business.' A crack appeared in his regal regard. A flicker of something that might have been concern. 'How are you this morning?'

She felt as if she'd been skewered with a hot buttered sword, had begged for more and been given it. Should she say that? She might have said it to the man. Not to the King.

'So-so,' she said instead. 'Ari chose not to call on me to spar with him this morning. He tells me my concentration's off.'

'Does he know I stayed the night?'

'He's head of my security detail. Of course he knows. Are you worried he'll gossip?'

'No.' Augustus didn't look worried. 'If there's one thing I'm learning about the Order of the Kite, it's how well they can keep secrets. If I wasn't increasingly wary of the lot of you I'd be impressed.'

'If you want to know more about the Order, ask.' She was serious. She'd been handing out historical information ever since she'd got here. 'There's not a lot more left to tell.'

'Really?' The huffing sound he made was an irritated one. 'I had two reports cross my desk this morning, both of them concerning you. One of them informs me that before you came here you were the Chief Financial Officer for a global not-for-profit organisation that distributes over half a billion dollars each year to charities. Lady Lianthe controls the company—which I assume is connected to the Order of the Kite.'

Sera nodded. All of this was public knowledge, or at least accessible knowledge if you knew where to look.

'You were being groomed to replace her,' he said next.

'I was, yes.' She squared her shoulders and avoided glancing at the report beneath his hand in favour of studying the hand itself. Long fingers, broad base and a signet ring with the royal crest on his middle finger. A kernel of need began to heat deep inside her. Those fingers were magic.

'And here I was trying to turn you into a humble employee so you'd have something more than courtesan to show on your résumé when you left here. More fool me.'

He was angry this morning. Clipped vowels, exact pronunciation. Sera eyed him warily.

'I have no complaints about the work I do here,' she said. 'The charity programme here has been honed over centuries, much like the one the Order oversees, and it's been illuminating to compare and contrast the similarities and differences. They're both good. Different, but good. Besides, you know why I'm here. There is no secret. I didn't come here to court business opportunities. I came here to honour an ancient accord between my people and yours and repay a personal debt I've been accruing since I was seven. I win, Augustus. You keep implying I'm here under duress. You're wrong. I'm here because I choose to be.'

He had the best sexy brooding face she'd ever seen. 'And where does last night factor into all this winning?'

'Last night can be whatever you want it to be. Forgotten. Repeated. Picked apart until it bleeds.' She was predicting the latter and sought to head him off. 'I enjoyed it.'

'You were a virgin.'

'And?'

'And now you're not.'

Apparently she wasn't the only one with slow brain cells this morning. 'I'll celebrate later. First let me reassure you that I have no regrets, no inclination to tell anyone else what transpired between us and no plans to force you to marry me now that you've claimed my precious virginity.' He looked highly sceptical and Sera bit back a sigh. She had no wish to trap him. That had never been the goal here. Helping him address his needs had been the goal and she was doing that, wasn't she?

Frustration looked remarkably like arousal on him. 'So you *don't* want to marry me?'

Panic hit her hard and fast. 'That's not even on the table. Marriage isn't for the likes of me. Courtesans don't marry.'

'Don't they?' He was getting colder by the second. 'Is it formally not allowed or is it something you personally just don't want to do?'

'You're angry with me.'

'Sharp as ever,' he clipped. 'Answer the question.'

'I've never considered marrying you.' She kept her voice even but it was a near thing. 'Courtesans and kings can be intimate, no question. They often grow quite fond of each other. I'm fond of you.' *Liar—you're in love with him.* 'But a wife's role is very different to that of a courtesan.'

'Really?' She hated his mockery. He did it so well. 'How so? You're already bound to me and under my protection.'

'For a time,' she injected.

'You take on hostess roles, offer me counsel and share my bed.' His lips twisted. 'And you're fond of me.'

She was. Very. 'Augustus, you're a king. I'm nobody. A trained companion.'

'You have connections worldwide and a powerful political faction behind you. You're not nobody.'

She searched for another excuse. 'Your people would never accept me.'

'Wouldn't they? Because, given the press you receive, I'd say you have a better than fair chance they're going to love you.'

'Because I'm an oddity. A throwback curiosity with a sharp brain, a pretty face and interesting clothes.'

'You're making my argument for me.'

She had other arguments. 'You want love. That's why you've stayed single so long. I can't give you that.' Her mother had loved deeply and paid a dreadful price. Sera had paid that price too and had no wish to repeat the experience. 'I won't.'

'What exactly is it you think we did last night, Sera?'

'It was good, I don't deny it. But I've been trained to please.'

Last night...what you did with him? That was love, a little voice told her helpfully. *Are you really going to deny that?*

'My mother loved and look where it got her,' she said doggedly. 'Even when she left him she couldn't escape him. She was never *free*. One day I'm going to be free. If I were to marry you I'd never be free. That other role—'

'Wife,' he offered, not at all helpfully. 'Queen Consort. Mother of Kings. Or Queens. Princes and Princesses.' His eyes slayed her with his intensity. 'Heart of a nation.'

Yeah. That. 'I'd never be free.' She retreated into silence. So did he. While the tension in the room threatened to choke her completely.

'Right.' Bitterness tinged his voice. 'Not as if you want to be royal. Which brings me to the second report on my desk. If you wanted to be royal, all you'd have to do is tell people who your father is.'

Sera swallowed hard, her mouth suddenly dry. 'What do you mean?'

He tapped at the folder and her gaze was inevitably drawn to it. 'I mean you're a king's daughter by blood. You simply choose not to acknowledge it.'

He couldn't know that. No one knew that.

'The only time my late mother spoke of my father, she spoke fearfully and never by name,' she offered steadily. 'She said he was a monster who had no time for daughters and I believed her. I don't know who he is but, even if I did, why would I want to acknowledge a man such as that as my father, high-born or not?'

Augustus leaned forward, elbows on the table. 'You know exactly who I'm talking about.'

She'd pieced it together over the years, yes, and then *held her tongue*. Confiding in no one. She wondered if ants felt like this when put beneath a microscope and burned. 'My birth certificate says *father unknown*.'

'Your father died recently. Your half-brother is a king and as a child you went to school with your half-sister. *If* she's a half-sister. Who sired *her* is a matter of speculation. It could have been the King's brother rather than the King. The point is, you have family. A royal family.'

And she wanted no part of it. 'You have *no proof* of any of this.'

'Haven't I?'

'Augustus, please. Leave it alone. It benefits no one.'

'You know who he is.'

Yes. 'I know nothing.'

'You're lying. You're a royal daughter of Byzenmaach. Does Cas's sister know who you are?'

'Claudia is my *friend*.' Sera stood, incapable of sitting still any longer. 'If my father is who you say he is, then you know he had no use for daughters. The *world* knows this. Yes, my mother was sent to contain him when he began to mistreat his wife. She was to offer other activities for him to focus on, less damaging ways to vent his anger, and she did but he was beyond her control. She failed, and fled and hid and I'm *glad*. I take no pride in the blood running through my veins—and you're only assuming it's his. The man was a tyrant and a murderer. His son, bless us all, is a far better man than he ever was and Byzenmaach is now in good hands. What would I add to that? What could possibly be gained?'

'Power,' he offered.

'I *have* power.'

'Royal status.'

'A noose around my neck.'

'Family,' he said softly, and at this she broke years of deportment training to wrap her arms around her waist and hunch forward as if preventing her stomach from falling out.

'I already have a family,' she whispered, and tried not to think of the pictures in the paper she'd seen recently. Casimir of Byzenmaach, half-brother, wholly in love with his new bride and bastard daughter. A king whose sister had recently returned from exile to claim her rightful place. 'I am Sera Boreas of the High Reaches, daughter of Yuna, pupil of Lianthe, member of the Order of the Kite, and courtesan until you release me. I need no royal titles. I want no royal duties.'

'Not even for me?'

'I don't know what you want from me!' she cried.

'Yes, you do. I've been saying it all along. I don't need a courtesan, Sera, I need a wife. And you, for all that you'll service me while I'm looking for one, aren't interested in the position. For what it's worth, I don't blame you. You have the world at your feet. Why take on royal duties when you don't have to?' His face hardened. 'But you can't stay here any more. I won't look elsewhere while you're here. And it appears I do need to look elsewhere.'

She stood immobile. 'I can't leave. The accord—'

'You can leave. In fact, I insist.'

He sat so still and silent. She couldn't read him. She didn't know what to say to him. 'By the terms of the accord—'

'I have the right leverage now to do whatever the hell I want. And, believe me, Sera, and with no disrespect to you or your secret Order, I've had enough.'

* * *

If anyone had ever asked Augustus of Arun what it felt like to be in love, he couldn't have told them. He'd never been in love before, not once. Not until Sera Boreas walked out of his office and took his beaten, bleeding heart with her.

He put his hands to his face and took a couple of deep breaths. It didn't hurt any less but breathing was a function of living and he still had to do that.

Sera had chosen freedom over duty. Freedom over *him*, and it was a fair call. Last night had been brilliant but he'd been reading too much into it. Passion did that. Wanting something too much did that. So they'd made love. So what? Courtesans did that. Didn't mean she wanted to stay and be his wife.

He reached for the phone.

'Get my lawyers in here. I'm drafting a written offer of marriage to Katerina DeLitt.' Another proposal that was likely to be rejected but it would serve a purpose and he didn't have to present it to Katerina yet. 'I also need you to find out what Sera weighs, double it, and I want that weight in gold removed from the vaults. I want a copy of my offer of marriage to the Baroness DeLitt and the gold delivered to Lianthe of the High Reaches and I want it done today.' He needed to stitch up the gaping hole where his heart had once been and he didn't need an audience. 'And then I want Sera and her guards escorted from my *goddamn home*. Today.'

CHAPTER TEN

SERA STARED UNCOMPREHENDINGLY at the letter Augustus's private secretary had just handed her. It hadn't taken long to read.

'Lady Sera, you are free to leave,' Augustus's secretary said firmly. 'The terms of the accord have been satisfied, or close enough. I've made arrangements for you and your retinue to stay at a hotel in the city.'

Ari stood beside her, arms crossed and his face impassive. 'It's eleven at night.'

'It's a five-star hotel with round-the-clock check-in,' the older man countered. 'Organised and paid for until the end of the month, should you wish to delay your return to the mountains. They're expecting you.'

'How? How has he satisfied the terms of the accord?' asked Sera.

'The King has an offer of marriage on the table and believes the terms of the accord have been satisfied in principle, milady. Lady Lianthe agrees. *Double* your weight in gold has already been delivered to her.'

'I—' She needed to call Lianthe. She needed to speak to Augustus. 'Is His Majesty in? May I speak with him?' Not that she had any idea what she was going to say.

Thank you? How did you do it? Are you really going to cut me loose, just like that?

'He's not in.'

There'd been no evening event written into his schedule this morning. Sera knew this because the man standing in front of her had been emailing her Augustus's daily schedule every morning for several weeks.

'May I see him in the morning?'

'His Majesty has a full schedule tomorrow. He needs to finish everything he put on hold today in order to accommodate your wishes.'

'My wishes?'

'Your wish to leave.'

'Right,' she said faintly. 'That wish. The owls—'

'Will be taken care of. Your belongings packed and returned to the High Reaches. There's a palace vehicle at your disposal. It's waiting for you at the south wall entrance.'

Funny how freedom felt a lot like dismissal.

Sera nodded. Manners before breakdown. Discretion over protest. 'I'll leave a letter for His Majesty on my desk. Will you see that he gets it?'

'He'll get it.' The older man seemed to soften and sag. 'The question you should be asking is: will he read it?'

Ari waited until the King's secretary had left the room before turning silently towards her, eyebrow raised.

'I need to ring Lianthe,' she told him. 'Alert the others that we might be on our way.'

He nodded and reached for his phone, heading over towards the entrance doors but staying inside the room where once he might have stood outside the doors to give her more privacy. Sera walked in the opposite direction and made her call from the bedroom.

Lianthe picked up on the second ring.

'Is it true? Have the terms of the accord been satisfied?' Sera asked without preamble.

'Well, he doesn't have a wife and he doesn't have an heir but he does have a valid wedding proposal in play and I have no reason to believe it will be rejected. He also informs me that your presence is no longer required and has threatened to expose your connection to the Byzenmaach throne if I don't agree with him.' Lianthe drew a heavy breath. 'So I agreed with him. I'm not sure where he got his information from. I can't imagine you told him.'

'I didn't.' Sera closed her eyes and tilted her head towards the sky, only the sky wasn't there; it was only the ceiling. 'He had us investigated.'

'That information's not available.'

'Nonetheless, he got it from somewhere.' The sudden sting of hot tears welled beneath her eyelids. 'He asked me to marry him. And I didn't know what to say.'

'I suspect that says it all.' The other woman's voice was soft and soothing. 'What a pity. I find his utter ruthlessness on your behalf quite admirable. He must be very much in love with you.'

'He's trapped, that's all. He's being forced to take a wife and his heart's not engaged with any of the available candidates. I've watched him. He can drum up polite friendliness towards them if pressed.'

'And what does he drum up for you?'

Stories from his childhood and an insatiable sexual hunger that had left her wrung out and panting. Challenge and temper and unexpected moments of understanding. 'More. But Lianthe, I'm not cut out for love. Courtesans don't love. They serve, willingly, and I have. We were doing well. No one ever said anything about *love*.'

'You have something against it?'

Yes. 'I don't believe it brings happiness.'

'Your mother was an extreme case. She had a soft heart and the man she fell for, he wasn't soft at all.'

'Neither's this one. He's difficult and demanding.' And passionate and protective and a demon in bed. 'And petty and powerful and…' Gorgeous and supportive of her charity schemes and… 'He's a king in need of a queen. There'd be oaths to Crown and country. I'd be accountable for every minute of every day. Who would want that?'

'Who indeed?'

'It's a lifetime sentence of duty and reckoning and being judged. And usually being judged wanting.'

'Indeed.'

'Who'd want that?' she repeated.

'Not you, clearly. You probably wouldn't rise to the occasion at all, even if you loved him. Which you don't.'

'I don't.'

'Well, then.' Lianthe sounded disturbingly cheerful. 'When are you coming home?'

'Want to talk about it?'

Augustus scowled at his sister and wondered, not for the first time, why he'd allowed her to invite herself to dinner. She said she'd missed him—which he very much doubted, given how busy she was. She'd wanted a catch-up—which usually meant pumping him for information or delicately *revealing* information that might be of interest to him. The fact that he'd banished the only other woman who'd ever come close to providing him with this type of relaxed political conversation was not lost on him. 'Talk about what?'

'The rumour that you've proposed, or are about to propose, to Katerina DeLitt. The abrupt midnight departure of your courtesan.' Moriana waved an airy hand towards him from across the dining room table. 'You choose.'

Sera had left four nights ago. The people of the High Reaches would be coming to collect everything that belonged to them, Lianthe had said, but she hadn't mentioned when. Stepping into the round room only to find Sera not there was driving him insane. The soft hoot of owls mocked him. The tapestry wheel of pleasure haunted him. So many things they hadn't done yet. Perhaps he should be thankful.

'I choose silence.'

Moriana allowed him that silence for all of thirty seconds, and that was only because she had a mouthful of food.

'You want to talk to Theo about it?' she asked when her mouth was empty again. 'Or Benedict? Benedict's surprisingly insightful when it comes to matters of the heart.'

It stood to reason he would be, what with all that practice. 'Thank God he's not here,' Augustus offered drily. 'Sera Boreas has gone, the accord has been honoured to everyone's satisfaction, and I'll be married by the end of the year.'

'So you say. But to whom? And please don't tell me

you're madly in love with Katerina. I know you. And you're not.'

'Since when has love ever been a prerequisite for marriage?'

'Since when has love ever *not* been a prerequisite for you?'

'Not everyone is cut out for the kind of love you and Theo share.'

'You're not so different from me.' Moriana raised her chin and regarded him haughtily. 'You want that kind of love—you always have.'

He offered up a careless shrug and cut into his meal, ignoring his sister's scowl. She hated it when he refused to engage. Said it was a stalling tactic that had no place in open conversation.

'Augustus, I love you. You know this.'

Uh-oh.

'But I've had a dozen calls this week from people here in your palace, begging me to come and strangle you. At which point I would become their ever so reasonable Queen.'

Augustus snorted.

'I'd probably have to renounce Theo to do it, of course, and this baby currently in my belly would probably be kidnapped back and forward between palaces until he ran away and joined the circus, but at least your palace employees wouldn't be suffering.'

'You're pregnant?' She didn't look pregnant, even if she did look more vibrant than usual. He'd put that down to their argument, or the wine she…wasn't drinking. So much for his keen powers of observation. Sera would have caught that one within five minutes of being in the room.

Moriana nodded and offered up a tiny but self-satisfied smile. 'I'm barely nine weeks in. We're keeping it quiet until I'm a little further along, but I wanted to tell you now and in person.'

'Congratulations.' He meant it. 'Are you well?' Was she happy about it?

Theo would be ecstatic with an heir on the way.

'I'm as well as can be, given that I can barely keep dry toast in my stomach before lunchtime. Augustus, I'm so happy. A mother. Me!'

Envy had no place in his heart. His sister was happy and deserved to be. He could wait, and one day it would be his turn to puff with pride and joy because his wife was pregnant. But there was only one woman's face he could see in that particular daydream. Sera, with her slender frame, luminous grey eyes and flawless skin.

The same woman that had chosen freedom over a life spent with him.

He didn't blame her.

He'd done everything in his power to set her free.

'You could go after her now that the accord has been satisfied,' said Moriana, and he blinked because he thought they weren't having this conversation, only apparently they were. 'You always did have trouble with the *she was duty bound to serve you* part.'

'If we're using the argument that Sera's now a free woman, she could come back at any time. Do you see her here?' He didn't need Moriana's answer. 'Neither do I.'

'She hasn't returned to the High Reaches,' Moriana said tentatively.

'Perhaps she's sick of serving them too.'

'I have it on good authority that she's in Byzenmaach, at Cas's Winter fortress.'

'She's *where*?'

'Visiting Cas's sister.' Moriana eyed him with blatant curiosity. 'They know each other. Studied together in the mountains as kids.'

He hadn't told Moriana about Sera's parentage. He hadn't told anyone. He'd tried telling himself that such effective leverage could be used over and over again if he kept it to himself but the truth was he'd never go against Sera's wishes to keep her father's identity a secret and he'd never use that particular leverage again. He was done with it. He was done with *her*.

'So what are you going to name this baby? Have you given it any thought?'

'I've given it no thought at all yet.' Her eyes glinted with sharp humour.

'And the due date is when?'

'Thirty-one weeks from now, apparently. You could drop in on Claudia or go see Tomas about how to get rid of the remaining owls in the round room. They shouldn't be too hard to catch, seeing as I have it on good authority that you're feeding them.'

'Lies.' All lies. 'And the baby's health? How's the baby's health?' Why couldn't she be one of those expectant mothers that talked of nothing else?

'Good try, brother.' Moriana outright smirked. 'Should you be fortunate enough to be invited to see beyond the veil of Theo's outright terror at the thought of becoming a father, I should warn you he will talk of nothing else but baby names, giving birth and raising children. Honestly, I think it broke his brain.'

It was Augustus's turn to grin outright. 'Really? Theo's gone gaga? I'd like to see that.'

'You have no idea.'

'I'm thrilled for you both.'

Moriana looked positively tearful as she set her cutlery down and reached for her napkin to dab at her eyes. Their late lamented mother would have scolded her twice over. First for her unseemly display of emotion, and then for inappropriate use of tableware. Such scolding would have once sent his sister spinning into the depths of despair but the new, improved Moriana didn't seem to care.

'Have you really proposed to Katerina DeLitt?' she asked, because she was a sneaky, *sneaky* woman, not above using tears to disarm him.

'I've drawn up an offer, yes.'

'Have you sent it?'

It was still sitting on his desk. 'Do you have anything against her?'

'Nothing at all, apart from the fact that you're in love with someone else. As a woman who's been in Katerina DeLitt's position before, she has my utmost sympathy. If you had any sense, you wouldn't even consider proposing to her in your current condition. If she had any sense she'd refuse you.'

'Maybe she will.'

Sera had refused him.

His sister regarded him solemnly. 'Will you at least meet with Sera again before you take such an irrevocable step with someone else?'

He gathered up the icy reserve he rarely wore around his sister and pinned her with his gaze. As dear as she was to him, and pregnant along with it, her interference was unwelcome.

'I didn't want to talk about any of this with you, but I heard you out and now it's your turn to hear me. No, I will not seek out Sera again. I've had my say already and her ambitions do not include becoming my Queen. I will not discuss this with you or anyone else ever again. And if you don't like my answer, feel free to leave.'

CHAPTER ELEVEN

CASIMIR OF BYZENMAACH's Winter fortress perched atop a mountain pass. Sera had reached out to Claudia and asked if she knew of a place where she could exercise and clear her head and it was a measure of their friendship that the other woman had instantly invited her to stay.

Accepting that invitation without disclosing the secret of her parentage made Sera the worst friend in the world, but up here in the mountain pass, with Tomas's falcons soaring overhead and dawn breaking softly over the horizon, she felt a peace steal over her that she hadn't felt in days.

She finished her forms and bowed to the valley below and the rising sun and turned to find her hostess sitting silently on a rock behind her, watching. So she bowed to her too and watched the other woman smile.

'That was beautiful,' said Claudia. 'But then, you always have been very beautiful.'

'My lot to bear.' Always making waves, being coveted or even despised for no other reason than she'd drawn someone's eye. Glazed stares, suspicious glares and people wanting to possess her.

Augustus had wanted to possess her from the beginning.

It was a miracle, really, that he'd withstood that urge for as long as he had.

'Whose heart have you broken this time?' Claudia asked.

'One does not kiss and tell,' she replied quietly and picked up the towel she'd brought with her and put it to her face.

King Casimir and his family were at their Summer palace in the city, not here. She'd wanted to meet him. She hadn't wanted to meet him. Those two thoughts did not coexist peacefully.

She didn't know what she wanted any more.

Lowering the towel, she closed her eyes and drew fresh breath, feeling at home here, in a way that had everything to do with cool mountain air and not having to view the sky from beneath a web of steel and glass.

No endless dinners, galas and fund-raisers to oversee.

No severely tailored work clothes.

No king to serve.

No duty.

'I don't know what to do any more,' she confessed. 'I have no plans, no direction, no thoughts for the future. I'm finally free and all I'm doing is looking over my shoulder at what I left behind.'

Claudia nodded. 'I know that feeling. Here.' She opened a small basket at her feet. 'I brought breakfast. The food here is amazing.'

Sera spread her towel on the ground and sat cross-legged, and for a time they feasted on meat pastries and sweet milky tea. But Sera wasn't quite ready to let go of her friend's earlier comment. 'Do you ever think you should have stayed in the mountains?'

'I'm of more use to the people of the High Reaches if I'm advocating for them here, so no. I shouldn't have stayed in the mountains.'

'But do you like it here?' Sera watched as the other woman's gaze tracked a falcon in full flight. 'Do they treat you well?'

'They treat me like a princess, because that's what I am. Some treat me like a newfound friend and confidante and I like that. Some can barely look at me but dream of the day I was taken from them, nonetheless. It's not always easy but I'm making my home here.' Claudia reached for a paper napkin. 'I wanted you to meet my niece. Face of an angel and an absolute terror. Wants to be a Samurai this week. I thought you two could bond.'

'I'd like to meet her.' A niece. She blinked back sudden tears.

'Hey.' A warm palm snaked out to cover her forearm. 'What is it?'

'Nothing, I—nothing. I'd like to meet her some day.'

'Hardly a thought to induce tears—although some of the guards here may beg to differ.'

Sera smiled, as she was meant to smile. 'Thank you for inviting me here.'

'Stay as long as you dare.'

'Another day, perhaps. After that I don't know. I need to keep moving.' Searching, so that she didn't keep remembering nights full of politicking and quiet confidences and one night in particular when she and Augustus had forgotten their roles and let honesty rule them.

'May I do a visualisation exercise with you?' Claudia reached out and took both of Sera's hands in hers.

'It's one I've found useful whenever I find myself adrift. Close your eyes.'

Sera nodded and closed her eyes.

'You're standing at a crossroads. Seven paths to choose from, radiating out in all directions. Some safe, because you know where they lead. Some bright and beckoning and full of new adventures. Others dark and seductively forbidding. On some paths you can see family in the distance and maybe you're not sure of your welcome because they look so happy. What else could they possibly need?'

Sera opened her eyes and searched the other woman's face for some sign that she *knew*.

And found nothing.

'Close your eyes.' Claudia moved her thumbs in soothing circles over Sera's skin. 'Someone stands beside you at that crossroads. Someone you'll never leave behind because you carry them in your heart like a talisman. Someone whose path was chosen for them the minute they were born. They couldn't follow you even if they wanted to. All they can do is be there at the crossroads where your lives intersect and watch you make your choice and let you go. They'll fight for your right to do that, you see. Of all the gifts they can give you, it's the most expensive.'

Sera trembled. 'I know who you're talking about.'

'Do you? Because it could be anyone. It could be me.'

Sera snapped her eyes open and saw nothing but love and gentle understanding.

'It could be me saying I'm right here and ready to be whatever you need me to be,' Claudia repeated quietly. 'Close your eyes and breathe.'

Sera closed her eyes and breathed.

'Whenever I do this exercise I see Tomas beside me. Whoever heard of a princess and a falconer? He won't even lay a hand on me, can hardly bear to look at me, but I swear to you I'm laying down a new path for us, brick by brick, just in case he ever wants to walk my way. It's not so easy to live a royal life, you see, and those already there will never force the issue. You don't need to mention my regard for Tomas to him, by the way, unless it comes up in conversation. At which point, go for it and use embellishments.'

Sera opened one eye and arched her brow.

'Shut it. No winking,' her sister of the heart replied with a tiny grin. 'I'm trying so hard not to make this about me. Close your eyes and open your heart.'

Sera obeyed.

'I know there's someone there beside you at your crossroads. I know you can't move forward without resolving your feelings for them. Doing that is your next step and it might be the most important step you ever take.' Claudia moved forward; Sera could feel it even if she couldn't see it. The other woman's cheek brushed hers, comfort, solidarity and warmth, as she whispered, 'You know who you see.'

They walked back down the mountain in the crisp morning air, Claudia looking skyward more than once and smiling softly when a falcon appeared and circled above. 'They questioned Tomas for days after I disappeared,' Claudia told Sera. 'He was eight years old and the last person to see me and they grilled him over and over again, with no mercy given for the fact that he too was a child.'

'And now he uses falcons to track your every movement?'

'Not my every movement.' Claudia sprang from one step to the next, her feet sure as they made their way down the rocky path. 'He's been training himself to wait longer and longer each time I come up here before flying one of his hunting hawks to find out where I am. We're up to almost an hour.'

'And do you help him with the birds?'

'You know I do.' Claudia had skills of her own in that area. 'Watching that man work is a pleasure I have no words for.'

'And how will you manage to steer him towards romance if you're the Princess in the castle and he's but a mere falconer?'

'By putting my own spin on this Princess gig and getting out of the castle a lot,' Claudia offered drily. 'It helps that Cas is so utterly overcome by my return that he lets me do whatever I want.'

'He didn't reprimand you for staying away?'

Claudia might have been kidnapped as a child—for her own good, as it turned out—but she'd had chances to return over the years and had never done so. Not until her father had died and her brother had taken the throne.

'It wasn't safe for me here. You know that.'

'But it is now.'

Claudia nodded and looked to the sky and let the early morning light caress her face. 'It is now.'

Coffee was served on their return, set up on a little table on a balcony overlooking a walled garden. There was also fresh fruit and bread, and an array of northern delicacies to tempt them.

'Is this all for us?' asked Sera because, frankly, half a dozen more people could have joined them and it still would have been too much food for one sitting.

'They're making up for all the years I was gone. It's what people do around here.'

'Every day?'

'Every damn day.' Claudia reached for a royal blue folder sitting on the table. 'Mind if I look through my morning mail? The palace keeps me informed as to the news of the day.'

'And you trust this information?'

Claudia laughed. 'Oh, Sera. The look on your face. If something of interest comes up I look into it. Did you not rely on the Arunian palace for information?'

'Not really. I have my own sources.'

'I find these ones useful and I don't have to go looking for them. They even present them in order of palace importance. Very informative in itself, would you not say? Take this one, for example: it's item one and it's a note from the desk of Moriana of Liesendaach, formerly of Arun, telling Cas that there's been an assassination attempt on her brother but rumour of his death is a gross exaggeration. Is that not good to know?'

'What?'

Claudia passed the sheet of paper over without further comment, and picked up the next item. 'And here's what the tabloids have to say. Hmm. Your good King was in a bad part of the city last night. Two people in custody, Augustus and a minor in intensive care.'

'A minor?' Sera wasn't tracking too well any more. Hadn't been since the words *Augustus* and *death* had been mentioned in the same breath.

'Here.' Claudia passed that one to Sera too before

picking up her coffee in one hand and sifting quickly through the others. 'That's all the information I have. Do you have anyone you can get more information from?'

'Not at this hour.' It was still too early for regular workday hours, and for all that Augustus's executive secretary often stayed late, he rarely began his day before nine. 'Unless the entire communications team has been called in to deal with this. Then there might be someone there willing to give me more information.'

'Would you like to use one of our phones?' Sera asked.

'They'll think the call is coming from the Byzenmaach King.'

Claudia raised a dark brow. 'And? Not as if there aren't advantages to that approach.'

The woman had a point.

She found a phone and made the call to Augustus's office number and waited impatiently for someone to pick up.

The call appeared to get diverted and Augustus's secretary answered on the sixth ring, his voice curtly polite and the strain in it evident.

'It's Sera,' she said.

Silence.

'I'm staying at the Winter fortress in Byzenmaach and heard the news this morning.'

More silence.

Don't hang up... 'How is he?' She cleared her throat. 'Please.'

Claudia was watching her from the doorway. Ari stood sentry on the other side of the room, silently watching them both.

'He's in intensive care,' the older man said finally and Sera let her head droop so her hair curtained her face.

'And his condition?'

'He needs someone to fight for him.'

'I can fight,' she said, blinking back tears. 'I know how to fight.'

'Yes, I know. We all know that. But, if I may be so bold, don't come back if you're not planning to stay. He let you go once because that's what you said you wanted and it nearly destroyed him. Don't make him go through that again.'

'I won't.'

'Would you like to put that in writing?'

'If you tell me where he is, I'll put it on a billboard.'

'He's at the Sisters of Mercy Hospital in the capital. They have a helipad, and I assume you have access to a helicopter and a pilot. Tell them to go through me and I'll clear your way for landing.'

It was more welcome than she'd ever hoped for. 'You're probably going to get into trouble for this.'

'I probably am,' he countered drily.

'That's a debt you'll be able to collect on, should you ever need something from me in the future.'

'Do you still have your guards with you?'

'Yes.'

'Then I'm calling that debt in right now. Bring them. The King's head of security quit this morning in a fit of temper. There's an opening.'

'I'll bring them.' She couldn't resist the next question. 'What happened?'

'Which version would you like, milady?'

'Your version.' She trusted the older man's take on palace events.

'In that case, the answer's very simple. Most people have a healthy sense of self-preservation. My King has lost his.'

It took three tries to put the phone back in its cradle and the third time Claudia's hand was guiding her. 'I need a helicopter,' she said.

'Then you shall have one.'

'And a pilot.'

'I shall fly you myself.'

Which was how Sera managed to get from Byzenmaach's Winter fortress to the Sisters of Mercy Hospital in just over an hour, her guards flanking her as she strode from the helipad towards the building. She had her travelling cloak on but didn't bother with the hood. Memorable entries were her speciality, and she had every intention of brazening this one out.

Augustus's secretary stood waiting for her and opened the door as she approached.

'How is he?' A question that carried with it everything her world had narrowed down to. Because there was only one person she wanted to walk beside in this world and if he wasn't alive…

If she never got that chance…

All the colours of the world would be gone.

'Please. How is he?'

'Follow me,' he said. He avoided her gaze and supplied no other answer. Maybe he had no answer for her. 'Is his sister here? His father?' Had Augustus's next of kin been gathered?

'They're about.' The older man swept them through a long hallway with security guards at either end. Guards who nodded and straightened to attention as they passed by. She thought Ari's barely leashed displeasure at their carelessness in letting an assassin get close enough to their King to do damage might have something to do with it. That or her own scathing, stormy gaze.

'Ari and Tun will relieve the guard detail on the door to the critical care unit,' she said, and smiled tightly when the old courtier blinked at her sheer hide. 'You were the one who wanted them here. No one said anything about you commanding them.'

'Perhaps you will allow His Majesty's guards to brief your men on what actually happened last night before you sweep them aside,' the older man advised. 'The King occasionally goes into the city by himself and in disguise. He did this last night.'

'And you *let* him?'

'Freedom's irresistible to those who've never had it.' They'd reached the end of yet another long corridor with guards stationed at either end. 'You can go in.'

'Is anyone in there with him?' It wasn't that she was putting off walking through those doors. She simply wanted to be prepared for whoever she might find.

'His sister's just stepped out.'

There was never going to be a better time.

There was one bed in the room she entered and it was empty, machines switched off and the bottom sheet rumpled, the top sheet pushed aside. Augustus stood to one side of the window on the opposite side of the room, his face pale and wan, his chest bare, his shoulder bandaged and his left arm strapped tightly to his chest.

His eyes widened at the sight of her.

'Hello,' she said awkwardly, caught completely off guard. Not that the sight of him standing there didn't fill her heart to overflowing, but this really wasn't the kind of intensive care she'd imagined. 'I… Ah, you can stand.'

He raised a quizzical eyebrow.

'And…uh…walk. That's good. Brilliant recovery.' She'd been had, but right now she didn't give a damn. 'So good.'

'What are you doing here?' If she was drinking him in with her eyes, he was doing much the same to her.

'I was—'

In the area and just thought she'd drop by? Hardly.

'That is to say—'

He was waiting for her to say.

'I was visiting Claudia, my friend who is not my sister, and she has this mountain…'

He looked sceptical. 'Of course it's not her mountain, but it's a mountain nonetheless, and I was up there thinking about you, and me, and whether there could ever be a "you *and* me" that wasn't all about honour and duty and sacrifice. A you and me that *does* involve those things, sure,' she said, and contradicted herself completely and stumbled on regardless. 'Because you're you and there's no getting away from your duty as King, but above all that, or maybe underneath it, I was wondering if there might be a "*you and me*" who could be together and we could make a point of building some freedom into our lives, keeping the courtesan's quarters open as a place where you can be you and I can be me, and there could be holidays in the mountains and I could show you things you've never seen. And maybe at some point, if you haven't already proposed to Katerina DeLitt, that is, we could talk about you marrying me.' She tailed off, wishing he'd say something. 'Because of love.'

'Was that supposed to make sense?'

Yes, yes, it was, and if it hadn't she'd try again. 'I'm in love with you.'

'Why?' The tiniest tilt of his lips gave her the courage she needed to keep going.

'Because you let me in, even though you knew this was going to get messy. Because you let me try and be all those dozen different things I was taught to be, no matter the cost to yourself. Because you put my needs before yours and fought for my right to be free in a way you can never be. And I *am* free now and I'm still being selfish, because when I heard you'd been hurt there was only one place I wanted to be. So here I am.'

And there he stood.

'Of course, you might not have much use any more for the love of a former courtesan and that's okay too.'

'No reciprocation required?' he asked softly.

'No. That's not love. Love is standing here and feeling so much relief and joy that you *are* okay. And then turning around and walking out that door if you ask me to.'

She wanted to stay. She so badly wanted to touch him. But she didn't have the right to.

'Come here,' he said and she walked closer and fought every twitchy bit of muscle memory not to sink to the floor at his feet. He'd never wanted that from her.

'If there's such a thing as love at first sight, I felt it the first time I ever saw you.' He touched his fingers to the tie at her neck and tugged it loose and then used both hands to push her travelling cloak from her shoulders until it pooled in a puddle at her feet. 'First time you ever curtseyed for me, I was torn between wanting to keep you there for ever and never wanting you to lower yourself in front of me again because I wanted an equal. I *needed* an equal. And you stayed and triumphed, no matter what I threw at you, and I realised I'd finally found one.' He traced the line of her cheek with the backs of his fingers. 'Always knew I'd have to let you go.'

'You did.'

'And yet here you are.' He threaded his fingers through her hair. 'And I think you should know that I have no intention of ever letting you go again.' He kissed her gently at first and then somehow it became all-consuming.

They were both breathing raggedly when finally he broke the kiss. He rested his forehead against hers and huffed a laugh before taking a determined step back. 'I had a plan for if you ever came back. It involved rather more clothes and no bullet wounds on my part, and there was possibly a fantasy moment of you wearing ancient slave jewellery mixed up in there somehow, but I did have a plan and it went something like this. I love you. I want you by my side from this day forward and not as my courtesan or employee.'

He got down on bended knee and tugged his ring from his finger and held it out to her. It was a dark blue cabochon sapphire with the royal insignia of Arun overlaid in diamonds. 'This one's heavy, I know, but it's yours if you'll take it. There'll be other rings, I promise. Sera, will you marry me?'

'Yes.' A lifetime of royal duty in exchange for the opportunity to walk beside the man she loved and who loved her in return. 'Yes, I will.'

He put the ring on her finger and she looked at it and then at him. 'I know what you mean now about having someone kneel at your feet. It's very disconcerting having all sorts of thoughts running through your mind about what they might do while they're there.'

'Tell me about it,' he said with a glint in his eye that promised exploration. 'And don't spare the details.'

'Another time, perhaps. Once you've fully recovered from your...did you say *bullet wounds*?'

'I may have been an idiot in your absence. You're likely to hear about it at some point. I believe there's a *Bring Sera Back* petition circulating through the palace as we speak. Or perhaps everybody's signed it by now. There was a jar circulating too. People were putting gold jewellery into it, trying to raise your bodyweight in gold as an incentive to woo you back.'

Sera blinked. 'They what?'

'Good thing there's not much of you.'

A knock on the door preceded the entry of Moriana of Liesendaach, formerly of Arun. She took one look at Sera and her brother, still on bended knee, and said, 'Oh, now that's a pretty look.'

'Do you *mind*?' Augustus asked her.

'Oh, no. Not at all. Please. Continue. Don't mind me.' Moriana waved away his concerns. 'Hi, Sera.'

Sera waved and the ring on her finger glinted.

Moriana's smile broadened. 'Does this mean I can have my six gold bracelets and Theo's two golden goblets back? Because Theo did, in fact, get into trouble for donating those goblets to the cause. Not only are they insanely heavy, apparently they're two thousand years old.'

Sera leaned forward and put her lips to Augustus's ear. 'I think you should get up now,' she whispered. 'I promise to make it worth your while later.'

The smile of unfiltered joy he bestowed on her was

one she wanted to see at least once every day for the rest of her life.

'We're getting married,' Augustus said.

Moriana rolled her eyes but her smile almost rivalled her brother's. 'I never would have guessed.'

'And I need to speak with my future wife about exactly how quickly we can make that happen,' he continued regally and pointed towards the door.

'I can help you there.' Moriana was enjoying herself way too much. 'Royal weddings take time. Months. Years! And involve processions.'

'Out!' He sounded so commanding.

'In the mountains of the High Reaches there's a ceremony called a binding,' Sera offered quietly. 'It involves two people pledging their hearts into the other's safe keeping. There are four witnesses, one for each point of the compass. It's very simple. Will you do it with me?'

'I'll do it today and every day for the rest of my life,' he promised, and touched his lips to hers.

When Sera finally surfaced, Moriana was gone and the door to the room was firmly closed.

'How soon can we break you out of here?' she asked, and placed a gentle hand to his shoulder and then to his heart.

'They're being overly cautious,' he grumbled. 'I can be out of here tonight.'

Uh-huh. She'd like to see him try.

'One week,' she promised. 'One week today and with the mountains as our witness I will bind my heart to you.'

EPILOGUE

AUGUSTUS STOOD DRAPED in the ceremonial black furs that also served to keep the bitter cold at bay. He wore his royal uniform beneath the borrowed cloak because, for all that he was standing on a mountain with a blizzard closing in, he was still the King of Arun and carried the hopes of his people with him.

He'd been in the mountains for two days and had stayed in a sprawling fortress every bit as grand as any he'd ever stayed in. Sera had shown him the horses, the falcons, the temples and the steps carved into a mountain path that wove its way ever skyward in suicidal fashion. Only for her had he risen and bathed and dressed before dawn and climbed those icy steps, grateful for the burning torches carried by others and the chain ropes beaten into the rock centuries ago and the heavy-duty gloves lent to him by Ari this morning.

A High Reaches binding was not for those who lacked courage and the journey there was part of the process.

His sister and her unborn babe were here, swathed in ceremonial garb and red-gold furs. She would take the East point on the compass, the new dawn. The Lady Lianthe stood to the North, a guiding light, the voice of experience. His father stood to the South, the foundation stone for all that would grow. Princess Claudia of Byzenmaach took the West point and, while darkness and betrayal rode with her as part of her past, she wore love like a shield and had cloaked herself in purest white.

The sky overhead was a vivid blue, a perfect complement to the snowy white and the occasional slash of rocky grey.

There were the four points of the compass, an invisible circle connecting them, and only two sets of footprints within that circle.

They met at the centre, where a goblet of melted snow sat on a stony plinth, and if Theo thought his goblets were heavy they had nothing on this one.

Sera wore a cloak of grey to match her eyes and he couldn't wait to see what was under it. Something similar to bridal wear, she'd told him demurely. Beyond that, he'd have to wait and see.

Her hair had been coiled atop her head and dressed with diamonds.

She wore a fine platinum necklace, matching earrings and the royal ring he'd given her one week earlier in lieu of an engagement ring.

She was loving and giving and his and he'd never felt more blessed.

There would be a wedding, of course. A royal one with cavalries and balconies and a kiss in full view of the people. It was expected. It was tradition. But this… this moment here was deeply, emphatically personal. Simple words meant for no one but the one receiving them.

Four witnesses, a sacred mountain, a cup full of water and a vivid blue sky.

And then Sera spoke.

'My heart is pure and true and yours,' she told him. 'I offer it from a position of knowledge, power and freedom.'

It was all he'd ever hoped for.

'I accept this priceless gift and I will never let you down,' he promised and drank from the goblet.

And then it was his turn to say the words. 'My heart is steadfast and often guarded because it carries with it the weight of a nation but to you I offer it freely and without reservation. It's yours.'

'I accept this priceless gift,' she said, and drained her goblet. 'And, let all here bear witness, I will never let you down.'

* * * * *

MILLS & BOON

Coming next month

A VIRGIN TO REDEEM THE BILLIONAIRE
Dani Collins

'I went to the auction for an earring. I kissed a man who interested me. I've since realized what a mistake that was.'

'It was,' Kaine agreed. 'A big one.' He picked up his drink again, adding in a smooth, lethal tone, 'I have half a mind to accept Rohan's latest offer just to punish you.'

'Don't,' Gisella said through gritted teeth, telling herself she shouldn't be shocked at how vindictive and ruthless he was. She'd already seen him in action.

He smirked. 'It's amazing how quickly that little sparkler brings you to heel. I'm starting to think it has a cold war spy transmitter in it that's still active.'

'I'm starting to think this sounds like extortion. Why are you being so heavy-handed?'

'So that you understand all that's at stake as we discuss terms.'

She shifted, uncomfortable, and folded her arms. 'What exactly are you asking me to do, then?'

'You're adorable. I'm not asking. I'm telling you that, starting now, you're going to portray yourself as my latest and most smitten lover.' He savored that pronouncement with a sip of wine that he seemed to roll around on his tongue.

'Oh, so you blackmail women into your bed.'

For a moment, he didn't move. Neither did she, fearing she'd gone too far. But did he hear himself? As the silence prolonged, she began to feel hemmed in and trapped. Far too close to him. Suffocated.

'The fact you didn't hear the word portray says more about your desires than mine,' he mocked softly. He was full out laughing in silence at her. So overbearing.

'I won't be blackmailed into playing pretend, either,' she stated. 'Why would you even want me to?'

He sobered. 'If I'm being accused of trying to cheat investors, I want it known that I wasn't acting alone. I'm firmly in bed with the Barsi family.'

'No. We can't let people believe we had anything to do with someone accused of fraud.' It had taken three generations of honest business to build Barsi on Fifth into its current, iconic status. Rumors of imitations and deceit could tear it down overnight.

'I can't let my reputation deteriorate while I wait for your cousin to reappear and explain himself,' Kaine said in an uncompromising tone. 'Especially if that explanation still leaves me looking like the one who orchestrated the fraud. I need to start rebuilding my name. And I want an inside track on your family while I do it, keeping an eye on every move you and your family make, especially as it pertains to my interests. If you really believe your cousin is innocent, you'll want to limit the damage he's caused me. Because I make a terrible enemy.'

'I've noticed,' she bit out.

'Then we have an agreement.'

Continue reading
A VIRGIN TO REDEEM THE BILLIONAIRE
Dani Collins

www.millsandboon.co.uk

LET'S TALK
Romance